SEÇONDS

ENDORSEMENTS

In *Seconds*, Abigail Wilkes has written a fascinating journey through questions of identity and purpose. Readers are drawn into a world that is both familiar and magical, following characters that strive with what it means to be valuable, powerful, and loving. Come for the supernatural powers, evocative settings, and well-drawn characters, but stay for the serious contemplation on what lies in the depths of human hearts.

—Joshua Haveman, Executive Pastor—Grace Community Church: North Liberty, IA

SECONDS

ABIGAIL L. WILKES

ELK LAKE PUBLISHING INC

PUBLISHING THE POSITIVE
Plymouth, Massachusetts

COPYRIGHT NOTICE

Cover and Interior Design: Derinda Babcock
Editor(s): Mary White Johnson, Deb Haggerty

PUBLISHED BY: Elk Lake Publishing, Inc., 35 Dogwood Drive, Plymouth, MA 02360, 2021

_____

Library Cataloging Data

Names: Wilkes, Abigail L. (Abigail L. Wilkes)
Seconds / Abigail L. Wilkes

p. 23cm × 15cm (9in × 6 in.)

ISBN-13: 978-1-64949-342-2 (paperback) | 978-1-64949-343-9 (trade paperback) | 978-1-64949-344-6 (e-book)

Key Words: Speculative fiction, different worlds, culture differences, values & virtues, family relationships, government oversight of personal lives; mandated birth control.

Library of Congress Control Number: 2021943161 Fiction

THIS BOOK IS DEDICATED TO THE 65.5 MILLION.

ACKNOWLEDGMENTS

JESUS. Thanks for your infinite love and freedom.

Thank you, Reader, for being amazing and going on this journey with Miki and me.

Many thanks to tea, especially black and with a hint of almond or vanilla. I love you. Also, dark chocolate, my constant companion.

Thanks to my family. Libby and Mom for babysitting so I can write. Libby, your rock-star is showing. Lee for the amazing maps. Thanks for being my in-house artist like no one else could. Johnny. For putting up with obsession, early morning wakeups and writing sessions. Thank you for supporting my passion! My kids—Ditto, and for grounding me when I might have floated off to Thoth and never returned. Thank you for the snuggles after I wrote a particularly important death.

The Abortion Survivors Network for being brave enough to share your stories so I could share this one.

My coworkers at Changes Thrift Store for listening to my rants about the craft of writing.

My fabulous beta readers through my online writing groups. Also, thanks to Molly, Kaia, Melissa, Kailey, and Mom for beta reading my books. Hanu, thank you for your gut honest feedback which only made this book the best it could be. Also, thanks for the name inspiration! I'm sorry I shortened Hanumiki. Sorry, I lied. Not sorry.

Deb with Elk Lake Publishing, Inc. for giving me a shot! MJW—the best editor a gal could ask for and for putting up with my incessant questions and over-the-top positivity. Cristel for the A+ advice about the first chapter and generally being extremely helpful. Thanks to Derinda for the great cover!

Thank you to Josh Haveman for endorsing my first book and being a stellar English teacher and avid lover of the Lord.

Thank you to all my fabulous ARC reviewers and instagrammers who helped me out!

To all the people who heard "I'm an author," and didn't look at me like I was crazy.

Thank you to ancient Egypt for amazing ideas and an amazing language. And God for creating it.

Thank you to the Rocky Mountain Roastery Cafe for being my office space. Also, thanks kitchen table, my mini desk corner, and that big old clunker of a desk I was so glad to upgrade from but so grateful to have. Thank you, wrist pads, for saving me from carpal tunnel.

Thanks, Dad, for saying writing wasn't a career plan. Here's the first step to proving you wrong.

If I forgot anyone, it's because I'm only upright because of Jesus. You are all amazing!

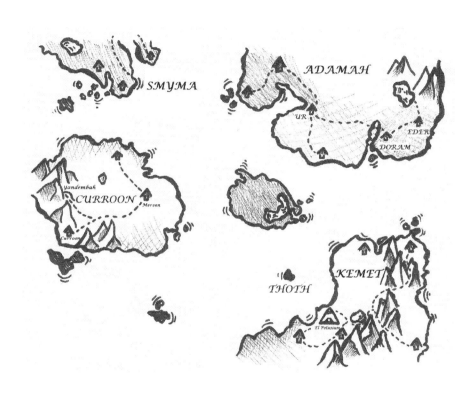

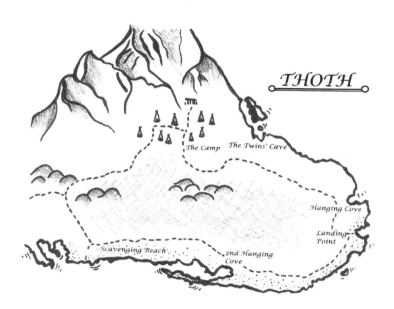

THOTH

The Camp

The Twins' Cave

Hanging Cove

Landing
Point

Scavenging Beach

2nd Hanging
Cove

CHAPTER 1

Someone like Tiye shouldn't have even had a job, let alone such a prosperous one. She hadn't had a break day for three weeks and five days, the longest streak since she'd started working at the cloth shop four years ago. She shut the wooden door against the sandstone frame with a thud. *I shouldn't curse the extra work. Others have died before even getting the chance for a single day.*

She choked on the humid air. What a foolish thought.

Tiye turned from the door, leaving the shop—and the thought—behind. Her purse jingled against her hip as she made her way through the market. Three dozen stalls with white canopies and stone tables lined the fifteen-foot-high walls. The cobbled road north led to the bulk of the Lower Pyramid, where hundreds of sandstone houses were stacked on each other, including her own.

Tiye hesitated in front of the wine merchant's stall. Tempting though a bottle was, the wine would cost the past week's wages, and she had two unopened ones back home.

The merchant, dressed in a plain toga like Tiye's, pulled the bottles off the counter.

"Unless you are going to buy top tier, I'm done for the day." He waited, fingers tapping on the countertop.

Tiye turned away, not bothering to explain she couldn't afford top tier. He could tell by her plain white toga and simple topknot. She was a standard Lower Pyramid dweller, not some embroidered, headdressed fool from the Higher Pyramid. The tunnel leading to the elites' houses sat on the far side of the market. Steelmen guarded the entrance as usual. They wore teal half-togas and matching linen headdresses. Their bronzed chests were bare, and they clutched long spears as if wanting to use them.

Tiye shivered.

Steelmen.

They didn't know her true identity, but that didn't make passing them any easier. She turned away from the wine stall, the smooth linen of her toga whipping around her ankles. The road swarmed with people leaving the market for the day, chatting about their wares.

Overhead, the waterfall drummed. The city wasn't a true pyramid, since one side was built into a mountain. The lake at the top fed the waterfall, which channeled through an aqueduct built a thousand years ago.

Things could have been different a thousand years ago. Perhaps someone like her hadn't needed to hide. She shook the thought off and turned for the road home. The long days were wearing. Maybe the time had come to open one of the wine bottles she had in her house.

"Are you the cloth woman?" A small boy slipped in front of her. A ruined strip of linen served as his loincloth, streaked with the dust of the bustling city.

"The shop is closed for the day. You can get what you need tomorrow." Tiye's bare heels scuffed the road as she stepped past him.

"Here." Clammy fingers pressed something cool into her palm. He scampered away without another word and slipped into the thinning crowd.

A rock sat in Tiye's hand. Rough, uncut, with a symbol scratched hastily into the top. It wasn't even a rune in the language of El-Pelusium, the city.

No. Her breath hitched.

He wouldn't have been so foolish. She dropped her hand, neck burning. But even if someone saw, they couldn't know what the rock meant. She shoved it into her purse, where it clinked against her day's pay.

True, she hadn't seen her father in months, and she missed him, but it was for the best. The fewer chances they gave people to see them together and draw unwanted conclusions, the better.

Tiye steadied her breathing and set off down the road again. Her father must miss her worse than she thought—to have sent that message. She could visit him in a few days under the guise of fitting him for a new toga. Jabarre, her employer, often did personal fittings for other Council members.

The high wall of the Lower Pyramid blocked the setting sun as Tiye rounded the corner. The first of the sandstone houses lined the road. A thin haze of cooking smoke wafted into the light breeze, scenting and disrupting the humid air. Evening lamplighters went ahead of her, jugs of oil sloshing between them. In an hour the daylight would be gone, and only a few stragglers would still be out in the city.

Tiye slowed, grabbing her purse. Her father had used the rock before, but he'd always been discreet about leaving it at her door or in the cloth shop's window. Things must be urgent for him to use the boy. She jerked around, her elbow catching in a woman's side.

"Hey! Watch it!" the merchant spat, grabbing her basket of herbs closer to her chest. Tiye bowed in apology and hurried back into the market. Only a few merchants remained.

And the Steelmen.

They still guarded the tunnel, more for formality than anything else. Tiye threw her shoulders back and marched passed them. At least her pale skin and black hair kept her unremarkable.

The tunnel rose gradually for half a mile before it opened into a bridge. Another tunnel began on the other side. The houses of the Lower Pyramid sat under the bridge, with the aqueduct running beside it and over the city.

The sun gave one last ray of heat before setting into the distant ocean. No sign of anyone. A tingle burned up the nape of Tiye's neck. Had someone followed her?

She had been foolish to come up here without a plan. The rock in her purse dug into her hip, as if digging its truth into her soul. That innocent rock could get both her father and her banished if anyone knew what it meant.

She stumbled to a halt and into a dark doorway. She could not afford to be caught, now that she'd involved her father. Or he'd involved her. Her breath hovered in her throat, hot and thin. The Steelmen could have gotten bored and followed her to question what she was doing in the Higher Pyramid.

A torch flickering on its last lick of oil lit the street as dusk settled in. She let the rhythmic crashing of the waterfall soothe her heartbeat. She had survived four years out here alone without being banished. She could go one more night.

Forcing back the urge to shudder, she stepped back into the street as if she belonged in the Higher Pyramid.

"H-help me!" A voice, low and desperate, cut through the noise of the rushing water.

Tiye bit her tongue, and the sharp taste of copper flooded her mouth. A man sat in the shadows on the side of the bridge, dirty and smeared with red paint.

No, not paint. Blood.

The red stains stood out against his pale skin, gleaming in the night. His eyes were wide, frantic. Before Tiye could step back, his blood-encrusted hand shot out and grabbed hers.

"Please." The man's voice cracked. "Help me."

"Miki." Another man's voice, firm and deep. The bloody stranger dropped her arm, his eyes flashing to the newcomer.

Father. The name was on her lips, but she kept quiet. Tiye stepped away from the bloody man toward the torchlit mouth of the hall and her father. He wore a linen headdress edged with glass beads. A white toga, plain apart from a teal belt with gold embroidery, covered his torso. His feet were bare. The enclosed hall where he stood led into the heart of the Higher Pyramid and away from the stacked sandstone houses of the Lower.

"Please! Woman, if you don't help me, they will banish me—" The stranger's voice cut off in a choke.

Tiye paused halfway, looked at the man and then at her father, whose dark eyes flashed in warning. The injured man was too dangerous to be near. She sprinted the last ten yards to safety, and her father's warm fingers wrapped around her wrist.

Something moved behind the bloody stranger.

Steelmen. There were at least a dozen of them, spear tips dancing as they marched up the road and onto the bridge. The stranger fell to the ground, his sob breaking the night. Tiye's father went to the door in the hallway that was his front door and wrenched it open, the massive wooden planks creaking, and she stumbled into the house. The door slammed shut, a bang that resounded against the stark walls. Her father did not speak, and a tightness in her chest kept her from voicing her fears. One look into her father's lined face proved he shared the same thoughts.

The man outside was a Second. He wouldn't have spoken of banishment otherwise.

Her father smiled, but the smile did not reflect in his eyes. "You are fine. He didn't know who you were. It was a coincidence."

"Yes." The word was inadequate.

"I know that look, Miki. Trust me, you're fine. Come, let's eat while you're here."

Her father retrieved a lamp from the low table by the door and moved further into the house. The walls were bare, apart from intricate pictographs like those carved into the houses of many of the elites of El-Pelusium. Tiye's finger twitched at her side, as if wanting to trace the lines of those engravings as she had when she was small. But that had been Miki, her father's child.

Her father lit the remaining torches lining the walls, their fire contained inside glass globes, something her own modest house did not have. The sparsely decorated room was unusual for someone of her father's station, but for her, it was home. A warm evening breeze drifted through the open balcony beside her, blowing the gossamer linen curtains inward. She couldn't imagine how others envied such a large sky-wall when her heart raced just standing in front of it. She felt vulnerable, unprotected.

"Years have passed since you've had to fear who might look in through there, Miki. Come, relax and eat with me." Wood scraped on stone as her father set a bowl of fruit on the bench between them. "I shouldn't have asked you to come." He frowned, the lines of worry crossing his forehead.

"Why did you?" Her breath didn't catch up with her words, and they came out in a wheeze. She cleared her throat and tried again. "Using a boy was risky. What's going on?"

His frown deepened. "There were rumors of a hunt for a Second. I wanted to make sure you were safe."

"That was the man outside," Tiye whispered. The irony of her father's actions tonight, of all nights, wasn't lost on her.

Her father paled but didn't broach that topic. "It's the new High One. I'd hoped she wouldn't be the sort of ruler her father was, and I would be able to sway her to our cause, but it's proving harder than I first thought. The other Council members want her to redouble efforts to find Seconds—"

A scream cut through the evening, making Tiye jump. Her hand smacked into the bowl of fruit, sending red and orange berries rolling across the open floor as far as the bedroom entrance.

The man outside. Tiye edged closer to the sky-wall, where the street beyond lay visible. The man knelt, bent over in the street, a pool of red polluting the bricks under him.

"They won't be able to banish him if he's dead," she muttered under her breath.

"Miki, come away."

"What are they doing to him?"

"Miki," her father's voice more stern this time, "you don't need to watch."

"But how did they know he was a Second? Five years have passed since they found one."

That day had been cold, the coldest the Pyramid's mild winters had produced in her memory. A shiver raised the hairs on her arms at the thought of that man. Pale and scrawny from years of living in the sewers, enduring a life that hadn't saved him. The Steelmen paraded him past the cloth shop on his way to the boat for banishment, just like the ones before him. Tiye hadn't wanted to see, but Jabarre, the owner of the shop, had insisted, laughing too much to notice when she ran away and vomited in the storeroom.

"Stop watching." Her father's fingers dug into the crook of her elbow and yanked her back. "No good will come of it. All you have done is ruin my fruit."

A splash of orange stood out against the thin palm-weave rug. She sighed. "I'm sorry, I just—"

"I know. Me too." His icy fingertips brought goosebumps to her arm as they fell away. "Let's finish in the other room so we do not have to see." But his face drained of color. He was as frightened as she.

Thud.

Sharp pain in her palms as her nails dug into them.

Thud. Thud. A fist on the wooden door.

"Councilman Bast, we must speak with you!" A Steelman.

She exhaled a gust of nerves and tried to suck it back in. She shouldn't have come, not after a year of staying away.

Her father tugged her across the room and into the bedroom. "You must go into the cellar."

Wood creaked under Tiye's feet. "No, not that. Father—"

"Miki, you must go down there. Being with me won't protect you, not after what just happened. Go!"

He lifted the edge of the small bedside rug and the attached cellar door opened with a groan of forgotten hinges. Without another word he spun from the room, head held high like the Councilman he was.

The cellar gaped before her, a black mouth waiting to devour her. This was worse than the man outside, most likely a Second, being beaten and then being banished. Going into the cellar was something she'd hoped to never do again.

The door beyond opened. Her father's deep tones filled the house. A man's apologetic voice answered. Feet scuffed the floor as the Steelmen moved inward. She had to go now.

A gulp of fresh air. Closed eyes. Tiye threw herself into the cellar, fingers wrapping around the rough edge of the door above her and pulling it shut. The rug would fall back into place on its own, just as her father had designed it to do when he'd hidden her as a child.

Her fingers found the latch in the darkness and flipped it closed. Silence and darkness settled. Breath hovered in her lungs and blood pounded in her ears. Hours, days, years of her childhood spent down here, in the same darkness, the same nerve-grinding fear. The only difference was now the cellar door brushed her head instead of being a few feet above her.

Tingles took her fingers, moving from her heart to the tips of her extremities. The poison of anxiety hadn't touched her for so long. Closing her eyes, she sucked in another breath and wished it away.

"A Second?" Her father's voice came through muffled but was calm, practiced. "You are sure? That is a serious accusation, gentlemen." Nineteen years of her life, and more before her, had prepared him well for this.

"Yes, Councilman Bast. I am aware of the gravity of the charge. Councilman Montu suspected him. He commanded us to call the Council once we caught the Second ..." The husky voice moved away and grew too muffled to hear well.

Tiye stepped back, exhaling. So they were not there for her, not yet. Either way, her father would not want her out of the cellar until they left. She turned in the darkness and brushed the stone wall. Keeping her hands on it, she traced the familiar grooves in the stone further back to the main cellar. The scent of stale air from a long-forgotten room hit her face.

Her knuckles thunked against wood. The cabinet sat as it always had. She pulled the torch out and lit it with the tinder her father kept fresh, even if five years had passed since she'd used it. A box of crates sat in the corner, filled with a child's pictograph tablets and blankets for the pallet of goose down in the opposite corner.

This was Miki's place. Yet why did it feel so familiar?

"Because I am Miki," she whispered. "I am Miki." The words settled around her, the name resting on her shoulders like a cloak she'd refused to put on for far too long, only to realize the chill in the air without it.

She was Miki for the first time in fifteen years. Just for tonight, she was home.

"Home." The word echoed for a second before vanishing into the dark at the back of the cellar ten feet away. Sinking onto the small bed, she dropped the torch into a ring on the wall with a *clunk*. There was nothing left to do but wait.

To the far side, the cellar's secondary entrance stared at her. A half-sized door made for a child. She could go through that door, leave her father's house, and return to her own—Tiye's—home. She almost raised her hand to the leather knob, but paused. Two long strokes of a hot iron had left the wood of the door charred black and indented. If it had not been formed by a small boy's shaking hand, it would have been a recognizable character of the alphabet.

Kamu. The exceptional one. A name meant for a boy who would be the one to get away with being born Second. A name fulfilled, at least as far as Miki knew. With a sigh, she sank back against the bed pad.

"I miss you, Kamu." Every time the cellar swallowed her, she whispered those words. Every time since she was four—when he'd vanished. A brother she did not really know given to a family halfway across the world, so he might have a chance at a fair life. Or so her parents had told her. She could inquire about him, but her father would never answer. After all, he probably did not even know.

Miki shifted, lying with her hands folded across her stomach. Breath in her throat, she waited.

Another thud, louder this time.

She jumped up and took the stairs two at a time. The cellar door flung wide before she reached it. Her father stood above, face pale, the creases in his forehead twice as deep.

"I must go to the Council Chamber. You should return to your home if you do not want to stay the night in the cellar."

"Will they banish him?"

Her father held her gaze. "I love you, Miki."

"What is it?" The last stair creaked as she moved up into the house.

"I will find you after the verdict, but with news like this, I am sure the city will tell you before I get a chance." He turned, straightening his headdress.

She followed him back to the main room. The sky was now dark, and the sky-wall was a hole of glowing pins as torches burned throughout the Pyramid below.

Father turned and placed a kiss on her forehead. "Hurry home to Tiye's. I am sorry I asked you to visit. I will find you in the city next time. Better to not risk coming up here. Try not to worry, Miki. Your name—"

"It means *Victory*. I know. That is too much pressure to put on me."

Her father turned for the door.

"You have earned it," he said, and stepped into the night.

Miki closed her eyes, putting the moment in the cellar behind her. She could not afford to be Miki any longer. She was Tiye—*Light*—again, an easier name to live up to. She stepped into the night. The street was dark apart from a scattering of torches, casting little light on her father as he retreated up the dim tunnel to the Higher Pyramid. She turned right, heading to the Lower Pyramid.

The blood of the Second still glowed on the stones of the road, a sickly warning to all other Seconds who might dare to enter a world of Firstborns. Tiye's stomach somersaulted. She hurried past even as the blood slithered between the cracks of the stones to follow her. The question which had plagued her nightly for her entire life burned again.

If that was what happened to a Second-born child, what would they do to a Fifth?

CHAPTER 2

"Did you hear?"

"About the man?" The woman's voice dipped to a whisper, but her voice still carried across the textile shop. "The one they say is a Second?"

"Confirmed as a Second, you mean." Jabarre's scratchy voice rang out.

"Confirmed? When? There was a trial?"

Tiye could picture Jabarre's thin face screwing in concentration just before he nodded once, sharp and precise. His way of elevating his knowledge above others. But she did not look up from the fine weave running between her fingers, richer by far than the cream she'd spared for her morning coffee. She might regret the expense later, but the day of a Second's trial warranted cream to smooth it over.

Jabarre cleared his throat, which only worsened his dry tones.

"A trial, yes. Not even an hour ago. The news was all over the city. A boy told me right as I arrived. He'd been there himself. The royal messenger."

"You mean—" the woman gasped, "—you mean *she* was there?"

"Yes." Jabarre said no more for a moment. Tiye ran the cloth between her fingers one more time, doing a twelfth inspection. The fabric was fine enough for the very person they gossiped about. She laid it over the flat counter in front of her, the only furniture in the textile shop apart from shelves of cloth.

The floor behind her creaked in protest as the customer stepped closer to Jabarre. "Things must be serious then, if the High One herself was there."

"Of course things are serious! He is a Second."

The fabric slipped from between Tiye's fingers and the corner dusted the ground. A brown smear tainted the milky white. She snatched it up, not daring to see if Jabarre or the customer noticed.

"Banishment?"

"And the second finger removed on each hand."

The woman gasped. Tiye's teeth grated together. If only she had stopped to help the man. He could have hidden in the cellar with her … no. That was something Miki would do, not Tiye.

The cloth lay in a perfect triangle, ready for wrapping in the palm leaves stacked to the side, but Tiye didn't move toward them.

"The amputation seems barbaric, but I suppose he earned it, being the first Second-born they've found in half a decade."

"Hmm." Jabarre's bare feet brushed the stone floor and his shadow fell across the cloth working table. "Is her order finished, Tiye?"

She jumped, startled, but covered it by reaching for the palm leaves. "Yes."

"Then wrap it up. My client does not have all day."

The palm leaves crinkled beneath her fingers, releasing the fresh scent of citrus already permeating the small shop. A string of twine topped the package off. Jabarre's spindly fingers snatched it away before Miki could offer it to the woman clothed in a toga of the exact white she had just prepared.

"Four bags of grain," Jabarre said as he held the package aloft. The woman motioned to four lumpy bags sitting against the wall.

"Thank you for the interesting conversation, Jabarre. I'll be back within the month for the same." She accepted the package, tucked it under her arm and made her way through the door curtain into the busy Lower Pyramid beyond.

The sun bit into Tiye's eyes through the open window. Business in the Lower Pyramid moved slowly. Customers and merchants alike stopped to put their heads together and gossip. Shops lined the road before the Great Tunnel began, the Tunnel which wound to the very top of the Higher Pyramid where the High One lived. But today there weren't people streaming up the road as there usually were. A Steelman barred the way, feet spread and head up. He wore a half toga, leaving his chest bare. A plain teal headdress, much smaller than the one her father wore, sat on the man's head.

If the High One had sent her personal Steelman to stop the usual trade in the Great Tunnel, she knew what effect the sentencing of the Second would have. Almost as second nature, Tiye wound her long black hair into a topknot. She had to be Tiye today, in every way.

With a sharp snap, the curtain covering the doorway smacked against the wall, and another woman stepped into the shop. Her second chin wobbled as she advanced on Tiye.

"I need four rolls of linen, plain, and one roll embroidered. Tell your master I have a goat for him."

Tying her hair off with a leather strap, Tiye headed for the shelves of cloth behind her.

Jabarre approached the newcomer. "Kleo! Have you heard?"

"My dear man, who hasn't?"

"Banished, they say."

"Tortured first, too. But did you hear about the goat herder's daughter?" The air in the shop thickened, and Tiye's hand froze above a stack of embroidered yellow on white linen.

"No. Is she a Second too?" Jabarre's tone was casual, but to any who knew him as well as Tiye did, he was restraining the urge to shake the woman for more information.

"No. She nullified."

A stab of pain hit Tiye's chest, and her hand fell away from the shelf.

"She was pregnant? Wasn't she the one who tried to petition against nullifications?" Jabarre chuckled under his breath. "Oh, how the proud fall."

Kleo's laugh bounced off the stark walls, fading only when Tiye's attention fell on the fabric in front of her. Delicate lines of thread ran in every direction, compounding until the most intricate pattern covered the surface. But Tiye didn't see any of it, only the goat herder's daughter.

"I'd say they've shown her the error of her ways." Jabarre stepped behind her again, and Tiye snatched the cloth from the shelf and moved toward the folding counter.

"Apparently, she didn't want to face the consequences of having a Second-born after all. Besides, it's not like it would have been a person. She wasn't pregnant with a baby, but a curse." Kleo pounded her fist against the open palm of her other hand.

The fabric slipped from Tiye's fingers again, but this time the whole bolt fell to the ground. The thud echoed through the shop. She sucked in a breath, but too late.

Jabarre snatched the cloth up as if it were life itself. His face glowed with anger as he set it back on the counter.

"Go fetch the palm leaves." The scratch in his voice only magnified his curtness.

Tiye nodded once and turned from the room. The back storeroom was only a few feet away, but the moment her bare toes found the dimmed room, she gasped. Her fingers shook against the stones at her back.

The Second. The nullification. She hadn't been so close to either in many years. Miki had, but that wasn't who she was anymore. Light blinked through the rear door Jabarre never used. Safety was out there. Away from the cloth shop and the gossips inside.

She ripped the top half of the stack of palm leaves up and stepped back into the shop. Jabarre glared and stepped forward now that Kleo was outside fetching the goat. "What in the name of the High One was that, Tiye?"

"I've been having pain in my hands recently. I can't help it. They just spasm." The lie came easily enough. Her fingers still pulsed with the erratic beating of her heart.

"Find a tonic or salve for them. These are expensive fabrics and expensive customers. You know that." He leaned in closer, thin nostrils flaring enough to make his nose average size for once.

"I know. I'm sorry. It won't happen again."

Jabarre dropped a hand on the counter in front of her. "You are making me feel as if you are fifteen again, freshly orphaned, but you aren't. I've invested four years in training you since then. I won't find anyone else. Have the rest of the day off. Go find that tonic for your spasms."

Tiye nodded and turned for the door just as Kleo reentered with a brown goat struggling against its lead. Jabarre accepted the goat and took it through the back room to where an animal pen for payments sat outside.

"Have you ever nullified? You seem the proper age to have had a Firstborn." Kleo filled the doorway, looking Tiye up and down as if reading her skin for signs of childbirth.

Tiye sidestepped. "No." The street was so close ...

Kleo moved with her. "Well, when it happens, be smart about it. We don't need any more of these cursed Seconds running about. Or Thirds. Years ago, I heard a woman down by the wharf hid a Third for three months. Three months! Can you imagine? But the neighbor heard it screaming, and they sent it to Thoth with all the other mongrels."

"They banished a baby to Thoth?" The words were out before Tiye could stop them. The door threshold creaked beneath her foot.

Kleo pulled back, chins wobbling and eyes wide.

"Of course! What else were they to do with it? Can't kill it once it's out, that's a worse curse than letting one stay in El-Pelusium."

"Who would take care of—" Tiye bit her tongue. Now was not the time. She couldn't risk everything by speaking so openly. Miki hovered in the back of her mind, waiting. Tiye forced a smile for the customer but fought against the fog in her brain. Miki had to stay buried, or the anxiety would come again.

Kleo's eyes narrowed, but Jabarre's return kept her from voicing whatever malicious thought she was having.

"The payment is fair," he said. "Same order next month?"

"No. This is all I'll need until winter. My husband says we shouldn't spend so much with a Second being uncovered. I think he is right." She gathered up the packages he had finished and elbowed her way past Tiye to the street.

"Curse that Second!" Jabarre slapped his palm against the stone counter. "If she's thinking that way, so will everyone in the city! At least the Council members will still need robes. They can't meet naked, can they?" He picked up another package off the counter. "I forgot about this. Take this to Councilwoman Edrice. She requested it late last night but expects it by midday. I trust you can make it in time?" His intense glare and even more intense scowl told her there was no other option.

Tiye accepted the crinkling palm leaf-wrapped package. Jabarre vanished inside the shop, the uncorking of a bottle following soon after. Her tongue tingled and her mouth watered. Perhaps she could spare a stop at a wine stall for a fresh bottle. But the sun burned almost at full height. There wouldn't be a chance until after the delivery.

Sighing, she turned into the market. Top-knotted heads were still together, arms still intertwined, folk trying to make sense of the gossip and the Second. Most of the shops were outside, the owners not being as wealthy as Jabarre. White painted posts and rails divided them from one another, and the goods lined the fences, forgotten while conversations blossomed between customer and seller.

"If they found one, do you think there are more?"

"Of course there are. I've been saying it for years." A rotund merchant with a chicken tucked under his arm shook the bird to emphasize his point. Its eyes bulged as its head wobbled.

The other man nodded. "But how will we get them all—"

Tiye turned from the conversation before the anger clouding her mind released along with Miki. There was no point to it. Things had to remain as they had for the past four years.

The Steelman in front of the tunnel to the High Pyramid stood as he had before. A group of merchants approached the Steelman, arms laden with food and sweet delicacies.

Tiye did not need to step closer to smell the cinnamon and cloves. The closest merchant, the same rotund man with a topknot so small someone could have gripped it and pulled out all of his hair, stepped up with the food. He muttered words too low for her to catch.

The Steelman shifted, relaxing the spear into the crook of his elbow and took the offering.

"The High One will not tolerate Seconds. The Council is worried the fiends may act on her life after this morning, so no one is allowed up the Pyramid who does not live there."

"But what of the man they caught today? Can you tell us more?" The fat little man leaned in farther.

"Excuse me!" Tiye slid between the merchant and the Steelman. "I have an urgent package for Councilwoman Edrice. You must let me pass."

The merchant choked on his gossip, and the Steelman stared at her.

"Urgent? Cloth?" He eyed her package.

"Yes. I will hurry and come straight back." Her voice didn't shake, thankfully. *May this be the first and last time I ever speak to a Steelman.*

"Fine. I'll come looking for you if you aren't back in an hour." He moved aside and waved her on with his spear.

Tiye nodded and slipped past. Blood swooshed in her ears as she rounded the corner, following the tunnel as it wound upwards. In fifteen minutes, the Lower Pyramid was far behind her. The sun stabbed at her eyes, and the darkened stones from the Second's blood were brown and dull in the light. She did not look. Her bare toes scuffed the stones outside her father's house.

She did not stop. Councilwoman Edrice lived farther up. The hard stone jolted her with every footfall, but she kept running. Last night was only hours ago. She had not planned on returning to the Higher Pyramid again, let alone this soon. Her blood bounded like the waterfall above the city. The ever-growing anxiety lessened for a moment. The waterfall. Yes.

The wind was hot, as it always was no matter the season. Stale and dry, even with the waterfall spreading its moisture through the city. Tiye hurried higher up the Pyramid. The market and the gossips were far below now. If she turned, she no doubt would see the whitewashed fences hundreds of feet below, but she entered another tunnel, the last stretch before the waterfall and the palace itself.

The stones were painted yellow and teal in patterns too intense to stare at for long. The colors flashed in Tiye's peripheral vision, but she did not stop to look. The roar of the waterfall covered her footfalls and those of any who might be following. She had not passed a soul. Surely there was no one to follow her. Moisture tickled her skin, and the next corner presented a large hole in the wall where water thundered past on its way down the aqueduct to the farms beyond the Pyramid.

She slowed. The water brought back memories of peace, and of the rare days when her mother dressed Miki up as a small shop girl to deliver her weavings to those who lived even higher than them. To The High One himself, the father of the current High One. On the way back they would stop and stare at the water, pretend it was cleansing El-Pelusium, taking away the fear of Seconds.

The bite of cold-water spray stung Tiye's fingertips, and she pulled her hand out of the water with a gasp. The tunnel remained empty. A shiver not born of the cold water trickled up her spine. The waterfall was so close. She hadn't seen it in years. A peek of the full falls would be glorious, but she had to keep going. Edrice lived a little way on, not too far now.

The sun burned twice as strong on the Balcony, the lone open stretch of road at the High Pyramid. The rest of the road was built into the cliff to protect it from the waterfall. Miki stepped to the railing, the crashing of the water covering her footfalls and the pounding of her heart. She turned. The tip of the Pyramid where the royals lived sat nestled into the waterfall itself. The water crashed against it, cascading down the sides and funneling into the aqueduct. Green algae gleamed beneath the water, decorating the stones.

"My mother once told me she climbed the waterfall, but I didn't believe her." A voice, clear and amused, cut through the pounding of the water.

Tiye lowered her eyes, breath in the back of her throat. A woman stood before her, a woman close to her own age with rare caramel hair loose around her shoulders, though her teal embroidered and beaded headdress hid most of it. A white toga covered her, but her wide belt was decorated with the same teal and yellow patterns of the tunnel behind them.

There was only one person this could be, and she was the last person Tiye wanted to see.

The High One of El-Pelusium clasped her hands in front of her and stepped out from the shadow of the entry to her palace. The wind from the waterfall picked up the strands of copper hair left free from the headdress and threw them about her face, but she did not swat them away. Living under the waterfall was ingrained in her.

Tiye sucked in a breath of the thick, moist air and choked.

"This tunnel is closed to commoners." The High One tilted her head, but her voice did not hold accusation. "How did you get up here?"

"I walked." The words were out before Tiye could think.

"Very amusing." A smile pulled at the edge of the High One's mouth then slipped as a shadow crossed her face. "You're not with the Seconds, are you? Not here to stab me?"

"What? I—no. I have a package to deliver." Hundreds of gossiping merchants, their buzzing chatter filling her ears, threatened to bring Miki out. Miki was so close now, hovering in the forefront of Tiye's mind. Tiye pressed two fingers to the bridge of her nose to clear the buzzing, the same two fingers the Second had lost just hours before. She dropped them, heart pulsing faster.

"Sorry. I just figured the Council would want me to ask." The High One chuckled.

"Is Councilman Bast up here?" Tiye's hand tingled with the urge to clap it over her own mouth.

"Yes. He is in the Council Hall for the meeting. Do you know him?" Curiosity sparked behind the High One's brown eyes.

"No. I don't. I just met him once at the cloth shop where I work."

"Ah, a weaver? Are you up here to deliver your goods?" The High One stepped closer and the mock smile came back. Her eyes dropped to the parcel of palm leaves in Tiye's hand.

Shifting it to both hands, she took a step back.

"Yes. I should be going now."

"Wait." The word cut above the thundering water, stern and sure. A command.

Despite the almost painful tingling of adrenaline shooting through her toes, warning her to turn and flee, Tiye paused and turned back to the High One.

The woman's eyes narrowed, taking her in. She clicked her tongue. "What is your name?"

"Tiye."

"I'm Ptolema."

"You are the High One."

"Yes, but I'm also Ptolema." Her cheek twitched.

Tiye stepped forward. "Is there something I can do for you, High One?"

Ptolema's shoulders slumped and the headdress shifted. She raised a thin hand to set it straight.

"You think they would have designed this to be lighter, considering I have to wear it all day, and my neck is only so thick." A red tinge took her face. "Forget I said that."

Tiye stepped back. This woman was responsible for the torture of the Second. She encouraged nullification of the rest of the Seconds. Now she was trying to make a joke. Bile rose in the back of her throat.

"I've got to get back to work." Her neck smarted as she offered a head dip. Dirt crunched under her heel as she turned.

"It was nice to meet you, Tiye …"

But Tiye was already halfway down the tunnel, hand over her mouth to keep herself from screaming. She'd almost gotten back to the market before she remembered the package was still in her basket.

CHAPTER 3

The strange woman sprinted down the tunnel as if a Second was after her. Ptolema could call out to the woman, order her to come back and finish their conversation, but they had not really been having one after all. No one apart from Council members conversed with the High One.

If only someone else would. Maybe then she could bear the hours-long meetings. She could have someone to laugh with over the stuffiness of the Council members, and to giggle at their preening over the best headdress. She could have a friend.

The cool mist of the waterfall caressed Ptolema's face. The sun washed her with warmth, sending comforting rays down her torso. She didn't have much longer, but every moment away from the Council chamber was worth it. The tunnel was an empty black mouth. Even the colored pattern was dim, the rays of the sun not yet long enough to light it up. Eight weeks as High One seemed like eight years. Had her father really been gone that short a time?

A stab in her chest brought her hand up, a pain as familiar as the ones that plagued her every hour since his death. The skin on her collar bone flushed warm, not cool as it should be with the waterfall mist falling across her.

The muted murmuring from behind rose louder, the voices of the Council members echoing off the red sandstone. Perhaps they'd noticed she'd been gone too long.

Of course they had.

There was no escaping their eyes anymore. She would be High One of El-Pelusium until the day she died. Sighing, she turned away from the colorful light refracting against the waterfall. The entryway to the Palace stood as it always did, lit by ever-burning torches. The eight-inch-thick wood panel door stood open, the sun illuminating the deep groovework of a nameless master carver, centuries deceased.

The time had come to return to the chamber. Nausea swirled in her stomach, and Ptolema took a steadying breath. Chamber was not the right word for the stuffy room filled with men and women who smelled more of rotten fruit than of humans.

Ptolema made her way through the door, her palm fiber woven slippers swishing across the stones. She suspected the floor would be icy-cold if she went barefoot, like the woman she'd just met and even many of the Council members. They found no need for shoes, so why did the High One need them? *Stupid tradition. Like so many of them.*

With a dip of his plain teal headdress, the Steelman standing before the entrance to the Council Chamber pulled back the sheer curtain. The scent of rotten berries wafted across her like a putrid breeze from a dead animal. Ptolema forced a smile and stepped down into the room. The walls were bare, as in the rest of the Palace, and the room provided no seats. The Council members milled about the large room, their voices echoing off the arched stone beams above them.

"There must be a decision."

"It was a tragedy, I tell you."

"No one expected—"

"But without proof of more we can't act ..."

The voices died down as Ptolema made her way through the crowd of fifty Council members to the lone stone-carved chair at the end of the hall. Her bottom smarted just to look at it again. A cushion would prove she was too weak to sit in the chair, so there wasn't one. She bit back a sigh as she settled onto the unforgiving stone. The Council members parted into the three groups they had sorted themselves into earlier that day for the trial of the Second. With a nod, she signaled for the meeting to continue.

The man at the front of the center group stepped forward, his slippered feet sticking out from under a green embroidered toga. A bold fashion statement. But then Montu always did have a flair for the excessive. Ptolema kept her snicker to herself, sucking it down before she gave herself away.

Montu bowed low. "High One, as required by our ancestral laws, we have divided into three groups and voted amongst them without bias from the others to reach a decision in the matter of the Seconds."

Ptolema raised two fingers and waved the other group leaders forward. "Present your plan, please."

The leader of the group to the left cleared her throat. She wore no slippers, and the heat of jealousy shot up Ptolema's spine.

"We stand with the decision to send out Steelmen to search all homes in the Lower Pyramid for Seconds." Councilwoman Edrice's voice was cold, calculating.

Ptolema's mouth twitched, threatening to drop into a frown, but she held it straight.

Montu stepped even further forward, the ends of his toga brushing the dais on which the throne sat.

"High One, my group has reached the same decision, but we would take the matter a step further and see that sterilization is enforced after having a first child. Nullifications are not enough."

"Sterilization is a drastic measure and dangerous to the patient." The leader of the third, and smaller, group stepped forward. Mid-fifties, age-worn face. His bald head gleamed under the torchlight that shone even during the day—the Council Chamber had no windows in order to foil eavesdroppers and prevent anyone from committing the grave offense of seeing the members without their headdresses on.

Ptolema adjusted her own headdress with a slight incline of her head. If only she could remove hers for even five minutes of the meeting. She waved Councilman

Bast forward to speak. To her, this man was the kindest in all the Council. Ptolema would never tell a soul, but she harbored a deep fondness for Councilman Bast that Montu or Edrice would never earn.

"This was an isolated incident. My group feels it would not be prudent to search the city or even react beyond sentencing Pilis. We must not weave fear through the Pyramid."

"Pilis?" Ptolema leaned forward to ease the pain in her bottom.

"The man we sentenced to banishment on Thoth this morning, High One." Bast said the name of the dreaded island without so much as a shoulder flinch.

"He was not a man, but a curse, a Second who must be destroyed," Montu said.

"Without the unanimous vote of the entire Council, we can't move forward against Seconds," Bast countered, and looked to Ptolema.

This was her moment. Her gut roiled with nausea. Edrice's and Montu's eyes were on her as well, not to mention those of the other forty-seven Council members. Two months of this and still her fingers glazed with cool sweat.

Ptolema pulled herself to her full seated height, headdress included.

"Councilman Bast is correct. We cannot do anything without a unanimous decision. Until more evidence of a resurgence of Seconds can be proved, we need not meet again on this matter. Thank you." She rose and the pressure on her rear end lessened. *Thank goodness.*

The groups dispersed. The door was so close, Ptolema could almost taste the fresh air. She swept through the hall, only to have a fierce voice stop her.

"We will have to decide something soon. Even without more Seconds showing themselves, this man was proof of their existence." Montu followed her out into the corridor.

"Of course they exist." Bast stepped between them, massaging his temples. "Men and women love each other, and nature happens."

"Dangerous nature, Councilman Bast. Or have you forgotten your history? If we allow those cursed results of nature to run rampant, our city will be destroyed—"

"Mythology is not the same thing as history," Bast cut in, voice sharp. "Have you found the missing Tablets? Have you been poring over the Forgotten Histories without us?"

Montu swelled, his face deepening to a savage purple. "How dare you—!"

Ptolema held a hand up.

"Gentlemen, I have decided for now. Please leave it at that. Now, if you will excuse me ... ?"

"Of course." Montu swallowed whatever threat he had prepared to dole out on Bast's head and offered a half-hearted bow. He turned away, no doubt to seek solace in his misery with Edrice. She stood in the back of the chamber, her face a cloud of annoyance.

"You did well, High One. Your father would be proud," Bast whispered, low enough for only Ptolema to hear.

She smiled. "Thank you. Though I'm not sure the others agree."

"Your father was a young High One once too. They all accepted him with time." He dipped a bow and turned to depart down the tunnel.

"Councilman Bast, wait."

He paused mid-stride, his already sagging shoulders dropping an inch further. His weariness washed across her, and Ptolema almost sighed. Now wasn't the time. She pressed closer to him, the refreshing scent of oranges wafting from his toga.

"Did my father ever mention anything the missing Tablets of History might have said?" It was a shot in the dark. No one had ever known anything written on the Tablets.

Bast turned, his face more haggard than she had ever seen it. He shook his head. "No. It's been hundreds of years, High One. No one knows."

"But knowing what they said would make this all easier."

"Perhaps, but then human nature is still in play. Good day, High One." A shadow crossed his face, darkening the deep lines. He turned away, not bothering to stay and argue with the rest of the Council, whose bickering echoed off the dim walls. Ptolema couldn't blame him.

Fools, the lot of them.

A tingle of the rebellion of her childhood touched her fingers, and she giggled. Too low for anyone to hear, of course, but it felt good, until something brushed her elbow.

"My apologies, High One," muttered Edrice.

"How old is Councilman Bast?" Ptolema could still see his back fading away down the corridor.

"Fifty-two, I believe. Your father selected him from the people's nominations, even though he was hardly a day past his twentieth birthday." A touch of scorn entered Edrice's voice, but she covered it with a chuckle.

"Thank you, Edrice." Ptolema left her with no further explanation and headed back up the Pyramid, the roar of the waterfall her only company. Fifty-two? He could have been seventy judging from the wrinkles on his face. Either way, he didn't know any more than the rest of them about the missing Histories.

Torchlight flickered in the library's doorway as she approached. She hadn't made her way through those shelves in such a long time. The knot of nausea from the Council Chamber returned, but this time the face of her father accompanied it.

Two months.

The last time had been with her father the day before he passed into eternal sleep. She brushed the wooden door frame. Smooth, forgotten. Maybe there would be one tablet in there to remind her of him. One story.

Ptolema entered, expecting to turn toward the shelves which housed the fabled stories, but her feet took her the opposite direction. Toward the older shelves and the dust-covered tablets.

"Mythology is not the same as history," she murmured. Bast's retort to Montu. What had he meant? The familiar thrill of curiosity gripped her as she moved further back into the shelves. Perhaps a tablet on Seconds and their rebellion would set her mind at ease. She could return to the Council Chamber tomorrow with a clearer verdict to soothe Montu and Edrice. Not that she cared about soothing them, but she had to appear wiser than they if she ever hoped to win their respect.

Her fingers danced across tablets, some so old their titles were no longer legible. She had read a tablet from this section once, long ago as a child with her father. What had it been called? Something about the rebellion, of course.

"If you are looking for the Tablets of History, you won't find anything before the Seconds' Rebellion, and even that one is missing." A man's low tones drifted from the darkness beside her.

Ptolema spun to the left. The flickering torchlight deepened the shadows under the eyes of the thin man sitting in the corner, his legs crossed under him. He wore a black toga, a rare color in El-Pelusium, and his hair hung just past his ears where it flipped out.

She crossed her arms over her chest. Two strangers in one day? Either luck or misfortune favored her. Tradition dictated she shouldn't speak to either of them.

Fling tradition out the sky-wall window for all I care.

"You're not from the Pyramid." She made it a statement, not a question.

The man nodded, his green eyes flashing. "Correct. I am not."

"So what are you doing in my library?"

"Reading." His eyes widened in mockery of her question.

Ptolema held her tongue for a moment. This stranger was as odd as the first. He studied her as intently as she studied him.

"Maybe I should have been more specific. How did you get into my library? We reserve it for Council members and royalty."

"Ah, yes. I should have expected that question." He set the tablet down with a scrape of stone on stone and shuffled through a hidden pocket in his toga. He pulled out a folded bit of parchment and held it out. "An official invitation from High One Kentimentiu to peruse the library of El-Pelusium."

The stranger should have risen and brought the paper to her, not made her stoop low to see it, but curiosity drove her forward. The man handed the letter to her. The paper was light, expensive. She unfolded the letter and saw that the symbol for her father sat in the lower corner. Signed. There was no mistaking the curling ends of each letter. The words were a brief invitation to do just as the stranger said.

"You know my father is dead?"

"My condolences. I heard just before I arrived."

"So then you know by the laws of El-Pelusium, this letter has no power?" Ptolema held it out, the torches casting shadows across her dead father's writing. The paper shook slightly, but the stranger made no note of it.

"Are you asking me to leave?" His green eyes flashed as he smiled.

He was daring to joke with the High One. He was daring, and refreshing. Ptolema offered him the letter back. "I will allow you to stay if it was my father's wish. But I require a reason."

"I am a student of history. Your library was the last on my list in completing my studies."

She glanced down to the tablet in his lap. The age-old etching was worn from the touch of many hands pulling it from the shelf. "How can you even see that?"

"I feel more than I see." He ran a finger over the letters. "This is a story older than this city. A myth about a creator and the rise of man. But you won't find historical tablets of this age."

"I know. They are missing. Everyone knows that."

"Then why are you looking for them?" He held her gaze.

"I wasn't looking for them. I need to see if there is a tablet holding any further information on the Rebellion of the Seconds apart from what the missing Histories held, and—"

She stopped. Perhaps she shouldn't be telling the stranger these things. But what did it matter? Maybe he had come across them. If her father had trusted him to come into their city, their library, there must be a reason.

Perhaps her father had known his fate and wanted someone like this to provide Ptolema knowledge.

Maybe she was simply desperate, looking for straightforward answers to impossible questions. Ptolema drew herself up. She was High One now. She could make her own decisions.

"If you are a student of history, perhaps you can help me. I need to see what is wrong with the Seconds, where it started."

"Ah. Well, you won't find that either."

"For a stranger not from El-Pelusium, you know much about my city and my library." She stepped toward him, arms crossed. "Do all students of history know so much?"

"For being High One, you know very little." The man stood and stepped toward her. "I also study countries, cultures, life, and myth. I travel from library to library, growing my own library of knowledge. In just a few days here, I have learned all you once learned, most likely in a childhood of study."

Such gall! But there was something about the way he spoke, the light sarcasm, the dry wit, that made her want to laugh. Instead, she offered a token of peace.

"What's your name?"

He stopped just short of her and dropped into a bow. "Radames at your service, High One."

"Just Radames? No land, no family name?"

"Just Radames." His beak-shaped nose was the only feature of interest on his face.

When he offered no other reason for his single name, Ptolema waved to the shelves of tablets. "My father told me the Tablets of History went missing the night of the palace fire, at the end of the Seconds' rebellion, either stolen or lost to the flames. But even if the fire ruined the tablets, there would be at least some trace of them left, wouldn't there?"

"So you think they were stolen?"

"They had to have been. But it happened hundreds of years ago. We will never know for sure." She ran her hand along a row of tablets.

"True."

"And the reason the Seconds can't be trusted? Why is that tablet about the Rebellion missing?" The tablets were cold under Ptolema's fingertips, silent, keeping their mysteries to themselves. Her nail caught in a rough crack on the edge of a tablet, and she winced.

"Because it was never recorded." Radames pulled the offending tablet from the shelf with a grinding noise and ran his index finger over it. "These are what people witnessed, or invented themselves for the enjoyment of others. What you are seeking came into being organically after they murdered half your ancestors and the Pyramid burned three hundred years ago. Now time has forgotten it."

"And how do you know that?"

"You've heard the oral account of the rebellion your entire life, correct?"

"Of course. We built our society upon it." Ptolema shifted under his fierce gaze. How unfair of him to make her feel so insignificant. "Everyone knows there used to be many Seconds and even Thirds. But eventually they rose and tried to take the Pyramid. They inflicted significant damage before the Rebellion ended. The next High One banished all future Second-borns to the island of Thoth." The words came out automatically, as if she recited them again to her childhood tutor.

Radames nodded as she spoke, stroking his chin. "Is that all you know?"

Ptolema stepped back, cheeks burning.

"Do all people from wherever you are from have so little respect?"

Radames held up a hand. "I meant nothing by it. It's an honest question. Do you not know the cause behind the rebellion?"

"I—" She turned to the long row of tablets, their rough edges dark in the shifting shadows of the lone torch. A time from years ago hovered in the deep recesses of her mind, when her father brought her to the library to explain the missing Tablets of History. "It was something bad. Something truly awful. My ancestors were more scared than any enemy could make them."

"That is correct."

"Where did you learn so much of my people's history?"

"Sometimes the best place to keep your history is in the minds of those who witness it from afar, unbiased."

"So you know what the missing Tablets say? You can tell me?"

Radames eyed her for a moment, thumb and forefinger circling the groomed bit of hair on his chin. "I do not know what they say."

Ptolema could not stop a scoff from rising.

"Then why are you leading me on to think you did? You are wasting my time." She turned away from the shelf. She should be in her room, going over papers the Council members sent her.

Cold fingers dug into her wrist. "Ouch! Don't touch me!" She jerked her arm out of Radames's grasp.

"I am sorry for the force, High One, but I think you should hear what I have to say." He held his hand up. "I mean no harm. I came here seeking knowledge for myself, but now I see my true purpose. Let me help you."

"I have no reason to trust you. No way to know your true intentions." Why was she even still talking to him? "I could have your hand removed for touching me." She turned away and moved for the exit.

"Again, my apologies, but I think your father would want you to hear what I have to say."

Ptolema paused mid-stride, catching herself in the back of the heel with her other foot. A firm arm slipped under her, stopping the fall before it happened.

Radames pulled away. "Are you all right?"

"You knew my father?"

"High One Khentimentiu entertained me once. I was journeying home after a year on the road. He had already been High One for seven years, though he was only just into his twenties. Young, like myself, but his instincts were good. A man to respect."

Her father had become High One at only fifteen, far earlier than Ptolema. Her own age of twenty-two wasn't that young, and she needed to stop letting the Council members treat her as if it was. And if this man knew her father, perhaps he knew things which could help.

As if guessing her thought, Radames bowed. "Please, High One, let me help you."

She resisted the urge to straighten her headdress and stared him down. "Meet me in my chambers tomorrow evening."

Radames nodded. "Thank you."

Ptolema turned and swept from the room, her toga snapping behind her. The thrill of renewed curiosity vibrated with each footstep back up to her rooms. People hated Seconds, even feared them. That had stayed the same for at least three hundred years. Something horrible had spurred that hate, that much she knew. Her father had told her many times. One child was exceptional, a blessing. But there was something that happened between the firstborn and the second, and between all the following births. Something evil.

Maybe fate, and her father, had sent her Radames in her hour of decision to finally tell her what the Histories had forgotten.

CHAPTER 4

"I'm pleased your hands are better today, Tiye."

"Thank you." She handed Jabarre a freshly laundered stack of linens.

"I am even more pleased the High One has come to her senses and will allow us up today. This sale only happens every three months, and I need it." He pressed the linens into the bottom of a cloth lined basket.

Tiye coughed to cover a shudder. Why had the High One wanted to speak with her yesterday? She was just a commoner from the Lower Pyramid. If Tiye had let Miki slip out for even a moment, the High One wouldn't have been so friendly. Arrest. Banishment. Fingers removed.

Too much, Miki whispered in the forefront of her mind, louder than she had been in four years, apart from the time in the cellar. Tiye almost stepped toward the door, but not to follow Jabarre. The street outside led back to her small house. The straw pallet rarely seemed like home, but this morning she hadn't wanted to leave. After wandering through the hazy Inner Pyramid last night to clear her thoughts after her run-in with the High One, she still ended up vomiting the moment she got home. A strong glass of wine took away the acidic taste lingering in her throat, but it hadn't erased the High One from her mind. Restless sleep plagued her until well past midnight. Even then, the conversation with the High One lingered.

"Would you like to come?"

"What?"

Jabarre stepped out of the shop and placed the basket of linens on a wheeled cart. "Would you like to come to the Higher Pyramid? It's not every day anyone is welcome up there. Have you ever seen the waterfall up close? I'm assuming you didn't get the chance yesterday since the Steelmen wouldn't let you pass. You are fortunate Councilwoman Edrice hasn't complained." An unspoken 'yet' lingered in his tone.

Tiye shrugged. "I'd rather not. Doesn't seem all that exciting."

"Are you sure? You get quite a magnificent view of the whole Pyramid from up there. Not to mention you may get a glimpse of the High One, if she graces the market with her presence."

Bile tickled the back of her throat. "Yes, I'm sure. I'll keep the shop here open."

"All right, then. If any of my major customers come, send them up to me." He slung a satchel of thread over his shoulder and pushed the cart up the road, joining a line of merchants desperate to get through the tunnel to the Higher Pyramid.

Tiye slouched onto the bench under the window. She should have brought another bottle of wine. Jabarre didn't allow it at the shop, but he wouldn't be back until sundown.

A scuffle of feet slapped the stones outside. A shadow fell over her as a woman stepped into the shop. Tall. Very tall. Unbelievably curly black hair. Eyes wide. Tight toga leggings. Skin taut and pale.

"May I help you?"

The woman ignored her and flattened against the wall, fingers curling against the molding. "Kal, hurry."

The stone bench scraped against Tiye's exposed heel as she jumped up, but the hiss of pain stayed locked in her throat. A man stumbled through the doorway just as a shout split the square outside. He was almost as tall as the woman, with hair flipping out just past his ears. His toga was ripped and splotched with mud. He yanked the woman out of the doorway. "Quick! Get down!"

"Did you need something?" Tiye approached, though her gut twisted.

The man shoved a small sack toward her. "There's five lotus nuts in there. Please let us hide in here."

A shadow passed the doorway. Two Steelmen, plain headdresses, bare chests. They paused in the street outside, scanning the market. Tiye looked away, heart in her ears. They weren't there for her, but that didn't make things any easier.

The man pressed closer to the woman and held her protectively against the wall.

"We've got to go." His pale face lost any color it had left as the Steelmen moved toward the cloth shop's door.

"Kal! That's Mandisa's neighbor," the woman whispered. Another woman walked behind the Steelmen, short and so thin a lick of wind might have sent her toppling to the ground.

The man shoved the woman to the side. Something white flicked to the floor, but he either didn't see it or ignored it. "Get to the back of the shop! I won't let them take you."

The couple seemed to have forgotten Tiye was there, scared as they were. The woman clenched Kal's hand, knuckles white. Tiye tried to step away from the window and the troubling couple, but Miki yanked her forward.

Seconds, Miki whispered. *They are Seconds.* Her fingers wrapped around the woman's hand, warm on clammy, before she could think. "In the back room. Now."

"What?"

"Go!"

The woman's face paled further. "How do you know—?"

"They will find you. *Go!*" Tiye pointed to the curtain cutting off the storeroom.

Kal moved first, dragging the woman up with him. The door flap brushed aside, letting in a light breeze. Tiye spun back to the door, breath in the back of her throat.

A Steelman stepped into the shop.

"Is anyone in here with you?" He scanned the saleroom, empty apart from Tiye, and Miki rattling in the back of her mind.

"No. My last customer left ten minutes ago." The lie came easily, and by some miracle, her voice did not waver.

The second Steelman started toward the storeroom, but the first grunted in exasperation.

"If you check every nook and cranny, this is going to take us until winter. She said no, let's go. We will find the Second somewhere else." He exited.

The other Steelman moved for the storeroom anyway. Tiye stepped to intercept him, not even sure of what she could say to dissuade him. The tingle in her hand flooded the rest of her body as she reached to yank him back.

"Go about your work."

The Steelman stepped away from the storeroom—now empty—and left the shop.

Tiye exhaled with a shudder. The back door stood ajar, and the alley beyond was deserted. They must not have bothered to hide. Nausea rippled through her belly.

Seconds. The Steelman had confirmed it.

Tiye staggered back into the shop, gripping her head. She rested her forehead against the warm sandstone wall by the window where the couple had crouched. Something crinkled beneath her toes. Squinting, she pulled the creased and mud-splotched parchment out from under her foot.

—who am I?

The words drew her eyes like a Firstborn was drawn to a sense of self-worth. Tiye pulled the paper out between her fingers and spread it flat against the linen folding bench with a crunch loud enough to call the Steelmen back.

[begin block letter]

Kal,

I hate this. I hate it all. You say I'm me. But who am I? I can't hide from one me forever while pretending to be the other me. It's going to end sometime. I think Mandisa's neighbor knows about Dalilah. I think it is time to go. Meet me tomorrow in the Lower Pyramid.

With love, no matter who I am,

Dalilah

[end block letter]

The words, so familiar, yet so confusing, drew Tiye in again. This Dalilah made it quite plain how she felt. More importantly, Dalilah was the Second. It might not be as plain to someone else, but her words too closely mirrored Miki's struggles, before Miki chose to be Tiye.

"A Second," she muttered. She knew it. She wasn't the only one. Well, maybe the only Fifth, but not the only unwanted member of society. Tiye exhaled and sank to the floor to relieve her shaking legs, but doing so did nothing to relieve the pressure in her head.

She had found another Second. A Second who was on the verge of being caught. And by helping them, she had put herself in danger, especially with this letter. The man had been foolish to drop it. If the Steelmen found it …

Tiye stood again, pulse spiking. She ran back to the storeroom and fumbled for a torch. None. A bucket and a flint box would do. The letter went up in a puff of smoke, red lines eating at the betraying words of Dalilah until only ash remained. The faint heat touched Tiye's cheek, and she shuddered.

Nineteen years of hiding, of not looking for any signs of other Seconds. Nineteen years, all gone in one day.

CHAPTER 5

"Someone named Radames is here to see you. He says he was invited." The guard scowled. The teal headdress did not mix with his olive skin, and it lent a sickly green pallor to his face.

Ptolema waved him aside. "Yes, I invited him. Please let him in."

The man's frown deepened, but he stepped back through the doorway, the sheer curtain fluttering down behind him. The wooden chair grated against the stone floor as Ptolema pushed back from the desk. It was one of the few chairs in El-Pelusium, but it wasn't much more comfortable than the stone throne. Rubbing her constantly sore rump, Ptolema stood. The patterned and jeweled headdress gleamed at her from the far corner of the room. With a sigh, she crossed the empty chamber to retrieve it. She could have met with Radames in the larger of her four rooms, but this one, being smaller and more intimate, made her visitors feel privy to her life and thus her power. Puffed-up egos could be quite helpful. She needed any tactics she could muster against the ruthless Council members.

Ptolema faced the roaring waterfall as she settled the headdress over her hair. The evening air, though still warm in the late summer, blew through with a damp chill after passing through the cascading water. Hundreds of tons of water plowed down from the mountain above to pour across her sky-wall. A short wall edging her balcony proved all the protection she needed from the water. The familiar scent of wet stone and algae clung to her room.

Home.

It was almost enough to make her forced smile real. But a reason to leave the papers stacked on the desk for even five minutes, gifts from the ever thoughtful Council members, was reason to smile. One day she would burn the endless reports of theft, solutions to rout imagined impending risings of Seconds, ways to ensure she held the throne eternally, and other such nonsense.

As if.

But maybe Radames's information could mix up the tedium. With any luck, she might learn things her father never knew. Ptolema straightened her headdress in the washbasin's reflection by the doorway. She leaned over the bowl until her nose was six inches from the surface. She traced the line of the scar above her left eye, faint but visible. The balm sat on her desk. Should she cover the scar as she so often did?

She stroked it again, passing over the three-inch groove. A clumsy child she had been. Mother's face, torn with grief. A wet rag pressing against the cut. Blood streaming into her eye. Pain, so much pain.

Ptolema pulled away from the washbasin, eyes closed, shutting out her mother. Now was not the time. Radames could see her without the balm, as so few did.

Her slippers swished across the floor tiles as she made her way to the ring of stone benches and sank onto one of the gold-edged pillows. Finally, a forgiving surface for her much abused rear.

"Radames, High One." The guard's voice came from the hall just as a hand parted the curtain. Radames stepped into her chambers as Ptolema sat straighter. In the shifting light of the sun coming through the pouring water, Radames's toga was deep blue, not black. He was taller than she remembered. His eyes were twice as piercing but his nose was less beak-shaped. A pleasant change.

She gave him the honor of a nod. "Good to see you again, Radames."

He moved forward, feet bare without his leather sandals. He took a seat opposite her without asking, but she did not bother to correct him. He was foreign, after all. She couldn't expect him to understand cultural taboos.

"I've been looking forward to this meeting." His green eyes shone in the reflected light from the waterfall. "Although I must admit I'm going to have a hard time hearing you with such a loud roar right above our heads," he added loudly, jabbing a long finger upward.

"You'll grow accustomed to it. It's nothing more than background noise to me."

"I suppose it would be." He gave a pleasant deep chuckle.

Ptolema's shoulders relaxed. This man knew her father, and he knew some forgotten history of El-Pelusium. Both things were good. He wasn't a Council member out to trip her up. Another good mark on his record. Still, she couldn't let her guard down too much. She waved a hand over the empty fire grate between them. "Where is it you traveled from?"

"As I said, I am widely traveled." He smiled and reclined on the bench with one hand on the back. The smile transformed his face from one she would have called middle-aged to quite a few years younger.

"Yes, but where do you call home?"

"A place far from here you surely would not know. A small mining village of little significance." The smile slipped for an instant, only to be back the next moment stronger than ever.

"Does this village have a name?"

He shrugged. "It's too long for you to pronounce properly. But it hardly exists anymore, and means nothing to anyone outside its borders. After all, it's your home that I am here to discuss, is it not?"

Ptolema adjusted the pillow beneath her rear. She rested her elbows on her knees and stared Radames down. One of the few times in the past two months she could act as herself.

"What do the people in your village say of my Pyramid?"

"Not very much, I'm afraid. They never leave and so know nothing."

"Is that why you became a traveling scholar? To break the mold?"

"Yes, I suppose that could be why. I always blamed it on an insatiable curiosity."

"And what is it that people in other cities say of El-Pelusium?"

"I take it you don't get many visitors?" The smile was wry this time.

Ptolema frowned. He noticed too quickly. But then, they didn't exactly try to hide the fact.

"We get merchants, but they never come further than the Lower Pyramid. They are afraid. And the dignitaries of other nations, well ..." She sat back with a dismissive wave of her hand. "They prefer to send letters. I have been lucky to entertain one so far in just two months of power, and can look forward to only a handful more before I retire."

"Out of curiosity, who was the one you entertained? I may know him. My travels have taken me to many cities, and I have spoken with many dignitaries and rulers."

She managed to stifle a gasp with a cough at that, but she made her comment a statement, not a question.

"Really."

Radames held a hand up in surrender, as if reading her face.

"Take no offense, High One. I have placed myself in many precarious situations in order to grow my knowledge, many times with people you would suggest I run from." He chuckled, but his eyes darkened.

"No offense taken. My father warned me such things do not always go well. But visitors are beside the point. I want to know more about my people. Radames ..." Ptolema met his gaze and pulled herself straight, "what can you tell me of the Seconds?"

Radames said nothing for a moment. The noise of the water heightened to a crashing boom He pulled his arm off the back of the bench and cleared his throat. "High One—"

"You can call me Ptolema."

"Ptolema, what is the most you know of the Seconds' Rebellion?"

"A Second-born tried to overthrow the High One. He claimed the High One was evil because he was a Firstborn.

The Second had a mysterious power which helped in the rebellion. Many other Seconds and even Thirds"—a shudder swept Ptolema's back—"went up against the High One. They burned half the Pyramid and killed the High One. But someone killed the Second and banished the rest. They put our current single-child law and banishment of Seconds in place." She shrugged and sat back. "That's all anyone knows anymore."

"And that is what they teach in the schools?"

"Yes. Some instructors add to it for drama's sake, but what I just said is all we can count as true."

"Well, at least it ensures no more will be forgotten."

"My great-grandfather started it. All children learn by age three."

A frown tugged at Radames's thin lips. "But they do not learn why Second-borns are feared?"

"We teach them the danger of Seconds. Of what they have done. What they can do."

"And what is that?"

"Radames, I don't mean to offend you by mentioning such things." Ptolema shifted on the pillow, still uncomfortable, though it had more to do with the topic than her rear end.

Radames held her gaze, and she looked away, not sure why. When he cleared his throat, she looked back to find his eyes closed.

"The ability of Manipulation has been around since the dawn of man, High One. Speaking of it will not offend me."

She inhaled so fast the air whistled through the slight gap in her front teeth. Most everyone in the Pyramid refused to talk of Manipulation, and the subject had essentially become taboo. "So you know of it?"

His eyes remained closed. "There was a time I did not, but I won't be so ignorant again."

"So Manipulation is real?" Ptolema leaned forward, the pillow slipping from under her and landing on the floor with a thump. "That's the advantage the Second in the rebellion had?"

"That is what those in my homeland say."

A shiver worked its way up her spine. Her father had only spoken of Manipulation once, and even then in two short, clipped sentences, his face yellowed by the liver disease that would claim him.

Don't ask, Ptolema. It's ... Death. An uncontrollable curse, inbred.

He had been frightened of Manipulation up to his deathbed in this very chamber. She shivered.

"What is it?"

"Manipulation is power. A way to force the elements of this world to follow your commands. It's evil, High One." Radames's eyes opened, sharp and green, like the deepest part of the ocean Ptolema had seen once as a child. "Never underestimate it."

"And this is what the Seconds have?"

"Manipulation isn't something you *have*. They *take* it. A Firstborn has no ability to do so. That keeps them pure. But each birth after the first redoubles the power. Seconds, since they are more common than Thirds or anything beyond, are the natural ones to fear. With a word they can Manipulate nature and bring destruction to us all." The sun slipped behind the Pyramid at his words, and a chill seeped into the room.

Ptolema sat back, uneasy gurgling sounding in her stomach. If a Second could move stone, he could rip the Pyramid down. Uncontrollable, her father had said. "It makes so much sense," she muttered. "But if that's true—"

"It is, Ptolema," Radames's voice was sharp, cold. He frowned. "I have encountered these Manipulators. I wish I could say the myth has exaggerated their power, but in truth it underestimates them."

The water thundered past the sky-wall, leaving the veranda sprinkled with wet splotches. To have the power to stand under that mist and move it ... What would it be like to whisper a command and redirect the waterfall's flow? If she'd been alone, she might have reached out to brush the water, but not with Radames present. Not with so many unanswered questions.

"How do you know this?" she said. "It's not that I don't trust you—"

"But you don't trust me." His light laugh swept over her like a warm breeze. "It's quite all right, Ptolema. The scrolls of Smyma were the most helpful, I must admit. They speak of strange boulders taking out city walls on their own accord. They never considered someone might be behind those boulders. Even my own village, as ignorant of the world as they were, knew of the Manipulation in El-Pelusium. Knew of its consequences. The ancient stories were passed down to keep us afraid." He leaned forward, eyes narrowed with intensity. His left hand balled into a fist, and he shook it while he spoke. "My village witnessed the destructive power of Manipulation firsthand. It is the driving force behind my journey for knowledge."

His new intensity stole Ptolema's breath, but she leaned forward to meet him.

"The only time my father talked about Manipulation, he said it was because of a curse a thousand years ago," she said. "A Second-born High One murdered his sister to take the throne. Father didn't say any more than that. Who put the curse on us?" The stone edge of the bench cut into the backs of her thighs, but she didn't relax.

Radames clicked his tongue. "Ah, that is the greatest mystery. We might never unravel it."

"But there were Manipulators in your village? Was it close to the Pyramid?"

"It was high in the Northern mountains. Our tales said we were distant descendants of people from El-Pelusium, but that's all I know. My research never showed why only the Pyramid and my village had the power, and why Manipulation hasn't surfaced anywhere else. My village stuck to themselves. They didn't travel or marry outsiders. I'm sorry I can't tell you more." His apology looked genuine as he scowled at the empty fire. His hand clenched in his lap.

Ptolema leaned back. Well, he couldn't have known everything.

"Why did you speak of your village in the past? Is it now gone?"

Radames's hands relaxed, and he pulled back.

"If you need confirmation of what I have told you, ask a member of your Council." His eyes flashed in the depth of the green. "You may be surprised how tongues will wag when not held back by societal stigmas. One of them will be brave enough to speak about Manipulation with you, even if they would never do so in a hall full of their peers. Better yet, if you can manage it, speak to a commoner. Someone who doesn't stand to gain anything from admitting their genuine feelings." He stood and dipped a bow.

Ptolema did not move. Radames had not earned that status even if he had achieved a private audience with her. And he had dodged her question. Still, she was grateful.

"Thank you. I will think on what you have said. Are you leaving El-Pelusium?"

He stroked his chin, considering. "I have a mind to continue my travels tomorrow. Unless there is something you suggest I should read, or a sight to see before I leave?"

Ptolema did not offer the branch he wanted. "Travel safely."

"It's been a pleasure, High One. I have one last tidbit of advice. Further proof will present itself. You have caught one Second. How long before there is another?" Radames bowed again and left the room, dark toga swirling about him.

Ptolema stood the moment the veil fell back over the doorway, and the doors thunked shut beyond it. She stood on the veranda and let the mist of the waterfall dance upon her face, remembering the times she had stood here with her father, asking him where the water went.

"Down there," he would say, and point to the miles of Pyramid stacked below her. "It keeps us safe. It brings life."

But the Seconds brought death, if Radames was correct. Ptolema walked to the edge of the veranda, her skin covered in a fine layer of moisture. A low wall stopped her from being able to walk off the veranda or touch the powerful water. The lights of the lower Pyramid were just being lit, small pinpricks of fire glowing far below. Perhaps someone down there would speak with her about

Manipulation, the one word no one dared utter anywhere, much less in the presence of the High One, Firstborn of all Firstborns. A crime against all things the founders of the Pyramid cleaved to a thousand years ago.

The same rebellious streak her tutors so often tried to lecture out of her resurfaced as it had in the Council Hall. She rubbed her sore rear end and smiled, wondering what it would be like to walk through the Lower Pyramid undetected. How would it feel to truly see her people, perhaps even find a friend?

She turned away from the sky-wall, wiping the mist off her face with the sleeve of her toga. She could be a High One trapped by the mistakes of her ancestors and the threats of the future. Or she could be a High One who looked for a way out.

CHAPTER 6

Miki. Miki. Miki.

The name flitted through Tiye's mind. What had been foreign and unwanted the day before now sounded warm, as it hadn't since childhood.

Miki.

Her true name.

Tiye would not have helped Dalilah and Kal, the fugitive Second and her lover. Miki would have, and did.

A poof of dust rose from the road as she turned onto her street. She sneezed, holding an arm over her face to catch the sneeze just in time. The linen in her elbow carried the scent of oranges, like her father's house. Her gut twisted.

Miki.

A grunt, and an elbow dug into her side. A man in a half toga mumbled an apology and continued on his way. A tingle resonated at the base of her skull.

A cat ran across the road in front of her, a streak of black. Tiye stumbled to a halt but avoided tripping over the animal. Grumbling, she rounded the corner and her home came into view.

The door stood ajar, a dark sliver between wall and wood. Gravel crunched underfoot as she stepped forward. She should turn and flee. Maybe her father had come? He wouldn't be so foolish as to leave the door ajar, not after the other night. Rough wood met her fingers, and she almost drew back, thin breaths rattling in her head.

The door was jerked inward, leaving her hand hanging a foot from the High One's face.

Tiye choked.

"Oh, I'm so glad you're home, Tiye. It took me half the morning to find out where you live. The Steelmen of the Lower Pyramid were beyond helpful. At least two of them can't keep their eyes off you. Did you know that? It's amazing what someone will admit to the High One." Her caramel hair hung free to her shoulders, unfettered by any headdress. A plain toga draped across her. Nothing to show who she was.

The punishment for seeing her without her headdress was death! Tiye staggered back. "W—what? Your head—"

The High One waved the words away. "I chose to come like this. You won't be arrested. But you should know the Steelmen find the Lower Pyramid's cloth woman quite attractive." The High One beckoned toward the inside of the small house. "Come in, come in. I've been waiting for an hour. I can't wait much longer, or else the Steelmen will start looking for me."

"You've been waiting for me?" Tiye's leaden feet did not move.

"Yes. You're the only commoner I know." Her face fell. "That sounds so pathetic." Her chuckle held a hint of remorse. But she perked up again the next moment and clamped her cool fingers around the other's wrist. "Come in. This is your home after all."

The High One was in her house, and she hadn't come to arrest Tiye. Was she horrified about the small, sparse space? A bed pallet, table, and a cabinet in the corner holding Tiye's few belongings were the only furniture. There were no decorations. A fire grate sat in the wall at the far end, dark for now. Tiye let the woman guide her to the stone table and its low benches.

The High One did not sit herself, but grimaced and stepped away to grab a bowl of lotus nuts sitting on the windowsill.

"These are quite the delicacy. The cloth shop must do well for you." The High One popped one into her mouth and smiled. "Well, say something. I remember you had a tongue when we met at the waterfall."

Tiye cleared her throat. "Sorry. I'm just a bit confused."

A pink hue flooded the High One's cheeks.

"I would like to get to know you, Tiye."

"Get to know me?" The woman had to be insane.

The High One sat on the bench across from Tiye, frowning.

"Cursed stone benches. You really should get some cushions made. They're allowed for someone of your station." She popped another nut into her mouth and smiled. "Look, I spend all day sitting and listening to people older than me drone on about what they think is right. I nod and say my part. But for once I want to hear someone else's point of view, someone who hasn't been warped by the Council."

At least the bench was there to hold Tiye up. So this had nothing to do with Seconds. Just a lonely High One.

"I am very busy, High One."

"Ptolema. My name is Ptolema. I'm a guest in your home. Please don't call me by that absurd title."

"All right." But Tiye could not bring herself to say the name. "Perhaps we can speak another time." She choked on her tongue and didn't suggest they never speak at all.

"Oh, come now. You are finished with work and don't have a husband to entertain. The Steelmen seem to know much about you." She winked, as if Tiye should let a Steelman court her. "What better way to spend an afternoon than chatting with me?" She flashed a brilliant smile.

"High One—"

"Ptolema."

"Have you ever been inside someone's house in the Lower Pyramid?"

Ptolema's face twitched. "No."

"Then you can see why I am a bit out of sorts." Tiye made to stand.

"But that is exactly why I am here!" She grabbed Tiye's wrists and pulled her back onto the bench with an *oomph* of expelled air. Ptolema flushed. "Do you have any wine?"

"Wine?"

"Yes. The liquid, alcoholic kind? Red, perhaps, or purple?"

Tiye slid off the bench and moved for the pantry in the corner beside her bed pallet. She cleared her throat and pulled the cabinet open with a squeak. Two bottles of wine stared up at her, each worth ten days' wages.

"Red or purple, High One?" Her voice squeaked and then cracked.

"Please, call me Ptolema. I'll take red. Purple is too sweet."

Tiye pulled the bottle down and brought it to the table where Ptolema had already set two wooden mugs. She beamed and motioned for Tiye to pour. Tiye stared for a moment at the red-tinged cork. The woman didn't deserve her wine. Her hard work. The only thing which brought her pleasure in her life. Her fingers tightened around the thin clay neck of the bottle.

"Do you need an unstopper?"

"No, it's open."

"Ah, so you are a wine drinker yourself."

Tiye nodded, her neck smarting at the motion. Her tongue tingled in anticipation, yearning for the dry notes of the wine. She pressed her thumbs against the cork, which came up with a satisfying *pop*. The deep red liquid filled both mugs and left the bottle half empty. Tiye set the bottle on the table and slid into the bench across from the High One.

The woman held her mug aloft in a salute of sorts, then threw it back and drained half the wine in one go. Her mug scraped against the table as she set it back down. She stared into the contents as if searching for words or answers.

Tiye tilted her own mug back, the smoky wine slipping into her mouth. She suppressed the urge to groan in satisfaction as she set the mug back down, still almost full. Wine was to be savored, not guzzled But then the High One could afford to drink as much wine as she liked.

"Tiye, what do you think of the Seconds?"

Tiye tried to cover a cough by sipping more wine, only to splash it on the table. She jumped up to fetch a rag. When she turned back, heart hammering, the High One was still staring at the contents of her mug, eyes crossed in concentration, frowning enough to pull a scar over her left eye down toward her eyebrow.

"Do you think they are an inherent danger?" the High One said. "Most of the Council seems to think so. After all, they've thought that way for three centuries."

This could not be happening. The High One of all El-Pelusium, the Firstborn of all Firstborns, could not be sitting in Tiye's home asking her opinion of Seconds. A chill crept toward the tips of her fingers.

Ptolema spoke again before she could answer. "I met a man, Tiye. He knows things, more than any member of the Council. He's been to the greatest libraries of the world, and he thinks the myth of the Seconds is true."

"I'm not sure it is." The words rushed out without a thought.

"Have you heard of Manipulation, Tiye?" Ptolema leaned over the table, her hair spilling across the surface.

"I—" Tiye swallowed. Ptolema hadn't come because she believed Tiye was a Second. Still, her heart thudded in her ears, drawing in the blackness to her peripheral vision and the familiar chill to her hands. The anxiety waited, ready to pounce on her mind.

"You can tell me. No one knows I'm here." Ptolema's hand crept across the table and squeezed Tiye's.

Tiye nodded, head heavy.

"Yes. I've heard." *Manipulation.* The cursed word hovered at the back of her throat, but she didn't dare let the syllables out.

"Radames, the man I met, claims this is the reason Seconds can't be trusted. He says they used Manipulation during the rebellion to kill my ancestors." Ptolema stuck a finger in her mouth and chewed on the already mangled nail. "Imagine, Tiye. They could rule this world."

"Well, then I would say that's good evidence that the story isn't true, since Seconds are not ruling El-Pelusium," Tiye said, perspiration beading on her forehead.

Pushing the boundary, Miki whispered in her mind. Tiye shivered and bitter bile stung her tongue. If she didn't fight back against the anxiety ... her behavior would be a dead giveaway to the High One that she was a Second.

"Only because we have banished them all." Ptolema began on another fingernail.

Tiye curled her fingers against her thigh, tearing her toga. Curse it all, she had to get herself together. The anxiety suffocated under a wave of something stronger. She couldn't reach across and strangle the woman, though her hands tingled at the idea. She compensated by lifting the wine to her lips again. The liquid trickled into her mouth, a soothing cool to the heat of the conversation.

Ptolema took Tiye's lack of response as affirmation of her comment. "We can't give Seconds the chance to Manipulate if this is true. We'd have to try even harder to find them all."

Tiye choked on the next swallow of wine and set her cup down with a loud scrape to cover the sound. She had to get Ptolema off that train of thought.

"But this man could be lying. If he is just trying to eradicate Seconds, he would *want* you to try harder."

Ptolema paused at that. She lowered her chewed nails and tapped the table. "But he is a foreigner. What cause would he have to lie?"

"There could be any number of reasons." Tiye leaned over the table in earnest now. "Has a Second ever caused you any harm? Have you ever met one?"

"No, of course I've never met one." She pulled away, affronted. "Have you?"

"No."

"Then you can't know if they would hurt you or not. Manipulation is a serious thing, Tiye. If Radames is right, we've been too lax on the Seconds and those who allow them."

Manipulation.

It all came back to that. To look in the High One's face and at the deep worry on her forehead, Tiye would think people went around killing using Manipulation every day. She dropped her gaze to her hands. Her smooth fingers. No power hid there. Nothing. The power was a myth. "High One—"

But the High One was pushing herself up from the bench.

"I've enjoyed this. You should come to my rooms for tea tomorrow morning. We can speak on this matter further."

Tiye jumped up after her. "I'd rather not."

The High One's laugh echoed around the small room. "You are hilarious, Tiye. I think we are going to be the best of friends." Her face went somber. "Think on what I told you. I can't delay much longer in making a decision regarding what to do about the Seconds." She turned, pulling the loose cowl neck of her toga up over her exposed hair. "Tomorrow, ten o'clock. I can't wait."

Then Tiye was alone, the silence only magnifying the words the High One had spoken.

We'd have to try even harder to find them.

Dalilah's pale face, Kal's wide eyes. Tiye slumped back onto the bench. The edges of black crept closer, drawing her in. Her fingers locked over her head, unwilling to let her straighten or curl them.

The darkness was coming.

Her breath came shallow, each inhalation pushing more pressure against her chest. A groan echoed in her throat, but there was nothing to do, nothing to stop the feeling. She closed her eyes as the waves of anxiety hit her, pulling her under, crushing her. A black death she could not escape, no matter how hard she tried.

"Tiye?"

Her father's voice. She opened her eyes, but the black did not recede. It heightened, increasing the pressure in her chest. The fingers clamped across her head grew clammy and stiffened further.

Footsteps moved closer. A warm hand pressed against her forehead. "Miki," he breathed. "Oh, Miki, you're all right. I'm here."

She needed to be alone, as she would be in the basement. Couldn't he see that? Alone with no chance of being caught or getting him caught. Alone in the darkness she grew up in.

Another hand pulled hers, smoothing her stiffened fingers out. "Shh, you're all right. Let it pass."

Tiye inhaled deeper this time. If it passed, would she be all right?

Yes. Yes, she would.

She inhaled a second time, letting the warm hair fill her lungs. The blackness receded half an inch, letting in her father's face, creased with worry. One more inhale, followed by a deep exhale, and the blackness faded.

"What are you doing here?" Her voice was a croak.

Her father's eyes were darker than usual. Something would have to be urgent for him to come to her home. "It's Hemeda. We must go to her."

"Hemeda?" Her sister's name pierced the air, as cold as her sister's voice the last time they had spoken. "She won't want to see me."

"Today might be different. She is—" He swallowed and pulled Tiye off the bench with bony fingers. "She is very sick."

"Sick? With what?"

"Hurry." Her father ducked back out into the oncoming evening.

Tiye hesitated long enough for a ball of worry to knot tight in her gut. What could possibly be wrong with her older sister to make her father so worried?

The blackness threatened again, but she balled her fists against it. No. Not again.

She ripped an over-tunic off the hook on the wall and hurried out the door. She followed him at a distance, never seeming to walk with him. They made two turns, then veered sharply to the left to enter the Inner Pyramid. The thick stone walls rose above her, like the crushing fear in her mind. Tiye exhaled, shaking, but kept following her father past the rows of stacked houses. Cooking-fire smoke mingled with the mist of water that rushed through the aqueduct in the Inner Pyramid's walls. The air was always hazy in here, just one of several reasons Tiye preferred to stay out.

Her father vanished around a corner. She lowered her head as she passed a gaggle of young Inner Pyramid girls, their topknots adorned with feathers. Several merchants hurried by, their arms laden with goods to take to the market for the morning.

One more turn and a door met her at a dead end. A breeze from far above tickled the end of Tiye's nose from where the air found its way into the enclosed Inner Pyramid through a sky-window.

Miki.

The name hovered on the air. Gravel crunched as Tiye jerked around. No one stood behind her, whispering the name, although she had heard it. Swallowing a lump in her throat, she turned back to the door. Tiye would never have come to Hemeda's home. Tiye did not have a sister.

"Miki." This time the name came from her own lips, softer than the wind itself. Today she had to be Miki again. Yesterday, with the fugitive Second, she had been Miki as well, even if she hadn't accepted it. With everything that was happening, there was no other choice.

The wood of the door was rough under her palm as she pushed it open. Stepping inside, Miki held her breath. The house was plain like most in the Pyramid, but fine weavings hung on the walls, gifts from her sister's merchant husband. He traveled more than he stayed at home.

Her father stood in the well-lit home, frowning. He was alone in the main space of the house, but flickering torch light shone through the doorway into the bedroom.

"Did you tell her I was here?"

"No. I did not want to give her the chance to refuse to see you." He ducked through the bedroom doorway.

She stepped in after him. The scent of herbs and spices hit her first. Sharp, bitter, clean. A large down-stuffed bed pallet took most of the space in the room, and on the bed lay Hemeda, dark hair spread about her head like a bird taking flight. Everything about her screamed sickness, but no distinct smell of malaise lingered in the room. The healers had done their work well.

Hemeda's large eyes met their father's, and she groaned. Even sick, her face held the same beauty Miki had envied as a child. Thin, with puckered lips and round eyes. Even in the bed, her tall frame showed, her feet pressing up against the edge of the blankets. The familiar glow of jealousy stirred in Miki's belly but vanished the moment Hemeda grimaced with some unknown pain. She massaged her temples with a pale hand.

"Father, I don't want to talk about it." Her voice held exhaustion, something unusual for Hemeda.

"I thought it might do you good to see family."

Miki attempted to shy back toward the doorway, but her sister's gaze shifted to her at the movement. Hemeda's eyes narrowed, and she inhaled with a hiss.

"You brought her? Are you completely mad?" She pushed herself up on her elbows, grimacing at the effort. "You're mocking me, aren't you? Showing me what I *did*."

What had she done? Miki stepped back again, but their father clamped his fingers around her shoulder, pulling him to her. "She's your sister, Hemeda. It's been years since you saw her."

"You're endangering my entire household by bringing her here."

"Grandfather Bast!" The squeak of a small boy's voice echoed off the walls behind them. A boy who came no higher than Miki's waist darted into the room and threw his arms around her father's legs.

A smile pulled at the old man's face, then vanished, replaced with creases of worry. "Good to see you too, Moises. If I promise to take you to the waterfall tomorrow, will you leave us to discuss grown-up things?"

Moises wilted and shot a glance to Miki. "Who is she?"

"This is your—"

"No one. That is no one," Hemeda's voice regained some strength, and the tone burned Miki's cheeks. "A cloth woman from the Lower Pyramid. She is helping your grandfather."

Miki lowered her hand, half-ready to give Moises a hug. She had seen him several times, following his mother through the market. When he was an infant, she had even held him when her father watched him in his manor. But no longer. Hemeda made sure she did not. A stab of regret hit Miki, and she let Moises run back to the main room without embracing him.

"Don't you ever tell my boy this woman is his aunt." Hemeda pulled herself up, pointing a wavering finger at their father. "She's not. She shouldn't even be here."

"Hemeda—"

Miki cut her father off, "I told you she wouldn't want to see me. We should go."

"Wait." Her father moved to the bed. "How is the pain?"

"Manageable." Hemeda's discolored face said otherwise. "But I want her to leave."

"Hemeda, why did you do it?" Father whispered.

She raised bloodshot eyes to Miki. "Because it's the law."

"That never stopped your mother," he said, a disapproving glow in his dark eyes. "It only did when she died. She died during a nullification, Hemeda! The same procedure you had!"

Hemeda clenched her jaw, muscles popping in her cheeks. "I did it because I don't want one of those," she breathed, looking at Miki.

Miki stepped forward despite the ice in her gut screaming *no*. "You nullified?"

The word pierced the stillness of the room, sucking away everything but the pain on Hemeda's face and the soft groan from their father.

Her sister looked away.

"Hemeda, that child—"

"I don't care. I can't be like you, Father. I can't hide a child just to watch it disappear like Beren or be sent away like Kamu. I can't live in fear every day, waiting for it to use its power against me." She spoke to the covers on the bed, avoiding his eyes.

Miki edged closer, annoyance rising. Everyone was talking about power today. If they weren't all so afraid, they might see. Knotting the edge of her toga between her fingers, she muttered to herself.

"I don't have any power."

"She is your *sister*, Hemeda."

"No. You made the choice to keep her in this world. I don't want any part in the repercussions of that." She looked up, brown eyes holding Miki's. "You aren't my sister. You aren't *anything*."

Miki took another step closer, and Hemeda shied back against the wall, face screwed in disgust.

"Remember the cellar, Hem? You used to hide with me after Kamu left. We would play High One in the Dungeon. You were always the High One, and I was the prisoner." Miki kept the sob from her voice. "I remember though, there was a time when you let me be High One. No one had ever made me feel so alive." Two girls in a dark hole under the floor, pretending their way out of an awful situation.

Hemeda looked to the wall, speaking to it instead of Miki. "Take her out of my house. Don't endanger my son again."

Her father's fingers dug into Miki's arm, and he pulled her toward the door. Moises was sitting just beyond, a box of small toy Steelmen made of real steel at his feet. He made to jump up, but his grandfather held a hand of caution.

"Go see your mother. She needs you."

Moises' face fell, but he obliged.

"I told you not to bring me here," Miki mumbled.

Her father spun on her, eyes blazing with a vigor they rarely held. Not since her mother died had Miki seen him look that way. She stepped away, taken aback.

"Your sister is blinded by this foolish society, but I won't let her die like your mother. I need to find a physician. The healer she hired to perform the nullification was not good. One look at her face shows it." He turned for the door.

"Father," Miki placed a hand on his arm, where the warm skin on his wrist was a comfort to her. "This isn't your fault. What happened to Mother won't happen to Hemeda."

He exhaled, all his fight gone. "Where did I go wrong, Miki?"

"Nowhere." But the words held a bitterness. So much could be different. So much—Miki forced the thoughts aside. There was nothing to be done.

"I'd better get going. The High One has called another Council meeting in the morning." Her father stepped outside.

The High One. Miki stumbled on the way out the door. She cleared her throat and grabbed her father's wrist again. "Father, I know where to find a better physician.

Actually, I could probably get the best in the whole of El-Pelusium."

"What?"

"I can ask the High One."

Her father's face tightened. "And how do you know the High One?"

"I stumbled into her and she came—" She couldn't tell him that. The thought was ludicrous. "She just wanted to talk."

"Miki, I wouldn't think I'd have to tell you she is the worst possible person for you to talk with."

"I know, but she could help Hemeda."

Her father glanced back to the house behind them. "So be it. But be careful. Please."

Miki nodded and turned down the road. Careful. Was such a thing possible anymore?

CHAPTER 7

Ptolema slipped past yet another Council member, holding her breath. The woman shouted something but Ptolema ignored her. Exiting the tunnel before the great waterfall, she shielded her eyes with a hand. He had to be somewhere. The ships didn't leave until later in the afternoon. Another Councilman dipped his head as she walked past. She came to an abrupt halt, feet almost tangling under her.

"Have you seen the foreigner? Did he come this way?"

The Councilman pivoted back to face her, startled. "Foreigner, High One?"

"Yes. He wears dark robes. Did he come this way?" Movement shifted in the side of her vision and Ptolema looked down the decorated tunnel. A Steelman. Sighing, she turned back to the Councilman.

"I did see someone wearing dark blue, quite an unusual color for the Higher Pyramid. May I ask who he is?" The man's gray eyes glowed.

"No, you may not. Where did you see him?"

The Councilman raised a hand to his nose as if to scratch, thought better of it and stepped back. He stared at his feet. Good thing, too. Scandalous, to be selfish enough to scratch your nose in the presence of the High One.

"I saw him not ten minutes ago, speaking with Councilman Montu and Councilwoman Edrice—"

The rustle of Ptolema's toga as she spun away overrode him. She moved as fast as she dared, not running but not quite walking toward the Council Hall. The tunnel was dim, but she didn't wait for her eyes to clear. She knew the way. Her stomach shivered with relief. If he had left, then she was alone. The stone archway to the Council Hall stood unguarded, and no Steelmen announced her.

"I can see why you might feel that way. Most of us feel the same." Councilman Montu's voice reached Ptolema first as she stepped through the doors.

"I just don't want this great city to fall into the situations others have." Radames stood off to the side next to Montu.

"If only we could get her to—" Edrice stopped as her eyes slid to Ptolema, her face paling.

Ptolema granted her a wide smile. Of course they had been talking about her. She strode into the Hall, shoulders high and the smile firmly in place.

"Ah, Radames, I am so glad I caught you."

Radames stepped away from the Council members, his eyes widening in surprise. "I was just on my way to the boat when these two snatched me for quite an enlightening discussion. Did you know they have been writing their own resolution to the matter of the Seconds?"

"Have they now?" Thankfully her voice conveyed nothing other than mild interest.

Montu, however, backed away as if guessing her annoyance. "This is quite the intelligent gentleman you have been entertaining, High One. I will be sorry to see him go."

"I need to speak with our guest alone." Ptolema stepped away, toward the dais where her throne sat.

Edrice and Montu exchanged a look. They left the room, showing enough propriety to not glance back over their shoulders. Radames eyed Ptolema curiously, the look strange over the beak-like nose. He wore only the toga and sandals she had first seen him in.

"This is your traveling attire?" Ptolema crossed her arms over her chest.

"I already sent my items to the ship with a pageboy. There's not much. A bag with a scroll for my records and a spare toga. Best to travel light." His eyes glowed with a strange intensity Ptolema suspected had nothing to do with the affairs of his travels.

"I'd like for you to stay in El-Pelusium. You can have a room here in the Higher Pyramid. We keep half a dozen available for dignitaries, but we never use them. You aren't expected elsewhere, are you?"

Radames's expression did not change. "Stay, High One?"

"Yes. It seems you have already made an impression on the Council members, something I find a challenge myself."

Radames let loose a loud laugh. Ptolema started and glanced around just to make sure something else had not caused it. When she turned back, Radames was wiping a tear from his face with the back of his hand. His fingers were long and weathered, as if they knew use in a special craft, though she hadn't heard him speak of being an artisan.

"What do you find so amusing?" Ptolema resisted the urge to glare at him.

"The Council is a pack of rats, fighting each other for the largest bit of cheese." Radames's smile faded, and he cleared his throat. "They want to help the city but also want to make sure they feel a benefit."

"Right. That is why I need you to stay. I can't get honest advice from any of the Council members." A face rose in Ptolema's mind, old, wrinkled, kind. She shook it aside. Councilman Bast was a good man, but his moral compass was immovable.

"Am I right in guessing you spoke with someone else concerning the Seconds?"

"Yes. I found someone in the Lower Pyramid I could trust." Ptolema had enjoyed the meeting more than any she had been to. To be in a commoner's house, eating common nuts, was almost fun. But Tiye had been so disagreeable. Ptolema frowned. "She didn't seem to agree with you."

Icy fingers encased Ptolema's, and Radames leaned to her level, eye to eye. "But do you agree something must be done?"

"I think so, but that is why I need you here."

His fingers tightened around hers. "Then I will stay. I will help where I can."

"Thank you." The relief swelled again, and the smile returned in honesty this time. "You can't imagine how hard it is to work with the Council members." She attempted to pull away, but his fingers pressed tighter around hers.

"Are you prepared to do what is necessary, High One?" Green eyes glowed under dark, thick eyebrows, like a hawk surveying a new prey.

Ptolema shuddered but stopped it before it reached her hand.

"I am prepared to discover what is necessary." She pulled her hand away and stood taller. "I will not act rashly and without thought. If the Seconds must be done away with, I have to make sure we are not harming innocents."

"Exactly my—"

"And I want to be absolutely positive the Seconds are dangerous. Manipulation is evil, but I need evidence."

Radames studied her, his long fingers tracing a circle on his cheek. "High One, no one has Manipulated in daylight for hundreds of years. Catching a Second in the act will not be easy."

"I know, but we must ensure the truth of all of this."

His eyes darkened, but he smiled.

"Of course. Councilman Montu informed me of a hunt for another Second that is underway now. Do you plan to force them to Manipulate?"

Ptolema choked. "What?"

"You didn't know?"

She turned to Radames, heat in her face. "Montu said this?"

He nodded.

"That vile sneak-about! He should have made an effort to tell me."

"It's becoming clearer why you need me, High One. Perhaps I can find out more things of this nature for you."

"Please call me Ptolema. And yes, see what else the Council members might be up to behind my back." She inched closer, only to freeze. No good would come from appearing too eager. Without him, she was lost in a pack of rats who knew no more than she did. Her father had passed on before she was prepared to deal with all of them.

"I am at your service." He hesitated, then smiled. "Ptolema."

She moved for the door. "I have already had your rooms set up. I have a meeting now, but will you join me in my rooms for dinner?"

"Joining you would be my pleasure." His footsteps echoed behind her, the slap of sandals on stone. "I have a feeling this is going to be a great partnership."

CHAPTER 8

The upper corridors of the Higher Pyramid funneled straight to the High One's chamber, yet Tiye took her time. The paving stones were cool underfoot here, with no direct sunlight to warm them as they did in the Lower Pyramid. She paused outside the Council Hall. Was her father inside listening to hours of circular arguments? Stepping closer, her feet found nothing but smooth floor beneath them. No bits of grime or even a stray pebble. Higher Pyramid, indeed.

Still, prickles ran along the edges of her arms. How many Seconds had been sentenced inside that room? She shivered as she turned away. The hall wound up to a flight of stairs and past several doors, each one veiled by a transparent curtain.

You go up until you can go no further. That is where the High One lives. A voice, soft and familiar, wove through Tiye's memories. Her mother—no. Miki's mother.

Any thought of the past vanished as the last door stood before her.

The door was made of two massive carved pieces of wood, their engraving rivaling the doors at the entrance to the Higher Pyramid. A Steelman stood at attention in front of it, tanned hand clasped tight around a spear. His dark eyes narrowed as she approached. Tiye edged away from the Steelman against her better judgement. The High One herself had asked for her to come, but nothing could erase the knots in Tiye's gut.

The man turned to her, his bare chest glowing in the torchlight. "You are the one the High One is waiting for?"

The knots loosened but did not vanish. Tiye nodded, neck stiff.

The Steelman stepped aside. The muscles in his forearms strained against taut skin as he pulled open one side of the massive door. "You can go through."

The scent of lavender and crushed mint greeted Tiye as she stepped through the door into a foyer. A sheer curtain hung on the other side. She waved it aside and entered the chamber of the High One. The room was large, but smaller than she had expected. Plain white walls. A low stone table with gold-lined cushioned benches.

The High One herself sat behind a desk in front of a sky-wall four times the size of the one in Tiye's childhood manor. She gasped before she could stop it. Cool air flowed from the sky-wall, pulsing out in invisible waves formed by the waterfall as it rushed downward. Streaks of gold and flashes of red lit the water from the afternoon sun behind it in a shimmering, dazzling display of art. Her breath wouldn't come. Tiye couldn't peel her eyes away, even as she could sense the High One standing at her desk.

A chuckle broke through her trance, and she started. The High One stood beside her, staring up at the waterfall with a half-smile on her face. She had the look of one remembering times long gone.

"I hated the waterfall when I was younger, you know. It was so loud. Once I asked my father if we could make it stop. He gave me a spanking." Ptolema chuckled again. She turned back to the desk and pulled her headdress off. Her caramel hair cascaded down the back of her teal embroidered white toga.

"Goodness, it's nice to have that off." She set the headdress on the desk and motioned for Tiye to take a seat by the stone table where a tray held a copper tea set.

Tiye eased herself onto the bench but made no move for tea until Ptolema poured herself a cup of the amber liquid and settled back to stare at her with curious eyes. "I'm so glad you came, Tiye. Today's been filled to the brim with manipulative Council members and myths I can't fully untangle." Sipping her tea with one hand, Ptolema massaged her forehead with the other, her thumb directly pressing against the scar over her left eye.

Tiye returned to her tea before the High One caught her staring. The liquid flooded Tiye's mouth with rich orange and berry.

"How was the cloth shop today? Busy? Full of gossips?" Ptolema's voice held a hint of excitement, and when Tiye looked up, she found the excitement mirrored in the High One's bright eyes.

Tiye lowered her cup. "It was fine."

"Oh, come now, there has to be more."

"It's boring, honestly."

"But there *is* something going on. I can see it in your face." Ptolema set her own cup down and leaned forward. "What is it?"

Tiye chewed on her tongue, then sighed. "A friend of mine. She's sick."

"Sick? With what?"

"Well—" Tiye stopped. Could she dare say the cause? Ptolema had been raised to think nullification was right. But Hemeda needed the help. Tiye met Ptolema's anxious gaze. "She nullified. The procedure didn't go well."

"Oh." Ptolema sat back, frowning. "Well, that is worrying. Has she been seen by a healer?"

"Yes, the one who performed it. But he was not a master. She needs a real physician."

"I have a staff of them. I can send one to see her. Maybe even two or three, just to be safe." Ptolema stood and went to the doorway.

"I would be very grateful if they could see her in the morning."

"No, no. They will see her now. Steelman!"

The man stepped into the room, eyes wary. He took one glance at her naked head and his eyes widened, then snapped shut.

Ptolema froze, seeming to realize too late her mistake. But she shook it off and cleared her throat. "Steelman, go to the physician quarters and send at least three to the house of—" she turned to Tiye.

"Oh—Hemeda of Bast."

Ptolema's eyes went wide. "Bast? As in Councilman Bast?"

"Yes." Tiye held back a shudder.

"Oh." Ptolema waved the Steelman out the doorway. "Well, you heard her. Hemeda of Bast."

The man dipped a bow, turned around and struck the door frame with a crunch of bone on stone. The Steelman muttered an apology and ran from the room. Ptolema took her seat, one elegant thin eyebrow raised. "You didn't mention you were friends with the daughter of a Council member."

Tiye shrugged. "I mentioned I met Councilman Bast once. That's how."

"Ah." Ptolema sat back. "You're more interesting than I first thought."

A scoff caught in Tiye's throat. If the woman only knew just how far the intricacies of her life extended. Their gaze locked, and a smile tugged at Tiye's stony lips. The sensation was so strange, so unusual, a chuckle echoed in the back of her throat.

Ptolema's more common smile spread over her thin face.

"I knew you had a smile in you!" She stood and grabbed Tiye's hands, her own cool as if the waterfall were a part of her. "Would you like to see the gardens?"

"I—" A flutter took Tiye's belly. The idea of the royal gardens suddenly sounded appealing. "I would like that very much, thank you."

Ptolema grinned, a child instead of a twenty-two-year-old High One.

"You're going to love them. My father rebuilt them for my mother before she died." Ptolema led her through a door into another chamber. White walls and rug-lined floors. "Are you close with your parents, Tiye?"

"They're both dead." The words, half true, rolled out with only the smallest hint of her practiced memorization.

"Oh, I'm sorry to hear that." Ptolema's fingers wrapped tighter around Tiye's hand. "My mother died before I could remember her. She fell."

"Fell?"

Ptolema led her through one last door. An open veranda greeted them, lined with plants of every shade of green imaginable. Pinks, oranges, and blues dotted the garden, plants Tiye could not put a name to. Spiked ferns of a vibrant purple lined a path through the gardens, and Ptolema continued down it.

"A Steelman found my mother's body beneath the sky-wall in the room we were just in. They think she fell. Probably slipped on water and toppled right out." She spoke the words without a shred of remorse.

"Oh, Ptolema. I didn't know."

"They never published the story to the rest of El-Pelusium. They just said my mother died in her sleep. My father wouldn't have wanted the people afraid of the Waterfall. It's what gives us power, or so he said. Either way, I was quite young." Ptolema paused in front of a large bush covered in yellow petals.

"That's awful." Remorse cinched tight in Tiye's gut.

As if suspecting the guilt, Ptolema patted Tiye's hand.

"I'm fine. I never really knew her, and my father was a good parent." A sad smile played across her face. She dropped Tiye's hand and kept walking. The garden path wound toward the edge where a half wall was the only thing stopping them from toppling down to the Lower Pyramid like the deceased High One's wife. A string of orchids on a vine lined the wall, and Ptolema plucked one off. She tucked it behind her ear, then plucked another and offered it to Tiye.

"But what was your mother like? I have always wondered how having a mother would be. Did you sit and braid each other's hair like in the stories?" Ptolema giggled and spun a third flower blossom stem in her fingers.

Tiye stared at the pink flower. Her mother. A woman whose care for her children, legal and illegal, had run deeper than the waterfall.

"I was only eight when my mother died, but eight years was enough time for me to know her." The smell of fresh rain clinging to her soaked toga after an unexpected shower on a trip to the market. Light grey eyes laughing at Tiye's insistence they go for one last dance in the rain. Fresh picked nuts on her mother's lap as Tiye curled up next to her once they were home and dry, happily snacking.

Safe. Loved. Even if the fear of being caught never left, her mother had made life as normal as possible.

"I can see in your face how much you loved her," Ptolema said, smiling.

"We may have braided each other's hair once. I wouldn't have been very good at that age."

Braids. Her mother's fingers flying down the back of her head. A sharp rap on the door. Her mother's hands pulling back and her face paling.

"Into the cellar, Miki! Go!"

Tiye shuddered even though the air was warm in the garden. She had gone into the cellar that day having a living mother and emerged with a dead one.

"I'm sorry, Tiye. I shouldn't have brought it up." Ptolema's cool fingers squeezed her wrist. "Want to walk further down? There's a magnificent orange tree around the corner."

"Don't be sorry. It was a long time ago."

Ptolema yanked her down the cobbled path.

"How old are you? Twenty? You can't be much younger than me."

"Nineteen." No matter if Ptolema knew her true age. There could be hundreds of nineteen-year-olds in the Pyramid.

"And you've been apprenticing at the cloth shop since you were thirteen, like usual?"

"No. I didn't start until I was fifteen." Her father had still been anxious, but she couldn't live in the cellar forever, trapped without experiencing life. Her missing brother Beren had been right about that at least.

"Why did you start so late?" Ptolema rounded the corner and a flowering orange tree filled the path. No fruit hung on its branches yet, but it was marvelous all the same, the way the sun caught the petals. Orange fragrance filled the air, sharp and satisfying.

"My father. He had health issues, and I didn't want to be away from him." Both a truth and a lie. He had already lost so many loved ones. To live in the city, to take a new name … he had lost Miki the day she decided.

"You sound like a dutiful daughter." Ptolema stood in front of the orange tree and plucked one of its buds. She sucked the middle. "They taste like oranges. Have you thought any more about what we talked about at your house?"

"High One—"

"Ptolema. Please, Tiye. I need some moments like this, or I'll go mad." She flicked the bud to the ground and sank onto a bench under the tree.

"Ptolema." A shiver traced up Tiye's back. "I am really not comfortable talking about this." Especially with her.

"I know, and I'm sorry. I just think it's time someone asked these questions. My father's and my tutor's answers never seemed sufficient. If I'm to rule, I need to know how my people feel."

Tiye sank onto the bench beside Ptolema. A tremor shook her hand, and she shoved it under her rear. "I'm glad you care so much."

"So you still think Seconds may be innocent?"

Telling her that once had been dangerous enough, but twice? She stared at this High One, not much older than herself. This was a farce. They couldn't be friends. If she told Ptolema what she was, there would be no more garden walks. The truth tugged within her, yearning to be free.

But it never could.

Ptolema grasped Tiye's hand.

"We should make this a weekly thing, don't you think?" Her light brown eyes glowed in the light of the setting sun. Eager.

Weekly wouldn't go unnoticed. Tiye shifted on the seat. She should leave now, refuse to come back, but there was something about Ptolema. Her honesty, not to mention the beautiful gardens. A taste of a life, of a friendship Tiye could never have. "Ptolema, I—"

"Ah, High One, I've been looking for you." A man strode from the way they had come, robed in the deepest blue fabric. Heavy eyebrows sat over a beak nose. His height left him almost brushing the bottommost leaves of a tall palm on the edge of the path. He smiled at Ptolema, but when his eyes found Tiye, the smile faltered.

"Radames, a pleasure to see you. Did I miss a meeting?" Ptolema stood and approached, hand outstretched. She had to be astoundingly friendly with him to offer her hand, though this High One seemed to do things differently from her father.

Radames took her hand and shook, but did not take his gaze from Tiye. His eyes narrowed quickly enough for her to stand. A cold knot which had only just vanished re-tightened in her belly. The air stiffened, and the light breeze shifted away. Ptolema was speaking, her voice echoing in the dull air, but Tiye didn't really hear it.

A blue vein pulsed in Radames's neck. He met Tiye's gaze with no smile, only dark emerald eyes. The knot in her belly clenched further. There was something wrong with him, something she could not put a name to. His eyes bored into her as if he knew her secret. As if he knew she was a Fifth, and knew her true name.

"Tiye, I'm so sorry to cut this short. Maybe you can return tomorrow?"

Tiye blinked and the light breeze returned, kissing the tip of her nose. She cleared her throat.

"Yes, of course. Thank you for the tea." She bowed and turned away. The heat of a pair of eyes dug into her back until she rounded the corner and passed into the shelter of Ptolema's rooms. She picked up her pace, sprinting past the sky-wall where Ptolema's mother had met her death and through the doorway into the corridor. The Council Hall blinked through her peripherals and then darkness took her as she ran down the tunnel, not caring if a Council member saw her.

Every beat of her blood urged her away from the man in the dark toga.

CHAPTER 9

"Stop!"

Tiye slowed at the frantic shouting. Her home lay just two blocks away, on the other side of the commotion. Four Steelmen hovered in the street, their white headdresses almost touching the colorful awnings over the entryway of the nearby pottery shop. The largest of them, a man whose back almost groaned audibly under the strain of his muscles, lunged forward toward something the other Steelmen blocked.

"Please! She's harmless! Don't do—" A Steelman's spear butt jabbed into the man's gut. He doubled over and thudded down onto the stones. Rolling to the side, he raised his eyes to Tiye.

The moisture vanished from her mouth.

Kal.

His eyes widened in recognition, but the Steelman bore down on him before he could say anything. The spear pole cracked against his raised forearm and he rolled back, groaning.

Tiye fell into the wall, rough stone scraping away her skin. She stifled a hiss of pain. The other three Steelmen pulled a struggling woman to her feet. Dalilah's tall frame seemed hard for them to manage. She fought wildly, ripping her long arms out of their grasp, only to have them pinned back to her side and tied with rope. Crimson slicked the side of her face, pooling below a gash at her hairline. Dalilah pulled away again from the Steelmen, only to have the shaft of a spear plunge into her foot. With a shriek, she toppled to the ground.

"Dalilah! Stop it! Don't let them have a reason to kill you—"

"Quiet!" A Steelman's sandaled foot sank into Kal's stomach.

"No!" Dalilah cried. "Kal, don't let them take me!"

The tallest Steelman's fist cracked against Dalilah's jaw.

"You're a filthy Second. You don't get to talk." The gap-toothed sneer on his face hinted at what he might do if she tried again. He turned to his subordinates. "Bring her to the Cells."

They hauled Dalilah off the street and out of her own blood. Kal rolled over, and a foot pressed against his rib cage.

"Don't move, or you get to come with us."

Dalilah and her captors moved toward Tiye, who scrambled inside the house behind her.

A woman muttered a curse, dropping a bowl of fruit with a crack.

"What are you doing in my home?" She pulled brown hair out of her wide eyes.

Tiye leaned against the corner and dug her fingers into the cracked window frame. The woman quieted as the Steelmen moved past her doorway.

Kal didn't follow. Tiye couldn't see him, but his cries echoed in the street.

"No, no, Dalilah, no!"

The Steelmen and their prize turned the corner, leaving only a splattered trail of blood.

The woman's hot breath wafted across Tiye's ear. "Did they catch another Second?"

She didn't answer. She left the house, the woman stuttering behind her. Kal lay where the Steelmen had left him, curled in a fetal position, his body shaking with sobs. Tiye's hand trembled over him, wanting to touch and comfort him. But she couldn't bring herself to do it.

His bloodshot eyes rolled upwards, meeting hers.

"Why did you do it?" he whispered in a tight breath.

"What?"

"Why did you turn her in?" Kal hissed the words through red-stained teeth.

"I didn't. I swear it."

"Liar. You were in the cloth shop. You saw the Steelman coming for her." He pushed himself up on one bruised arm.

"No, I helped you," Tiye whispered. She had to be careful. The woman from the house hovered at the window. People were watching.

"Then why did this happen?"

"Her neighbor. The woman who brought the Steelmen to my shop."

Whatever color was left in Kal's face drained away.

"They're going to banish her ..." His words ended in a sob.

Tiye almost dropped to her knees, almost pulled him to her in a comforting hug to tell him Dalilah wouldn't be banished, that he would get her back. But it wasn't true. She turned away from Kal.

"I'm sorry."

"Wait—"

She slipped down an alley, not stopping to see who might have witnessed her traitorous exchange.

Tiye's house held a gloom deeper than usual, even at midnight. The moon and stars were gone, and the darkness was complete. The shutters blocked out the lamps in the road. The stone wall chilled her back, but she sat against it anyway, a bowl of nuts between her palms. Silence pressed against her. She had spent the rest of the day hiding from any noise in the street, but this was worse.

A sharp rap sounded on the door. The bowl tumbled out of her hands, spilling its precious contents across the small room.

"Tiye, open up! Please!" Kal's voice shook.

Tiye jumped up, despite her muscles screaming in protest. The door creaked open when she pulled it, and

Kal pushed his way through, still reeking of blood and desperation. She eased the door shut behind him and slid the bolt home. The Steelmen preferred daylight to showcase their stunts, but she wouldn't put anything past them now.

Kal sank onto the low bench where Ptolema had sat just the day before. He was her opposite—withered, afraid, beaten.

Tiye slipped in across from him. "How did you find me?"

Kal massaged his temples. "Easy enough. You're well known in the richer circles, Tiye the cloth woman."

"You shouldn't be here."

"I have an idea."

Her stomach somersaulted. It would be reckless, whatever it was. "I want no part in it."

He stared at her, brown eyes hardening. "Why did you cover for us in the shop?"

"Because I don't like El-Pelusium's laws." She caught her fingers intertwining, an old nervous habit.

Kal leaned across the table. "Why would you care so much?"

Her throat was full, clogged by the desire to not speak. She cleared it anyway. "Everyone is supposed to live, no matter their birth order."

"Then you should help me get Dalilah back. I heard you know the High One."

"What? Who told you that?" Tiye's back went rigid, the bench painful under her rear end.

"Did you really think you could go to the Palace twice in one week and no one would notice?" Kal's eyes narrowed. "Maybe you are too much of a fool to help me after all."

"So what if I know her? She's not going to listen to me and let Dalilah, a known Second, go free."

"Maybe. You can't know until you ask." He leaned even further forward, the beads of sweat on the end of his nose catching in the candlelight.

Tiye stood and gathered the nuts off the floor, plopping them back into the bowl. The sound broke the tension of the conversation, but Kal's eyes followed her every movement.

She turned back, the low glow of the candle casting a shadow over Kal's face, illuminating his nose to twice its length. Tiye sucked in a breath. The strange man from Ptolema's gardens, Radames, glowed in her mind, a sharp, dark face of anger. She couldn't see him again. She didn't know why. There was no logical explanation. The bowl scraped against the surface of the table and she stepped away.

"No. I can't ask her. I'm sorry."

"Sorry?" Kal muttered in disbelief. "Dalilah is bound to be banished, as good as a death sentence, and you are just sorry?" He stood, sending the bowl and nuts flying back to the floor.

"This has nothing to do with me." She turned away, even as the false words turned to ash in her mouth.

"I'm going to bet it has everything to do with you." Kal spit, the saliva hitting the bricks inches from Tiye's toes.

Her fingers twitched at her side, her heartbeat steadily increasing. He knew. He had to know. She turned back to him. A satisfied smile split his face, even though his own hands shook.

"You know nothing about me." She stepped closer, hands balled at her sides. "I want you to leave my house."

"I'd bet Dalilah's freedom on your being a Second."

"Maybe I just sympathize with them." Her feet left perfect sweat imprints on the stones as she moved for the door. "Please leave."

"Tiye." Kal cut in between her and the doorway. "You are the only person who can help." His shoulders slouched, the feigned defensiveness fading away.

She found the end of her toga tie, the linen calming under her nervous fingers. "What do you expect me to do?"

"Ask the High One for a pardon. Say the evidence against Dalilah is a sham."

Closing her eyes, Tiye rested her forehead against the rough wood of the door. For a moment, the wood against her skin was the door to her cellar. A shiver crept up her back. Her entire world had become the cellar. Her breathing pinched into tight bursts and she clamped a clammy hand over her mouth to deafen the odd rasps.

"Tiye?"

The room tilted and she shut it out. The swirling only worsened. There was no door to hold her up, no floor beneath her feet. She reached out for support, her hands brushing cold stone. The walls of the cellar. No! She couldn't be there, not again. Not so soon. She stumbled back from the door. A shaking hand pressed against her back. She blinked.

Kal stood beside her, eyes squinted in confusion. "Are you all right?"

No, she was not all right. She was not even sure of who she was. The cellar remained outlined in her vision and if she were to turn to the side, her bed pallet and stack of tablets would be there. Not Tiye's things, but Miki's.

She was Miki. She couldn't deny it any longer. It was time to cast the lie of Tiye away forever and embrace the name she had been born with.

Kal's hand registered on her bare arm, and Miki jerked away, breath vibrating with the resurgence of her childhood anxiety at the acceptance of her real name.

Kal followed, eyes widening with understanding. Her icy hand pressed against her even colder forehead. This could not be happening.

"You *are* a Second!" Kal leveled a shaking finger of accusation at her nose. "Admit it!"

No, not a Second. Something worse. But the words were too heavy on her tongue, the explanation too much. A groan rose in her throat and she turned for the door. Miki ripped it open, revealing a dark street dotted with a scattering of almost burnt-out torches. Bits of hope remaining for Dalilah and the Seconds hiding in El-Pelusium.

"I'll go tomorrow after I work. You should probably find somewhere to hide, just in case they decide to arrest you as well." She held a hand toward the door. "Good night."

"Thank you!" The thin sticks of Kal's arms wrapped around Miki's head, pulling her into a musty, bloody embrace. He sobbed into her neck, the hot tears reeking almost more than the rest of him. "We have to protect each other," he muttered into her neck.

She pulled away and gave him a halfhearted pat on the back. She wouldn't admit what she was, as if that would deny what he already knew.

"Keep your head down. I'll find you with the High One's answer tomorrow evening."

His arms snaked back for another hug, but Miki danced to the side to avoid it.

"Thank you, really. I know this will work. I know it." Kal's tears melted into a smile that would not have been nearly as confident if he knew just how slim the chances were for his plan to work.

CHAPTER 10

"High One, they have captured another."

"What?" The scroll fell from Ptolema's fingers, and she didn't bother to stoop and catch it before it slipped into the fire before her. Her slippered feet hit the floor as she stood from the end of her bed. "A Second? When? Who?" She twisted her toga on as she walked, not caring that the man had seen her in her under-slip.

The Steelman didn't raise his eyes as he made his way back to the outer door and spoke.

"Yes, a Second. Four hours ago. They are holding her in the Cells." He stepped aside at the doorway to let her pass, but shrank back and bowed as she whirled on him.

"Four hours ago? Why wasn't I notified then?" Heat rose to Ptolema's cheeks, but she resisted raising her hand to strike him.

"Councilman Montu insisted they should interrogate her first to ensure she was a Second before bothering you." The Steelman adjusted his headdress to keep it from tumbling to the floor as he pulled himself upright again.

"Councilman Montu is far too considerate," Ptolema spat. "Take me to the Second now, then call the Council to the Hall."

"Of course, High One," he mumbled as he tripped over his own bow on the way to the corridor.

The corridor was silent, but heads popped out as Ptolema strode past open doors. They knew.

"Did everyone know before me, Steelman?"

"I couldn't say. I was just following—"

"Yes, of course. Just hurry."

The man muttered another apology as he turned down a dim flight of stairs. The cells were hidden from prying eyes in the heart of the Higher Pyramid. They reached them in fifteen minutes. A last pair of Steelmen stood guard at the wrought iron door and both bent at the waist as she approached. A draft tilted her headdress, but she held it firm with satisfaction. For once she hadn't forgotten it. Perhaps she was finally truly becoming High One.

"Gentlemen, I will speak with the prisoner. Now."

The Steelmen backed away, eyes on the ground. The iron handle was cool under her grip and when the door creaked open, an even colder gust of air hit her face. Damp air. She shivered. She should have brought a cloak.

"Ah, High One, I'm relieved they finally informed you." The warm voice of Radames eased the annoyance filtering through Ptolema's veins. He stood at the bottom of a small flight of stone steps, iron bars at his back. The round cell was built in the middle of the circular chamber. Steps encircled the entirety, allowing observation of the prisoner from all angles. The ceiling rose at least a hundred feet above them. Only Ptolema's rooms were higher.

She granted Radames a smile.

"At least someone with sense was notified. I'm going to gut Montu and make him eat it," she said, stomping down a step with each word.

Radames chuckled. "If only he could have fooled Councilman Bast as long as he wished. But Bast found out and put the woman's trial off until tomorrow. You have him to thank for that, I guess."

"Yes, perhaps I'll let Bast do the gutting of Montu." Ptolema descended the final stair and chanced a look into the cell pit ten feet below. A woman, streaked with the crusty red brown of dried blood, lay huddled to the far side. "Why hasn't that injury been attended to?"

Radames clicked his tongue. "She is a Second."

"Yes, but the blood could spread disease, and there is no use letting her die before we can sentence her."

"Sentence me to Thoth?" The woman's voice came from below, weak but defiant.

Ptolema clenched the railing until her knuckles turned white.

"Are you a Second?"

"What's the difference? They've all already decided my fate." The woman's thick black hair fell in front of her face, but it failed to hide the heat in her words.

"She's a Second, High One. I can feel it." Radames pressed in closer to the cage, his nostrils flaring as if the woman's stench was too great for him to bear.

"Feel it?"

"I once told you I had experience with Manipulation, did I not?"

"Yes."

"Well, I can feel them."

"I've never Manipulated, please—" The woman cut off with a groan and pulled her injured foot closer.

"No, you have not, but that doesn't mean you can't." Radames inhaled, his nostrils pulling wider.

Ptolema gave the air a tentative sniff. Nothing. Just drafty air. "She doesn't seem dangerous."

Then Tiye's words floated up from the depths of her memory.

"... this man could be lying. If he is just trying to eradicate Seconds, he would want you to try harder."

Ptolema cast Radames a sidelong glance, and the ease she felt at his presence lessened.

"I know, that's the beauty of it," he said. "But you can't trust a Second, High One. It's in their nature from the moment they are conceived."

Was it? Tiye didn't seem to think so, but then Radames had seen much more than her new friend had. Ptolema turned to Radames.

"The Council will meet at first light. I'd like for you to be there."

He dipped a quick bow. "It would honor me."

"I will stay here alone for a moment in preparation."

"I would advise you not to do so." His eyes darkened.

"Thank you, but I will be fine. The Steelmen are just outside. Good night." She turned to face the cage.

Radames hesitated, but only for a moment. The sound of sandals slapping against stone echoed through the open chamber, until the door creaked open and thudded shut. Ptolema stared at the woman below, who shifted, raising her blood and dirt smeared face.

"Who gave me up?"

A thrill tingled up Ptolema's spine. "You admit you are a Second?"

"I deserve to know who gave me up."

"I don't know who it was."

"Was it that wretched shop girl?"

"I honestly don't have a clue." Ptolema studied the woman. Mid-twenties, maybe. She would have been beautiful if not bruised and bloodied. "You can't Manipulate?"

"That's a myth. No one can, especially not Seconds."

"Do you know others?"

"No." The woman slipped her injured foot away from her body and groaned. The hole in her foot no longer bled, but the skin was green.

Ptolema almost backed away but caught herself mid-stride and held her ground. "Did you know Pilis, the other Second we caught?"

The woman looked up, scowling. "I don't want to talk to you. Please go away."

"You can either hinder or help your position. You might as well answer my questions."

The Second twitched as if considering attempting to stand. One look at her worthless leg proved that would be impossible. She sighed and leaned her head back on the bars. "You have to promise you won't go after my intended."

"We must bring him in if he is a Second."

"He's not. He is a Firstborn." A half smile grew on the captive's face.

A First wanted to marry a Second? It was absurd, going against everything Ptolema had been taught. Going against nature. The woman had to be lying. Still, an icy knot grew in Ptolema's belly. She cleared her throat and the feeling passed. "If you can give me another Second, we will spare your intended and chalk it up to his foolishness."

The Second's cheeks reddened, but she had the sense to keep her anger to herself. Head down, she studied her injured foot.

"What is your name, Second?"

"Which name do you prefer?" the woman mumbled in defiance.

"What do you mean?"

"I have two. The one my parents gave me when they gave birth to me illegally and the one I hid myself under."

Aha. So that was how she had done it. Ptolema's shoulders relaxed from a pressure she had not known was there. She was getting somewhere.

"Give me both."

"My name is Mandisa. My true name is—" her lips quivered, and she shuddered. "My true name is Dalilah."

Ptolema leaned away from the railing. This was too much, too personal, knowing her true name. Would it help? Would the name uncover more Seconds? Ptolema inhaled the chilled air and crossed her arms over her chest for warmth, but did not allow her shoulders to hunch. She must stand tall. She must be regal.

You are the High One of the greatest Pyramid in the world. They cannot see you as weak. Her father's words from just eight weeks ago, his last to her on his deathbed, fluttered into her mind. They rested softly against the raw irritation of the past few days and the matter of the Seconds. What would he do?

Banish the woman. Banish anyone. Just as her father had done. Ptolema shivered. Hadn't he been the loving father to everyone as he had to her?

She knew the answer, but she ignored it.

The woman shifted below. "I might be able to give you one Second. If I do that, you will spare my intended?" She pulled herself upright, clinging to the bars in front of Ptolema for support.

"Yes." Ptolema's fingers clenched around the iron bar again.

"The shop girl. She had to have been a Second. She wouldn't have jumped to hide us so quickly when the Steelmen came if she wasn't." Dalilah's face glowed with hope.

"Who is she?"

"I don't know. She was also there when they took me. Pale as a toga. Knew the same could happen to her."

"But you don't know anything else about her? What shop does she work in?" Ptolema leaned over the railing, fingers biting into it with force enough to bring prickles of pain to their tips. If she could find another Second before the Council, they couldn't go around her again.

The woman licked her dirty lips and looked away.

"She had dark hair, like mine. Plain as a cat. Talked little. We ran into the shop to get away. I don't know which one it was. That's all I know."

Ptolema forced her shoulders straight again. Dalilah's information was virtually worthless. Any girl could be plain and quiet. Searching every shop in the Pyramid would take months.

"If you can tell me more information about this girl tomorrow at your trial, I will spare your intended. You will remain here until then."

"High One—" the Second's voice was small, having lost all of its fierceness, "I'm a person too."

Ptolema turned away, her slippers gliding easily up the stone stairs. A part of her wanted to turn back to the woman and agree, even if she didn't. The door opened before she could touch it and when she stepped out, Radames stood before her, face calm.

"Have you learned anything?"

"I suppose I should discipline you for not going to bed as I instructed."

"So you are angry with me?" His upper lip twitched.

"No," she sighed. "It's nice to have someone do what they think is right for once."

The lip twitch morphed into a warm smile. "I stayed here to help and support you. I'm not about to run off to bed."

Ptolema chuckled. His presence was soothing now she was away from the Second. This man had put aside his own goals and plans to see her through this. Her doubt in the cell stemmed from fear of the Second, not fear of Radames. She turned down the hall. "I'm sorry I doubted you in there."

"Is that what that was?"

"Could Manipulation be making me feel that way?" The Steelman behind her shifted, uneasy, and she looked at him. "Send for the Amputator. The second finger from both hands. Tell him to do it well. The woman is already injured." Bile rose in Ptolema's throat at the words. She could change the law just for the brutality of it, but she was too new to power for something like that to go over well.

Radames slipped his arm through the crook of her elbow. "I heard the Amputator did an excellent job on the other Second."

The Steelman tapped the butt of his spear on the floor and dipped a bow.

"It shall be done, High One." He stepped into a fast walk and vanished out of the corridor.

"I am curious why you cut off the fingers before the trial." Radames eyes shone with mild interest.

"If they admit what they are before the trial, it becomes mere ceremony. Things will be far simpler in the morning when the woman enters the Council Chamber missing her fingers. They will all see her hands." Ptolema sighed, her shoulders seeming far heavier than they ever had before.

"You don't like the amputation?"

"Am I that obvious?"

Radames chuckled. "I'll admit I don't see the purpose. Why does it matter how many fingers they have once they are banished?"

"I agree. Though the Council would riot if I changed things so early in my tenure."

"Ah, I see." Radames gave her arm a gentle tug, directing her down the hall. "You asked if Manipulation was making you feel uncertain in the Cells. The woman was not Manipulating with nature. I would have felt its power. You must still be careful. She could trick you. That is another aspect of power."

Ptolema walked with him down the hall, almost as she had done with her father months before when his health failed.

"Walk with me, Radames, and tell me what you make of her."

CHAPTER 11

Tiye,

Please meet me in my gardens tomorrow at noon. I would love to finish our discussion from the other day. This time I will provide lunch! I look forward to it,

Your friend,
Ptolema

The paper was finer than any Miki had ever held. Smooth, delicate, nearly as thin as a blade of grass. The discarded envelope lay on the table, only something a royal would use. Ptolema's official seal and title was stamped across the top in traditional symbols. It read: *High One Ptolema of El-Pelusium, Chief City of Kemet.*

Did the errand boy who dropped it off find it odd that the High One wanted such a personal note sent to someone in the Lower Pyramid? But he wouldn't have read it. The seal wasn't broken.

Miki ripped the envelope off the table and shoved the paper back in, fingers shaking. Today of all days. Perhaps Ptolema would be excited to see her a day early. Perhaps everything would go well.

Maybe.

She shoved the letter deep into her bag, in case Steelmen gave them any trouble on the way up. The doorknob creaked under her shaking fingers. but it was too late to change her mind. The sun glinted off Kal's black hair as he waited in the street for her, as he jumped toward her impatiently, but she cut her arm downward through the air and hissed. He couldn't approach her, not now. Kal's eyes widened at his mistake and he turned down the alley.

Miki took a parallel side street and entered the tunnel into the Higher Pyramid. The Steelman at the entrance did not glance her way, but the fine hairs at the nape of her neck stood on end. Kal veered closer to her with every step until he walked only a foot in front of her.

"What happened to lying low until tonight?" Miki muttered under her breath.

"I had to come. I have to know."

"Fine, but you'd better appreciate the risk you are putting us all in."

He nodded.

"And stay out of the Palace once we get up there."

He choked on a protest and slowed, letting her pass him. The journey through the tunnels had never taken so long. Every merchant seemed to crane their neck to get a better look at the pair of them. Sweat slicked Miki's fingers, the basket slipping in her grip. She adjusted it once, then twice. Kal kept his distance, but the Steelman who took Dalilah would recognize his face.

Finally, the sunlight of the open road before the Higher Pyramid struck Miki's eyes and her step quickened. She raised a hand to signal for Kal to wait, but a shoulder thumped into hers. She stumbled backward with an *oomph*. The stout man muttered an apology and continued down the road. Miki's heart beat in her throat as she tried to signal Kal again. Another person, a topknotted woman in her sixties, almost bumped into her. Sidestepping, the woman caught Miki's gaze.

"Have you heard?"

"What? Is something going on?" More people hurried away from the Higher Pyramid, heads locked together as if passing information. The pit of Miki's stomach sank.

Kal caught up with her, no longer bothering to pretend they weren't walking together. "What is going on?"

The older woman straightened her toga and leaned toward Miki, eyes glowing. "They've finally done it. Now that they've caught another one—"

Kal sucked in with a hiss, earning Miki's elbow in his rib.

"—the Council has passed an edict. All Seconds are to be hunted down. No more waiting to see if they slip up."

"What? Did the High One approve?" The words were out before Miki could stop them.

The woman eyed her. "Yes, she was the one who called the meeting."

"You're forgetting part of it." A fruit merchant with a basket still strapped to his hip, sidled up to the woman. "Anyone found harboring or associating with a Second will be subject to punishment as well."

The woman snatched a pear from his basket and handed him a slip of silk in exchange.

"Serves them right. I mean, how could anyone think to even talk with a Second, let alone hide one?"

Kal's wide eyes met Miki's. She stepped away from the two gossips and whispered to him.

"We can't do this. It's too late."

"No, please. We have to try."

"Both of us have associated with Dalilah. They will arrest us."

Kal raised a hand as if he might object, but then whipped around. Rocks crunched on the stones beneath his feet as he broke into a sprint. He bobbed through the crowd, one frail man against the world.

Groaning, Miki started after him. If he managed to get to Ptolema, if he even so much as mentioned Tiye, everything would be over. The basket tumbled to the ground, bits of wood chipping off and showering the stones. She picked up her pace until the street streaked by, filled with the excited faces of Firstborns without a clue to what the edict meant. She should call out to him. Make him stop! Her breath hitched in her throat. No, too dangerous. She pushed harder.

Darkness overtook her again as the tunnel began. Torches flitted by and the small windows added light in small bursts. Kal ducked around a corner. She followed, hands knotting in the ends of her toga. Curse him! Curse it all!

The light grew, as did the faces she recognized. Councilwoman Edrice skirted out of her way, face shining with alarm. She didn't know who she was, of course, but people rarely ran through the corridors of the Higher Pyramid. Miki lowered her head, praying none of them had been to Jabarre's apart from Edrice.

Shouts echoed through the hall. She had to get to Kal before he ruined everything. She plunged ahead, the same urgency pulsing from her head to her blood to her feet.

Kal's back met her nose before Miki had time to see it. The scent of sweat saturated the folds of his and she pulled back, coughing.

"It's her," he whispered, breathless.

Miki looked up, knowing she shouldn't, knowing who it was who stood across the corridor outside the Council Hall. Ptolema stood framed in the doorway. Her headdress was twice its usual size and framed in an assortment of colorful feathers. A chain of teal beads hung across her brow, highlighting the teal embroidery in her toga. Flecks of yellow and purple accented the toga as well. Her head was high, her shoulders straight. A different Ptolema than the one Miki knew. This was the High One.

"We can't talk to her now, Kal," Miki breathed. "We have to go."

"I can't let—"

The man Ptolema was speaking with turned as they exited the Hall. His near-black toga swirled on the floor, mixing with Ptolema's colorful one. Polluting it. Miki stepped back, breaths coming thinner. Kal's fingers pried at her arm, but his words came through a muffled veil.

Radames.

He was behind the edict. He had to be. Ptolema wouldn't have passed such a blatant thing on her own. Miki's mouth ran dry.

But maybe the High One would have.

Another man stepped from the Hall on the heels of Radames. Face creased in worry, Bast caught up with Ptolema and bowed. Whatever he was saying was too low to hear, but Radames was not pleased. He stroked his beard while his eyes darkened. Her father needed to be careful. This was not a man to meddle with.

The pressure of Kal's fingers on her arm loosened, then vanished. A cry rose in Miki's throat. It cut through the jabbering of the Council members. Her father turned, eyes widening. His lips moved, soundlessly muttering her true name.

"High One! You must pardon her!" Kal streaked across the hallway and made it within a foot of Ptolema. A Steelman leaped forward, spear flashing out before Miki had time to cry out a warning. Kal crumpled to the ground, spear embedded in his side.

Shrieks rose, then stopped abruptly. Kal writhed at Ptolema's feet. "You ... must ... pardon ..." The moans overbore the rest of the words. Beside them, Bast's wide-eyed gaze met Miki's. *Go now,* he mouthed.

"That's him, High One. He was with the Second when we caught her." The Steelman wiped the crimson spear tip on the back of Kal's toga, leaving a long bloody smear.

Radames stepped forward, frowning. "This is what I was talking about, High One. This man is only the beginning of other Firsts who will betray you if we don't ferret them out. "

Fingers of blood trickled through the cracks between stones, reaching for Ptolema's silk slippers. She stepped back, eyes only on Kal. He shivered, a hand out into space. Lips quivering, he spoke. "Help ... her ..." He swallowed and exhaled one last word. "Tiye."

His arm smacked the floor, dead weight. His shivering ceased.

Miki raised a hand to her face. Her cheeks, fingertips, blood were ice. This wasn't what was supposed to happen. Dalilah wouldn't have wanted this.

"Tiye?" Ptolema's voice shook, and when Miki looked to her, her eyes were wide as if she saw someone she recognized, but not who she expected.

Miki stepped back, the Council members parting around her. She shouldn't have come, she should have told Kal no. But he lay still in a pool of his own blood, no longer caring what happened to her. Ptolema did not move toward her, but the tight lines of her face said enough.

Miki turned, toga tangling around her ankles as she ran from the Higher Pyramid.

Within moments, the shouts of the Steelmen followed her.

The door of her cellar gleamed in the noon sun from the window high above the Inner Pyramid, the hinges shining as if inviting her in. Miki slammed into it, pain shooting up her shoulder. Fingers fumbling with the latch, she yanked it open and slipped into the musty darkness. The lock slid into place on the child-sized door and she stumbled backward, hands groping over the stone in the dark. A scrap of something sharp bit into her palm and she cried out. Sinking her head into her hands, a sticky warm moisture stained her cheek, then her forehead.

The Steelmen were only five minutes behind her. Maybe she had lost them in the Inner Pyramid. Her gut clenched. It wasn't that easy.

"Curse you, Kal!" Her fingers caught in her top knot and she yanked, her hair cascading over her shoulders. If it wasn't for him—

Noise in the street. Shouting. Another voice answered the shouts. Words too muffled to make out. Miki clenched her hands tighter around her head.

This was it. Her worst nightmare.

Her breath hit her forearm, hot and clammy at the same time. Footsteps sounded on the stone outside the door. Her breath quickened. A low groan slipped through her teeth. A *crack* echoed through the small cellar as something collided with the door. She flinched and her teeth dug into her bottom lip, the taste of blood filling her mouth.

Another shout sounded above. A thump on the trap door at the top of the stairs. Miki exhaled.

Please, let her father be okay. Maybe he escaped, maybe he claimed he cast her out as an infant. The pathetic excuse brought a cry to her throat. Her hands clenched tighter. She shouldn't have come here. Anywhere but the cellar, the surest place to lead back to her father. But there had been nowhere else. This couldn't be happening, this couldn't be—

Light flooded the cellar, polluting it with the warm illumination it usually never saw. A Steelman shouted above her and the pounding on the cellar door paused.

"She's got to be down here. Why else would Councilman Bast have built this? Come on!" The stairs creaked under several pairs of feet.

Miki didn't raise her head. One hot tear leaked out onto her forearm.

"I'm so sorry, Father." The words were lost in the tangle of her arms.

"There!"

Miki's heart thundered through her ears and she tried to focus on it, but the pinching of a man's fingers around her arm was too real to block out. Someone jerked her upright, loose hair snapping about her face. A Steelman in the teal headdress of the High One's Personal Guard held her as he shouted back up the stairs.

"I got the Second!" Then he sneered down at her. "The High One wants to see you."

Miki's muscles gave out, they were shaking so badly, but another Steelman stepped up and caught her before she hit the ground. They escorted her up the stairs, though her legs still shook to the point of being useless.

Her father's bedroom was a mess, pillows strewn across the floor, their stuffing ripped out. The main living room was worse. Smashed bowls and fruit juices smeared in colorful streaks across the floor.

Her father knelt near the sky-wall, head down. Bits of red decorated his toga where it was torn and ripped. His bald head sported a large blue bump. A cry rose in Miki's throat and she jerked toward him. The Steelman's grip only tightened, bringing stabs of pain to her forearm.

Her father looked up and her gut somersaulted. His face was awash with bruises and cuts. His left eye widened as she met his gaze, though his left was swollen shut.

"Miki! I'm so sorry, so sorry—"

"Quiet, you Second lover." A third Steelman granted him a backhand blow across the face.

"No!" Miki jerked against the arms holding her and thudded to the floor. Pain burned in her side.

"Miki!" Her father tried to move, but the Steelman hit him again.

The pinching fingers found Miki, and the room shifted. She struggled against the hold of the two Steelmen, but they carried her into the street, only leaving her with the image of the horror washing over her father's beaten face.

CHAPTER 12

This could not be happening.

The waterfall raged overhead as usual, but it was only a distant annoyance to Ptolema. Her large toe met the base of her desk as she passed by for the twentieth time. She bit back a cry, clutched at the toe, and threw herself onto the benches at the fire.

"This can't be happening," she muttered.

"You have to sentence her. They can't hold her in that room forever." Radames moved away from the veranda where he had been staring out into the water. This was the first time he had spoken since the death of that man outside the Council Hall. The image of the traitor, pale and lifeless, his eyes still pleading for his lover's life, burned in Ptolema's mind. She rubbed her toe harder, but the image didn't go away.

She stood again, ready to continue pacing. Radames slipped in front of her. "I am sorry, High One, about all of this." The words were soft, concerned.

Ptolema's shoulders sank as she exhaled, defeated.

"She's my friend. How can she be a Second?" The letter she had written to Tiye just yesterday morning sat on the desk, crumpled and bloodstained. The Steelmen had brought it to her with the news of Tiye's capture.

Ptolema refused to look at it.

"Their lies run deep. It only goes to prove the extent of their evil." Radames moved closer. He squeezed her shoulder.

"It just doesn't make sense. She never seemed evil."

"The worst evil never does." Radames's eyes darkened, as if seeing something else, something far away, and he frowned. "But you do have to deal with her. The Council will not wait much longer. They want revenge on Bast in particular."

Bast. The man she once considered the best in the Pyramid. A hand of ice clutched Ptolema's heart. Things made so much sense. Tiye knew Bast and his daughter because she was his *other* daughter.

"Ptolema, I know you don't want to hear this, but this is a perfect example of how deceitful Seconds can be. If we hadn't discovered her, she would have worked her way further into your trust and it could have been too late." Radames's hand fell away from her shoulder, leaving it as cold as the waterfall. He looked back to the sky-wall, hands crossed behind his back.

Ptolema shivered. The young man in the corridor. So young ... Tiye's face replaced his. Would she, Ptolema, never have any friends for fear of their intentions and hidden identities?

"If you don't sentence her soon, your authority will be undermined," Radames spoke to the waterfall.

"I know," Ptolema breathed. "I need a moment. I will be back soon." She headed for the door, heart pounding, then hesitated. She spun back to the desk and ripped the crumpled letter off, and then went back to the door.

"It wouldn't be wise to speak with her." Radames turned from the waterfall, his eyes boring into her.

"I have to. I spoke to the other Seconds before their banishments." The cloth of the doorway veil was cool between her fingers as she brushed it open. "I'll be in the Council Hall in a quarter of an hour for the trial. Assemble the Council Members, please."

"Ptolema, be careful—" The outer door cut him off.

Ptolema wound down the stairs and through the dim halls to the Council Hall instead of the Cells. Ptolema had sent Dalilah to the boats that morning for banishment. The woman would never know what happened to her lover. Guilt tugged at Ptolema, but she shook it off. The man had been a fool.

She passed the entrance to the Hall and made for the small door to the side. No one guarded the door, just as she'd asked. She gripped the small key in the inner pocket of her toga, cold and hard.

The key slipped into the lock and turned with a click. Ptolema stepped through into the large storeroom with a slight creak of hinges. A sharp intake of breath came from the far wall. The room was empty apart from Tiye, huddled in the corner, knees to her chest, toga riddled with dirt. Her hair hung in front of her thin face, lank and matted.

She scrambled up at Ptolema's entrance.

"Ptolema! I can explain!"

Ptolema's vocal cords strained to give the speech she had practiced, the calm statement of her crimes, but it would not come. Tiye stared at her. Plain and quiet, just as Dalilah said. How had she not seen it?

Because she had not wanted to.

She stepped forward, despite the shake in her ankles.

"You lied to me."

Tiye raised a mud-streaked hand. "No, I just never told the whole truth. You wouldn't have understood. You are the High One."

"Yes." The intensity of the word brought a tingle to Ptolema's palms. "Yes, I am, and I was foolish enough to befriend a *Second*. A Second, Tiye! Me, of all people. I don't know a thing about you. Your name isn't Tiye, is it?"

Tiye glanced to her feet, confirming it. "No."

"We'll get the truth from your father if you don't tell me."

"No!" She stepped forward. "No, please, don't hurt him. All he's ever wanted was life for us."

Ptolema clutched at her toga. "Then tell me your name."

Miki met Ptolema's gaze, her breath coming in thin rattles. The High One's face was taut and pale. Her hands clutched at her toga as if a wind might blow it off. Muscles cutting tight lines in her arm, Ptolema tightened her grip, a paper crunching in her palm.

"What is your true name?" Her teeth clenched over the words as she asked again.

"Miki of Bast." The name hit the cool air of the storeroom, immediately thickening it like some unleashed curse. The room spun.

Ptolema considered the name for a moment. "Victory," she murmured, then spoke louder. "It doesn't suit you."

"I know."

Ptolema said nothing more for a moment, her eyes searching Miki's face. She shoved the paper in her hand forward. The letter from yesterday.

"I wrote this to a friend," she whispered.

"I never asked to be your friend," Miki bit back. Ptolema thought she was the victim here? "We only met three times."

Ptolema didn't move, hand with the letter still extended. "Did it ever occur to you I considered you a friend? I've never had more than one casual meeting with anyone unless they wanted something from me."

Miki didn't respond.

Ptolema dropped her arm. "Did you hate me from the moment you met me? Were you lying when I asked about Manipulation?"

"I told the truth. I can't Manipulate. No Second can."

"Lies," Ptolema breathed. "Dalilah said the same, but you must be covering for each other."

"No, Ptolema—"

"I am the High One! Don't you dare call me differently." Ptolema strode closer until she was a foot from Miki's nose. "You are a liar and a fool, Miki of Bast." Her brown eyes glowed, and not with friendship. "The time has come for you to be sentenced." Ptolema turned and strode to the secondary door leading into the Council Hall.

"High One, wait, please!" Miki ran after her, bare feet slapping the stones.

Ptolema ducked out of the room, replaced by a stern-faced Steelman. His thick fingers encased Miki's arm and with a jolt, he pulled her into the Council Hall. Fifty pairs of eyes bore into her, so fierce she thought she might combust. She closed her eyes to block them off, but her skin still prickled under their gaze.

The Steelman yanked her forward, and she followed blindly. Voices echoed around her. Squinting her eyes tighter shut, Miki focused on her breathing. She was going to be okay. Banishment would only take her away from the hate in the Pyramid.

And from her father and the only life she knew.

"Miki of Bast," Ptolema's voice rose through the chamber and she let the name sink in.

Miki opened her eyes. She stood in the center of the circular Hall, Council Members ringing her in.

Ptolema sat on the stone throne, face dark.

"I charge you with being a Second-born of the Councilman Bast, who is charged with harboring a Second-born."

A Steelman, helped needlessly by a glowing Councilman Montu, brought Miki's father forward, twice as bruised than just hours before.

Even as her heart begged her to go to him, Miki's feet stayed firm.

"She's not guilty, High One," Bast croaked.

Miki flinched at the raw voice as her father's swollen eyes met hers.

"No," she said, "and neither is he guilty, Ptolema."

As one, the Council Members sucked in their breath at her casual use of the High One's name. Ptolema paled even further, her fingernails audibly scratching against the stone armrest of the throne. The lone pillar of darkness in the Hall, Radames, stepped forward and whispered into her ear.

Ptolema nodded once and released her grip on the throne. "You have already been found guilty by your own testimony not five minutes ago. Bast, were you harboring any others?" Ptolema's voice projected around the room, the echo against the stone pillars magnifying it.

"You look well, High One. I am glad." Bast dipped his head.

Radames stepped forward. "You will not address her unless answering a direct question. Understood?"

Miki's father's eyes did not move from Ptolema. He said nothing more. Miki bit into her lip, resisting the urge to run to him again.

"Were you hiding more Seconds?" Ptolema asked again, her jaw barely moving as if the act of speaking hurt.

"No," Bast answered.

"You hid one child for nineteen years. Did you hide any others?" Ptolema pressured.

Kamu. Beren. Boys Miki would never forget. She looked to the floor lest her face give her away.

Her father did not speak at first. Radames stepped forward again.

"Answer the High One."

Her father sighed. "They're not different from you or me, Ptolema. They deserve to live."

Again, the Council Members sucked in a breath. Montu motioned to the Steelmen. They stepped forward, ramming the butts of their spears into Bast's back. He doubled up and fell to the floor wheezing.

"No! Father—" Pain flared in Miki's back, but she held her ground, teeth gritted against it.

"You will not address the High One by her true name," Montu began, standing over Bast's crumpled form.

"If you beat him, I will never hear what he has to say," Ptolema cut in, voice thin. "Bast, we have reports of your wife giving birth at another time apart from your two daughters. Is this true?"

Miki sucked in a breath. Did someone know of Kamu and Beren? Her father's features were laced with pain.

"Yes." He picked himself up off the floor, a hand to his ribs. "Everyone knows my wife died during a forced nullification."

Miki's hand curled at her side. Neta, one of the sisters she never knew.

"If it was forced, then she was caught breaking the law. You should have been arrested then," Radames cut in.

Bast's gaze slid to Radames. "I say forced nullification, because given the choice we would not have done it. A friend discovered the pregnancy and brought her own physician to attend to my wife, leading us to believe she was against nullification. However, he took the child out of my wife—" clenching his fists he stood erect, a sob in his voice, "—killing them both."

Miki stiffened. Her father had never spoken of the nullification or the death of her mother. He still did not look her way, his face glistening with eleven-year-old tears.

Ptolema paled further, so white she could have been the statue of the ancient ruler at the city gate. Radames leaned close and whispered something. She nodded. He straightened and cleared his throat. As one, the gaze of everyone in the Hall swiveled to him.

"What happened to your wife could have been avoided with sterilization. But what I find most troubling in this confession is that not only did you have two children—" He paused, face contorting in what could almost be pain. For a moment, the hall was silent and Radames's lips moved without sound. Ptolema stayed focused on Bast, as if she didn't notice the strange moment, worry written on her face.

Finally, Radames cleared his throat again, and the moment passed. "What I find most troubling is you attempted to have a Third and would have, if not for your brave friend who put a stop to it."

"If you could lie to me my whole life, what stops you from lying now?" Ptolema's low voice broke in. She stared at Miki's father, eyes bloodshot.

He met her gaze evenly. "Ptolema—"

Montu did not even have to signal for the Steelmen to ram their spear butts into her father's back this time. He collapsed to the floor once more with a gasp, clutching his ribs.

"Father!" Miki managed two steps before something caught her in the back and she careened into the stone floor with a grunt of pain. Through moist eyes she caught Ptolema staring at her father, an expression of ice and worry mixed into one.

"Councilman Bast, you are stripped of your position and all possessions, including your home."

"No! Ptolema, please! He will become destitute, you know that. He could die!" Miki made it to her knees before the Steelman's grip tugged her back.

This time the mention of the High One's true name brought a hush to the crowd. Ptolema's cheek twitched, and for a moment, she was the cheerful girl in her mother's garden, only wanting a friend.

Ptolema leaned forward, the image gone. "Then your father should not have broken the law. You, Miki of Bast, will be banished, sent on the next boat to Thoth."

Thoth. The name rang through the Hall as an echo to Ptolema's voice as each Council Member whispered it. Miki said nothing. Thoth was a place of nightmares, where her mother and father warned her she must never go. The island of banished ones. Harsh as the people sent there. A shudder worked its way up her spine. She knew things would come to this, but hearing the name was different from knowing. It was reality.

"Her fingers, High One?" Montu stepped closer to the dais, face glowing.

Ptolema stared at Montu as if he had spoken something grotesque.

"No, please, High One—" Her father was cut off with a heel to his head.

Miki knew she shouldn't run to him, shouldn't scream for it all to stop, but her body moved anyway. Someone shouted behind her, but there was only her father coughing on the floor. Pain flared through her back and she tripped only a foot from him. Another blast of pain, and the world went black.

CHAPTER 13

Wind beat against Miki's face, sharp blast after sharp blast. She jerked her arm, and rough cord bit into her wrists. She grunted and tried to turn. Something hard vibrated up against her back. Gray sky blinked into focus, accompanied by bursts of sea spray.

The boat taking her to Thoth.

"Good thing you woke up. We're almost there." A gruff voice rose above the squall.

Miki craned her neck as far as she could against the wooden wall of the small boat. A miniature elderly man sat at the stern, hand on the rudder beam. A sail full of wind floated above them. The boat could have held twenty men, but no one else was on board.

The man chuckled. "Not so many getting banished these days. Although you two are a record now."

Miki slipped her bound hands over her legs and pulled her knees up, but the bitter wind still blasted through her toga. Couldn't the Firsts have given her a cloak for the trip? Or shoes? Of course not. They considered her only a rat.

The boat rocked as the old man stood. "Ah, there she is. Not a pretty sight, but a sight, I suppose." His leather pants and cloak fit snugly, not giving the wind a chance to snap them, as it did with Miki's toga. Sea spray soaked them.

Deep gray choppy waves rolled in every direction. Her father's maps showed Thoth somewhere to the South East, but the exact mileage wasn't stated. Twenty or two hundred, she hadn't a clue. The area on the map fit two crooks of her forefinger perfectly, but it was over twenty miles in all estimation.

"The cursed Back Current is coming up. Oy! Get up, woman, you are on the rafts!" He raised a hand and shouted toward a pile of blankets at the front.

A hand extended from the blankets and rubbed the foot now sticking out the end. A woman sat up with a start, blankets spilling about her. One long, black braid tugged against her long face in the steady wind, the same color of the bruise on her forehead.

Dalilah.

This mess rested on that woman's shoulders. If not for her, Kal would still be alive. Tiye would still exist. Miki's hand twisted within the rope at the thought of tossing her overboard.

"This is as far as I go. If I get any closer, the Back Current will suck me in and I'll be stranded with you on that island." His eyes narrowed and he looked past Dalilah.

Miki saw it in three seconds.

A white line of sea foam roared a hundred paces away. She braced against the side this time, but there wasn't a jolt. The wave raced away from them, toward the fog in the distance. It stood as a near-perfect semicircle on the horizon and stretched out of sight as if encircling something hiding behind the fog.

"Stand up, girl, hurry! They doped you with too much sleeping tonic and I don't have time for you to wake up properly. I don't want to hang around that current longer than I need to." He gave a dry chuckle which morphed into a coughing fit. "This almost isn't worth the pretty sum they pay me anymore." The old man offered Miki a hand.

She accepted and he yanked her up. Dalilah staggered upright. The blankets tumbled to the deck to reveal a pile of wooden planks, rough and less than five hand spans long.

The Boatman moved for them, shooing Dalilah off with a wave of his hand.

"All right now, you each get one and only one raft. We can't waste any more on you. Hold tight with both hands and you should make it over the Back Current. The rest will be easy. It'll push you straight to land." He offered one plank to Dalilah.

She scoffed through a tooth-chattering shiver. "You want us to float the rest of the way?"

"Aye. As I said, I won't get any closer and be stuck there for all eternity with the likes of you. Now go. I've got a wife and warm stew to get home to. Though I bet that's more than you'll have on that island." He shoved the plank into Dalilah's gut.

She grasped it with a scowl. Miki accepted hers before he could do the same to her. The Boatman herded them to the edge.

"Now jump. The current is closer than you think. It runs a good fifteen feet down, so when you sink after you jump, it'll grab you and pull you toward the island. Just make sure you make it up for a breath or you won't get there in this life." He rammed a fist into Miki's back and she staggered against the side of the boat.

"This is madness!" Dalilah clutched her plank with white knuckles, staring at the rolling waves.

What other choice did they have? Death here in the waves or death at the Boatman's hands. A wicked and well-oiled blade gleamed in his belt. The absence of Steelmen proved the Boatman wasn't as frail as he looked. He stared at her as if reading her thoughts and pulled the knife from his belt.

"Jump. I won't say it again."

Miki held out her hands. "Cut this rope and I'll jump."

"I don't know about that. They told me you were a particularly dangerous Second. I don't want you—" his voice dropped, "—*Manipulating* at me."

"I can't Manipulate."

"They all say that, and I don't believe you any more than them. Now get off my boat."

She clutched the plank to her torso as well as possible with bound hands. If it didn't support her and the current didn't take her to land, her banishment would be short.

Dalilah shivered beside her, staring at the waves. No one else could die because of all this. There was only one thing to do.

Miki inhaled thick, salty air, and jumped. The wind howled as she plunged down. Crushing cold. Crushing silence. A muted thump. Suffocating blackness. No sense of direction. Or air. Her lungs burned.

Something grabbed her. Yanked. Jerked. She shot forward. Or back. It was impossible to know which. Ice stabbed her limbs. Fire gripped her chest. Miki spun. Pain tore through her leg. Right or left. Both. Either. She twisted and the pain worsened. The burning in her lungs heightened. Another tug and the water changed. Warmer, but still cool. Salt tickled her tongue. She coughed and inhaled water. Rhythmic waves replaced the roaring speed. Her fingers sank into the pebbly sand as she flopped onto the beach. The water receded and Miki rolled over, retching.

Alive.

Her lungs protested and she coughed, saltwater spewing into the already drenched sand. Dalilah sputtered beside her, then choked and gagged. The woman dragged herself further out of the water. No rafts in sight. Had the Boatman known they were useless?

Miki stood on shaking legs. The island she had not seen through the fog on the gray waves stood before her, a jagged coastline of ragged rocks. Not a slip of vegetation. A crooked sign stuck from the pebbles on the beach:

THOTH. PLACE OF SECONDS. STAY AWAY.

Under the bold carving was etched in a rough hand:

Eshaq's Domain

"I knew it. I knew you were a Second."

Miki turned, holding her bound hands as close to her torso as possible for heat, but the icy wind cut through her anyway. Dalilah stood two feet to the side, her free hands wrapped around her chest and toga leggings plastered to her by seawater. "Looks like you got what was coming to you, ratting me out like you did." Dalilah spit, the drops vanishing among the wet pebbles.

"I didn't turn you in," Miki mumbled, and turned away. Of all people, why did she have to be banished with this woman?

"It's pointless to deny it out here. I knew Kal would find you and turn you in." Dalilah raised a finger of accusation, only to drop her hand with a shudder. Instead of a full pointer finger, it ended in a little nub of angry red tissue. Her gaze dropped to Miki's bound hands.

She pulled them tighter against her chest. No pain and no missing fingers. Montu had suggested it, but Ptolema hadn't ordered the amputation.

Dalilah said nothing, only balling her own ruined hands into fists and wincing.

"Kal is dead," Miki whispered. The green algae-slicked boulder in front of her outstripped the need to look at Dalilah.

"What?" Pebbles and sand shifted behind her. Dalilah grabbed Miki's shoulder and jerked her around. "What did you say about Kal?"

"He died trying to reach the High One. He was trying to get a pardon for you. I told him it was too dangerous."

"Dead ..." Dalilah's hand dropped, and she staggered backward as if Miki had slapped her. "But he's a First—"

"It doesn't matter anymore. They changed the law. Any First helping a Second is as guilty as the Second. It's ... it's deranged," she finished in a whisper. The only person she had ever known besides her father who wanted to help a Second was dead. But that life was over.

She took in their surroundings again. The shoreline rose to the left, a small cliff jutting above the water. To the right it continued flat against the oncoming waves, but with clusters of large rocks and boulders. The land behind them was scrubby and rocky. No sign of a road or posts pointing the way to wherever the banished ones lived.

"But he is dead? Oh, Kal ..." Dalilah's knees hit the sand.

A man's cry cut through the air.

Miki jerked toward the cluster of boulders behind them. The cry sounded again, this time ending in a gurgle.

Someone else was there! She darted forward, balance thrown off by her bound hands. Sand sprayed up over her legs and through the rips in her toga as she darted toward the boulders. The cry split the empty terrain again. Miki slipped around a rock and staggered to a halt a foot away from a ravine.

A man hung below her from a stake rammed into the rock, suspended by a rope looped over his hands. His green eyes darted to Miki and widened.

"Help—!" A wave cut him off, the water splashing as far up as his forehead. It receded, leaving him sputtering. "Help, please," he gasped.

A dark night lit by torches. A man lying in his own blood. The first Second discovered in five years. "Pilis," Miki breathed.

His eyes widened further at his name just as another wave beat into him. Something white flashed past Miki and Dalilah knelt at the edge of the ravine, arm out to him. It was too far by a foot. She could never reach him. Miki threw her rope-bound hands over a bulge in the rock. She jumped off the rock, her grip anchored by the rope. Adrenaline pulsed through her as she dropped to the icy surface of the rock and reached for the stake holding the man's ropes. Kal had died, but Pilis would not.

His rope hung just inches away. Her fingers stretched further. A wave rose below and shot up Miki's nose. She fell back, coughing.

Dalilah shouted something, but the drumming of the waves covered it. Her shout vanished into a scream. Miki flung her rope over the knotted rock again and scrambled back up. She flopped on to the ground, only to find a leather wrapped foot pressing her back down. Muscles cut along the leg, but they were thin, as if the man had never eaten a decent meal. He stared down with curious— and rare—blue eyes.

The man standing above her muttered something to a woman beside him, his dread-locked hair swinging at his shoulders. The woman shared the same stunning blue eyes and thin frame. Her short dark hair hung just past her ears. Her gaze slid to Miki. "Who are you?"

"Tiy—Miki."

"Tiy-Miki? Their names are getting odder every year," the woman muttered.

"No, it's just Miki." She tried to sit, but the foot pressed harder. She fought back a cough.

"Well, Miki, you and your friend are interfering with Eshaq's judgment." The woman leaned over her, yellowed teeth standing out from her tanned skin.

"He's going to drown if we—"

The man's fist shot down toward her. Light exploded as Miki's head snapped against the rock. The world spun. Ringing vibrations and pain. She blinked through tears of pain and the man's face hovered in front of hers, the rock under her feet and two more men holding her upright.

The man wiped his bloodied knuckles on his leather jerkin.

"First rule: never be interfering wi' Eshaq's judgment." The words came haltingly, as if not familiar with his tongue, but his blue eyes flashed.

Pilis cried out below them just as a wave rose so high the spray soaked Miki's feet. Her captors did not react. No one spoke. The waves beat against the rock, one after another. It was like the waterfall in El-Pelusium, but angrier, wilder. The dreadlocks man held up grime-encrusted fingers and flaked the dirt out from under his nail with the edge of a rough stone dagger. The woman did not move.

Pilis did not cry out again. He was dead, then. Miki's panic rose, threatening to bring on her anxiety. She gulped for the cold, salty air and gasped as it hit her lungs. The man eyed her, as if annoyed she made such a loud sound. Two more men and a woman came from the beach, hauling Dalilah between them. Her nose bled, and when her eyes met Miki's, they were wide with fear.

The first man and woman, apparently the leaders of the band, stuck their heads together again. The outlines of their thin faces were identical. Siblings? Twins, even. Twins didn't exist in El-Pelusium, though Miki had heard stories of them from other lands. Was Thoth a fairy-tale land? Miki choked her curiosity down as the pain pounded in her head. She closed her eyes, but an elbow dug into her side.

"There be no getting ou' of this that easy." The captor on Dalilah's right chuckled, harsh, mirthless. His brown hair shone with a telltale layer of grease, and his ribs could be seen even through the animal fur wrapped tight across his torso.

"My brother thinks we should take you to Eshaq. It has been a while since we found so many new citizens." The woman stepped closer, her blue eyes boring into Miki. "Although the last one didn't turn out so well."

Pilis's body thunked against the rock below, rhythmically rocked by the waves.

Miki shivered. The blue-eyed man chuckled. His sister frowned and swung her fist in a wide circle, a signal of some kind. In one swift movement, their captors drew into a tight group. They moved away from the shore, Miki's feet stumbling over jagged rocks and thorny ferns, the only plants in sight. Sucking in air through her teeth, she tried not to cry out. Dalilah whimpered behind her.

So this was Thoth.

CHAPTER 14

With the thick gray fog hiding the sun, Miki couldn't be sure how many hours had passed. The landscape remained consistent, with rocks, ferns and low shrubs, all of them so brittle the persistent wind should have blown them off the island. No plant over a foot or two tall existed, and the distinct lack of any buildings was unsettling. They had banished a fair share of Seconds over the past three centuries. By now their offspring should have formed a civilization, no matter how crude.

A sharp barking cut over the rough terrain. The woman raised a hand and whistled. The man escorting Miki stepped away.

"Don't move." He broke off from their group and cut out over the rock. The barking sounded again. It ended in a yelp and a snarl.

"W-what was that? Dalilah asked, breathless from the hike.

"Coyote." The blue-eyed woman spoke to the horizon.

Miki's escort crept toward a cluster of rocks, spear held aloft. Another bark. He rammed the spear down. The animal yelped. A mass of gray jumped from behind the rock and sped off the other direction, yipping. The man pulled another coyote up and slung it over his shoulder where it blended it against his fur tunic. He rejoined them. He passed the animal off to the blue-eyed woman and grabbed Miki's arm again. The march resumed, the dead animal swaying across the woman's back.

The band followed no trail, but picked their way through the rocks at an amazing pace. All of them wore variations of animal hide, mingled with a few bits of cloth stitched to make a shirt or pants with the leather and fur. The man whose fingers bit into Miki's arm even wore a half toga, like the Steelmen, only made of hide and not expensive linen.

His index finger was missing. A small nub pressed into her arm along with the others.

Heat rose in her cheeks. Would they notice hers were intact and relieve her of them? The *swoosh vroom swoosh* of blood through her ears drowned out the far-off crashing of the waves and the crunching of gravel under their feet. Pinpricks of light dotted the edges of her vision. Maybe an anxiety attack would spare her being conscious for the removal of her fingers.

Her extremities went numb. They were both freezing cold and pulsing with heat at the same time. Wine, she needed wine. Three good sips would drive the darkness away. She inhaled, but the air was thick, putrid, filled with the reeking scent of fish. It blasted across her face, ice cold.

The blackness receded, overwhelmed by the stench. Beside her, Dalilah held her free hand over her face, face screwed in disgust. The woman holding her other arm captive rolled her eyes and snickered.

"Where are we going?" Miki asked.

The blue-eyed man did not slow his march but veered left without warning. Miki stumbled into his sister.

"Sorry," Miki mumbled.

The woman's eyes narrowed, but she turned after her brother. The course led back toward the coast where small jagged peaks rose from the far side of the island, waves crashing against their backs as if hoping to break them down.

Something moved along the base of the mountains. Miki's feet tangled under her and she stumbled to the ground. Pinpricks of pain flared along her exposed skin as rocks and thorny sage raked her palms. A firm hand forced her back up. She winced as a bit of a shrub came up with her, embedded in her calf.

The blue-eyed man continued up ahead, but his disjointed voice floated back.

"Second rule, be watchin' yer step."

Clenching her teeth against the pain, Miki stepped after him, jerking her arm out of the other man's grasp.

"I don't need your help."

He chuckled. "You willna be thinkin' that much longer."

As if in agreement with the man's cryptic tone, she stumbled again, but steadied herself before falling. More movement at the base of the hills. The closer they came, the clearer the outlines of tents stood against it. A silver fog, mingled with the smoke of cooking fires, shrouded the camp, making it hard to see in its entirety. The red glow of flames pierced the fog, and shapes moved in front of them across the camp. Seconds and their descendants. At least two hundred, if not twice that.

The blue-eyed man and his sister pulled ahead of the group and slipped through the throng of tents. Miki made to follow, but her guard tugged her the other way.

"We be waitin' for Eshaq." He led her toward the far end of the camp where a shallow cave stood among the rocks. Stained animal hides hung on all sides and a chair—a throne?—which looked to be made from driftwood stood in the center, more animal furs draped over it.

The inhabitants of the closest tents edged toward the cave, their eyes wide in the lights of the fires. Flames cast long shadows on their gaunt faces. The banished ones wore the same clothes as Miki's escort. Some were fortunate to have leather wrapped around their feet, but most were barefooted. Miki caught the gaze of a teenage boy, and he stared back with a dirt-streaked face and fierce eyes. She shivered. Here was the largest group of her people she had ever seen, and it unsettled her. But it shouldn't.

The Firsts were wrong. Ptolema, Radames, and the Council were wrong. These people were the same as them. But looking at the ragged civilization, that was hard to see.

The boy scratched his nose. Miki's gut dropped with a sickening gurgle. His forefinger was gone. But he couldn't be older than fifteen. Not all those present were missing fingers. Natural-born citizens of Thoth, descendants of those who were banished, surely. Maybe they wouldn't notice her fingers were intact.

"Ho! Two newcomers? I be hopin' I won't be forced to send ye on as I was with the last one." A man stepped into the cave, wearing as many furs as the entire group which held Miki wore. The furs hid the man's true size, giving the illusion he was fat, but judging by the others on the island, and his hollow cheeks, he wasn't. His skin flushed red in random blotches and the wisps of his gray hair drifted in the wind, as if longing to leave him bald.

"May I present Eshaq, Master of Thoth," the female twin announced without any fanfare.

Eshaq flashed Miki a yellow smile as he marched to the makeshift throne and threw himself into it with a loud creak.

"So. Names, both yer real and false ye used back in the Devil's City." Eshaq waved at the cave behind him and the blue-eyed man melted out of the shadows. He held a tablet, if it could be called that. He pressed his rock dagger into the rough slab of granite and gazed expectantly at Dalilah.

Shivering, she stepped forward. "Mandisa. D-Dalilah."

The knife moved across the tablet. The man flung a dreadlock out of his eyes and looked at Miki. So fierce, yet so much like her lost brother Kamu, even though his eyes had been gray.

"Name, or I'll set him on ye," the man on the throne barked.

Miki started. "Tiye. Miki of Bast." Her true name came on instinct.

"Of Bast?" The old man leaned forward on the throne, a gnarled hand on his knee. "What do ye be thinking this is, some court that cares of yer ancestry? Ha!" He spit to the side. "If ye are noble born, which ye must be to say yer surname, ye'll be finding this life hard." The gleam in his eyes betrayed his pleasure at the prospect.

Miki lowered her eyes, taking in the trampled earth beneath her. No sage covered the ground, though small stumps littered the circle. Rocks lined the area as if cleared out.

"Ye'll be finding life hard here either way. I am Eshaq, ruler of Thoth. Ye'll be used to referring to us as 'banished ones' or 'Seconds,' but ou' here, on my island, there be none of that. We be one community." His voice cut out against the wind as if he was used to yelling to get his point across.

Miki's father had never referred to Seconds as 'banished ones.' He knew their value. To never see him again ... Even this dreadful Eshaq couldn't—

"Third rule: always be looking at Eshaq when he be speakin' to ye." Leather-wrapped feet slipped into Miki's vision, and she only had time to look up before the fist flew into her nose.

The fires multiplied, sparking red, yellow, and white as her eyes snapped shut. Gravel crunched underfoot as she stumbled backward. Agony gripped her nose and exploded into her head. Crying out, she cupped her nose and blinked, water pooling in the edges of her eyes.

The blue-eyed man stared at her. No anger, no remorse. Miki stepped back before he could punch her a third time, but he turned and resumed his place at Eshaq's side. A son? A favorite thug? Whichever he was, a white-hot ball of hate for him glowed in her belly.

"Atsu be correct." Eshaq waved a hand to the man. "We have many rules here and ye must learn them if ye wish to survive."

"Well, we shouldn't be punished for not knowing them now." Dalilah's voice wavered.

"If ye used yer common sense, ye might have figured some out to keep yer friend from receiving Atsu's fist."

"We are *not* friends," Dalilah spit.

A wide grin pulled at Eshaq's face, revealing the yellow teeth.

"Well, isn't that nice? I suppose ye would like to share a tent then, since ye be not friends."

"No—" Dalilah was silenced with a kick from the woman who had escorted her.

Eshaq cracked his knuckles, pulling back on each one methodically. "Ye be right. We have no tent for ye. Ye be not yet members of our community. We don't know ye, apart from yer names. Now we will pick one of them for ye and no complaints now. Ata?"

The blue-eyed man's identical sister stepped forward, her short hair ruffling in the wind. She no longer held the coyote. She turned her gaze first to Dalilah.

"Dalilah means weak, beautiful one. You are weak, but you are not beautiful. You will be Mandisa." She spoke with no accent, her words flowing clear in a way her brother's and Eshaq's did not.

Dalilah sputtered a response, but Ata turned her attention to Miki. Her breath hovered in the back of her throat. The name meant nothing. She had overcome that on her own.

"Tiye means deity of light. We can't have you thinking you are a deity. Miki, however, means victorious. I'll admit I'm stumped on this one, Atsu."

Her twin shifted on his feet and flashed her a frown. "She be Miki." No explanation.

The woman nodded. "Aye. You will be Miki. You were victorious enough to reach Thoth through the Back Current."

Miki shivered. This was victory?

Eshaq leaned forward in his throne, the wood crying out under him. "The rules be simple. Do not interfere with my judgments. Look at me when I speak. Work diligently and bring all yer finds to the large tent—"

"Finds?"

A vein in his cheek twitched, but Eshaq did not lash out. "Aye. From now on ye are to work as fishermen, craftsmen, cooks, or scavengers who hunt the coasts for items of value or things that be helping us survive. Ye work for us to keep us all alive. This be a community. No putting yerself first anymore."

Miki scoffed, choked it down, and covered it with a cough. Did Eshaq never put himself first? Her neck burned under the gaze of her guard, as did her forehead under Eshaq's and two sets of blue eyes. She coughed again. Ata's eyes narrowed, but her brother did not step forward for another blow.

Eshaq cleared his throat and pulled himself erect in the chair.

"If ye be sick, Miki, I will throw ye into the sea. We don't know ye yet and can't waste a healer on ye."

"No, I'm fine. Just a tickle in my throat."

His eyes narrowed. Atsu set the name tablet down on the ground.

"Fourth rule: No be lyin'." His accent, thicker even than Eshaq's odd lilt, hung in the air between them.

A retort burned in the back of her throat, but she ignored it. Her nose still throbbed with the impact of his last punch.

Eshaq nodded. "Aye. Fifth rule: Do no try to leave. Ye will only end up dead. The sea is twice as vicious as me, and we be having no boats. Surely ye saw the dangerous Back Current as ye rode in. There be no way past it."

The Boatman had already taught them that lesson plain enough.

Atsu looked to Ata, but she did not return the look, although her shoulders stiffened. Her brother continued the sharp stare, but Eshaq's voice cut over it and Atsu dropped his eyes.

"There be only one more rule and I won't speak it. Use yer common sense and don't break it."

"How are we supposed to keep a rule we don't know?" Dalilah argued.

Eshaq pursed his lips and studied her for a moment. "I think Ata be wrong."

Ata dropped her brother's gaze and faced Eshaq. "What do you mean by that?"

"This one may be weak, but I think she be beautiful." His eyes glowed with an unsatisfied hunger.

Dalilah stepped back, her arm brushing Miki's. Cold as the wind.

Ata said nothing and stepped away, her face firm as the stone behind them. Eshaq stood.

"Ye will begin working now. The fishermen are ou' already, I don't know yer cookin' or craftin' skills, and I don't trust ye to scavenge yet."

Atsu slipped up to him and leaned into his ear, whispering. A grin split Eshaq's face, pulling the age-weathered skin taut. "My lieutenant here be correct. We should give ye hard labor until ye prove we can trust ye. It just so happens we are digging a new pit to the west o' the village to store the valuables. Ye will help." He waved Ata over to him, and she obliged. They muttered amongst themselves, the trial apparently over.

A firm hand pinched Miki's shoulder and forced her around.

"This way, if it be pleasin' you," the guard said in a mocking tone.

There was no choice but to follow him out of the throne room and into the foggy evening. Dalilah and her guard stepped in behind them, and they made their way back across the camp. The onlookers faded away, back to whatever tasks they were assigned. The guard led Miki to a cluster of men hefting shovels over the ground on the far side of the camp. Most of them were topless, wearing anima-hide duplications of half togas. One man lowered himself to the ground as they approached, and Miki's gut back-flipped. He only had one leg. So many things could have happened, yet Eshaq ... Was that his form of justice, along with drowning innocent men?

"Clear out," her escort barked. "These two be finishin' this."

A visible wave of relief passed through the group, although more than one cast a curious glance at Miki. She stared back. A crude shovel handle was pressed into her hand and she winced. Pulling it away with her other hand, a sharp slice of wood jutted from her palm.

"Work until dark, then work four more hours. If you can't judge time by the moon, work until the sun comes up." The guard handed Dalilah another shovel, one with even more splinters. She grimaced but took the implement without complaint.

Their escorts turned away, the man yelling over his shoulder. "And don't think of running off. There be nowhere to go." His chuckle followed him into the smoke of the dozens of campfires hovering across the valley.

Soft earth crumbled into the hole as Miki stepped closer. She lowered the shovel and its bent tip nudged more dirt downward.

"You're making it worse," Dalilah said flatly. She stepped around the other side of the hole, arms folded across her chest, the shovel abandoned.

"If you don't do this, I know they will hurt you." Miki's shovel bit deeper into the earth, and she brought a load up to fling over her shoulder. The tool was unfamiliar to her hands, but it appeared straightforward enough.

Dalilah did not move to help, but kept her thoughts to herself. Miki plunged the shovel into the hole again until, within fifteen minutes, the side she stood before was noticeably deeper. She threw a bit of her old life behind with each shovel full of dirt. What was her father doing now? Begging for food in the street outside of Jabarre's? She frowned, sob threatening. No, he wouldn't beg, no matter how bad his situation got.

"What are you crying over?" Abused metal sank into the dirt besides Miki's shovel as Dalilah joined in.

Miki did not raise her gaze from the dark earth, picking out the specks of metallic gravel within. Her father was miles away. He was gone from her life. Her fingers clutched at the shovel handle, shaking. With an inhale, she pushed the dark cloud of anxiety away from her mind. She wouldn't let the anxiety get her, not out here with Dalilah.

"I said, what are you—"

"I'm not crying." The words slipped through her lips with little more than a whisper. Miki blinked and the black rushed back, blotting out the pinpricks of shine in the dirt. Blood thundered through her head in a frantic rhythm. Pain tingled in her lips, sharp, hot. Acrid copper tickled her tongue and she choked the blood down. The shovel fell from her fingers, the ground rushing closer. The earth, cool and moist, accepted her knees with a soft *thwump*.

Was someone calling out her name? Was a hand pounding on a cellar door far above?

No.

She gasped, clawing at her eyes, trying to bring the dirt and shovel back to sight, but her hands wouldn't move, frozen in the lock of panic. A sound squeezed out of her throat, unintelligible. Someone spoke above her, but the words only came through a veil of pulsing blood in her ears.

Frigid cold blasted across her face. It spilled down the nape of her neck, where it settled, burning her skin with its ice. Gasping, the dim light of late evening flooded into her eyes as she batted with her muddied palms at the water streaming into her face.

"Good, still alive then." A shovel sank into the dirt by Miki's left thigh and Dalilah leaned closer, dark hair falling into her vision. "Do you think Eshaq would let me off easy if you died on my watch?" She stood. "Because I seriously doubt it."

Fingers tingling with the receding pain of the immobilization, Miki wrung her hands together to massage the last bits out. The water had worked at least, but she wouldn't bring herself to say thank you. The shovel handle granted her another splinter and she hissed as she pushed herself up.

"What is wrong with you?" Dalilah's hand curled around Miki's right shoulder, squeezing far beyond the friendly point. "Don't you realize they are watching us?"

"I didn't do it on purpose." Miki shrugged the woman's hand off and stepped back.

"Well, don't do it again. If I'm to be stuck with you, you better not bring me trouble." With a grunt, Dalilah plunged the shovel into the dirt.

Miki fiddled with her hands, tracing the line where a thin sliver of dark wood showed under the waxy skin. Pinching her nails around it, she tugged. It came free, leaving a thin streak of faint red. The sliver vanished into the dirt at her feet.

"Do you think they really don't have any boats here?" she asked, without glancing up.

"Yes. They're idiots." Dalilah threw herself into another shovelful of dirt.

"It's just odd. They've been here for centuries as a civilization, and no one ever thought to build a boat?" Miki leaned against the shovel, the end butting into her chin.

"They are backward, ignorant savages. I'm not surprised they don't have the courage to build a boat. Besides, it wouldn't work anyway." Dirt scattered across Dalilah's feet as the shovel tilted in her grip. Cursing, she jumped backward.

"But there's got to be a way off." Miki pressed the shovel back into the earth.

"There's a *back* current. You were in it. You felt it. The current will only shove every boat that tries to cross back to the island. Haven't you ever studied it?"

No. There hadn't been any reason to study Thoth. All of her father's energy had been taken up ensuring she never ended up here.

"And do you think these people would want to get away? They wouldn't like the Pyramid and would be caught anyway. All other land is weeks away. They wouldn't make it. Eshaq seems happy enough. Either way, we don't have a boat, so it's pointless to talk about it." Dalilah hefted herself into another shovel full of dirt, turning her back away.

She was right, but the coast, only a few yards away, called to Miki. The fog still lay heavy around them, but a thin slip of pink glowed through. Sunset, then. Her teeth dug into her lip.

The hours eked by. Even when the sun vanished, the moon did not rise through the curtain of fog. The shovels beat rhythmically into the dirt until Dalilah's came less often, disrupting their pattern. Miki couldn't stare at the dark earth beneath her any longer. Dalilah's weary face was the only thing to focus on.

"Has it been four hours past sunset?" Dalilah slurred.

"Probably."

Dalilah's shovel thudded into the earth, soon followed by her rear end. "Good."

The tents behind them were silent. Not even a child's cry split the dark night. If they were not to have a tent yet, where would they sleep? The dirt steamed beneath Miki's bare toes, warmer than the brisk night air. How could it look so inviting? She wrapped her arms together against the ocean breeze. An island should be sunny, not chilly and fog covered. Her knees sank into the fresh dirt. A strange but wonderful kind of warmth.

"What are you doing?"

"We have to sleep somewhere." Miki huddled up in the dirt, almost feeling her old blankets bearing down around her.

Dalilah didn't retort. Perhaps she was finally too tired to mouth off.

An animal howled somewhere in the night. White hot pain flared through Miki's abdomen. She drew her knees closer to her chest, only to have the pain attack her lower back. With a cry, her eyes flew open. Leather-wrapped feet and wiry legs stood against the hazy purple of dawn.

Atsu.

Miki rolled away. Pain spiked along her neck. The man's angry toes followed her, jabbing every inch she left exposed. A rock met her free hand and Miki pulled up against it, clinging to steady herself. She spun around, hands outstretched.

"Stop it! Stop!"

Atsu's knee jabbed upward, catching her in the chin. The rock met her back and forced all the air from her lungs with an *oomph*. Dropping to the packed dirt, she rolled into a fetal position just before another blow crunched into her shins. His foot found a sliver of leeway between her legs and rammed with the strength of a trained warrior against her ribs.

A cry rent the still morning, and it wasn't her own. Blinking through the tears, Miki caught Dalilah cowering under Ata's solid punches. Atsu stepped closer, cutting them out of her view. His blue eyes shimmered in the early light as he knelt in front of her, almost at her level. A thin finger scratched a small nose as he assessed his prey.

"Why?" Miki croaked.

His eyes narrowed, as if considering. A dreadlock slipped from the knot on his head and fell in front of his face.

Miki clutched at the pain in her ribcage. His eyes flicked to the injury, but he said nothing. He pulled away, waving an arm to his sister. His silence buzzed in Miki's ears, deafening even the thudding of the blood through her brain.

Ata shot her a frown, making up for her brother's composure. Then she turned and followed Atsu into the oncoming dawn.

"What? Why would they do that?" Dalilah sobbed, rolling onto her side to face Miki. Miki's stomach churned, even as her own pains burned. Blood slicked Dalilah's face, streaming from a gash on her cheek and staining her ruined toga. She drew her knees to her chest and shook with a sob.

Miki stretched her legs, testing the pain in her ribcage. It burned fiercer at the movement, but nothing she couldn't bear. Her palms pressed into the soft dirt and she pushed up. The camp brightened behind her as a flare of light rose above the horizon.

The sun. It existed on Thoth after all.

They lay in silence for close to fifteen minutes, Dalilah's sobs punctuating the stillness. The pain in Miki's abdomen heightened with each passing minute. Would Atsu be back? Would the twins keep beating them after every failed job?

The clouds hung heavy above her, deep gray, threatening rain. Would Eshaq expect them to keep working if it stormed? Too many questions. Too many unknowns. Her stomach rumbled. She hadn't eaten since El-Pelusium, more than a day ago. Dalilah's sobs came less often. Was she thinking over the same things?

Miki rolled onto her side. Pain flared through her gut, but she flinched it away.

"I'm going to find some food." Dirt crumbled away beneath her as she stood. She straightened, twinging at the pain shooting everywhere.

"Don't leave me out here," Dalilah wheezed. She pulled herself up, a hand to her face, though it didn't hide the cut Ata had given her.

"Maybe we can find food and find somewhere to hide out the rest of the day." Miki staggered toward the camp.

Dalilah followed in silence. They'd passed a cook tent on the way into the camp yesterday. This place seemed communal. Were they allowed food from the pot?

No one tried to stop them as they entered the camp. The few faces peering from tattered tents were children or the elderly. Was everyone else at work already less than an hour after the sun came up? Smoke swirled fifty feet to the left, in front of a wooden framed tent. Miki's stomach twisted tight. The robust scent of cooking meat called to her. She veered for the large black pot hanging over a fire.

"Ye canna make it out here without someone watchin' out fer ya." The man who had escorted Dalilah from the Landing Point slid in between Miki and the pot. His eyes widened as he took in the bruises covering her face. Her hand twitched at her side, but she didn't cover her cheek.

Dalilah caught up to Miki's side, gasping, but still managed to speak.

"You can leave us alone for all the help that comment was." She tried to step around the man and her shoulder thumped into Miki's.

The man grabbed her arm and yanked her back.

"Are ya daft, woman? Do you want the Mad Twins to do this every time you fail to bring back finds?"

"No." Dalilah didn't pull back.

"Then ya need someone to take yer side."

"Someone like you?" Miki's stomach gurgled. The soup was so close, bubbling lusciously in the pot behind the lunatic.

The man released Dalilah's arm.

"Aye. I'm Lukmon. Eshaq trusts me. If ya stick with me, the twins canna harm ya." He shot Miki a glance but his most penetrating gaze he saved for Dalilah's long face and curves.

"I don't need a guardian." Miki stepped past him to the soup, dead grasses crackling underfoot. The scent of mustard and what must be wild coyote meat was too strong to ignore any longer. She swiped a wooden bowl from the stump beside the pot and ladled a healthy portion of soup into it. Hopefully this was allowed, though she would faint if she didn't eat soon, so it hardly mattered.

"Good thing I wasna talkin' to ya," Lukmon chuckled. "So will ya take my help, Mandisa?"

Miki slurped down half the soup in one go. Her belly throbbed with the fresh bruises, but she forced more food down. Dalilah said nothing, but her gaze burned into Miki's back. Was she asking for advice?

Dalilah stepped up beside Miki and grabbed another bowl.

"It would be wise of yeh to be thinkin' on it." Footsteps shuffled away, grasses crackling beneath and gravel skittering.

Miki drained the rest of the soup as Dalilah ladled some for herself. Miki led the way to a boulder at the edge of the camp. No one else was around. Perhaps they would go unnoticed here. She sank onto the packed black sand. Dalilah followed and sat motionless, staring silently at her still full bowl.

If they were to be stuck out here together, perhaps it would be wise to breach the hostility rolling off the woman even in her silence. Miki cleared her throat.

"Kal was a good man. He would have done anything to free you. I'm sorry about what happened."

Dalilah lifted the bowl and took a sip. When she brought it down, her eyes hardened.

"Kal is dead. It doesn't matter what he was." But a choke in her throat denied her words. She stared unblinking at the soup.

Miki closed her eyes and leaned her head against the boulder. So much for trying to patch things up. Dalilah didn't move beside her, apart from the slurping of soup. After fifteen minutes she mumbled, "I've got to make the most of life here. No matter what."

Gravel crunched. Miki opened her eyes to see Dalilah standing up. The bowl clattered to the ground, empty. The woman stared back toward the camp.

"Dalilah?"

"Kal wouldn't want this for me. He would want me to find a life," she whispered, as if trying to convince herself.

"You can't be thinking of taking that man up on his offer—"

"You know nothing about me. You spent your life in the Pyramid with a caring, well-born family and working as a privileged shop girl, but I fought hard for my place. My mother's nullification failed. They killed my twin, but not me. They didn't realize I was still there until too late. The moment I was born, they threw me to a poor family without children. That family saw me as a slave, not a child." She spit into the sand. "I escaped when I was six years old. I met Kal when I was ten. He caught me stealing from his mother's kitchen. He was the first person to see me as a person with worth." Her words thrummed with intensity. "I'll find nothing like that again."

She swallowed hard and stepped away from the boulder.

"I won't let Kal's sacrifice leave me in another sort of slavery, digging through junk for that madman. If this Lukmon is the only person on this forsaken lump of rock to find me worth protecting and give me a better life, so be it."

"Dalilah ..." But what could Miki say? That Lukmon was nothing like Kal? Dalilah had to know that. She had her own reasons. Miki had often wondered what life was like for the other Seconds in El-Pelusium. Dalilah had a point. Being born to a noble family, a family who wanted her, made a tremendous difference even if the danger increased because of the public aspect of her parents' lives.

Dalilah strode away without any sort of farewell to recognize the end of their journey together. The bitter wind cut through Miki's ruined toga.

She was alone.

CHAPTER 15

"There must be a new resolution about the Seconds before the end of the month, High One. We have found three in two weeks! Delaying even a moment after we caught Bast was preposterous!" Montu threw his arms in the air, purple embroidered toga exaggerating his fury.

Ptolema fought the urge to shift on the throne and set one hand on the arm.

"I am working on a resolution I will present to the Council in a few days. You can hardly expect things to move much faster after so many developments. We must ensure everything is in place."

Radames nodded where he stood at the edge of the room. He had agreed waiting was the best strategy. Things done rashly could backfire. But judging by the scowls across the room, the Council did not agree.

"What if by moving too quickly we draw out more Seconds who are not as tame as the last three?" Ptolema offered. Radames feared this, and rightly so. "If anyone has advice for the resolution, they are welcome to keep it to themselves."

Montu shuffled forward, all faux piety.

"I am sorry, High One, but that is not an option. Since you are not yet twenty-five and have no High Advisor, we cannot leave you to make this decision alone."

Whispers and nodding heads ran through the hall. Ptolema's fingers curled against the throne's arm. How dare he speak so? And in front of the whole Council. Not even waiting to suggest it in private. Ptolema drew herself up the extra half inch she had until she was straight as possible. She had seen her father do it on numerous occasions, calling on the full extent of his control. "I do not need a reminder of our customs. A High Advisor is not necessary or mandatory. My father—"

"Did not find himself in trying times such as these." Edrice stepped up beside Montu, followed by three more Council members. They didn't meet Ptolema's gaze, but stared at their bare feet and manicured toenails.

They had planned this ambush. She had no choice but to either defy them in front of the whole Council and risk an upset, or give in to their demands. Her index fingernail cracked as she dug it too far into the stone.

"We suggest you either name a High Advisor or allow this session to remain open until sunset for any opinions on the matter of the Seconds Resolution to be voiced and voted on." Montu dipped a bow, as if that made his words inoffensive. The Council stood as one, silent, eyes locked on her.

"I ..." What was she to say? Giving each of them the chance to say their piece would muddle the whole thing. A truly powerful resolution would be impossible. So much truth would be lost in the bloat of vanity. But she couldn't pick one of them to be High Advisor. Maybe if Bast hadn't been a traitor ... but he was.

Movement flickered at the edge of the room. Radames's gaze locked with hers. Sharp greens. Arms crossed, waiting for her answer. Pity he couldn't help with this.

Ptolema yanked her hand off the throne's arm. "I choose Radames as High Advisor."

Radames's arms dropped. His eyes widened.

"You can't choose a foreigner!" Montu sputtered, his face reddening.

"I can and I will. There is nothing written against it." Ptolema faced Montu again. He couldn't see her uncertainty. Her desperation to avoid letting him be her choice. Radames had shown up in the nick of time and had been a wise friend so far.

"There is nothing written against choosing a foreigner, because there is nothing written stipulating who the

Advisor must be, apart from at least thirty years old and versed in El-Pelusium law and history." Edrice commented dryly.

"Radames knew my father and probably knows more of El-Pelusium than any of us. He is a student of history and has traveled to every great library in all of Adamah, including our own."

"It is true," Radames said with a humble smile.

"We must accept your decision." Edrice bowed lower than Montu had, her purple headdress almost sweeping the floor. Ptolema forced her smile to remain small, satisfied and not gleeful. Edrice knew when she had lost. They had assumed Ptolema would pick a Council member, because it was traditional.

Montu looked from Radames to Edrice to Ptolema and back again. His gaze darkened, but only for a moment before a sickly smile wiped it away.

"As you wish, High One. May his advice be prudent and wise." He turned and swept from the Hall. Edrice and her companions followed him out. The rest trickled out, whispering. Disgruntled? Good.

When they had all gone, Radames approached the throne.

"I am honored, Ptolema. You could have picked any of them."

"And be heckled to death? No, thank you." She slouched, the pressure and weight of ruling lifting. "But thank you, Radames. You've been there when I needed you."

He dipped his head. "I am doing what I can to find the truth."

"I'm such a fool." Ptolema rested her head back against the stone throne. At least the Council members hadn't known how close she had gotten with Tiye—no, Miki. If Montu had known she had spent time with the Second in the royal Palace ... Ptolema shuddered.

"You aren't a fool. You have a heart for your people. How were you to know what that Second was?" Radames sank onto the stone steps before her, his dark blue toga swirling against the red stone.

"But her of all people ... When you met us in the garden, could you feel?"

"In a way. There was something in the air, though it wasn't the same as with the other woman."

"You could have told me."

"I had to be sure. That is quite a serious accusation to make of a friend of the High One." A smile flickered under green eyes.

"Being High One makes everything hard."

"Well, I suppose as your new High Advisor, I've got to make it easier." The smile broke through.

Perhaps she had been rash in choosing him, but perhaps it had been a good move as well.

CHAPTER 16

Two more days on Thoth changed nothing. Dalilah didn't reappear, unless one glimpse of her across the camp hanging on the arm of Lukmon counted. The man's words appeared true, as much as Miki didn't want to admit it. Dalilah hadn't been given any duties as far as she could tell. Unless they were indoors and much kinder.

They had sentenced Miki to scavenging on the coast by herself. Muscles stinging, every tendon crying for rest, she sank into the rocky sand. But it wasn't a break. She pulled herself back up, a cracked shell clenched in her palm. Blisters throbbed on her skin from the shovel, even though she had not used it today. It was a relief, but scavenging wasn't much better.

The broken shell shone dully in Miki's hand, pink and speckled. Would Eshaq find value in it? A dry chuckle rose in her throat. She had no idea what that madman would find value in. Three days in his camp had proved he loosely held the settlement together and was only driven by his thirst for power.

She tucked the shell into the pouch at her waist, wincing at the movement in her burning ribs. At least Atsu the Mad Dog had not beaten her again. But then she hadn't given him cause to. A wave splashed against the shore, the water hitting her knees like pricks of ice. Miki jumped backward, heels landing in soft moss. She tied the ruined toga up at her knees. Water dribbled down from the dirty fabric.

"It be true yeh be royal?"

Miki spun, her toe catching on a rock. She slipped and water rushed to meet her. The ice dug at her, stabbing every inch. Black, it was all so black. Squeezing her eyes shut, she twisted within the waves, but only disoriented herself. Her foot kicked against another rock and pain flared in her toes. But she had found the bottom. She kicked up. Fresh air cut into her skin.

"Yeh no a good swimmer." Atsu stood on the shore, dreadlocks tied up in a knot and thin arms crossed over his chest.

She couldn't decide which would be worse, staying in freezing water or getting out to be beaten by him. Every moment Miki paused, the fiercer the ice bit at her torso. She stood and walked out of the water, trembling fists a far cry from protection.

"Don't touch me."

He stared at her, curious facial expression not changing. He uncrossed his arms and stepped closer. "It be true yeh be royal? I be hearin' o' them."

Miki stepped back, arms still up. "No, I'm not."

His face darkened. "Oh."

The air sliced through Miki's wet toga, but even holding her arms to her torso wouldn't stop it now. Teeth chattering together and vibrating in her skull, she grasped at whatever warmth her chest offered.

"Yeh be somethin'. Yeh willna be admittin' it." Atsu mused, blue eyes sparkling.

Her feet squeaked in the sand as she trudged past him. She stooped and picked up the basket a woman had given her after informing her of the new job. Its lack of weight brought a ball of anxiety to her gut. Would Atsu beat her again if he saw how little she had found?

The scent of salt in the air doubled as he caught up to her. "Sometime yeh be tellin' me what El-Pel be like."

"No, I won't. Are you from the Pyramid or were you born here?" The question tumbled out before she could stop it. The people she wanted to speak with least always sought her out. Ptolema had been the same.

"Yes." The word hung in the windy air, awkward as all his speech was. He didn't bother to clarify which part of her question he was answering.

The familiar sensation of curiosity rising along Miki's neck vanished as the bruise on her nose from his first punch throbbed. She turned away from Atsu. A woman stood framed against the land, her short hair ruffling in the wind. She scowled and crossed her arms as Miki approached.

Ata.

The scowl deepened. Miki clutched the basket tighter, waiting for Ata to rip it from her grasp and criticize her finds, but Ata's gaze stayed fixed on the shoreline below. On her brother. She stepped down the small hill and met him, the wind carrying away whatever she had to say. With such a rigid back, it couldn't be encouraging.

Miki turned away. The problems of the mad sibling pets of the mad island ruler were none of her problems. As she neared the camp, the sun broke through the last line of clouds. Heat shot up her back. The dampness of her clothes drove it away. She had to get new ones, and soon, before the toga simply fell off.

The camp remained as it had been since they arrived—quiet, solemn. Most of the inhabitants were off scavenging or fishing across the island, and the few who remained were busy with other tasks. Miki moved for the center of the camp to dump her finds. Her first guess had been right. There were at least two hundred tents, many housing families or clusters of four or more people. They sat across the camp clearing with little organization. The largest was for storing the scavengers' finds, and another was the fish tent. Miki had found that tent by smell yesterday. Many other tents were little more than lean-tos with three walls, constructed of torn sails which washed up on the beach, or coyote hides. There had to be an entire pack nearby, judging by the howling at night. Did the mad twins protect the people from them? Or did the animals know to stay away lest they become someone's jacket?

Miki rounded yet another dirty lean-to. A child peered out, his thin torso covered in woven cloth.

"Moises, get back in 'ere!" An elderly woman with more wrinkles on her face than even Miki's father stepped out next to the child. A long gray braid hung down her back. Her eyes met Miki's and an eyebrow shot to her hairline.

"You're the newcomer, aren't ye?" Her soft accent was fainter than even Eshaq's, but it was there, as sure as they were on the island.

Moises. Miki's nephew who shared his name had all the privilege this child would never know.

"Ye look terrible, dear. Won't ye take these?" The old woman held out a pair of leather pants. "They were his mother's. But she isna coming back. The sea swallowed her." No remorse tinged her voice. Perhaps the sea swallowed mothers every day.

"Thank you." The leather was soft in Miki's fingers as she accepted the pants. Supple like the silk back in Jabarre's, a world away now. Would they interrogate him for unknowingly harboring her those four years? He was an obnoxious prude, but he didn't deserve to be found guilty. Whatever happened, Miki would never know, and worrying about her father far outstripped worry over Jabarre.

"She brought them with her, from that cursed Pyramid. That's the only reason they are so fine. Ye won't find another pair on this island," the old woman continued, as if trying to sell the pants she gave away. She herself wore an animal hide shawl and cotton dress with more patches than the original material.

"Thank you, really." Miki stared at the pants. Should she embrace the woman for her kindness? Her hands tingled at the unfamiliar thought. Her clammy fingers left small blotches of sweat on the fine leather, and she shoved the pants under her arm.

Black hovered at the edges of her vision and pain in her fingertips.

No.

Not again. She closed her eyes. This wasn't the Pyramid. She could speak with people here.

A gentle hand rested on her back. The old woman's breath misted across her face and Miki opened her eyes.

"It's all right. Ye don't have to hide 'ere." The woman smiled, the twin wrinkles at the corners of her mouth pulling outward.

Miki pulled her arms closer to her torso, pressing the precious pants to her chest. This must be what it might have been like to have a grandmother, or even a mother.

"Do ye have a tent yet?" The woman pulled away and swept Miki with a sharp gaze. Judging by her frown, she did not approve of Atsu's handiwork.

"No, I don't think Eshaq will allow me one—" She stopped. Her heart thudded louder and the pants hung heavy in her arms. Perhaps it wasn't wise to take them after all.

"Ah, a fool that man be." The woman waved a bracelet-covered wrist as if to wave Eshaq off the island. "Now come 'ere. Put these pants on. And I may even have a shawl for ye." She directed Miki into the small lean-to. There was hardly room for her to stand up. Heat returned to her body as she pulled the pants on. She shrugged off the ruined toga and accepted a woolen shirt and brightly woven shawl. The woman set it on Miki's shoulders and cinched it tight across her chest.

Miki grabbed one of the sun-weathered hands. "Thank you. I can't tell you what this means to me."

"Those rabid dogs of Eshaq's will drive anyone to their grave if he doesn't call them off. I just do what I can to make sure that doesn't happen. Good thing I'm the only one who's been 'ere longer than Eshaq, and he doesn't like it just enough to respect me." She chuckled and stepped away.

"How long have you been here?"

The woman picked up a flask and took a deep swallow, closing her eyes in satisfaction. Lowering the flask, she held it out to Miki.

"I've been 'ere longer than ye've been alive, I can tell ye that much." She chuckled, a soft, kind noise.

"And Eshaq?"

"Came ten or so years after me. Caught in the farms outside the city. Ye can go longer out there, ye know."

Miki raised the flask to her own lips, inhaling the sharp scent of a terrible wine. Her stomach tightened. The irony that Ptolema had made her drink her special reserve just a few days ago hit her. If not for that, she never would have had one last drink. She tilted the flask, hot liquid streaming into her mouth and tickling the taste nubs on her tongue. With a cough, she choked it down. Water pooled in the edges of her eyes as she handed the flask back.

A hand thumped against her back. "There ye go, get it all down. I know it's not the best, but it's a right delicacy 'ere ."

"What in the blazes was that?" Miki wiped the moisture from her eyes with the back of her palm.

"Fermented mulled sea wine. It's the only way to make alcohol on Thoth." The woman chuckled again. "I take credit for it, ye see. It's only been here as long as me. Maybe fifty years."

Fifty years. Nausea swept through Miki's gut. She wouldn't be there so long. She couldn't be.

The woman drained the contents of the flask. When she lowered it, a twinkle shone in her eye. "It's not as bad as ye think." The smile vanished, replaced with tight eyes. "Just stay clear o' those mad dogs."

"You mean Ata and Atsu?"

"Yes, those devil twins. Not a good bone in their bodies."

As if called to the mention of them, Ata and Atsu walked past the lean-to. His shoulders slouched as she leaned toward him, muttering. "—just won't do anymore—" Ata vanished around the center tent where Miki should dump her finds. Atsu followed, moving in an awkward gait that hadn't seemed to slow down his beatings.

Miki stepped away from the door, shuddering. "What is wrong with them?"

A small hand slipped into hers. Moises batted large brown eyes. "Old man Grundy says I'll turn out wrong like them because I was born here too."

"Boo!" The grandma swatted him over the head with a scrap of animal hide blanket. "Ye have me. They didn't. Besides, what have I told ye 'bout spending time with Old Man Grundy?"

"Sorry, Gamma." Moises hung his head.

"Go find the others. Masika promised she'd have lessons for you today."

Moises perked up and bounded out into the camp. Miki turned to the old woman. "Thank you—?"

142

"Name's Nenet. Mentioning my name might save ye some trouble from Eshaq and his dogs." She chuckled.

"They were born here?"

"No, Old man Grundy never gets 'is facts straight." A shadow crossed Nenet's face. "They arrived as infants, days old."

"From El-Pelusium?" It made sense, of course. If they found a woman who gave birth to a Second, they banished the child as soon as possible. But to see what they left those infants to endure was staggering.

Nenet stepped as far back as the tiny hovel would allow.

"Ye seem brighter than some others, Miki, but don't let it get to yer head. The twins won't like someone digging into their business, and Eshaq won't like someone asking questions. There are only two things that scare him. One is brains, and the other, well, I will not tell ye about that."

"Like the rule I can't break that he wouldn't tell me?" She couldn't keep the irritation from rising in her voice.

"Yes, just like that." Nenet smiled, bringing youth to her creased face. "Ye should run along with that basket. Come back though. I will find a place for ye to sleep."

"Thank you. I wasn't even sure if kindness existed on Thoth."

Nenet rolled her eyes. "If Eshaq had his way, it wouldna. But it does, don't ye worry."

An almost forgotten smile crept over Miki's face. A shiver of relief accompanied it as she stepped back into the chill. It didn't cut through her, and the warm shawl wrapped around her like an embrace. The sun's rays spread heat across the top of her head and she could have giggled, if not for the pain in her ribs and face.

The Loot Tent rose in the center of the camp, foreboding. She didn't know if there was anyone there to inspect her offerings, or perhaps deem them unworthy.

Fear was ridiculous. Next time she would fight back. Her fingers, however, trembled as she stepped up to the tent entrance. No one stood before the entrance as its flap snapped in the wind. The inside flashed when the canvas lifted, revealing a dull pile of gray and brown. Miki stepped through, her breath returning once the wind was blocked.

Wood, broken bits of metal, formless clumps of clay which could have once been a sculpture, and even a few pairs of waterlogged shoes. Junk. That was all they could find? This was what they built their society on? The broken shells in her own basket weren't so unappealing anymore. They tumbled into the mess with a soft clink.

She was about to turn back to the entrance when the edge of a tablet caught her eye, half buried in the pile. Miki climbed to the stone tablet, the pile shifting under her feet. She wrenched the tablet free. A muddy shoe toppled down with the movement.

Manipulation through History.

Blood pounded through her ears, the rhythmic *swoosh* drowning out the crash of the sea and the roar of the wind beyond.

Manipulation. Was it real? Her breath thinning, she ran a finger over the grooved words. Could anyone read on Thoth if this was how they treated a tablet? Maybe they didn't care. The words were so worn from water and years that only a fourth of them stood out. Miki couldn't be sure without more readable words, but it appeared the author was speaking metaphorically of Manipulation, not literally. A woman as beautiful as a Manipulated gust of wind. Or maybe as a gust of wind stirring flowers. Or a badger eating pine nuts.

Nonsense, illegible nonsense. She flung the tablet back into the pile. A loud crack rent the air as it hit an iron crate, the corner chipping off.

A shiver of relief tingled down her spine. Of course Manipulation wasn't real. A half laugh rose in her throat as the relief swelled. She stepped out of the tent and stubbed her toe on a rock on the other side of the tent flap, only for the breath to leave her lungs in a rush of air.

Atsu stood at the edge of the camp where the shrubby lowlands met the cleared area. His eyes locked with hers. Miki's nails bit into her palms.

She blinked and Atsu and his intense stares were gone. His slouched form slipped behind a line of tents only to reappear in the open scrubby land beyond. What was he up to? The wind picked up again, as if it could increase infinitely. Miki pulled the shawl closer. At least the new clothes kept most of the wind out.

Where could he be going?

No, it was nonsense to think like this. Pointless.

But what if there were boats? Atsu and Ata had exchanged a look when Eshaq mentioned them. They had grown up on Thoth. They could know of a way through the Back Current. If she could find the boats, she could leave. Go home. Find her father. Disappear into the wild. The sudden idea was so tantalizing, it drove away the leftover tang of Nenet's mead.

Miki moved around a large boulder and lowered her head as a group of men with fishing nets stretched between them entered the camp. They said nothing and she exhaled with relief. Her feet thumped against the moist earth until the cleared campsite land fell away behind her. Atsu still walked ahead, knotted dreads sticking above his head. The distance between them shrank too suddenly and Miki pulled back into the brush, heart in her throat. A slip of viewing space in the middle of a cracked rock afforded only Atsu's fading outline. The brush shifting under her with a crunch, Miki pushed back up. She had to stay on him.

He turned, veering behind a cluster of jutting boulders. They hid him but would also hide his view of her. Miki pushed up and glanced behind. The camp sat under a heavy layer of dinner smoke, its tendrils drifting hundreds of yards behind her. The sharp wind cut the smoke to the side, and Miki froze, heart pounding. Was that Ata's thin frame?

The wind cut back the other way. Ata and her disapproving glares were not in sight. Chest falling with relief for the second time in the hour, Miki ran toward the boulder Atsu had vanished behind, staying in a crouch. The rock was warm under her fingertips, a surprising change from the others. Miki leaned against it, breath in the back of her throat. If she didn't confront him about the boats, she would be here until she died, digging through freezing sand for trash to please Eshaq. A niggling of fear dug away at her belly as she leaned against the rock.

The boulder shook, vibrations shooting through her palm.

Hand slipping from the rock, she dropped hard to the ground. The crack sounded again. A muted *thwump* rose from the other side of the boulder. What was happening on the boulder's far side? A rock poked her palm, hard and unforgiving. She ripped it out of the ground and pushed up. Not even Dalilah deserved to be beaten like this. The wind barreled into Miki as she stepped around the boulder just as the last rays of the setting sun washed over her.

Atsu stood alone on the other side. Alone, apart from two large rocks hovering in the air beside him.

He turned, eyes the deep ultramarine blue of the sea. Not clear blue like they should be. The rock fell from her numb fingers. He was—he was … all she managed was a strained gasp.

Atsu blinked, eyes widening, but not returning to their usual color. Miki staggered backward, but he sliced his arms up, then back down. The unnatural rocks hovering beside him thumped to the ground. His gaze slid to the left, toward the boulder hiding his actions from the camp. The middle held a dent, whitened with repeated ramming of rock on rock. He caught her gaze following his and Atsu raised an arm again, fist clenched.

Air whizzed past her ear as the same rock she had held as a weapon betrayed her, acting on its own will. It slammed into her head.

Pain flared, white hot, and the world went black.

CHAPTER 17

Thousands of pricks of light broke the darkness overhead. Stars. The fog must have finally cleared away. Miki sucked in the air with a hiss. Fire ripped through her temples, concentrating on the right one. Cold registered against her back. Prodding and poking. Rocks.

Deep blue eyes flashing in surprise. A rock flying at her head ...

Manipulation. The mysterious last rule. Never Manipulate. The second thing Eshaq feared. And the reason her head throbbed.

Manipulation was real.

Gravel crunched under her back as she shifted. Eshaq had outlawed it. Why? The Firsts claimed it was dangerous. That had to be it. Atsu must be practicing Manipulation against Eshaq's wishes.

The brightest star of the lot, one positioned straight ahead, winked in and out. The unsettling silence of the night pressed against her, its chill burrowing into her joints. Perhaps Atsu had left her out here to die. He must not want her running to tell Eshaq, though staying here, reeling in her thoughts, seemed easier than anything else. Cold air ripped across her and her nose tingled with oncoming numbness, but it didn't matter.

What if the Firsts back in the Pyramid were right? Seconds might indeed be something to fear.

But that couldn't be true. Her father had taught her the opposite. Sworn vehemently that the Firsts were misguided in their fear. She couldn't Manipulate. Her siblings hadn't been able to.

But Atsu could.

Perhaps her father had been wrong, even about something so important. If Manipulation was genuine … Ptolema's fears had a real footing.

"Father, did you know?" she whispered to the twinkling sky. Her father's face, weary from loving the children he should never have had, rose in the dark expanse above.

"No," she whispered. Kamu and Beren hadn't been dangerous. Her father couldn't have known.

"I once be knowin' a man who be sneaky as yeh." Atsu's voice pierced the darkness.

Miki stiffened, more pain shooting up her cramped legs. A rock dug into her calf, but she didn't shift. Had he been sitting behind her the entire time? Silence stretched between them, but the skin on her head prickled under his gaze.

When it became too unbearable, she sat up. The stars spun, her whole world streaking silver, but she didn't fall back down. Brambles cracked as she stood on wavering legs.

"What do you want?" Weariness shaded her words.

"An answer." Atsu stood ten feet away, arms hanging idly at his side as if they had not channeled an evil power into rocks. "Be yeh like the man I once knew?"

Even with the light of the stars, the darkness made it impossible to see what shade of blue his eyes were. She backstepped, another rock catching under her heel.

"Do yeh be like the man who be a Third?" Atsu stepped closer, and the moonlight flooded his features. Clear blue eyes.

"A third what?"

He dug one fingernail under the other, prying free some dirt. He didn't look at her.

"We on Thoth be Seconds, but this man be a Third."

A Third-born. Her mother's soft tears. A silent birthday celebration in a dark cellar. A brother who couldn't bear to remain in the cellar, wasting his life. A brother who never returned. Beren would be twenty-one if he was still alive, but she had given up searching years ago.

"Yer silence be incriminating, Miki."

"Don't say my name," she whispered. It was poison on his tongue.

"Then what do I be callin' yeh, Third?"

"Don't call me anything. I am not a Third." Her hands vibrated with adrenaline, with fear that he might send a rock flying at her head. But he knew the truth, or at least part of it. "How can you Manipulate?" The word shivered down her throat. Cold. Evil.

Atsu raised a hand so slowly, Miki did not dare breathe. He tugged a dread lock from his bun. The hair tumbled down around his shoulders.

"Yeh 'ave broke a law, Miki Not a Third of El-Pelusium." The name came out like a title, though his tongue tripped over it.

"What law?"

"Yeh be looking for boats."

"No, I wasn't! You are the one who Manip—"

"Yeh be lookin' for boats or yeh be slackin' off in scavenging. Both be punishable offenses." Atsu reached her side in two strides. Fingers of iron snapped around her forearm.

"Will yeh—" He jerked his hand back and hissed. Shaking it, he stepped back, eyes wide.

Nenet's shawl still covered her arm, though it was the worse for wear.

Atsu tilted his head. For a moment, in the shifting shadows of clouds passing over the moon, he was a different person. A quiet, interested boy wanting to understand. Then the moon returned, and he grabbed her arm again without hesitation.

"Will yeh be coming quietly, Miki Not a Third of El-Pelusium?"

The instinct to bite at his arm was so strong Miki ground her teeth. She nodded once. His fingertips pressed harder, cold and warm at the same time.

"You haven't answered my question," she said. "How can you Manipulate?"

He ignored her. He escorted her away from the shore with no more words or attempts to use his unholy power. A thin noise built in the back of his throat, half murmur, half unintelligible notes as if he were trying to whisper a song. Miki didn't fight back or press the question. Nenet was right. He was a mad dog.

Atsu's murmuring trailed off the closer the lights of the camp's fires grew. A thin form materialized at the edge of the camp. Stern eyebrows, sharp jawline. Ata spared Miki half a glance before turning on her brother. She folded her arms over her chest. He nodded back. Her jaw hardened even further, but she jerked her head toward the throne room.

"We couldn't find her for two hours. Eshaq is livid."

Atsu stepped away, shaking his hand as if in pain from the contact. He muttered again under his breath and stared at his hand for a moment. Ata cleared her throat. He jumped.

"Move." Ata stepped behind Miki.

But Atsu's hand ... Surely she didn't stare at it for the same reason he did. It was perfectly intact. No missing forefinger, no odd gap between thumb and middle finger. No telltale nub of being a banished Second. Nenet claimed they arrived on Thoth just days old. Perhaps they had been granted that small mercy, just as Miki had. And Ata ... what about her?

But the woman stood behind, hands hidden in darkness. "I said *move*."

Forcing herself to avoid Atsu's odd stare, Miki headed toward the throne room. Shadows flickered against the cliffside, dancing in erratic patterns as men stoked the fire higher. Eshaq reclined in the creaking chair, a foot out on a stump and boots shed to the ground beside him. His balding head shone with the red light of liquor, like so many merchants in the Lower Pyramid after a day's work. Miki averted her eyes from his sneer when she stopped ten feet from him. The stale stench of sour drink hung heavy in the smoky air.

Dalilah stood in the gathered crowd, the man who had offered to protect her draping one arm across her shoulder. She looked away at Miki's gaze.

"Atsu! Lad! Where ye find this wretch? I be callin' her to check in on her finds and couldna find her."

"She be looking for boats." Atsu spoke to the ground and shuffled to his master's side.

Eshaq leaned back, the chair creaking.

"Aye, I be figuring she was ou' breakin' a law. Didna we say there be no boats?" The chair crashed back to the stone and Eshaq leaned toward her, intent.

The silence stretched for close to a minute before she realized she should answer. "Yes, but I wasn't—"

"Miki, ye broke a law. I be disappointed by yer lack of loyalty only three days after we took ye in." Eshaq hefted a wooden carved cup and took a swig of the sour liquor.

If beating and forced labor was considered "taking in," then Miki preferred to be taken out.

"Ye do realize one of my rules be no one leaves Thoth?"

She said nothing, tongue pressing against the ridges at the back of her mouth.

"This one be daft," Eshaq chuckled. "I said there be no boats, so looking for one means ye be havin' no brains." He leaned forward, face reddening further in the heat of the fire. "I see yer lack of brains isna getting ye very far here." He gestured to her face.

With the reminder, the pain returned to her head, twice as fierce. She closed her eyes, shutting out the unsightly lumps on Eshaq's face. A woman's gasp brought them back open.

"Like that, don't ye?" Eshaq's greasy smile shook with exertion.

What was he going on about? Miki blinked.

A stick the length of a forearm hovered in front of her, twirling idly as if at any moment it might choose to ram between her eyes.

The sweat on Eshaq's face doubled, and he swallowed. The smile slipped. "Defy my rules again, lass, and I be makin' ye hurt."

Eshaq was a Manipulator.

The crowd ceased murmuring behind her and the woman didn't gasp again. This was his secret to lording over Thoth. The way his victims died. The way *she* would die.

The stick plummeted to the earth.

"Atsu, take 'er beyond the camp and beat 'er. Be driving out what little brains she be havin' tha' encourage 'er to look for fairy tales when they don't be existin'." Eshaq raised the wooden cup, green-brown liquid spilling over his front as he gulped it down.

The sentence settled on Miki's shoulders, the pressure building in her throbbing head. It could be worse. Beating she had endured before. She would not be impaled by a cursed stick.

"And Atsu, take off a hand. Or 'er tongue. Whichever be causing ye less trouble. It be abou' time she be missin' something like the rest o' us." Spittle evaporated above the fire as Eshaq threw back his head and chortled. His own forefinger-less hands waved in the fire light. "Don't think I didn't notice, lassie! Ye can't be getting away wi' it as if ye were born 'ere."

Despite her instincts against it, Miki's gaze found Atsu's hands. Hanging idly at his side. Both whole. Ata stood beside him, glaring at something that couldn't be made out. Her fingers, all ten of them, clawed at her biceps as she crossed them over her chest.

They might be mad, but they were whole.

CHAPTER 18

"If you do this, I'll tell Eshaq what you do behind that large rock." Miki's bribe tumbled out in a mess of words and adrenaline. But he had to listen. This was all his fault, the false charges, the punishment.

Atsu jerked her across a small ditch on the eastern side of the camp, one of the few places she had not yet explored. It was pocked full of the sort of holes just waiting to twist her ankle, but he did not slow down. His hunched shoulders rocked with his determination and he did not respond to her attempt to keep her hand or tongue. Atsu's fingers dug into her forearm. He did not jerk away at her contact as he had before the trial. The midnight breeze rattled her teeth, and the moon illuminated a barren field covered with small rocks, like the shore she had arrived on.

As if sensing her confusion, Atsu turned to face her, and she thumped into his thin chest. He staggered back but recovered, giving her a blank look.

"Eshaq wouldna believe yeh if yeh told him I be Manipulatin'." The confession didn't hold the weight it might have. He blinked and his eyes deepened to dark blue.

Miki stepped back, heart jumping to her throat, but there was nothing she could do to stop the bush at her feet from pulling free from its roots and drifting around Atsu's head. Not a bead of sweat above his eyes. No rapid breaths. Manipulation for him was easy, pure, natural, unlike Eshaq's performance.

The fear slipped, replaced with annoyance.

"Stop it," she said.

"Yeh no fit in here, Miki Not a Third of El-Pel." Again, her name came across as one long awkward title. Atsu's eyes darkened in the pale light of the moon until the irises almost vanished.

"You mean because I'm not a barbarian like the rest of you?"

"No." A second shrub rose and danced with the first, this time around Miki's head. She gasped as a thin branch cut her cheek. "Yeh be too much a savage." Atsu blinked and raised a hand to the star-strewn sky. The shrubs dropped to the ground, each tumbling once before lying still. He blinked and his eyes returned to their natural color.

Too much of a savage? She stared at the shrubs, waiting for them to spring into the air again.

"Also, yeh be a liar. Liars do no fit in here. Typically." Atsu's left shoulder slouched lower than the right. His left leg bent at the knee about half an inch outward. If things had been different, she may have been curious.

"You're the liar. Hiding your—" she choked on the word, unable to say it, "—power from Eshaq."

"I be sayin' typically." His smirk said the rest. He was not typical. A shriek of steel and he drew a chipped, rusty blade from a sheath at his waist.

No, he couldn't do this.

He stepped forward. "Be giving me yeh arm, Miki Not a Third, the liar of El-Pel."

"I'm not lying," she whispered.

His foot caught her in the chest, ramming her to the ground. Rocks bit into her back, dotting her with pain. He jumped astride her, blocking the stars from her vision. The stench of iron and dirt moved closer as he leaned over her, a foot pinning her left hand to the ground.

Miki jerked her right arm upward, but his free hand snatched it from the air. "Tell yeh what, I be makin' yeh a deal." A gleam caught in his eye, suggesting it would not be the deal she had presented. "If yeh be lettin' me teach yeh to do what I do, what Eshaq be thinkin' he be doin',

I won't be cutting off yer hand, or tongue." A chuckle caught in the back of his throat.

"What?"

His fingers wiggled around her right wrist and his jaw twitched. "Yeh be a Third." His fingers tightened.

"I'm not a Third." Her pulse beat against the restraint.

He squeezed harder and her wrists throbbed. "Yeh are. I be feelin' it. Let me teach yeh to Manipulate and I won't be cuttin' you."

He was mad. A short dreadlock fell across his face and it swung between those blue orbs, ticking down her fate.

"No. I'll never do that." She cleared her throat and hacked a spit wad on his small, square nose.

He pulled back, wiping the spit with the sleeve of his leather jerkin. A thin smile danced on his lips. Standing, he dragged her back up, rocks littering the ground as they fell from her clothes. He was going to go for her tongue. She rolled it back in her mouth. Such a strange, useful muscle. How had she never considered it before?

Atsu pushed her forward and a downed log caught her in the ankles. It lay black and rotten, twice the size of any tree on Thoth. She twisted around, hoping to catch a moment to escape, but Atsu pounced again, hefting her arms up to the tree. A scrap of rope appeared from his pocket and slipped around her wrists and the log, lashing her to it. Another cord stretched across her ankle, rough and unforgiving.

"I be returnin' in the morning, Miki the Third, when ye be changin' yer mind." A thin strip of stars blacked out as he moved away, his form invisible apart from his shadow.

The night settled around her. Like the familiar embrace of the anxiety from childhood. Waves drummed in the distance. *Crash, sigh, crash.* Her breath matched the motion, the rhythm. The fear edging in at the corner of her consciousness paused, as if confused by this new tactic to keep her sanity. *Crash, sigh, crash.*

The night deepened without further threat from a panic attack. Atsu's last words filtered through the dark surroundings. No, she would not change her mind. He was madder than even Nenet believed.

Miki, the girl who lied about not being a Third, did not call out as Atsu expected as he jogged away. He should have taken her hand, but the idea to train her was too tempting. There was never a chance it would have been her tongue. She had such amusing things to say. They never made a slip of sense. He chuckled, only to choke on it as his bad leg throbbed when he misstepped.

The thought that the girl might let him teach her was so tantalizing, it brought a layer of bumps to his skin. What would it be like to witness the power a Third-born could harness?

If she could do it at all. Ata said it was a myth that a Third-born had more power. A lie spread by the liars in El-Pelusium. But then, Ata was not the one to listen to about Thirds. Not after what happened with the last one, not after how she had acted. A shudder passed down Atsu's spine. Five years was a long time, but Ata's hair remained short and her language different. She had not forgotten the Third, and she likely never would.

Still, Atsu's tongue tingled at the thought of it. Miki would agree. Why would she choose to lose her hand instead of receiving the greatest gift a person could?

He veered away from the Barrens where he'd left the girl and crossed down to the eastern shore. Ata would be waiting. The water was as still as he had ever seen, one smooth sheet of black stretching to the line where it met the stars. He turned up the beach, hopping up a pile of boulders until he was a good ten feet above sea level. A black hole met him, and he jumped, cool air rushing past his cheeks as he entered his true home.

The slap of his feet hitting the rock at the base of the cave echoed fifty feet back. Ata's face appeared from a small opening, her small, pointed nose scrunched in curiosity the way it always was when she couldn't wait to ask a question. "So? Which was it? Hand or tongue?"

Atsu gazed at her for a moment, recalling the days when she had dreadlocks as he did.

"Yeh shouldna have cut them off," he murmured.

Her thin face darkened, but a hand went to tuck a loose strand of hair behind her ear. "You promised never to bring that up," she whispered as she stepped out from the crack which led to the deeper regions of their cave.

Her fur shirt had a hole again at her elbow from pushing along the paths of the cave. He would have to patch that. He raised a hand to measure the hole, but she stepped back, cautious. "I've been thinking of him too much recently. It's her, it's got to be. She acts like he did." Ata stared past Atsu. "Sometimes I can't help but wonder what might have happened if you hadn't killed him." She didn't accuse. Just stated.

"Eshaq be makin'—"

"I know." She raised a hand and shook her head, short hair flipping about her face. "That isn't what I meant. I just …" Ata at a loss for words? A thing unheard of, unless it involved the Third. "I can't help but miss him," she finished, somewhat lamely. There was more than missing him going on. Why else would her hair still be short and her language different?

"Ata, I be—"

"Come on." She turned back to the tunnel in the cave's wall, face suddenly bright as if the conversation had not taken place. "Some good stuff came in today. A bracelet, one that looks like it's worth something to those fools across the water." The fabric at her elbow caught on a nib of shale and with a grating noise, it ripped clear to her shoulder as she stepped back in. She didn't stop, but headed into the dark, only turning once the light from the main cave's fire vanished.

With a sigh, Atsu followed. She needed to move on, forgot about the Third. In fact, better that she never mention him again.

The flicker of another fire sprung to life as the tunnel widened so his elbows no longer dragged on the stone wall. A torch hung from a steel peg rammed in a crack in the stone above a pile of glittering objects. Bottles, spare shoes, jewelry, an assortment of weapons in varying degrees of rust. Pride tugged at his chest as it did every time he looked on their stash.

The gentle lapping of water on stone reminded him of the real treasure. The boat floated fifty feet to the right, straining against its lead, longing to slip out the cave opening just wide enough for it. It wasn't large, only fifteen feet long. Mismatched pieces of driftwood formed the bottom and several scavenged togas brought by the more recently banished Seconds were sewn into a makeshift sail. It wasn't beautiful, but it floated. Still, it was worthless until they could figure out how to get over the Back Current.

The fear which always followed the pride wrung his belly into a knot, and Atsu averted his gaze from the boat. Ata leaned over the pile of their carefully gathered treasure—a lifetime's worth of stealing from Eshaq without being caught. Of playing the best sort of game and the most dangerous one they could.

Ata held up the bracelet in one hand and waved her other to Manipulate a stone tablet.

"Good thing Eshaq didn't notice this before me. He would have crushed it under his fat foot." She giggled and let the tablet settle on the ground.

Atsu plopped down to read it. "Manipulation through History."

"Only it's not just some history tablet."

The intoxicating excitement presented by the notion of training the girl who was a Third resurfaced. The letters of the tablet were worn by water and time. They weren't beautiful or rhythmic.

Her heart is wind. Air eats it. Fire devours more. Water can't find rest. She leaves it all with nothing ...

"It be nonsense," he mumbled. "Wait—" *Fire devours more* repeated a third time, with nothing between to make sense of it. Another line about Water. Atsu narrowed his eyes. A good fourth of the words or letters were missing, making it hard to make out the whole thing. There was no last remark at the bottom, only a half cut off sentence. "It be part of others," he breathed and glanced up to meet Ata's shining blue eyes.

"Yes!" she said.

"But what?"

"Remember when we were children? The tablets?"

A foggy afternoon over fifteen years ago ... "The ones we be findin'—"

"And lost." Ata stood and Manipulated the tablet back to the loot pile. "Too bad we won't ever find them again."

"That's what kids be doin', lose things."

She puffed out her cheeks with a sigh. "Well, we can hang onto it, just in case."

A smile spread across Atsu's face. This was Ata in her element. The expert treasure hunter, avid explorer, passionate rebel. The Ata only he knew. Even Eshaq had probably never witnessed her charming smile, the way it lit up her eyes, took away the tightness of her olive skin.

"We'll do it, Atsu, believe me. One day."

The smile faded from his lips and the spark in his sister's eyes dimmed. She knew, even if she pretended everything was okay. Even if she helped her grow the pile of treasure and build the boat. The calluses on his hands proved his betrayal to his own fears, own dreams.

He turned away from her expectant face. Now wasn't the time to argue over their future or the possibility of leaving Thoth.

"You never answered. Did she choose hand or tongue?" Ata slid up to him, slipping her arm through the crook of his elbow.

He cleared his throat. "Neither."

The arm within his withdrew. "What?"

"I—uh, be givin' her a third choice." Third, because she was a Third, the little liar.

"A choice Eshaq did not offer?" Ata's sharp tone fell flat.

Atsu's fingernails dug into the thick tangle of his dreadlocks as he moved to massage away the annoyance rising with Ata's words. "Aye."

"Why would you do that, Atsu?" Here was the Ata everyone on Thoth knew and feared with good reason. Her shoulders thrust backward, she stared him down, fire in her eyes.

"I be thinkin' the girl could be helpin' to our cause." He held her gaze but continued playing with the tangle of his hair. The idea which had been just a spark yesterday flamed higher as the water lapped gently against the hull of the boat.

"That is the most foolish thing you have ever said, including the thing about not returning to El-Pel." Ata's voice remained flat, but a vein in her temple throbbed.

Dangerous, very dangerous.

"Yeh yerself be sayin' yeh are no' strong enough to help me be Manipulatin' through the Back Current."

Ata's eyes narrowed. "What is your point?"

This sister of his had been his only companion for twenty-two years in the hell where their parents had dumped them. Surely she knew. She always did, she always understood. He swallowed. His throat hurt as it did when he spoke too much.

He turned, sandaled heel squeaking against the fine grains of sand on the stone ground, not looking back to the pile behind Ata or the boat. It sat as it had for the past two years with no purpose.

"Atsu!" His name fell as on deaf stone, and Ata's grunt of annoyance followed. She had learned decades ago how pointless it was to get him to speak when he had decided against it. Still, her footfalls followed his through the thin tunnel back to the main cave.

"Atsu, I know you won't say any more, but please think about what you are suggesting. We don't know this girl. We also don't even know if she *can* Manipulate."

They had learned as toddlers, on accident. They were trying to dig in the sand and suddenly, it became easier to move it with their minds. What would stop Miki the Third from learning as an adult with an experienced teacher? He could tell Ata he had considered this a hundred times over in the past day since Miki discovered him Manipulating, but his throat still ached.

Atsu crossed to the back of the cave and pulled out his collection of Eshaq's favorite shells. The last one had not been easy to acquire. The drunk had been counting them, as usual, before nodding off to sleep. Instead of dismissing Atsu for the night, he requested him to stay and listen to a tale of El-Pel.

A tale of thieves, vagabonds, murders, and worst of all, a High One with no conscience. What kind of society would call someone High One and let them do whatever they wanted? It seemed dangerous and ridiculous. Of course, Eshaq was the High One of Thoth, but only because Ata and Atsu allowed it. He didn't know. He never would. Unless the girl learned to Manipulate.

The large blue shell glimmered in the torch light, a magnificent piece. Eshaq had at least a hundred of them, but the slow disappearances were driving him even madder than he already was. A chuckle built in the back of Atsu's throat as he ran a finger over the smooth surface of the stolen item.

Eyes burned on his back. Ata. Her presence filled the small cave like a rogue wave. Strong, angry. Atsu clutched the shell to his chest and turned to face her.

"We have been too careful for too many years to let things fall apart now," Ata chided. "I know you don't agree with my plan, but it's the only one we've got."

Not anymore. He blinked.

"And Atsu, you can't Manipulate so close to the camp. I felt it yesterday, and I was only a few yards from the Throne Room."

"He canna feel it. He be too weak." The words burned his throat, but they had to be said. He had to Manipulate, couldn't she see that? Too long without doing it and without the time to hike hours away, and he would go as mad as Eshaq.

"Maybe. You don't know that. I'm almost as weak as him, but I felt it."

"Yeh only be as weak as yeh allow yerself to be. Yeh shouldna have cut yer hair or changed yer voice."

Ata's skin lost the rosy glow, returning to ashy olive.

"I will not be a mongrel like the rest of them." Her nostrils flared, thin and red, as her voice lowered. "I can't sound like someone who was raised on Thoth when I get to El-Pel one day." Her hand settled against his elbow. "Yeh canna either." The words washed over him, sweeping his gut with nostalgia. Of times before the Third, when they were in their early teens, when she hadn't begged the newer arrivals to the island to teach her their way of speaking. Of when her dreadlocks hung to her waist, swinging every time she sprinted up the coast on the lookout for shells.

He turned away, setting the shell back on the stone ledge with a light scrape. He could tell her how his heart constricted at her old speech, her real speech, but it was just another old argument not worth rehashing. "The girl who be a Third saw me Manipulatin'." There, that would turn her off it.

Ata's silence blossomed in the cave like a poisonous night flower. He should leave before she snapped. He stepped toward the cave entrance, placing a hand on the cool stone hand-holds to heave himself up.

A thin hand came down on his. "What do you mean she saw you?"

"I already be tellin' yeh." His throat throbbed with fire. He needed to stop speaking.

"If she saw you, she could tell Eshaq. She might figure out what we've been hiding." The level of panic in his sister's voice rose.

Atsu shrugged. "Not if she be Manipulatin' too." He pulled his hand away from Ata's and jumped up the hole, hands grabbing the rocks on instinct, propelling him upward with as little effort as it took to walk. Ata's anger followed him, a wave of heat, but he cleared the hole of the cave entrance and made it to the beach. His legs pushed out in front of him, long stride after long stride. She could catch him, but she wouldn't. That was another thing she learned not to do a decade ago. He smiled and ran.

CHAPTER 19

Two silver orbs reflected in the moonlight. They weren't tall enough to be Atsu unless he was crouching behind the jagged rocks. The early dawn was too silent. No waves beating the shore. If the eyes belonged to a coyote, it didn't howl.

"Miki?"

Her hands stiffened, the rope biting deeper into her wrists. "Moises?"

The boy slipped from behind the log. He smiled and looked to the ground, embarrassed.

"I be sorry I took so long. Gamma told me ye were in the Western Barrens, not the Eastern. I wandered 'round over there fer hours before I be figurin' it out!" Dirt squeaked under his small feet as he knelt in front of her, a knife in even worse shape than Atsu's extended in his dirty palm.

"Nenet sent you to find me?" Her chapped lips stung after the night outside.

Moises nodded, black curls bouncing vigorously.

Miki smiled, only to have it slide off her face.

"We have to hurry. Atsu could be back at any minute. Can you cut fast?"

Moises glanced over his shoulder. "The mad dog be scarin' me, Miki."

"Yeah, me too." The confession brought a shiver to her limbs. "That's why we need to hurry."

Moises looked back to her, face shining with determination in the pale light. The blade slipped through the rope and he jerked it back and forth. Five swipes provided nothing. He frowned.

"It's okay, just try doing it harder—" Miki sucked in a pained gasp as the knife slid across the top of her palm.

"Sorry!" But Moises didn't stop. He sawed fiercer until the pressure released on her wrists and the rope fell away.

"My feet—" The words died in Miki's mouth.

In the distance, a slouched figure bearing weight on his right leg jogged toward them. Atsu.

The sawing of the knife blade began at her ankles. Moises's white teeth dug into his lip.

"Gamma be proud of me."

"Yes, yes, just hurry!" The empty landscape shrank in around Miki. Where could they hide?

The rope snapped, Moises thudding onto his rump with the unexpected force of it.

"Go!" Miki grabbed at the rough fabric of his hide shirt and jerked him upward.

Atsu slowed, a hundred paces away now. The rising sun framed him and his half smile.

"Not yet," she muttered through frantic breaths. "Come on, Moises." Her fingers locked around his small hand and she took off, running not to the camp, or Atsu, but anywhere people weren't.

Moises's breath fluttered next to her as he struggled to keep up, but she didn't slow. She couldn't. Would Atsu take more than one hand or tongue when he caught them? A nest-like formation of rocks rose on the horizon. Miki shifted left, making for it. Perhaps they could take shelter and he wouldn't find them. Her gut wrenched, both at her exertion and the insanity of the idea. Only a small boulder field broke the landscape. He would find them and rip out her tongue.

The boulders radiated with the chill of the night as she threw the two of them behind the largest. Gasping for breath, she turned to Moises. His brown eyes were large as the rocks at their feet.

"Stay here, okay? Don't leave without me." Her idea was a slim one, but she had to do something.

Atsu's form slouched closer at a pace hardly faster than a brisk walk. Miki's hands scrambled over the ground, searching for anything.

"Your knife, Moises. Give it to me."

"You canna fight him! He be mad!" The boy's voice shook.

"Someone has to." She wrenched the rust-caked blade from Moises's shaking fingers. The knife was cold in her hand.

Someone has to defeat Atsu once and for all.

Rock shifted on the other side of the boulder. Miki pushed off the boulder. Atsu turned, a strange light in his eye as she jumped at him, knife extended. The blade sliced air.

Atsu spoke from beside her.

"Well, this be amusing," he said, the half-smile still on his face. "Do this mean yeh havena be changin' yer mind about my offer?"

Miki lunged at him. Again, the knife swiped down into air. Atsu danced left, then right. She spun, the landscape blurring into a gray-green blob.

Atsu's foot crunched into her ribcage. Miki staggered backward, and the world stopped spinning. Doubling over, she braced a hand against her abdomen.

"It be smart, keepin' the boy around," Atsu's hot breath blew across her ear.

Miki rammed the knife upward. But Atsu wasn't there. She whirled around. Was he Manipulating? She dodged to the side as his foot flew toward her again. Missed. She hit the ground with a crunch of pain in her elbow and rolled. Moises backed away, eyes wide. She should tell him to run, but then her only hope of keeping Atsu from using his power vanished. With the witness gone, her safety went with him.

Fingers clawed at her leg, forcing her to roll back the other way and jump up, the knife extended.

"Yeh be havin' no idea how to use that." It was a statement, not a question. Atsu's smile vanished, replaced with something else, something strange. His eyes glowed, but not with the dark blue of Manipulation. "Be runnin', boy. Be tellin' yer grandmother to stay ou' of my business."

Brambles cracked behind Miki. Feet thumped the earth. She didn't need to turn to know her only hope to save herself was fleeing across the island.

Atsu's eyes confirmed her worry.

"Worried I be crushin' yeh with a rock now that he isna here to see?"

The knife shook in her hand. "Someone has to end you."

He chuckled and sprung, knife whizzing across the top of her extended hand. Her blade fell to the earth, showered in drops of red. He kicked her back to the ground. Then he was on top of her just as easily as the night before, foot extended over her arm.

"Do it, Atsu." Ata's voice cut through the morning.

Atsu's cheek twitched. The knife hovered above Miki's wrist. Blood thumping through her ears, she almost didn't make out his word.

"Interestin'."

Ata's shadow grew across him in the rising sun's rays. Her short hair ruffled in the wind, giving an almost supernatural aura to her. She frowned.

"Do it. We can't risk confusing Eshaq. Not now, not when we're this close."

Miki closed her eyes. There was no way out.

The pressure of Atsu on her arm and torso released. His shadow crossed her eyelids, to be replaced with the burning sun. She blinked her eyes open again. He was gone. She pushed up on her injured elbow, only to grunt with pain and fall back to the ground.

Atsu stepped away, dreadlocks drifting behind him in the wind. Ata's leather-wrapped legs cut Atsu from her vision. Miki scrambled back, but the woman's foot pressed against her chest.

Ata leaned toward her, a perfectly silver blade held aloft.

"Stay away from him," she hissed. "I'm so close to helping him, and this is only making it worse."

A wad of hot saliva landed on Miki's left hand. Her breath pinched off as Ata's eyes hardened. Not the same as Atsu's. No amusement. No curiosity. Only hate. Then she was moving, a blur of brown and silver.

"No! Ata!" Another streak of brown dreadlocks flying between Miki and the madwoman. Atsu shoved his sister back just as her knife descended.

Blistering pain in her hand. Red on Ata's knife.

CHAPTER 20

Heat. Sharp, like hundreds of scorpions spreading their venom through her body. Miki groaned. Hard earth pressed against her belly. Cool. She gasped. The darkness gave way to the intense light of midday.

The heat attacked again, bursting into her left hand. She screamed and wrenched to the side, adrenaline mixing with the agony to wake her up. Fingers at each wrist held her back.

"Shh. Be still, Miki. If we do no' cauterize it ye could lose much more than a few fingers." A calm voice with less of an accent.

Miki twisted her arm against the burning pain. Nenet leaned into her vision, creased face lined with worry. She pressed a bloody rag to Miki's left hand. The heat lessened under the cool rag, but the pressure ... With a cry, Miki tried to yank her arm away.

Nenet snatched it back. "Oh, no ye don't. Moises!"

The boy stepped into the sunlight, staring at the mangled hand with wide eyes.

"Hold this arm down." His grandmother reached for a smoking rock. "One last burn should do it."

"No—" The protest croaked feebly from Miki's lips, and Nenet did not react. She grabbed the rock with a pair of metal tongs and pressed it to Miki's hand with a sharp hiss and the stench of burning flesh.

She screamed and tried again to wrench the arm out of Moises's and Nenet's grasp, but the scream had taken all her strength.

Nenet set the cursed rock back in the crackling fire beside them.

"There. Don't use that hand for a few weeks and it should come through all right." A frown pulled at her kind face, but she said nothing else.

"Ye be so brave," Moises whispered.

"What?" Miki said through pinched breaths.

"To be fightin' the mad dog like tha'." Awe filled the small boy's voice.

"Brave and stupid," Nenet countered as she stood. A tent sat behind her, but not their familiar lean-two. The canvas bore stripes of red and orange. Color. Nothing else on Thoth had color.

Miki pushed up on her right elbow. Tall grasses swayed just above her head. The dusty outline of the tents of the camp sat fifty yards away.

Nenet caught her searching gaze. "This is an old medic tent. Eshaq outlawed its use after the last medic tried to poison 'im. Today though, he is preoccupied with celebratin'."

"Celebrating?" The word croaked from her parched throat.

"Yes. He Manipulated his throne two feet into the air. Apparently he had been working at it for quite some time." Her eyes narrowed. "What were ye thinking, trying to fight Atsu?" She retrieved a tray of smoked fish from a stump beside the tent and offered it to Miki.

She didn't take it. A charred lump complete with pointer finger and thumb. That was it. The other three fingers were gone. Sliced off by a madwoman. A wry laugh caught in her throat. Where most other residents of Thoth were missing two fingers, she now kept her forefingers but had lost three others.

The scent of the smoked fish made her stomach flip, threatening to send up any remnants of food from yesterday. She waved Nenet's plate of food away with her good hand.

"Ye brought this on yerself, defying Eshaq's laws." Nenet set the plate down and wiggled a finger of accusation. "I do it all the time, o' course, but I am smart about it."

"No. He decided not to cut my hand off," she swallowed and gritted her teeth. "Then Ata did it. That madwoman cut my fingers off."

"Atsu decided not to?" Nenet shook her head. "Well, that could be why he brought ye 'ere and sent Moises to get me."

"Atsu brought me here?"

Nenet nodded. "Good thing too, or that hand would have gotten a lot worse."

Atsu had spared her. His sister cut her fingers off. Atsu saved her. Miki dropped her head into her good hand. Her injured hand twinged with pain.

Nenet massaged the bridge of her nose and sighed.

"I'm not sure what to do with ye. Ye attract too much attention." Nenet dipped inside the tent and returned with a strip of cloth. She tied it into a loop, slipped it around Miki's head, and lowered her maimed hand into it. "There. This should keep ye from usin' it."

"Where is Atsu?"

Nenet pulled away, a wary light in her eyes. "I'm not sure. I'd be careful getting too close to him. Just because he spared ye from his sister's wrath does not make him any less mad. Probably more so, actually. Ata is not one to cross."

The light in the woman's eyes as she slashed off Miki's fingers wasn't something to forget. Had she done it for amusement or to protect her brother? She didn't need to ask Moises or Nenet to understand that Ata did not know what amusement was.

"Thank you again, Nenet."

"I better not be rushing to rescue ye every other moment." She frowned, but a smile hid in her eyes.

"You won't." Miki adjusted her arm in the sling.

Nenet picked up the bloody scraps she had used to clean the wound and stepped away from the tent. "I should be going. There is dinner to prepare. Maybe ye should stay ou' here, just in case. Keep yer head low for a while, eh?" She turned and headed back to camp, Moises dogging her heels.

Did keeping your head low matter on Thoth?

Voices drifted from the edge of the camp. Two younger men swaggered toward the medic tent. Miki pressed her good hand into the ground and jumped up. She dodged around the side of the tent. It wasn't the time for them to decide to question her.

"He doesna miss, that what I be tryin' to tell ye." An accent smoother than Atsu's rose from the other side of the canvas as the men drew nearer.

"I be knowin tha', ye do no need to be tellin' me. All ye be needin' is to see Eshaq's face when the mad dog be tellin him he missed tha' woman's hand. Ha!" The second man's chortle accompanied him as two fur-clad backs passed by, neither one bothering to turn.

Miki pulled herself closer to the tent anyway, the taut canvas creaking behind her.

"I do no think he be believin' Atsu."

"Atsu wouldna be lyin' to Eshaq. They be too close."

"Aye, but Atsu do no miss …" The voices faded as the wind increased and the men vanished around the outskirts of the tents.

Miki let out a breath.

She crossed back into the tangle of tents across the narrow path. A leather-clad back appeared a few feet in front of her, and she stumbled to a halt. It was Atsu, standing slouched, muttering to himself. Something lay in his hands. Miki took a slow step backward, and a twig snapped under her booted foot. Atsu started, shoving the object into the leather bag at his waist.

He spun, eyes flashing as they met hers, but then he sidestepped, head lowered again. For once, he did not drill her with the curious stare. The absence of the stare and his usual strange comments unsettled her stomach.

But he had saved her, after all, even if he'd still gotten her into this complete mess.

He jumped past her just as she jerked back, fingertips brushing the exposed skin where his sleeve ended. With a hiss, he stumbled backward, grabbing at his wrist. His eyes met hers again, the usual curiosity replaced with surprise. "What be that?"

"What was what?"

"Nothin'." Atsu dismissed his own complaint, dropping his wrist.

Miki turned away, only to grunt as pain shot up her injured arm.

"She be sorry about that." Atsu's voice was distant, disconnected from his words.

"I doubt it," Miki muttered. She paused, something in his voice making her turn back. Atsu's eyes were on the ground again. "Look, I don't trust you." She cleared her throat. "But thank you. For disobeying Eshaq, for fetching Nenet."

The words lifted his shoulders, bearing away some unseen weight, perhaps guilt. He shifted the bag at his hip, moving the strap across his chest to the other shoulder. It was heavy, then. The muscles in his stick-thin arms strained with the effort.

"Eshaq be a fool," he muttered, eyes still lowered.

"If you hate him so much, why do you serve him?" The annoyance filtered through in her words.

Atsu's eyes met hers, a peculiar flicker lurking behind the clear blue. "There be nothin' else."

"You can't believe that."

The strange flicker in his eyes doubled. "Yeh don' be believin' in Manipulation, but it be real. It be a funny thing what people be choosin' to be believin'." His right hand caressed his left wrist where she had touched him by accident.

"That is different."

"It wasna different for the Third that Eshaq drowned."

Everything always came back to the Third. Miki scoffed and turned away.

"Let me be teachin' you, Miki. Please." The lack of his usual title for her hung heavy in the air.

Miki did not glance back as she walked away. There, she had thanked him. It was over.

CHAPTER 21

Why would people bother to live in the Inner Pyramid? Ptolema wrapped the nondescript toga tight about herself, even though no wind cut into her skin so far inside the stones of the city. The skylights far above let in enough light to make it appear dusk, and the flickering torches did the rest. It was no replacement for the actual sun shining down on her back.

A mother with her babe strapped to her chest drew closer. Ptolema stiffened into an uncomfortable gait. The woman walked by without glancing at her. Ptolema's shoulders relaxed. Just as the day she had visited Tiye—no, Miki. No one recognized her without the get-up of the High One. It was liberating.

The house at the end of the row of houses waited for her. What would life be like with a sibling, a sister? What if she'd had someone who shared her experiences, someone she could have run to after Father died?

But Hemeda of Bast hadn't been that person for Miki. They'd lived opposite lives.

Ptolema stepped up to the door. Her knock echoed through the house. After a minute the door creaked open and a small boy peered out from the inner darkness.

"Hello?"

"Is Hemeda of Bast here?"

He nodded twice. "She's sick."

Sick. The nullification. Of course. Ptolema smiled at the child, who by the records on her desk must be Moises.

"Can you take me to her? Tell her the High One is here."

His eyes narrowed at the title. "You don't look very high to me."

She chuckled. "Not today."

The door squeaked open the rest of the way and Moises stepped back.

"Have you come to bring news of Aunt Miki?" His eyes shone bright with hope. "Mother thinks I didn't know, but I do. I wanted to meet her, but Mother says they sent her away."

He hadn't met her? Even a five-year-old should have. Ptolema's surety faltered. Maybe Hemeda would not be accommodating. But this had to be done. Her slippers brushed the stone on the other side of the threshold.

"Can you take me to your mother?"

Moises sighed and shut the door behind her.

"She won't be happy." He turned and led her through the living area to a door off to the right. The room was furnished with stone benches and tapestries befitting a wealthy merchant. "She never is anymore." His voice was small, hurt.

Ptolema made to ask him why, but he stepped into the small adjoining room.

"S-sorry, Mother. There is a woman here to see you."

"Who is it?" She sounded weary.

"She says she is the High One." Moises glanced back out to Ptolema, a blush touching his pale cheek.

"Show her in. We must not keep the High One waiting," Hemeda said, no sign of alarm in her voice.

Moises motioned toward Ptolema and stepped back out of the archway. The room was larger than it appeared from the other side, boasting a large feather bed pallet on the floor and several woven wall hangings. The subtle scent of cinnamon incense floated on thin lines of smoke circling the chamber. Hemeda of Bast sat on the bed, looking much like her younger sister, but every feature more graceful, more enhanced, except for the blue touches of skin under her eyes and the sweat beading down her neck. Her black hair spread about her, tumbling down the pillows.

Hemeda shifted in the bed as if making to stand.

"There's no need to rise. I came dressed like this to not cause a stir. I wasn't sure you would recognize me."

Hemeda nodded slowly. "I saw you often as a child, and sometimes when I used to go to the Higher Pyramid market with my husband." She sat back on the pillow, a hand absently rising to her flat belly. "I knew someone would come to interview me, but I had thought it would be a Steelman or Council Member."

"You've been through a lot recently. I thought I would spare you that stress." And she couldn't let the Steelmen or a Council Member twist Hemeda's words. She had been foolish to grow close to Miki, but that act couldn't be taken back now. She must see the truth for herself.

"A personal visit from the High One is less stressing?" Hemeda asked with a sigh.

"I suppose not." Ptolema moved closer to the bed, the incense smoke curling around her head. "How are you recovering from the nullification?"

"Fine." Pinched, forced.

"I'm glad to hear that."

"You came because of Miki, not to check up on me."

"It is unavoidable, Hemeda, and I'm sorry it has to happen now." Ptolema drew a scroll from her belt. "Did you know she was your sister?"

"Of course I knew. How could I not? My father bragged about her often enough to remind me." Bitterness shaded her words this time. She leaned against the wall, supported by more pillows, her lank hair hanging to her breasts.

So the relationship was not good between them. That would make it easier to get answers. Ptolema dug a charcoal stick out of her belt pouch.

"Your father would not give us straight answers at his trial. I was hoping you could provide some."

Hemeda leaned back on the pillows. Her son jumped onto the bed beside her, but she brushed him off with a wave of her hand. "Go play, Moises."

He flinched but ran from the room.

"You don't mind answering my questions?" Ptolema held the stick over the paper. Thank goodness it didn't waver. If the woman knew how anxious she was, she might refuse to answer questions.

"What can it hurt? Everyone in my family is dead or banished now." She spoke softly, as if fearing the words. A shiver spiked up Ptolema's back. Hemeda massaged her temples, closing her eyes as if the words would be less true that way. "I am the Firstborn. By rights, my life should have been my parents' focus, but they ignored me and moved onto others." She inhaled, nostrils flaring. "Kamu was the first violation, the Second of Bast—"

"Miki is not a Second?" The paper slipped from Ptolema's fingers, fluttering to the floor. She heard a whisper of a voice out of her memory.

I'm not a Second!

Ptolema's mouth ran dry.

"No. Kamu is, or was, Second." Hemeda's gaze fell to her hands where her thumbs danced circles around each other. "He used to hide in the cellar with Miki. I remember being jealous I could not play with them. When he was seven, my father sent him away across the Great Sea. All Father said was that he would be safer with a family in another land." Hemeda quieted, as if she feared to recall those days.

"So Miki is a Third?"

With a sigh almost too small to catch, Hemeda continued. "Beren was Third and my favorite. We played games, pretending to be High One." Hemeda didn't so much as blink at her admission of her feelings. "He refused to live in the cellar with Miki after Kamu left. I think a part of him died the day his brother left us." His brother, not theirs. But Hemeda didn't correct herself. "Beren was six and Miki, four. After that, Beren started hiding in the city instead of the cellar to escape both the Steelmen and my parents. To him it was a game. He passed years like that until one day he hid and never came back. I don't know what happened to him."

"How old was he then?"

Hemeda's eyes did not move from Ptolema's face, but something flickered deep within those browns, recalling happier times.

"Nine. I remember Kamu would have turned ten that year. We held his birthday celebration in the cellar like we did every year after Father sent him away, and Beren never showed up."

Ptolema had visited the cellar after Miki's capture. So small for a family to gather in. Had it been only lit by the candle on top of a pile of biscuits for the birthday? Five shapes huddled around it, weeping, wondering what had happened to two sons and brothers, one sent away never to be seen again and another running from a similar fate.

Ptolema shuddered at a new realization. If Beren was a Third, then Miki was ... she almost couldn't say it, profane as it was.

"So Miki is a Fourth," she said more to herself than Hemeda. An invisible hand clutched her intestines, wrenching them with painful truth.

"Isis was Fourth. She died before she was born," Hemeda whispered.

"Nullified?"

Hemeda shook her head. "Stillbirth."

The paper lay at her slippers, but Ptolema did not bend to retrieve it. The information Hemeda imparted seemed sacred. Hushed, forbidden. Years of memories too bitter to recall.

"Apparently, the only way my parents could cope with losing each of their children was to have another," Hemeda mused, eyes on fire. "So along came Miki, Fifth-born of Bast."

"Fifth." The word hit the air, hollow. *Fifth.*

"There was another after her, but Councilwoman Edrice tricked my father into getting a nullification for my mother. She promised help for my mother's pregnancy. Mother had violent pregnancy symptoms and could not eat for days on end. Edrice's physician came to examine her, and they sent my father away for herbs. When he returned, they had killed my mother and the child. My parents had already named her Neta. So Neta was Sixth, though she never truly existed."

"How old were you?"

"Old enough to see a foolish man fall," Hemeda whispered.

Everything came back to Bast and the consequences of his actions. Because of Bast, a Second lived with a family not his own somewhere in the world. A Third possibly roamed freely, and a Fifth had remained hidden for nineteen years. But another question nagged at Ptolema.

"How did your mother hide so many pregnancies so close together? She must have been pregnant nine months of every year for so many years ..."

"Six years. She claimed sickness kept her bedridden until after Miki was no longer an infant. Everyone bought the lie. Then my mother claimed to be healed, and she reentered the public eye for four years. But then she became pregnant again, and someone finally got suspicious. I don't know if Councilwoman Edrice ever knew about the other births, but she was kind enough to stay silent for my father's sake after my mother died."

And kind enough to be the reason his wife died. Ptolema's fists curled in her lap. Kamu, Beren, Isis, Miki, Neta. So many innocent children, dead or with uncertain fates. She stood before she could ask another, too dangerous question. The paper crunched under her foot. So much for notes.

"I am sorry for your family's story."

Something close to confusion crossed Hemeda's face. That had been the wrong thing to say. Ptolema turned for the door before Hemeda could challenge her if she dared. "Thank you for your time, Hemeda."

"It kicked me," Hemeda's voice shook, though it was so quiet Ptolema almost didn't catch her words.

"Sorry?" She turned back.

Hemeda's hands clenched the bedspread, knuckles white.

"The baby kicked me the day before the nullification. I waited longer than I should have. I kept thinking back to my mother and was afraid it was going to kill me too," she whispered. She stared at her hands. "Something that isn't a person yet can't kick their legs, can it?" She raised hollow, haunted eyes to Ptolema. A tear trickled down her cheek and hung on the end of her nose. She didn't wipe it away. "They lied to me. My daughter kicked me before they killed her."

Ptolema stepped back, her stomach flipping. She raised a hand over her mouth. That couldn't be true. The physicians swore pregnant women carried nothing but a mass of undeveloped tissue at the point they did nullifications.

Hemeda doubled up with a sob and pulled her knees to her chest.

"Mother?" The little boy leaned through the doorway.

Ptolema turned and fled past him, her meal of peaches and cheese threatening to surface. The door slammed behind her. Anyone who looked up would see the High One fleeing down a street in the most undignified way. But none of it mattered. The shadows of five wanted but illegal children followed her, accompanied by the cries of a baby girl whose life had been brutally ended before she was ever born.

"I had my doubts when Ptolema chose you as High Advisor, I admit, but I am pleasantly relieved with the direction you are taking." Montu leaned closer to Radames as they walked down the hallway, his second and third chins dangling close to his gold scaled necklace. "She needs someone like you to hold her straight. She's flighty and sensational. Not good in a High One. Her mother had the same problem. Probably why she ended up at the bottom of the waterfall. Oh, please don't repeat that. Few know." Montu had the sense to look ashamed, but his vanity recovered. "But the problem I'm talking about, Radames, is not just Seconds."

Second is better...

"The problem is that Bast almost had a Third! If his mysterious friend had not stepped in and seen to the proper nullification of the pregnancy, there would be a Third walking around our city right now."

Third is best. Chanting from three decades ago pounded in Radames's ears, the red stone hall replaced with a dark cave, gaunt men standing above him. He slowed his pace and flicked his eyes back open. Torches lined the hall of the Higher Pyramid. El-Pelusium. Not the cave in his childhood village.

He had known Montu's gossip already, but a shiver still ran up his spine.

"But Bast failed. The Third never took a breath." Even as he spoke to fend off Montu's fears, the chanting resumed in the back of his mind. *Second is better but Third is best. Want to be best, Rad? Want to be alive?*

Radames shook his head, and the chanting ceased.

"But he tried, Radames. It's unthinkable! We've only had two in the Pyramid's history, and they were summarily banished without word getting out. Ptolema's father didn't want to start a panic. The one before that was a century ago, and nothing is even recorded of its fate." Montu's upper lip gleamed with sweat as he leaned closer still, his worry obvious.

Third is best, yet beyond that is better than all the rest …

"No," Radames muttered, jolting to a halt.

"Pardon?" Montu stopped as well, as if caught off guard.

"There are no Thirds to worry about." Radames clutched at his right leg, the pressure bringing a faint relief to the involuntary spasms which had been taking him again ever since he had entered El-Pelusium. A sign of some sort, perhaps because he was getting closer to his goal. Or closer to his fears.

Montu didn't appear to notice Radames's unease but barreled ahead with his argument.

"Still, I would feel much better if we send bribes to all the Nullifiers, asking them to report on any cases of Second and Third nullifications. We must know the moment they put threats down."

Radames nodded. "I will speak to the High One about it."

Montu stepped back and sighed. "She is too young by far, but there may be hope yet to ensure she makes the right choices."

"She is bright. It will not be hard." A frown touched his lips despite his words. Ptolema had spirit, and a mind to look for her own answers without letting them be fed to her.

His purpose in coming to the Pyramid was harder with her to deal with, but it wouldn't help to admit that. Radames added as an afterthought, "I am pleased your only enemy in the Council removed himself with his own foolishness."

A faint blush touched the edges of Montu's face. "I always knew Bast was a rotten one. You can smell them, you know."

"I have a feeling you are better than your peers at sniffing them out." Radames touched Montu's arm in a gesture of feigned complicity. "I would much appreciate you coming to me first if a Second, or Third, is found. I do not want to worry the High One until we interrogate them to discover just how dangerous they are."

Montu nodded, his small eyes narrowing in understanding. "Yes, of course."

"Certainly there will be a reward for any loyal Council Member who brings me information. I want to ensure the High One is safe. I—" Radames paused. Thirty years of planning, waiting, enduring. So close, he was so close. He glanced up the hall, but they were alone.

Montu leaned closer, a hunger in his round face.

"I have a score to settle, Montu. Surely a man such as you can understand that?" Radames lowered his voice. This was it, the moment for which he had come to El-Pelusium. The moment his life had prepared him for. "I couldn't tell the High One my entire story. It would frighten her and even you might not be able to stand it, but I want you to know these Seconds are dangerous. I want to spare this great city what I have gone through."

"Can you give me specifics?"

Radames needed this man if others were to be spared his history. They had to be. His throat threatened to close, to emit a groan of years spent in this very endeavor. He swallowed it down.

"It's too terrible to speak of here in the Upper Pyramid, or really in any part of the Pyramid ..." He left the words hanging.

The man did himself credit by picking the train of thought up. "Is it—that power, that *thing* they say Seconds can do?"

Manipulation.

Radames's leg leaped back into a twitch. Ignoring it, he nodded. "I am afraid so."

Montu gripped his hand in earnest, a gleam in his eye. "I will find you first, be assured."

Radames pulled his hand free and turned away without another word, the corners of his mouth stinging from the strength of the hidden smile trying to force its way through. So close, he could almost taste it. The smile broke free as he slipped into his secluded chamber and laughed. The sound echoed off the stark walls, unfamiliar.

A real laugh for the first time since he was a small boy. For once, there was light and hope in the abyss of his life.

CHAPTER 22

"It's no' awful." Nenet pulled the bandage off the charred lump of Miki's hand and turned to a fresh pile of wool and fabric.

"It's hideous." Miki wiggled her remaining forefinger and thumb, the burned skin pulling tight with a sting. Wincing, she relaxed her hand. "Why couldn't she have missed more of my fingers?"

"Her missin' at all is a miracle. Ata is known for her skill with a knife. It looks better than it should after a week." Nenet pressed a wad of wool to the wound and wrapped it with scraps of animal hide. Cinching it tight, she stuck three pins through to hold it. "Don't lose these. They are all I have left o' my life before."

The pins glittered in the firelight beyond the edge of the lean-to. Miki pulled her hand into her lap. "If you've been here over fifty years, you must have been only a child when you came."

"I was thirteen."

"But your accent—" Miki dropped her gaze from the broad smile on the woman's face. "I just thought you couldn't have been here long with just a faint accent. It seems everyone who has been here their whole lives talk differently."

Nenet nodded, *mmm*-ing deep in her throat. "That's true o' many o' them. Eshaq for certain, and the twins." She ran a hand over the marbled gray and silver of her hair. "But some o' us work harder than others to keep a bit of who we really are." The edges of her eyes crinkled as she smiled. "Others work harder to forget."

Miki's hand throbbed, but she ignored it. Nenet had to know everything about Thoth. Miki leaned forward as the older woman busied herself with cleaning up the dirty bandages. "Do you remember a Third on Thoth?"

The blood-soaked wool hit the coals of the fire with a hiss and puff of acrid smoke. Nenet's head snapped up. "Who told ye abou' that?"

The light in Nenet's eyes proved the connection to Atsu would only deter her from answering. Miki held her gaze steady. "Dali—I mean, Mandisa's guardian told her and she asked me about it."

Nenet snorted as she sank back onto the rug-covered ground. "Guardian is a loose term fer that fool. Thinks if he can dress 'imself in the best leathers he can make this all go away and bring El-Pelusium 'ere."

"But is he right? Was there a Third?" The rug pressed under Miki's thigh as she leaned forward.

Nenet considered for a moment before offering Miki a sliver of dried seaweed from a bowl on the floor. Miki waved it away. The stuff was so saturated with salt it was almost impossible to stomach.

"Yes, there was a Third. He arrived, what—four or five years ago now. He could Manipulate withou' moving. One moment he stood in front of ye, speaking, and the next, fire danced spirals in the air. It was the most remarkable thing."

"What happened to him?"

"Well," she leaned forward, the light of the fire elongating the shadows under her wrinkles, "he was a much better Manipulator than Eshaq, and our esteemed leader did no' like that. He kept the man close, monitoring his Manipulation. He probably hoped to improve his own skills." She half snorted. "Then one day Eshaq couldna stand it any longer. The constant whispering about the Third, the awed faces searching for him. The backhanded comments askin' fer the Third to take Eshaq's place."

"So he killed him for that?"

Nenet nodded. "Had Atsu take him ou' to the Drowning Cove and leave him. As the story goes, he stabbed him if he tried to Manipulate until he was too drained of blood and too exhausted to save himself. The mad twins were still young then, only seventeen, but the corruption had run its course already." She glanced over her shoulder, then back. "But just between ye and me, I don't think Atsu did tha'."

"Drown him?"

"No. Stab him. Ata had a fondness for the boy, ye see. Atsu hated him as much as Eshaq, but he loved his sister more. I do no' think he would have tortured her tha' way. Even mad ones have their own twisted sense of logic."

"What was his name?"

Nenet shrugged. "It was too long ago to recall, and he only stayed on Thoth a few months." She sighed, and a soft smile touched her lips. "He was a nice young man. Always ready wi' a smile and a tale o' the Pyramid." The smile slipped as she glanced back up. "Ye should keep this between us. Eshaq doesna like it being brought up. Neither does Ata." She paused as if to add an explanation but settled for staring at Miki, eyes glowing with unsaid words.

"I'm not a Third, Nenet." Miki met her questioning gaze, voice firm.

"I'd never have thought ye were." A smile pulled at her wrinkled lips. "But Miki, I'm proud o' ye for keeping yer head down this past week. No point in making Ata take the entire hand. I know Eshaq is hard to deal with, but once ye settle into life 'ere, it can be life. Ye know what I mean?"

"Living isn't the same as life." She shouldn't have said that. This place was Nenet's home.

Nenet's hairline rose with her elevated eyebrows. "Oh, was it living ye were doing back in El-Pel life?"

Heat touched Miki's cheeks. "No."

"Ah ha." Nenet flicked Miki's nose. "Then why not try to make one 'ere? Keep yer head down for a few months and Eshaq will forget about ye."

A few months was out of the question. Only two weeks had passed, and Miki couldn't take any more. "Nenet, are there really no boats here? There's got to be a way through the Current."

"I'm going to stop ye right there. Do ye want Eshaq to make sure Ata finishes the job?" Nenet cast a sympathetic look at her hand.

"But the boats—"

"Don't ye know people 'ave tried to get through the current? When we first settled Thoth, a dozen people died trying to get through. Every few decades someone else tries and we find their raft splintered on the beach and the bloated body stuck in some cove with jetsam. No point in trying, see? I do no want tha' to be ye." She fluffed out her ragged clothes. "I'm going to lie down fer the night. Would ye mind going to find Moises? He's probably off with a friend across the camp."

Miki pressed the knuckles of her good hand into the rough weaving of the rug and stood. "It's the least I can do for your kindness."

Nenet did not answer, her eyes already closed, chest rising and falling. Miki ducked into the night, the moon far above casting a wealth of light on the camp. Smoke swirled upward, no wind to disturb it. It was almost … peaceful. An animal howled in the distance.

Low voices settled around Miki as the villagers hunkered down for another chilly night. Where did Moises's friend live? There were a dozen boys his age and they could be anywhere. She headed toward where more of the younger families' tents were clustered on the western edge. There was no one in sight, just the low murmuring inside the tents she passed.

Laughter rippled on the wind. The beach. She veered left and crossed out of the camp. Orange lit the haze of fog as she neared the shoreline. If the sun set before she found Moises, it would be a challenge. He had to be far more familiar with the rocky terrain than she. In fact, had Nenet really needed her to find him? The boy had grown up here. Or was she trying to end an uncomfortable conversation?

Probably the latter.

The hair on the nape of Miki's neck tickled. For the first time in a week, no one was watching her. Moises would be fine.

Miki struck south down the coastline. Freedom, if only for one hour. Manipulation wasn't something she could figure out, and now even the idea of boats had been dashed as thoroughly as the rafts and bodies Nenet had mentioned. The only recent positive was that by some miracle she had managed to avoid Atsu since the day he apologized for her hand. She had seen the twins from a distance a few times while out scavenging or making her way to dump her finds in the tent, but that was it.

A chilly breeze scooped up a tumble of dead brush and flung it into her path. Miki jumped over it and slipped down the steep bank to the beach where she had first scavenged. The waves lapped happily at the shore, one churning up the sand after another. Miki closed her eyes, shutting out the endless expanse of stars and dark water. A frog croaked somewhere nearby. The breeze was cool, but it was refreshing as it caressed her cheeks. Her father was out there somewhere to the East, alone, destitute, abandoned. Nenet was wrong. No life awaited Miki on Thoth, even if there was no way off. There was no life here while her father struggled alone in El-Pelusium.

"Yeh be strange, Miki Not a Third."

The smile slipped away, and her eyes opened to the stars again, but the scene was different, darker with the presence beside her. It wasn't over with Atsu. She had been wrong.

"Ata saw yeh sneakin' away from camp first. She be tellin' me not to be comin'."

"Is she here?" Miki's missing fingers tingled.

Sand squeaked beside her as Atsu stepped up beside her. His dreadlocks lifted with each gust of wind, then settled back against his shoulders in a slow rhythm. His eyes were almost as dark as the water.

"Be waitin', Miki Not a Third," he whispered. His hand rose perpendicular to the sea. A stream of water sprung from the ocean and hovered between her eyes. The water pulsed in continual movement, flowing up through the air and back down into the water.

Miki reached for it, despite the flare of warning shooting in the back of her skull. The water stung her fingertip, cold and unwelcoming. The flow dropped, returning to the ocean. Atsu clicked his tongue but said nothing else. Miki did not turn toward him, but stared into the waves where he had forced the water out. "Nenet told me about the Third."

"I be tellin' yeh too."

"He was powerful?"

"Not as powerful as me." He shifted on his feet.

Miki raised her eyes to his "Is there a way off this cursed island?"

A smile pulled at one corner of his mouth. "Miki Not a Third, I be havin' a new deal for yeh."

"Your sister already cut off my fingers," she said bitterly.

"Aye, that be why it be a new deal. Let me be teaching yeh to Manipulate, and I'll be givin' yeh a ride off this island on my boat."

"I knew you had one!" Miki stepped closer despite herself. "Are there others? Does Eshaq have one?"

"Eshaq couldna be buildin' a boat if he be havin' seventy years," Atsu murmured. He frowned at the sand but then looked up at her. "No. Ata and I be havin' the only boat on Thoth. So will yeh be learnin'?"

"Why do you have a boat if no one can cross the Back Current?"

His mouth tightened. "Maybe someone can, if they be Manipulatin'."

The night breeze cut into Miki's torso as she considered. Learn to Manipulate. Go against everything she'd been taught for a chance to be free. If she stayed on Thoth, she'd go mad too. What would happen to her father?

"I'm not going to be here forever. I'm not going to become mad like you," she whispered, then louder. "You're saying you could get the boat through the Current?"

"It be too strong fer Ata and me to be gettin' the boat over, even while Manipulatin'. I be needin' yer help, Miki Not a Third."

Her hand throbbed, her heart ached, accompanied by a vision of El-Pelusium across the sea, her father wandering the streets as a beggar. Her remaining fingers clenched tight, nails digging into the bandage on one hand and her palm on the other. A far-off star twinkled above the waves, and she focused on it to keep herself from changing her mind.

"Yes. I agree."

A triumphant chuckle rose in Atsu's throat. His eyes were the deepest blue she had seen yet. She stumbled back, her heel catching on a rock in the sand. But she didn't fall, though she should have. A mound of sand rose and pressed up against her, forcing her upright.

"We be workin' on yer nerves. Yeh be too flighty," Atsu commented as if she were an amusing trick of the weather, or a wild pony sidling away.

Miki swatted at the sand, the grains falling back into their place on the shore. "It's only because you Manipulated."

"So will yeh be fallin' over every time yeh be Manipulatin'?" He stifled a chuckle.

"No, of course not."

Atsu turned and walked up the beach, farther away from the camp. His left leg sagged in a limp which hadn't been as pronounced before. He didn't complain as his pace increased, though he waved a hand over his head, indicating she should follow. To be alone with him longer. Miki sighed and broke into a jog, and slowed when she was five feet behind him. There was no need to get too close. He didn't acknowledge her but kept going.

They walked in silence for well on an hour, Atsu mumbling to himself every so often. What could a madman even teach her? Her gaze dug into his back, but he never turned.

The smooth beach vanished bit by bit, eaten away by the rhythmic lapping of the water until there was nothing but a rocky shoreline. The crags between rocks fell away to foamy whitecaps of the sea. A wave leapt up, drenching Miki's boots. The intense chill of the water stabbed at her feet, and she clenched her teeth to hold in a gasp.

"The water can be killin' yeh." A spark jumped into the night as Atsu struck two rocks together. They hit again with a crack and a second spark flew even higher than the first.

A wave of fire filled the air. Hot, blazing, impossible. Atsu stepped back, left arm extended, the flame following his movement. It shrunk to the size of a torch and settled into his palm. No skin crackled or burned beneath it.

"How—" She cut off. There weren't words for this. She had been taught to fear this. Real. Live. In control.

"First lesson: Manipulation be requirin' a start point. Yeh canna Manipulate something if it isna there to begin with." He turned away as if that settled everything he had just done.

"Wait—"

But Atsu moved up the coastline, jumping over holes in the rocky terrain in a bizarre sort of dance. The fire lifted from his hand, flying back to settle a few feet above Miki. The light exposed a dozen more crevices in the rock and she jumped after Atsu, thankful for the light even if she could not understand it.

The faint pink of dawn lit the shore by the time Atsu slowed. The unnatural fire still hovered beside him, casting shadows over the rocks where Miki had first set eyes on Thoth. Was it really only two weeks ago? The chill of the day's coldest hour dug into her skin even through the leather and shawl.

The waves rolled unceasingly in every direction. There wasn't any land across it. They were miles from El-Pelusium.

"We had to be coming out here or Eshaq might be feelin' it." The haze of dawn was a sharp contrast to Atsu's bright eyes. Bright, but dark. He reached for a strip of leather hanging from his belt and wrapped it around his mass of hair. Thoth's version of a topknot.

Miki's breath vibrated in the back of her throat. Could she really do this? Manipulate?

Atsu's eyes darkened further. The air warmed.

"Rocks be easiest. They do no' change like fire and water and so be havin' little resistance. Yeh be startin' with a pebble." He stooped, plucking a piece of gravel from the ground. "Manipulatin' be second nature. Like breathing. Open yer heart to it." His accent softened as his intensity increased.

Open her heart? What did that mean? She looked at the pebble. She could pick it up and throw it at him for all the trouble it would be.

As if guessing her thoughts, Atsu stepped away, hand with the pebble extended. "Yeh don't think. Yeh feel. The air be always humming in anticipation, waiting for someone to Manipulate it. Same with a rock. It be waiting." Again, his thick way of speaking fell away, as something near to passion replaced it.

"Does it vibrate too?" Her palm thrummed with the memory of touching the boulder Atsu manipulated against.

"No' in the way yeh be thinking." He blinked, the dark blue holding. "I be feeling it even in this tiny pebble. A connection between air, earth, me. Sparks of energy between us all, like a life force from a god."

"H-how do I ... access it?" Her tongue tripped over the words she never expected to consider in her lifetime.

Atsu raised his left hand and the pebble rose from his right palm. He said nothing, but the pebble buzzed past Miki's ear. She staggered away. Pain bit into her cheek. She jerked back with a cry.

"Do no' move. Watch." Atsu snapped his hand closed. The pebble dropped onto Miki's boot, red with her blood. "Now yeh try."

"I don't even know what it was you did."

Atsu met her gaze, considering the question. His hand pressed against the side of his neck, as if massaging some pain away. He swallowed. "Be opening yer heart. Focus on the pebble." He massaged harder and winced.

Miki exhaled, her nineteen years of resistance to this very action threatening to stop her. She couldn't do this. If her father knew ... no. Things were different now. This wasn't the stuffy halls of the Inner Pyramid or the dank cellar. This was the only way.

The pebble glinted in the rising sun. A piece of sea shale. It sat without acknowledging her gaze or intentions.

Atsu gave no other hints of how to move it. The ocean thundered against the cove where Pilis, the first Second found in the Pyramid in five years, had died. The fresh sun rays pierced through the faint lines of fog and spread like a blanket across her back.

Focus her heart. Sure.

She exhaled again and scoffed.

"I can't do this."

"Yeh can at least be tryin', Miki Not a Third of El-Pelusium."

She glanced up to find his eyes back to their usual light blue and the flame gone.

"I don't know how to try."

His cheek twitched. "This would be easier if yeh were a child."

"Well, I'm not." Miki picked up the cold, red-splotched pebble and held it in her palm. "Do I just think hard enough about it and it will move?"

"No. Believe with your heart. Move the rock with your heart." He massaged his throat, flinching.

"Right," she breathed. Her heart thrummed with the raw loss of her father and of the only life she knew. Of Ptolema's betrayal. Deeper still, it ached with the loss of her mother, the sisters who died before she could meet them, of Kamu and the life he might live across the world. Then there was Hemeda's rejection and the mystery of Beren. How was any of that supposed to help move a pebble?

The sun warmed her back stronger. The pebble slipped from her shaking hand and hit the gravel with a light *plip*.

"I can't do this." Miki looked up, but Atsu was not there.

"Be tryin'." Atsu whispered in her ear.

Startled, she turned. Behind her, his eyes blazed a deeper blue than the heart of the sea. Rocks hovered around them in a ring, with a flame bouncing between them all.

Frustration rose in her belly and she stepped away.

"Showing off isn't helping me."

"Defend." He blinked.

A whoosh of air. A rock the size of a fist crunched into Miki's side. She staggered back, only to be struck by an even larger rock. The flame flashed past before she could turn and look for another attack. Lights exploded in her vision as pain burst in her scalp amidst the cracking of rocks.

"Stop it! Atsu!"

But the attacks did not stop. Miki threw herself to the ground. More pebbles and shale bit into her exposed neck and hands.

"*Defend.*" The word pierced the throbbing pain in her head.

Pain. Defend against the pain. But all she could manage was to pull her knees to her chest and close her eyes. The stabbings of agony continued beating against her back. She rolled together tighter, willing him to stop. He had to stop. He was killing her. The thundering of her heart in her ears thickened.

Another attack did not come.

"Yeh be a liar, Miki the *Third.*" The gravel beside her ear crunched.

Sunlight five times brighter than it should have been bit into her eyes as she peeled them open. Atsu's leather wrapped knees.

Atsu rose and stepped back, his face a picture of surprise. He was standing. Cold air filtered beneath Miki. She pulled her arm out from under her, ready to push up and stand, to show him she wouldn't take it, but her arm only found air.

She hovered two feet off the ground.

Before she could blink, she crashed back onto the earth. She scrambled up, ignoring the sharp burning pain.

"What was that? What did you do?" Her chest ached, her lungs raw from screaming.

"Nothing. Yeh Manipulated yerself."

"What?" Miki's fingertips burned while the dead cold of a chill crawled down her spine.

Atsu folded his arms over his chest. "Yeh be lying. Yeh be more than a Second."

"But I didn't do anything." He was insane. She looked at the ground, at the rock speckled with her blood. But she had been floating. Or was she going mad? She turned back to him, blinking away a growing lightheadedness. "What happened?"

"I do no' know, but I could feel it." He squinted at her as if not sure she was there. "The moment yeh connected with the energy, I felt it. Hot. Bitter cold. Raging fire." His speech was almost eloquent compared to its usual gruffness. No lilt.

Bitter cold. Raging fire. *Nonsense.* She massaged her temples and inhaled a cool slip of air. The world stopped spinning long enough for her to take another gulp of air and face him.

"What are you talking about?"

"Yeh be stronger than Ata. She's no' going to like this."

Stronger in Manipulation? *Huh.*

"But I didn't do anything."

"That's why we use our hearts, no' brains. Brains get in the way. They overthink it."

"But how can I do it again if I don't know what I did?"

Atsu ran his tongue over chapped lips. He leaned back on his heel, eyeing her. "Yeh will." He turned and walked back the way they had come.

"Atsu! What's next?"

"Be stayin' here." His accented words floated on the light breeze, almost drowned out by the rhythmic waves.

She followed five steps before a rock flew into her path. She tried to step around it, only to have another zoom beside the other. Each step brought more. Ringing her in, cutting her off from the path.

"Atsu! You can't make me stay here! Tell me what's happening! *Atsu!*"

He slouched away, the gray landscape swallowing him.

CHAPTER 23

Ripples of light filtered through the curtain of roaring water on the other side of the sky-wall. Pink, orange, and purple danced across the floor of Ptolema's study. She paced through a blue shaft of light, then turned and crossed an orange one.

Fifth.

Miki was a Fifth.

Ptolema tugged on handfuls of her hair in frustration for at least the tenth time, but it didn't help. A week had passed since she'd visited Hemeda of Bast, and still the woman's story refused to leave her mind. Miki had spent her entire life hiding, watching siblings die or vanish, and Ptolema had thanked her by banishing her to Thoth.

But Seconds, or Fifths if there had ever been one before, were to be banished. They weren't to be born.

Unless that was wrong. The words rang hollow in her mind, like bells in an empty temple.

Her desk chair creaked as she plopped onto it, a rare wooden item in a land of stone. Her undressed hair hid the room from sight as she sank her head into her hands.

"Why, Father?" He had taught her the wrong things.

Radames wouldn't like what she had learned. She was unsure if he would listen to it. Perhaps it was time to try. She had avoided him for the past six days, and he'd noticed. Trying to elbow his way through the Council members after a meeting. Sending errand boys with stacks of letters and suggestions. Ptolema raised her head and peeked at the stack of parchment on the edge of her desk, still unread.

Had it been a mistake to ask Radames to be here? He had valuable information, to be sure. But so had Hemeda. So had Miki. Perhaps Ptolema had acted too rashly when she chose Radames for High Advisor. The truth about Tiye had made the pain too raw. She hadn't been thinking clearly ...

A fresh gust of moisture-filled air swept the room, and Ptolema shuddered. She couldn't delay much longer what was to come next. Everyone was begging her for a new Resolution about the Seconds. Ptolema crossed to her desk. Paper crinkled under her fingertips as she pulled the stack of Radames's notes off. The fire ate them hungrily. She could always thank him for his insights without mentioning specifics. She sat at the desk and pulled a fresh tablet closer. It was time to decide.

Ash. Rose hips. Juniper. A strange combination, but so like the scent of his mother, if the twenty-five years since her death hadn't distorted his memory of it. Radames pinched the rag between his fingers and held it before his nose. Water dribbled back to the basin, the pink rose petals dancing away as the water rippled outward.

So close. He was so close to ensuring what had happened to his mother would never happen again. The water cooled his fingertips, even though the brand he held to Bast had warmed his hand hours ago. *Traitor.* The man would forever bear the mark on his forehead, forever be an outcast.

At least the former Councilman had the fortitude to hold back most of his screams. Most. After all, pain wasn't what Radames intended. It was exactly what he was trying to avoid.

"High Advisor, the High One has returned." One of the personal Steelmen Ptolema had assigned him bowed low in the doorway, his teal headdress nearly touching the floor.

"Thank you." He waved the man away, then had a second thought. "Wait."

The Steelman paused in his retreat, still bent at the waist. "Yes, High Advisor?"

"Did you find out where she went last week? I had hoped to hear by now."

The man hesitated, a vein throbbing in his exposed bicep. "I had her followed as you requested," he whispered. "High Advisor, I am not comfortable—"

"This is in her best interest. Would you be comfortable if someone cut her throat while she was wandering around the Inner Pyramid?"

"No, of course not." The man bowed lower.

"Then you will continue to follow my instructions." Radames bit his tongue to keep the irritation out of his voice. He couldn't blame the man for not having the experiences he had. For not understanding. "Where did she go this time?"

"A merchant's house. She talked with his wife."

"Which merchant?"

"A nut merchant. I don't know his name, but his wife is the daughter of Councilman Bast—"

"Traitor Bast. Thank you for this information. Wait for me outside."

The man backed out of the door.

Radames dropped the wet scrap of linen into the bowl of herbs, and water splashed merrily to the floor. He slipped into a purple embroidered toga wrap, a gift from the High One herself. It covered most of his own deep blue robe, but he wouldn't take his own off. Not until his mourning was over and the debt repaid. He stepped out of the room. "You can stay here. Make sure no one enters."

The Steelman dipped another bow, but his eyes flipped to Radames's robe. Radames turned down the hall, hiding a smile. He would never have imagined things going so smoothly in the Pyramid. The years in the wilderness had not prepared him for it, but then, he had prepared himself with all those books.

If only books could have prepared him for the High One. The young ruler was increasingly hard to read. One moment she was chiming in on a Council meeting, agreeing with age-old customs, and the next day she undid all the Council's hard work. Interesting as it was that she was doing her own investigation into the Bast family, the news could yet prove ill.

The Steelman outside Ptolema's chamber dipped his head as Radames approached, a slight smile spreading on the man's sharp face. The smile faltered as he glanced over his shoulder.

"Are you sure she isn't aware?"

"I am quite sure," Radames said dryly. "Do you think she would allow you to stand guard over her if she knew?"

The Steelman's dark eyes narrowed in doubt.

"I don't like it, High Advisor. She is up to something." His fingers tightened around his spear.

"She is still High One."

"I know. Of course." He leaned in closer, words dropping to a barely audible hush as if Ptolema might hear them through the massive door. "I am honored you trusted me with this position, but I worry she might detect my change of loyalty—"

"You are one of the few loyal to the good of the people," Radames cut in, voice sharp. "If I cannot trust you to stand firm, who will?"

The man bowed. "You can trust me, High Advisor. I will die for El-Pelusium."

"I am glad to hear it." The man might need to fulfill that rash statement before everything was over. Radames shrugged off the shiver in his spine and grasped the door handle. "This will be a private meeting."

The Steelman nodded and said no more. Radames yanked the heavy door open. He stepped into the chamber before waiting to be announced.

Ptolema started at his intrusion, dropping a tablet to the desktop with a *thud*. Her face was paler than usual, if possible, with shadowy bluish circles underneath her eyes. Was she getting as little sleep as he?

"Radames." She blinked. "What are you doing here?"

She had been avoiding him. It was clear as the stiffness of her shoulders. No matter, he had cut around that. He stepped closer to the desk, dipping into a bow.

"It has been almost a week since we last talked, and I wanted to make sure you were well."

She slid the tablet under her headdress laying on the far corner of the desk and stood to cover the movement. Radames smiled, but didn't let his gaze linger. The Steelman had been right. She was hiding something from her High Advisor.

"This is a personal day, Radames. I am free to do what I wish." Her tone allowed for no argument.

"And I am glad of that. You need a rest day, but you hardly seem to be relaxing." He laid a hand on hers on top of the desk.

She pulled back. "Thank you for your concern, but I am fine."

"Councilman Bast is officially labeled as a traitor and stripped of all possessions. I thought I would tell you myself." He moved away from the desk and slid onto one of the stone benches around the fire.

Ptolema turned back to him, her teal embroidered robes swirling with the abrupt movement.

"Labeled? That's not what we discussed. He was to be put outside the Pyramid with nothing. That was all."

Radames nodded. "Yes. But to appease Edrice and Montu after the latest news, it had to be done." He kept his face still, though a sad smile lingered under the surface.

Ptolema stiffened. "What news?" She frowned, exaggerating the rough scar above her eye.

Not letting his gaze linger on her defect, he motioned for her to sit. When she did not, he continued. "We've discovered Bast's wife had a miscarriage between their first daughter and Miki. If you include the child they nullified, that is four conceptions. Four, Ptolema." He fought to keep a waver out of his voice.

Her eyebrow line flattened, making the scar almost unnoticeable once more.

"What is the difference? His daughter is banished and he is ruined."

"The difference?" He gestured impatiently. "Ptolema, if we hadn't banished Miki, we would have a Third walking free in the Pyramid. But on top of that, we now know that if the nullification on Bast's wife had not happened, there would be a Fourth-born eleven-year-old walking around with quadrupled power! A massive threat to you and your throne." A Fourth- born using Manipulation. Radames's fingers numbed at the thought.

Ptolema sat beside him, back straight. "But the child wasn't born. She died."

"But Bast still had a Third."

"According to the gossips. Honestly, Radames, I thought you were above such talk." She waved a hand as if to shoo the gossip away, but her eyes flashed.

What did she know?

Radames leaned closer, the heat of smoldering coals in the iron grate spreading along his chin.

"What did Hemeda of Bast tell you, Ptolema? I know you visited her."

The brown eyes met his, unwavering. "I asked about her welfare. She recently nullified, like a proper, obedient citizen." She emphasized each word.

A coal popped in the grate. Radames pulled back as heat flared along his foot. The piece of ash was caught in the breeze from the sky-wall and drifted from sight. When he glanced back up, Ptolema was standing at her desk, thoughtfully running her fingers in a circle on the wooden surface.

"High One?"

"I am sorry for my short temper recently, Radames. You have been a good friend and advisor in these troubled times." She sighed and turned to face him. "It's just ... I want to know why."

"Why?"

"Why do we hate them?"

Radames leaned back on the bench, the cool stone pressing against his back. "We talked about this, Ptolema. The wars—"

"No. The babies. Why do we hate them? They haven't had a chance to do anything. They don't even have a chance at life before we destroy them." Her shoulders sagged under the weight of her statement and she dropped her head into her hands.

Radames pushed off the bench and crossed the room in three strides. He pulled her into his arms. She leaned into him, a warm weight against his chest. Perhaps if he had ever been fortunate to choose a life which gave him a daughter, this is what it would have been like. The shuddering breaths against his chest. The soft hair beneath his palm.

"I know, I know," he whispered.

"What do you know?" She sobbed back.

"I know why we fear them," he whispered. The moment had come. "I've seen it. I've lived it."

Ptolema pushed off his chest and looked up at him. She didn't seem like a High One with the weight of the Pyramid on her shoulders. Perhaps she was just a girl who needed a father and a chance to make the world better.

The answer he hated was already on his lips.

"I come from a village in the northern mountains. You haven't heard of it, I can assure you, and you wouldn't be able to pronounce its name." But he could, and oh, how he hated it. Iztklarigkitsch. Iztklarigkitsch. Its singsong pronunciation danced in his mind, as if it would bring back two decades of hell. *Izt-klar-ig-kitsch!*

At his hesitation, Ptolema pulled away and leaned against the desk, eyes intent. Hungry for more. Radames turned his back, staring into the coals. So similar to those which used to burn night and day in Iztklarigkitsch.

"In—" his voice caught and he tried again, "In the village there were many powerful Second-born men and women. Individuals who could Manipulate fire, water, air, earth. It was common, and they pressured all Second-born children to learn, if they could."

Ptolema gasped softly behind him but didn't need to voice her next question.

"No, I cannot. I am Firstborn. No need to worry about that." He gave a wry chuckle. "But they tried hard to convince me I could." The fresh air from the sky-wall turned bitter, like that in the caves where he used to hide to avoid those fearful men, their whips raised high.

Iztklarigkitsch has no use for a dead one. Dead ones die, or we won't be able to make the High One a dead one too.

Yellow eyes. Brown teeth. Gaunt cheeks and the stench of half rotten living men.

"Radames?" Ptolema's quiet voice pierced the memory.

Radames's eyes snapped open and his nails dug into his thighs through the two layers of fabric. His left leg jumped into a twitch. He blinked and turned back to Ptolema, rooting himself in this reality. Warm, living, reality. No men hunting him, demanding he Manipulate. No men on a mission to kill the one they claimed was responsible for their centuries of misfortune. Ironic, that he now stood before a descendant of that very person, implying her guilt, and they were all dead.

"What happened, Radames? In your village?" Ptolema whispered.

Maybe she should have been as afraid to ask as her voice sounded. He spent years being afraid of the answer.

"Everything came to a head on my fourteenth birthday. The village hadn't always been so adamant about training Manipulators, but in the last fifty years of its existence, that was all they focused on. But a small village could only hold so many Manipulators, and it was only a matter of time before something would go wrong.

"They died, all of them, and took everyone else with them. My mother—" A firm jaw, kind eyes, and hair the color of raven feathers. "My sisters. Toddlers, nothing more. Dozens of innocents." Innocents who wanted nothing to do with the power forced upon them.

"I've been abroad ever since, trying to find ways to stop them. And trust me when I say that I've spent years searching. The plateaus of Curroon, the forests of Adamah, even Smyma's silk farms. Nothing even close. A few random outliers, but they weren't Manipulators. Curse or genetics, it's bound to your Pyramid alone."

"What about your village? How could they Manipulate?"

"Ahh." He pressed his thigh to cover the twitch again. He had never told anyone these stories. With good reason.

"I need to know, Radames, if I'm ever going to understand what is going on in my city."

He raised a hand.

"My ancestors are the same as yours. Do you remember the Seconds' Rebellion? Of course, we talked about it when I arrived. Well, that original Second had another sibling. A Third. Or so the tale went in my village. He and his surviving loyal relatives escaped the aftermath of the failed coup. They avoided banishment to Thoth and started their own village far to the North. Their goal was to train as many as they could to Manipulate, and then to come back to finish what their ancestors had started. But time wore them down. The North is not kind. Resources were too scarce, and life was cruel. They didn't have enough Seconds or Thirds. Soon the mission was lost in the evil of Manipulation." He stared into the flames. So like the ones which had destroyed his home, his family.

"I had put off visiting El-Pelsium for years, afraid of what I would find here. But I had already visited every library worth visiting. There was nowhere else to search, and besides, a Second hadn't been discovered here in five years. Coming to the Pyramid seemed safe."

"But you arrived after Pilis." Ptolema sank onto the bench beside him, frowning.

"Actually, I arrived the same day. It took me two days to find my way up here. I think I was afraid." The admission sent a shiver across him, even with the fire dancing mere feet away. "But I suppose destiny wanted me to be here when the Seconds reemerged."

"Did you really know my father?" Ptolema said, voice low.

"Yes. A year after my village burned, I was traveling on the same ship your father was on. We shared a late night discussion. Khentimentiu was a young ruler in need of a friend and I was ... lost. He provided insight without knowing my history. He extended the invitation for me to visit anytime. I didn't have the courage to take him up on the offer until it was too late. I sent him a letter last year explaining my need for his library, and he wrote back. I showed you that letter."

"Did he know the reason? Did he know your involvement with Seconds?"

"No. It hadn't seemed the time to tell him. I mentioned I needed information only his library might possess. He was a good man, always wanting to help a friend."

Radames's fingers flexed at his side, longing to still the tremble in his leg. So close. He was so close. "Ptolema, do you understand now why we hate Seconds?"

"I'm sorry." She looked to the floor. "Why have we never been told of that here? Manipulation is little more than an unspoken myth. Hardly a truth to fear."

"You fear it enough to forbid Seconds."

"Yes, that's true." Her voice held an unspoken argument. Ptolema reached for her headdress. "Thank you for telling me."

"Are you ending your day off just because of my little tale?"

"No. I was going to end it anyway before you came in. I called the Council half an hour ago." She adjusted the mass of feathers on her head. "Your history may help with the meeting. Would you be able to present it for them?"

"I don't think Edrice and Montu need any further convincing of the evils of Manipulation."

"No. Just the opposite." Ptolema strode for the door.

"The opposite?" Radames's sureness melted as the fresh air chilled his neck. He moved quickly and met her at the door.

"You are going to help me convince them that our fear of Seconds is perpetuating the danger of them itself. Without our fear, Seconds wouldn't turn to Manipulation."

Radames slipped between her and the door, pulse thundering through his temples. "But Ptolema, the men in my village had no fear. They used Manipulation for their own evil—"

"And forced the Second-born children to take part. Left to their own devices, the children never would have learned, and the cycle would have ended with their generation. You yourself said things only got worse when they tried to force people to learn." Her eyes shone with the surety of her logic.

If only her thinking *was* logical. But then, he hadn't told her the entire tale, and still couldn't afford to.

"Ptolema, I would strongly suggest reconsidering this action. I won't be able to tell my story again. It's too painful. And either way, I am not sure the Council will view it the same way you did." He braced a hand against the door frame, blocking her exit.

Ptolema smiled. "I know telling your story was hard. I'll tell the Council if you can't. But the more I think about the myth of the Seconds, the more I am sure we could end all this by doing away with it."

Doing away with it. Bile rose in the back of Radames throat. He had been so wrong about her. So wrong that she was attempting to do the opposite of what he needed her to do. "Ptolema," he croaked and cleared his throat. "It's been a long day. You should think on it."

Her smile slipped. "I know what I am doing, High Advisor."

The title cut deeper than she surely intended it to. Radames dropped his arm. "Give me a day, High One. A day to come up with a better plan. Even if Edrice takes your idea well, I know Montu will not. What you are suggesting will require a direct reversal of the events over the past few weeks. A direct contradiction to centuries of law. Do you see what I am implying?" He leaned closer, inhaling the scent of sage lingering on her robes.

She did not shy away, but sparks flickered in her eyes. "Are you referring to Disposal?"

"Disposal of a High One has not happened since the Seconds' Rebellion when they sought the judgment themselves."

"You read quickly, Radames. I'm sure half the Council doesn't know the last time that happened." Her voice betrayed her fear.

"Please take more time to think this through," he said. "A day, at least."

She stepped back, pearls and feathers shifting in the headdress. "You are a fine advisor, Radames. I will take three days and would appreciate your company." A weak smile played on her lips.

"I would be honored to join you." He dipped a bow, suppressing his own smile. One disaster averted. For the time being.

CHAPTER 24

"We should be drowning her, get it over with. Too much trouble, tha' woman." Eshaq spit a wad of gristle from his mouth and the coals hissed as his saliva sprayed into the fire.

Atsu's left eye was doing it again. Twitching. Just enough for him to notice, but not enough to draw attention. He blinked his eyes closed and when he reopened them, Eshaq's teeth were ripping into another leg of ox. Grease dribbled down his chin, but he didn't bother to wipe it away. Beside him, Ata glowered at the fire, probably agreeing Miki should drown.

The eyelid twitched faster. Atsu clapped a hand over it and it fluttered against his palm. Ata scrutinized him. As usual. He smiled back, but her gaze did not leave him.

Miki the Third couldn't drown. Nothing at all could happen to her.

Atsu lowered his hand, the twitching slowing. A bowl of the ox sat abandoned at his crossed feet. Probably stone cold by now.

"Do no' be likin' the ox?" Eshaq leaned across the small fire in the throne room, his face full of concern. "I be thinkin' you'd be glad the few we have in the pens are finally big enough to be eatin'."

"It be meat." Atsu pushed the bowl away.

Eshaq's large palm smacked against his hairless forehead. "Ah! Right! How could I be forgettin'?" He flung the bowl into the brambles beyond the clearing. "Sorry 'bout tha', Atsu. I'll be rememberin' one o' these days. But what have ye got against it? Ye'd be a larger man if ye ate just a bite a day." Eshaq belched.

The gurgling in Atsu's stomach at the stench of the meat couldn't be explained to someone like Eshaq, but Ata's hard gaze proved she knew.

"But as I be saying, we've got to be doin' away with tha' Miki. I do no' know where she is half the time and I do no' like it." Eshaq threw his legs out in front of him on the flattened grass. His court was in session.

"She be scavengin' often," Atsu offered.

Eshaq wiped his mouth with the back of his hand and shook his head. "I'd be believin' it if I saw her findings. Khep be tellin' me she only turned stuff in twice. If she be scavenging, she be hoarding it all fer herself." His eyes narrowed, and a vein throbbed under the streaks of gray on his temple.

"I be lookin' into it." Atsu dug one nail under another, unable to meet his eyes.

"Be lookin' into it but then drown her, whatever ye find. I canna stand the thought of her sneakin' around, especially with her noble background. Who be knowin' what nonsense tha' High One over in the Pyramid filled her head with." Eshaq drew one leg up, resting his arm on it as he leaned closer to the twins. "Ye do no' think they could have taught her, you know—" His eyes grew round with implied meaning.

No, they hadn't taught her to Manipulate.

"They are afraid of it there, you know that." Ata flung her own leg of ox into the bushes, all meat stripped from the bone. "Besides, they wouldn't teach her and then send her here."

Eshaq drew back.

"I reckon ye be right, as usual." A chuckle accompanied his words. "Only the ocean be knowin' what I would be doin' without yer wisdom, Ata. Praise the stars and the cursed luck which brought me here tha' I found tha' boat with the two of ye when I did. Who knows what could have gotten to ye, just days old." His cheeks glowed with the heat of the sour liquor in the cup nestled in the grass at his side.

There had to be liquor in his blood to make him talk like that. Atsu met Ata's gaze, and she narrowed her eyes for a split second. *Humor him.* The message rang clear between them. It wouldn't be that hard. The man had saved them after all. A half chuckle slipped from Atsu's throat and he choked it back down. Ata said nothing, even though her nostrils flared slightly.

Saved. Raised. Eshaq, father of the mad twins. Atsu shoved another strip of fish into his mouth before he could laugh, or worse.

"Ye and me. This island be ours." Eshaq beamed at the two of them and reached for his cup. "Atsu, yer hip doesna feel any better, do it?"

"I don't think it ever will."

"Maybe. Nenet doesna seem to think so. Thinks it happened when ye was born."

"Aye?" Atsu dug his fingers into the always sore hip.

"The liquor is making your tongue wag, Eshaq. You've never mentioned that before. We always assumed it happened when we were toddlers or something." Ata refilled the man's cup.

"Really? I must be feelin' sentimental. But aye, his hip was all mangled and dislocated. I be takin' ye to Nenet first thing. Poor wee babes. Couldna been more than a week old."

Atsu looked away. What did it matter? His hip was ruined, and had always been so. There was no changing it.

Eshaq frowned and leaned forward, knocking his cup over. The sour sea-wine hissed over the grass. He ignored it, all hint of sentimentality gone.

"We've got a problem."

Ata leaned closer to Eshaq, her face lit with false interest. "What is it?"

"Well, this Miki girl be just the start o' it. If newcomers keep turnin' up on the other side o' the island like this and are as belligerent as the last three, we could be facing some sort o' rebellion. Not to mention tha' Third, even if he be a few years ago now. I'm all fer growing our population and those numbskulls in El-Pel keep sending us people, but we have to be smart about it."

"We could use them against the Pyramid," Ata offered, voice low.

The knot in Atsu's throat enlarged, threatening to cut off his breathing.

"Nah. Tha' be crazy talk, girl." Eshaq made to take a swig from his overturned cup and grunted when he found it empty. "Ye know I be havin' no interest in tha' liars' den. I've got this nice rock and I be meanin' to keep it." Blew her suggestion off, just like the last time she had brought it up.

Atsu flicked a rock at his sister, eyes narrowed.

Eshaq guffawed. "Ha! Listen to yer brother, he be sayin' more with a pebble than I be with words."

Ata glowered back. She would come at him later, with more words than either he or Eshaq could ever muster. Atsu forced the corner of his mouth into a half smile, but the motion only drew his throat tighter. A no go. He swallowed and focused on the fire, away from his sister's coals-for-eyes.

"There be something though, something tha' would make me be considerin' tha' …" Eshaq trailed off, words far too serious for him, especially with the sheen of liquor sweat covering his cheeks. The air grew thick, no lick of a breeze present. This wasn't Eshaq, not as Atsu had ever seen him. The older man glanced over his shoulder, as if expecting to see one of the other men who usually comprised his guard.

Nothing moved through the gray haze of fog veiling the strongest rays of the noon sun. The far-off echoes of the camp dwellers bounced back off the rock face behind them, but Eshaq's words would not reach the workers in the scavenger tent.

"There be a legend from before my time 'bout some Tablets tha' could be changin' the fate o' us here on Thoth." The statement was more of a question. Eshaq waited for one of them to counter him.

"Tablets?" Ata cocked her head.

Atsu rolled his lips together to match the rolling of his gut as he considered the tablet they had found days ago. Coincidence. He did not like coincidences.

"It be a legend is all. Ha!" Eshaq pulled back, the moment gone. "I canna even read. A lot o' good some tablets would be doin' me." He chuckled again and reached for his cup a second time. The chuckle exploded into a rolling laugh. "Bite me! I spilled it, did no' I?"

Yes. Two times over. Atsu sighed and his fingertips dug into the hollow at the base of his neck but couldn't drive away the aching throb which held him more often these days.

"Where did you hear of these tablets?" Ata, always the inquisitive one. Couldn't she bite her tongue for once? Couldn't she see his throat hurt him?

Eshaq settled back into the grass, his laughing fit over, but did not return to his somber mode. "Ah, tha' Third we drownded, ye remember him?"

Ata paled.

Oh yes, she remembered him. As well as Atsu himself remembered him. The olive face, same tone as Miki the Third. Black hair, same as Miki.

Drown Miki. No. He wouldn't. Couldn't afford to. The Third had been different. Afraid, begging for mercy when Atsu had none.

He remembered the soft glances the Third shot Ata. She smiled more in those three months than ever before or since. One memory stood out above all of them. A day down at the southern beach six years ago, he hadn't been able to find Ata all morning, but there she was, sitting much too close to the Third, their heads bent together. Laughter rippling on the salty breeze.

"You don't have to talk like them, Ata. You're better than that." The Third grabbed her hand.

Atsu hovered twelve feet away, a rock hiding him from their sight, but he leaned around it, waiting for Ata to rip her hand away and curse at the Third.

But she glanced down at his hand on hers and smiled. "I be trying, but it be 'ard."

"You've been trying. It's hard." The Third chuckled.

"I've been. Trying," Ata giggled. "It be—it's hard."

Ata never giggled. Atsu scowled. She needed to get away from this man—no, boy. He was a year younger than them.

Only sixteen. And a Third. How could they trust him? But Ata didn't seem concerned, judging by the smile lighting her face.

"You should leave this place, Ata. I've been studying that Back Current and I think if we had enough power, we could get through. We could go back to Kemet. Such food as you've never tasted! We wouldn't want to go to the Pyramid, though you should see it. But we could go into the countryside. There are other people like us there, in hiding. They aren't mad like your Eshaq. We could live a normal life. Together." He pulled her closer. His free hand reached for her cheek.

Atsu raised his own hand. A stream of water shot out of the ocean and blasted the Third in the face. The boy jumped up, a handful of rocks floating beside him.

"Atsu, no!" Ata screamed, whirling on him, but too late.

The Third's rocks flew. Atsu waved the boulder in front of him up into the air. Thunder crashed overhead as the rocks cracked into it.

A stick cracked next to him and Atsu jumped. Ata's gaze burned into him, as if she knew just where his mind had gone.

"Tha' scrawny boy thought he could be bribing me into giving him power here, into letting him *Manipulate*. Can ye believe it?"

Absolutely. Atsu ran his left thumb nail under his right to distract from the ache in his throat.

"He be tellin' me 'bout the Tablets one day. Dropped it into an everyday conversation as if it were a load o' the finest silk I ever be seein'. I didna fall fer it, o' course. Drowned him soon after."

Atsu thought he heard a tinge of regret in Eshaq's voice. He chanced a look. Eshaq's eyes glazed, somewhere far off, maybe not even on Thoth.

"He was mad." Ata said, voice low, but flat. A flicker deep in her blue eyes proved she didn't believe it, although it was probably for the best if she could convince herself of it.

"Aye. Madder than us three," Eshaq added with a chortle. "Anyhow, back to the issue at hand. Atsu, ye'll need to be patrolling the Landing Point more often. Once every week. I be knowin' it's quite a hike, more than half a day, but it's got to be done. Ata, I'd be sendin' ye with him, but I'm thinking it'd be nice to have ye here, instilling fear in any newcomers we have."

"Of course." Ata took a sip of her own sour liquor.

Atsu said nothing, as was custom, but it wasn't custom holding his mind somewhere else. A time a decade and a half ago. Two children hiding a box with gray stone rectangles inside. He glanced to Ata, but she gave no hint she was thinking the same.

A yell drifted across the camp, answered by a laughing shout. Men enjoying themselves at the Loot Tent. Too bad Ata had found the best items days ago. Atsu dug into the rest of his nails. The dirt resisted, but after a good go, he pried a bit out.

A tingle shot up his back. Beside him, Ata inhaled. Eshaq muttered to himself across the fire, no doubt planning more drownings. Atsu straightened, a slow methodical process he had perfected years ago as to not draw attention.

A warning action.

Ata pressed closer to him, her knee tapping his. Had she felt the tingle too? Someone held the power to Manipulate close by. Impossible! Eshaq never held enough to feel it. Unless—

A shape flitted through the fog ten yards to the left of the throne room. A flash of black hair snapping as someone darted behind a tent.

Miki?

"Ata, I be goin' to take a gander at the Loot Tent. Be meetin' me there in a bit?" Eshaq rose on shaking legs, too full of drink.

"Sure." Ata's muscles did not loosen.

Eshaq belched, adjusted his fur cape and sauntered out of the throne room, his booted feet thudding against the flat rock path.

"Please tell me that wasn't the woman he wants to drown," Ata muttered.

"Maybe."

"Atsu, for the love of everything gray and terrible on this island, why is my stomach somersaulting with bad feelings?"

"Couldna say." Fire tore at his voice box.

Ata exhaled, slow and heavy. "If you think she can somehow, by some miracle, increase our chances of getting that boat out of the cove, then protect her. But if not, I'll finish what you stopped me from doing to her hand. And worse," she added as an afterthought. "We are so close. So close, Atsu."

"Hrrm," was all he could manage.

"Fine." She pushed off the damp earth but paused and whispered, "Don't let this Miki become like my Ren. It's not worth it, Atsu."

"This be different—"

"How? At least Ren could have defeated Eshaq. Your Miki knows nothing."

Atsu flinched at his sister's nickname for the Third. Another thing she needed to forget. Ata stared at him one moment longer before turning and slipping into the darkness.

CHAPTER 25

Icy fingers curled around Miki's arm and jerked her to a stop. Atsu appeared out from between the tents like a ghostly apparition. Nenet's lean-to sat just five yards away. So close, but not close enough.

"I be tellin' yeh to stay out there," Atsu muttered, voice hoarse.

"And I decided against it." She tugged her arm out of his grasp.

"Yeh be a fool. Even Ata could feel yeh walking around the camp and she be no' even tha' strong." Atsu stepped in front of her, crossing his thin arms over his even thinner chest.

"What are you talking about?"

"Yeh've been opened to the power of Manipulation. Other Manipulators will be feelin' the change in yeh for at least a few days."

Miki narrowed her eyes. "You could have explained that before you walked off."

"Yeh could be trusting tha' I be havin' a good reason." A half smile pulled at his cheeks but did not reach his eyes.

How could she trust the mad dog of Eshaq? Miki shifted on her feet. The scent of stew hung heavy in the air. Perhaps Nenet had left some for her. Her stomach rumbled, hollow.

Atsu cut her off with another claw-like grip to her forearm. "Be gettin' out o' here. Be meetin' me where I left yeh, after sunset."

"Fine."

"I be lookin' forward to it," he whispered as if his throat pained him. He stepped past her, back to the heart of the camp.

Miki rubbed her head. This was all too much. Something in the hoarse scratch of his voice worried her, but she couldn't spare time to interpret it now. She stepped up to the lean-to, hunger piercing her belly like the sting of a scorpion.

"Miki!" A streak of brown and Moises threw himself around her waist.

"Hey." She sank onto a floor mat, bringing him with her. "Got any food around here?"

"Got it right here," Nenet said as she ducked inside, a steaming bowl in her hands. The luscious scent of ox and thyme filled the lean-to. It was enough to make Miki choke with hunger. She accepted the bowl as Moises peeled himself off her.

"We were wondering if ye had taken up residence elsewhere." Nenet folded her arms over her chest. A disapproving grandmother.

"I'm sorry about last night. I meant to bring Moises home but then Atsu ..." Should she tell her only friend on Thoth the truth?

"Bah! The boy knows the camp better than he knows how to mind his manners. I just asked ye that to 'ave a moment to sleep." A cheeky grin split her weathered face. "But I'm glad ye are back. What happened with Atsu?"

"Eshaq wanted him to supervise my scavenging on the southern coast." Miki tipped the bowl back to cover the tinge of heat in her cheeks at the lie. The soup was piping hot, and she gagged as it singed her tongue. But the thyme in it brought a rush of nostalgia. Her father's signature herb. She forced the rest of it down.

"Eat more if ye want. You look a bit peckish." Nenet smiled to herself and ducked back outside.

Eyes bored into Miki's side and she looked up to find Moises staring at her, intent.

"What?"

"Be ye different, Miki?"

"Different?" Could he feel she had Manipulated, like Atsu warned? Moises wasn't a Manipulator, though, so he shouldn't be able to.

The boy blinked and scooted closer. "Ye seem different."

"I spent the night outside, maybe that's it."

Moises shrugged. Miki pushed the empty bowl to him and stood. She stepped out into the hazy afternoon, his gaze still digging into her back. Stepping around the lean-to cut her from his sight, but her heart still pattered as if it were on a dog racetrack.

"Nenet," she breathed, "is Moises a Second?"

Nenet looked up from the soup pot hovering on a tripod over smoldering coals. "My dear, everyone 'ere is a Second of some kind."

"Yes, of course." How foolish of her. This was Thoth, after all. Anyone could have the power to Manipulate. Still ... "What do you mean, of some kind?"

Nenet placed a heavy iron lid on the pot with a clang and turned to face her. "For example, Moises is the Firstborn of two Seconds. 'Ere that is normal, but in El-Pel I am sure he would terrify them."

"Why?"

She shrugged. "According to El-Pel logic, the Seconds who were his parents would have doubled their so-called power by having a child together. That would essentially make him a Fourth even though he is a First. Confusing, I know." She chuckled. "But none of that matters 'ere, does it?"

"No, I suppose not."

"Trouble coming." Nenet stepped in front of her, colorful shawl lifting as the wind returned. "Get inside."

Eshaq stomped down the path toward them, Atsu, Ata, and Dalilah's man at his heels. Determination and fury hovered around them like a swarm of black flies. Eshaq swatted another cooking pot out of his path, the owner falling backward with a shriek as the glowing coals and steaming soup spilled over the ground, catching her fur wrapped feet. No one stopped to offer a hand up.

"Get in—" But it was too late for Nenet's repeated command.

Eshaq marched up to her, a finger of accusation in her nose.

"Nenet, be movin' aside. Yeh have harbored this traitor for too long."

"Traitor? Aren't we all traitors and that is why we are here?" Her voice was light, carrying a mirthful irony.

Eshaq's eyes narrowed.

"Yeh know that's no' what I be talkin' about. Move. She has got to drown."

Drown? Miki's fist balled at her side, nails biting into her palms. He couldn't be serious. Atsu stood behind Eshaq, leaning backward as if the man carried a rank stink, but he didn't look in Miki's direction. His eyes were blank, far away. Mad.

"No, she doesn't. She's been 'ere only two weeks. Ye can hardly expect her to fit in so quickly. If ye act so rash, no one will respect you, that is certain."

Eshaq opened his mouth to speak but snapped it shut as his face reddened even more than it already was. He stomped around Nenet, flattening a stray bush. His clammy hand latched around Miki's wrist. She jerked back, but he smacked her with an audible *thwack*.

"Ye be on thin ice, girlie. If Nenet be speakin' fer ye, then ye will have one last chance." He tugged her arm to emphasize his point.

Miki stumbled forward, having no other choice as she tried to fight back the stinging pain in her cheek.

"She be my personal slave until she be provin' trustworthy. Tha' be final. One slip-up and it's the water for her," Eshaq growled at Nenet.

She shrugged. "Fine, do as you wish, but she sleeps here at night."

Miki shot Atsu a look and his blue eyes met hers this time. They narrowed.

"I'll go," she heard herself saying. "It makes no difference where I sleep or work. This place is hell either way."

Eshaq chortled. "See, she be havin' a brain after all!" He tugged her arm again and trudged up the path to the heart of the camp. The woman by the overturned cook pot moaned in pain as they passed, clutching at her blackened feet, but no one spared her a glance.

"Bye, Miki!" Moises's voice hung in the air, but she did not turn to see him. He was better off without her nearby. So was Nenet.

Her escort delivered her to the entrance of the Loot Tent. Eshaq released his clawlike grip, and she staggered away, rubbing her wrist.

"Be stayin' here until nightfall. Sort through the pile and discard any obvious junk. There be bins lining the wall. Fill those with the rubbish and take it to the Eastern coast where ye will dump it. Got it?" Eshaq leaned closer, rotten breath ruining the air.

She nodded. Maybe that would make him leave. Atsu hovered behind Eshaq, staring at his boots. Maybe Atsu could Manipulate them both out of this mess. But then the secret would be out and they would have to make a run for it without knowing if they could make it over the Back Current.

"Good. I'll be sendin' someone to check up on ye so do no' try to steal anything or try to run away." His watery eyes narrowed as if trying to see through her. He ran a hand across his head, flattening the remaining wisps of hair. He stepped away, apparently satisfied she wasn't plotting anything. "Come on lads, the festivities be waitin' down at the beach."

His posse moved away. Atsu did not glance back. This wasn't his problem. Her stomach clenched, wanting him to stay and offer a word of advice.

She was going as mad as he. Sighing, she turned toward the mound of junk.

"I be knowin' what ye are." A man's voice, pinched and nasally, rose from the entrance of the tent.

Miki inched around, back straight. She exhaled and faced Dalilah, arm in arm with the fur-clothed man who had taken her in. She didn't meet Miki's gaze.

The man stared down his long nose and repeated his words.

"I be knowin' what ye are." His shoulders stuck out like sticks even beneath his furs, and his back was as straight as one. As if he knew a secret. As if knowing he was better than she.

He couldn't know she was a Fifth. She had never told Dalilah. Her palms moistened with sweat and the *swoosh vroom swish* of her pulse pounding in her ears drowned out whatever the man was saying. She had to get this under control. There was no need to panic yet. She inhaled. Cold air slithered through her teeth.

"There's no place on Thoth for nobility like ye." The man spat to the side, saliva splattering over the rocky floor of the tent.

"I've never been nobility." The words came out in a rush. Of course he didn't know she was a Fifth. A hint of laughter hovered in her throat, but she kept it down. No need to get giddy.

"Ye be," the man said with a sneer. "I can see it in yer straight shoulders. Ye be trained to think ye are better than all of this and us." He motioned to the camp.

"No." Miki turned back to the pile.

"Liar." Wine-thick breath blasted her face, and he jerked her around.

"We should go, Lukmon. There's no point to this." Dalilah tugged at his arm.

"I be doing this for you, Mandisa. It be seeming to me this woman has a lot to do with yer misfortunes, as ye been sayin' yerself."

Dalilah blushed and looked at the ground.

"Eshaq be too easy on ye. Thankfully, I be fixin' tha'." He shook Dalilah off him and stepped closer with the slithering sound of steel leaving a sheath. A blade poked from beneath his fur cape, red-encrusted and deadly enough to make the need for a drowning irrelevant.

Something crunched under Miki's foot as she stepped back into the mound of loot. He couldn't be this serious. Even the Steelmen hadn't had any intention of murdering her. The blood surged in her ears, drowning out all senses except for sight. Lukmon's smile broadened, gleeful for the moment the knife would sink into her gut.

The air in the tent wasn't sufficient anymore. Miki jerked back, stumbled, and fell. Something jabbed her rump. A strangled cry rose in her throat. Lukmon moved, a blur of gray fur and sharp steel.

Miki rolled to the left, bringing her knees to her chest and her hands over her head. The air grew warm. Too warm.

Lukmon's harsh, horrified scream tore through her fear. Miki scrambled up, ready to run in case he came at her again.

But Lukmon wasn't running anywhere. A ball of fire swirled around him. The scent of singed hair stung the air and Miki tried to inhale, but the sulphuric air clogged her throat. Nose. Everything.

"Stop it! What are you doing to him?" Dalilah's shriek came from the other side of the blazing flames. "Stop!" Dalilah backed away and fell against the tent wall.

"I can't ..." Miki's words died. Heat glowed at her fingertips, comforting and soft. A small ball of fire sat in each palm, burning without harming her skin, as the fire had in Atsu's palm yesterday. She jerked her hands back, as if it might put the fire out.

The flame of the torch next to the doorway jerked in response.

Lukmon's second scream rose above the crackling of his furs. *"Help!"*

"Miki, you're killing him! Make it stop!" Dalilah scrambled further away as the flames around Lukmon roared higher.

"I—I don't know how!" She clenched her fingers over the balls of fire in her hands, but the flames poked between the cracks, lively and bright. Something tugged in the pit of her stomach, an insistence that someone else was Manipulating close by. The insistence tugged harder. The fire in her palms doubled.

Lukmon's scream burst from the ball of fire between her and Dalilah. It would bring Eshaq running.

A gust of air ten times more powerful than the day's breeze hit Miki full in the chest. She toppled backward. The comforting heat snapped out in her palms. Dalilah gasped.

"What be that, Miki the Third?" Atsu's voice, calmer than a mid-spring day, settled over the tent.

Rubbish shifted as Miki sat up, ignoring the pounding ache at the base of her skull. A pair of silk slippers ruined by salt water and mud slid down the pile to Atsu's feet. His sharp eyes smoldered over a half-smile. He offered her a hand, but Miki hesitated, while Dalilah sobbed against the wall of the tent. The smoking pile of furs at Atsu's feet groaned and twitched. Alive.

Atsu's hand didn't waver. Miki accepted with shaking fingers. He yanked her up. More trash clattered away beneath her.

"Yeh are too open. Yeh need to learn to close it off." His accent weakened again while he was under the thrall of Manipulation.

"I don't know what happened." Miki flexed her trembling fingers. No more flames. The torch at the door burned innocently, not giving a clue to what it had done. What *she* had done.

"You—you're a Manipulator? Both of you?" Dalilah stuttered, face whiter than the foam caps on the sea. Atsu's gaze flicked to her, and she shrank further against the wall, sagging into the patched canvas.

Lukmon groaned again and rolled over. He pushed himself up, face and hands black with soot, pink skin glowing with fresh burns.

"Cursed devils, the both of ye!" He straightened and spit to the side. The blade shivered in his palm. "I'll be guttin' the girl and tell Eshaq his favorite son be a blasted—"

Atsu's fist rammed into Lukmon's stomach, doubling him over. A flash of steel split the layers of Lukmon's furs open, exposing his gut. Atsu withdrew the knife and Lukmon stumbled backward, eyes wide. He hit the ground with a resounding *thud*.

Dalilah's hands flew to her mouth. Atsu turned toward her.

"Who be yeh more afraid of? Me or Eshaq?" Even someone as fierce as Dalilah could wilt in that moment. With blood on his hands and his eyes darkening to a wild, dark blue, Atsu was terrifying.

"You," she whispered.

"Then do no' say a word o' this to Eshaq. He wouldna be believin' yeh if yeh did."

Dalilah nodded, fingers raking across the canvas as she scrambled up. She shot one last look at Miki, harsh and full of meaning, before running from the tent.

"You really think she won't tell?" Miki muttered, breathless.

"Aye." Atsu rolled Lukmon's body over with his foot. Raising a hand, the fire from the torch leaped into it as if it had been waiting. Atsu motioned toward the body. The fire sprung upon it, devouring, biting. When he pulled his hand back, a charred corpse remained.

"We be saying he fell into a fire, drunk."

Miki nodded, neck stiff with the pain of falling onto the pile.

"Thank you." Twice now she had said those words, not sure he deserved them. The man who had beaten her more than once, who had tortured her into Manipulating. The fading remains of a bruise on her ribs tugged with pain as if to remind her.

Atsu glanced up, eyes normal again. His lips twitched as if he might respond, but his gaze—fierce, and ravenously curious—spoke for him.

Something cinched tight in Miki's gut. A muscle, or a burning ache vanishing. She couldn't breathe.

But then the moment was over and Atsu looked away, grabbing Lukmon's wrists. With a tug, both he and the body exited the tent, leaving Miki alone with the strange heat in her belly.

CHAPTER 26

The body rolled into the remains of the lunch fire by the main food tent. The weight left Atsu's hands, but not his shoulders. No one had seen, of course, but he shouldn't have done it.

But Miki had been in trouble.

His jaw twitched. He brought a hand up to massage it, flecks of red decorating his knuckles. His stomach churned.

"Shouldna have done it. Shouldna killed him," he muttered.

The swirling remains of smoke from the cook fire curled almost lazily into the air, not caring that a dead man sat amongst the embers. The dirt-smeared flap of the cook tent shivered in the wind and Atsu jumped back. He couldn't be seen near the body. He stepped around a pile of greasy pots and strode away, weaving his way through the jumble of tents. No voices arose at his passing. Everyone was down at the beach this afternoon. The annual Ritual of the Sea. Just a time for Eshaq to claim the waters chose him to lead them. Food, liquor, a few hours free from work.

Would Ata be down there? Eshaq forced them to make an appearance every year, even if only for five minutes. She could be back home by now. Atsu frowned. He would not be making an appearance this year. Too risky. His leg throbbed with every step. The shifting sand at the beach only made it worse as he focused on keeping his gait straight. Finally, the rocky cove rose beneath him, the dark opening nothing short of welcoming.

What was Ata going to say? Her face though ... That was certain. Tight eyes, pursed lips. It would not be good. The hole gaped before him. It was time to go. The jarring impact of feet pounding against the stone floor of the cave sent shudders through his back, but Atsu didn't move, only focused on the throbbing in his left eyelid.

"Shouldna have done it," he muttered.

"Atsu, did you make it down to the Ritual?" Ata slipped out the tunnel crack, looking at something in her palm.

His hands burned, flecked with the telltale blood. Water. He needed to wash it off. Pushing past Ata, he hurried down the thin tunnel, rock scraping across his shoulders. With a soft rhythmic pulse, the waves lapped at the shore of their hidden cove. His feet slapped against the stone, followed by the crack of his knees colliding with it. The icy water pierced through the pores of his skin. Red leached from his hands and vanished into the deep gray of the sea.

It was gone, but he shouldn't have done it.

"Atsu?" Ata's firm foot falls echoed off the cave walls and domed ceiling. "What happened?"

Words tumbled in his mouth, begging to be said, but they refused to come out. He rocked forward, then back. What had Miki done?

"What she be doin'?" he murmured. A face burning with the reflection of flame. Eyes wide in terror. A knot of energy so great, he felt it half a mile away. Why hadn't Eshaq felt Miki's power? Too drunk, probably. And Ata? Perhaps she didn't feel it because she was underground. Atsu rocked forward again, eyelid twitching frustratingly fast.

"Atsu?" Gentle fingers curled around his shoulder. "What happened?"

"He be going to hurt Miki," he whispered. The pain flared in his throat before her name left his lips.

Ata knelt beside him, forehead furrowed. Her hands, almost as cold as the stone, pressed against each side of his face as they had so often when they were younger. He closed his eyes, suppressing a shudder.

"Don't go to that place, Atsu. Just tell me what is going on."

He didn't want to go to that place. He didn't want to need the calming ritual of his sister's hands on his face, but his breath rattled in his throat. Some missed blood still shone on his wrists and speckled his leather arm bands.

"Who did Eshaq have you beat this time?" Ata's voice was thin, strained.

"He would be givin' us up, he would be ruining everything," he croaked.

Ata's hands fell away from his face and she sat back, eyes wary.

"Eshaq didn't make you do this?"

Atsu drew his knees to his chest, nodding. He shouldn't have done it. Taken the life from a human of his own accord. Eshaq was a monster, and responsible for the other deaths, the other beatings. But not this one.

"No' this one," he muttered, voice scratching against a raw throat.

"Who, Atsu?" His sister whispered.

A tight pinched face. Furs sopping with blood. Maybe if he didn't say the man's name, he wouldn't be dead. He would still be roaming the camp, beating anyone senseless he chose, under the guise of a greater purpose. Like himself. Atsu's nails bit through the leather pants, reaching his legs. No, not like him.

A weight pressed into his shoulders. Warm. Heavy. "Tell me who it—"

"Lukmon," he said, so low it was almost inaudible.

Ata withdrew with a hiss, the heavy warmth leaving his back. "Lukmon? He is one of Eshaq's favorites! His death will warrant retribution."

"No. He burned."

"Burned …how?"

Atsu tore his gaze from his knees. Ata sat a foot away, face ashen. Prying each finger away from his legs, Atsu straightened.

"It wasna me, Ata." His arms sighed with the memory of the cool air gushing from the pores of his skin. "No' at first, anyway."

Ata leaned in closer, as if there was someone in their cave to overhear.

"Are you saying Miki Manipulated?"

He nodded.

Ata's face regained the color it had lost. "She can do it, then. She can help us get out of here! With her power, you can both Manipulate our boat out past the Back Current!"

"She be different, Ata. She can—"

"Eshaq could never stand up to us if you and Miki can Manipulate. How strong is she?" Ata's leather pants creaked as she leaned forward, eyes blazing.

His sister's reversal of her opinion of Miki gave him whiplash. But there was still danger, especially after the spectacle this afternoon. He drew a circle in the cave's dust floor with his finger so he wouldn't have to see his sister's face. "Miki be Manipulating herself yesterday. Today she be settin' fire on Lukmon without tryin' and she couldna get it to stop."

Ata inhaled with a hiss. "Manipulated *herself*?"

"Manipulated the air around herself."

"But you said it was impossible! You have even tried!"

He'd tried, yes. Succeeded, almost. Pressure, so much pressure of the air swirling around him, willing him to rise from the ground. A flicker of movement followed by pain deep in his chest. Ata's reaction now proved why she could never know that detail. Atsu clenched his fist. The agony of his betrayal to this sister of his, the one person he had in life.

"Ata, I be sorry."

Her hand rested on his boot. "Is she stronger than you?"

A noncommittal shrug was all he could manage.

"Then it is a good thing she is on our side. Come on," Ata stood, tugging at his shoulders. "We need to check the boat and see if it is ready."

Check the boat. She said it so casually, like they had left the island dozens of times and knew what they were doing. Protesting would hurt his throat, so he remained silent, allowing her enthusiasm to take over.

Ata walked over to the boat and ran her hands over the ropes they had long ago salvaged from a shipwreck on the Western side of the island. They had snatched every bit of the boat before the scavengers got hold of it. Before Eshaq got hold of it. They had studied the ruins of boats for years and watched the boat that brought any new Seconds. The boat floating before them seemed a fair representation.

What if it sank the moment they sailed out of the cove and into the sea?

His stomach somersaulted, threatening to bring up the smoked fish he ate for lunch. And if they made it across the Current, they had no idea what was out there. He wasn't sure he wanted to live in El-Pelusium—a city that had rejected him as a day-old infant.

A strangled squeak rose in his throat and slipped out. It echoed around the cave, the most pathetic noise he had ever made.

Ata paused with her hands above the rudder control, a cracked piece of wood she had polished until it now shone in the torch light. She turned toward him with a concerned frown.

"Are you okay?"

Okay was not the word. But then she knew that. She knew how he felt about leaving Thoth. Even now, in her moment of jubilation, a vein throbbed in her temple, her brown hair pulsing over it.

"Miki be no Second." The words tumbled out under his sister's firm gaze. Why had he said it?

"She is a Third?"

Atsu shrugged. Maybe more. The power she had wielded earlier still resonated in his gut, still drew him to her. He shuddered. It was almost too much. Even now his skin tingled with the use of Miki's power, of the impact it left when his rush of air sent her flying backward and their two forces met. A spark of flame she had not seen. A connection she could not have felt or she wouldn't have let him leave so soon.

Fingers of heat curled in his belly, a reminder of that brief connection.

"Atsu, where are you? You know I don't like it when you do this." A soft hand rested on his elbow.

"The tablet—" His voice cracked, and he cut off. *Manipulation through History*. Maybe it had advice about someone like Miki. Atsu forced his gaze back to his sister's, despite the roiling in his gut and beading sweat in the small of his back. He stood, legs tight from the tension in his body. Miki's face tugged at his mind again, eyes glowing with confusion and power.

A fiery power still mirrored itself in him, smoldering stronger. He had to find her before she did something else, something worse. Surely seeing her again would set his mind at rest and the strange fire in his gut would leave. He had to see Miki the Third again.

Atsu turned away from Ata's boat.

"Where are you going?"

He couldn't answer. His words were gone for the day.

"Even if Eshaq doesn't suspect you of killing Lukmon, it's going to be a mess. You don't want to be a part of it."

Atsu almost chuckled at that, despite his throat. When weren't they a part of whatever their adoptive father did?

CHAPTER 27

Two days.

Two days of failure. Of inadequate excuses and backup plans. Radames pulled at the edge of his dark toga, having finally taken off the decorative one given to him by Ptolema. Permanently.

The girl wouldn't listen, that much was clear. He stroked his beard with one chewed nail, the rough edge catching. With a wince, Radames muttered a curse and glanced at the paper on the desk of his chamber.

Empty.

Not one plan he had presented to the young High One suited her. Suppressing a huff, he reached for the plate of sugared nuts, only to push it away. The goblet beside the nuts stood full of a deep purple liquid. Wine from the Northlands. Probably only an hour's hike from his home village. Radames's knuckles cracked against the metal with a clang, sending both the cup and its contents to the floor.

"Trash, all of it," he muttered under his breath. The wine trickled into the cracks of the stone floor, finding its way to the heart of the intricate design. The edges of the linen bedcover morphed from white to purple as it drank up the liquid. Radames threw the decorative gift robe in the mess, obscuring the worst from sight. He chuckled. *My apologies, High One, the marvelous robe fell into a bit of wine. I suppose I won't be able to wear it any longer.*

Perfect.

Footsteps scraped in the hall beyond his door. He spun back to the desk. The paper remained empty, and tomorrow was the third and final day to change Ptolema's mind. If he couldn't, El-Pelusium was lost to a madwoman who cared more for the cursed Seconds than the innocents who would die from the Manipulators' powers.

He started toward the door. Perhaps it was time to go back and rejoin her in her three-day seclusion. He chuckled dryly. At least it would break up the wait.

The Steelman outside the door stood erect, fresh at the beginning of a shift. Radames granted him a nod.

"Find Montu. Tell him I should like to speak with him tonight. In half an hour."

The man dipped a bow and turned without hesitation. Even the success of converting the Steelmen to his cause didn't dampen his more pressing failure. He turned down the hall, only to drop into a bow.

"High One."

Ptolema's slippered feet stepped into his vision, a stark white against the brown stones.

"May we talk?" she said.

"We are talking right now."

She chuckled, the lightest thing in the past two days of heavy negotiations.

"Always the clever one, Radames." Silk swished over stone as she stepped into his rooms.

His plan was on track with hers, then. Relief welled so tight his chest hurt, but he couldn't be too hopeful yet. Not until he heard her out, and she him. He reentered the room and heat flushed into his face. Her present still lay in the puddle of wine.

Ptolema glanced toward it and her smile slipped, replaced with a twitch of an eyebrow.

"You liked it so little?"

"I was foolish and set the wine on the bed. It toppled off, taking the toga with it. My deepest apologies. I had sent the Steelman to fetch a cleaning maid—"

Ptolema's sigh overbore his words as she let herself down into one of the few chairs in the Pyramid.

"I have to announce my decision tomorrow evening, Radames."

"You have made one, then?" He leaned against the desk to keep his telltale leg from twitching. The wood was sturdy beneath his fingers, like the walls of the caves he grew up in.

"I think so." Ptolema smoothed her teal and gold striped toga, a rare flamboyant piece, over her knees. "You will not like it." She did not blink or waver with the declaration.

Radames's jaw tightened. "Ptolema—"

"I know this is important for you. I understand the pain of your past."

The words only deepened her idiocy. She couldn't understand, because she didn't know. He stepped closer, and she stiffened in her seat.

"Have you felt the unnatural fire of Manipulation burn your cheeks?" His words came out hard and brittle. "The cut of a rock thrown at you by a man who stood hundreds of feet away? All done to make you be like them?" He wrenched the dark blue robe up over his knee, exposing the five-inch gash from one of those rocks and the reason for his leg twitch. The tissue long ago scarred over but remained as ugly as ever. Knotted and red and as angry as his soul.

Ptolema remained still, her hands clenched over the fabric on her knee. The cool air of the oncoming night wafted across the bare skin of Radames's thigh, as if trying to ease the decades of fire in that pained knot of flesh. He let the cloth fall back over it. The silence deepened, a vein in Ptolema's temple pounding beneath the edge of her headdress.

Radames cleared his throat to say more, but she cut in.

"I'm sorry, Radames, but we in El-Pelusium have felt none of that, and we won't. This is how I will ensure it."

"You talk in fairy tales, High One, if I may be so bold." His voice thrummed with barely constrained anger. She was just a child, playing a game she did not understand.

A sad smile played on Ptolema's lips, pulling the pale skin of her cheeks upward. "I am sorry you will not be by my side in this decision. You have been an invaluable High Advisor." Ptolema choked on the last word.

"It doesn't have to be this way. I can agree with your announcement if there is cause—"

She held up a slim hand.

"Any Second or beyond who uses Manipulation for personal gain or violence will be punished. I want to encourage the proper, safe use of their powers. I don't want them to feel trapped so that they think the only way out is to use it to harm others, or me. And I've seen no evidence any Second in El-Pelusium has these powers."

"I don't mean to offend you, but there is no safe use of Manipulation. All it takes is one Second to use it rashly one time. Many could die."

"Then we must be vigilant to educate them."

"What about Disposal? Montu will not take this lightly." One last straw to grasp at.

Ptolema blinked, a flicker of doubt deep in her eyes showing through. "I am certain Edrice and many of the others will stand with me. Montu does not own the Council."

The man certainly thought he did. Radames stepped back. "Then I am sorry I was not more help."

With a rustle of silk, Ptolema stood.

"I do hope you will be there tomorrow at the Council Meeting."

"Of course." He dipped a nod. He'd surely be there to watch the Council go into a fury, and to watch her destroy her great city. He wouldn't miss it, since she was so determined.

"I hope you will consider staying in any case." She offered a smile, but his title was conspicuously absent.

"I shall think on it."

Ptolema exited, the scent of sage following her out. Radames dropped his hand to his thigh, pressing against the fabric to feel the bump of scar tissue beneath. If two days hadn't changed her mind, a third would only cement her decision. He scraped a hand across the rough wood of the desk, but the cup wasn't there. He turned instead toward the wash basin by the door and the pitcher of wine sitting by it. Stooping, he retrieved the goblet. The wine, a lighter pink, splashed noisily into the cup. Subtle undertones of grapefruit and raspberry. A blend meant for a holiday. He choked the rest of it down in one gulp. If Ptolema wanted him to celebrate, so he would.

Something had to be done. He could not allow her to reverse centuries of safety.

A knock echoed through the chamber, interrupting his train of thought.

"Councilman Montu here to speak with you," the Steelman announced, eyes dark. He stepped back out of the room.

Montu. Yes, he had forgotten. Perhaps not all was lost to Ptolema after all. Not while the Councilman stood loyal to Radames.

Councilman Montu entered in a swirl of clean linen toga, his purple embroidered headdress wobbling precariously.

"Ah, good High Advisor, a pleasure to get your summons. I hope nothing is the matter, considering the calling of the Council members tomorrow." He seated himself in the chair his mistress had just vacated, none the wiser.

Radames ignored the man's assumption that his status was before his own. The golden platter holding the nuts was cold under his fingertips as he held it out to Montu. The Councilor declined with an idle wave of his hand.

"Any news on what our dear High One intends to announce tomorrow?" He relaxed in the chair, his feigned disinterest falling flat.

"Yes. She intends to free all the Seconds on Thoth and strike down the Banishment law." Bile rose in his throat at the ridiculous words.

Montu choked and stood, eyes wide.

"What? You can't be serious. Such a thing would throw our society into chaos. Forget the so-called danger of the Seconds. She could destroy the stability of this Pyramid!"

"So-called danger? Do I need to remind you again how very real that danger is?" Radames leaned against the desk.

Montu stiffened, eyes narrowing. "You promised you would never speak of that again."

"Of what?" Radames chuckled darkly, nausea clenching his belly. He held Montu's gaze, his eyelids stinging from the urge to blink and body groaning to run to the wash basin and relieve the feeling in his stomach.

Montu's shoulders snapped into alignment and his eyes darkened.

"This is not a game, Radames. You are a visitor here, nothing more."

"A surprising change of tone in addressing the man about to save your city." Radames set the plate on the desk with a muted clang of metal on wood.

Montu's eyes sparked with curiosity. "Save this city?" He folded his arms across his chest in a flurry of white.

"El-Pelusium will remain free of Seconds and their evil power. I shall see to it myself." The nausea vanished at the change of subject, at the prospect of averting disaster. This was it, the defining moment. Ptolema had left him no choice. A small voice tugged, begging him to reconsider. But there was no chance. The girl had put herself in this position.

"I trust you, Radames, though many of my colleagues say it is unwise." Montu hesitated. "What do you need me to do?"

Radames held back the smile tugging at his mouth. "Wait for the Council meeting tomorrow. That is all I need."

"What will you tell Ptolema?"

"A great many things."

The hall's vast silence bore down on Ptolema's shoulders as she slipped further down the Higher Pyramid. So many tunnels left unguarded and too few Steelmen in sight. A thing she was finding to be common over the past three weeks.

Radames had been there for three weeks.

Radames did not agree with her about the Seconds.

Still, it could all mean nothing. Ptolema pulled the over-toga closer about her shoulders, the teal fabric fluttering in a slight breeze from the open road just yards ahead. Even now she could see the torches lining it, twinkling but alone. Where were all the Steelmen?

A man stepped into the meager torch light, spear clutched tight against his side. A teal headdress, white half toga. Suppressing a sigh of relief, Ptolema hurried up to him.

"Steelman, where have you been? My door has been vacant for hours." The sight had been shocking, to say the least. When had the High One's personal Steelman dared to venture away without her permission?

"I am sorry, High One," the man replied with no hint of remorse.

"What reason do you have to be away from my door?"

"My sister. She has a sickness." The man shifted on his feet and glanced to the floor.

Liar.

Ptolema's teeth dug into the rough of her tongue before the accusation slipped out. An absurd claim. Only Council members and the Royal Family lived in the Higher Pyramid.

"Why did you not call for a replacement?"

"I forgot?" The response hit the air as a question.

Ptolema couldn't stop the snort this time.

"A High One's Steelman has not *forgotten* in three centuries. I should have you hung for such an infraction."

His fingers tightened around the spear, but he did not take his eyes off the floor. "Again, I am sorry." Not a hint of fear in his voice.

A flare of warning triggered in her mind. Her fingers mimicked the man's, clenching around her over-toga. The humiliating bow and forehead scraping the floor were not happening. The Steelman shifted, clearly eager to be away.

"Return to your post at once, and do not let it happen again."

"Of course, High One." He bent two inches downward, a poor excuse for a bow, then straightened and slipped down the hall.

Ptolema shivered. Any loyal Steelman would run back to his post, proclaiming his apologies the whole way.

Any *loyal* Steelman.

She moved toward the open road at the base of the Higher Pyramid, the breeze digging into her chest, bringing a constant chill. She considered the possibility that her Steelman's loyalty had been suborned or bought. But that was impossible.

"Ah, there you are, High One." A door opened, revealing the warm glow of light behind Edrice's tall frame.

"Good evening, Edrice." Ptolema pulled the over-wrap tighter about herself. Couldn't she get anywhere in the Pyramid without meeting a Council member? She cleared her throat. "There is a meeting tomorrow, have you heard?"

"Care to hint at what it might be about?"

If Radames and Bast were the two extremes, was Edrice the moderate? The time had come to trust someone else.

"Edrice, I have made a decision about the Seconds that is going to be hard for Radames to swallow."

"Ah." Edrice folded her arms over her chest. "You are ignoring the advice of the High Advisor?"

"For the time being. Have you heard his story?"

"I admit I have heard some gossip concerning him." The Councilwoman frowned.

"Then you know why he can't make an unbiased decision in this matter. I think it is for the best if he does not attend the meeting tomorrow. Would you be able to arrange that for me?" Her earlier polite invitation to him had haunted her, considering the defiant glow in his eye when she left his chamber.

Edrice's face smoothed over and her hand fell from the doorframe of her home. "You wish him to be distracted?"

"Something like that."

"It will be difficult."

"Then tell the Steelmen to not let him leave his chamber. He will respect my wishes."

For a moment Edrice did not respond. Her toga fluttered about her ankles in a light breeze as she remained in the doorway. Finally, she spoke, voice lowered, carrying a warning.

"I would not be so sure of that, High One. He is a proud man. I hear the Steelmen are drawn to him."

Ptolema frowned. "What do you mean?"

"I cannot rightly say, but be careful with them, and him." She stepped back into her home, long fingers digging into the wooden door. "I for one do not want involvement in stopping Radames from attending the meeting. I am sorry." She shut the door with a squeal of hinges, cutting the warm light from the street.

A Councilwoman had just refused a direct request from the High One and then closed the door in her face. Ptolema's cheeks burned as if Edrice had slapped her. She stepped toward the door, but something held her back. Ptolema bit into her upper lip, the taste of blood flooding her mouth.

Edrice would only be so bold if she had more reason to fear Radames than the High One. The Steelman would not have abandoned his post at her door unless he had a greater duty to someone else.

Ptolema was losing her own Pyramid.

CHAPTER 28

Minuscule cracks spiderwebbed across the fist-sized rock at her feet. Miki squinted, and the lines wavered, but the rock did not move. She had done this twice before, both times unintentionally. Staring at a rock was not going to make her open herself to the power of Manipulation.

Atsu shifted ten feet in front of her, crossing his arms over his chest. His face didn't hold any sign of impatience, but the air resonated with it. Unless it was just her own, mirrored back to her tenfold.

"Yeh be overthinkin' it." Atsu moved toward her, leather boots crunching over the gravel that so generously covered the southern tip of the island. His leather leggings glistened with a sheen of sea spray as he knelt before the rock. It flew skyward.

"You keep saying that, but I don't know what it means," Miki muttered, unable to keep the irritation out of her voice.

The rock zoomed around, almost exuding an impossible sense of joy. Atsu blinked. The rock dropped to the earth with a thud. "The two times yeh have Manipulated, yeh werena thinking about it."

"Because the first time you were beating me." It seemed ages ago, not just a few days. The bruises were fading, but still dotted her body with proof.

Atsu's cheek twitched, but he did not offer a defense for his actions. "The second time yeh Manipulated to defend yerself again, pulling power from the closest element—

the torch." The accent, softer than usual, brought a warm glow to his voice.

She nodded. She'd thought as much. "Please don't tell me you are going to beat me again so I can defend myself."

Atsu pulled the rusted blade from his belt and dug the tip under his opposite thumb nail. His telltale nervous habit. The Atsu who wanted to teach her to Manipulate, the one who spoke more like a civilized human, seemed to be less of a mad dog than the one who did Eshaq's bidding.

Atsu's eyebrows twitched under her gaze and he raised his eyes to hers.

"Self-defense isna the key. It's no' thinking about it. Yeh *felt* it those times." He balled his hand into a fist and shook to emphasize his point. With the movement, the air warmed at least ten degrees, brushing across Miki's cheek.

She exhaled and squared her shoulders.

"Again, then." The rock remained where Atsu let it fall. Instead of looking at it, she focused her gaze on the white caps on the sea just five feet away. Atsu insisted on working close to the water. It was an element, he said, one of the most powerful. The water rose and fell in rhythm as it always did. A replacement for the waterfall in El-Pelusium. A strange new sense of peace washed down from the crown of Miki 's head, as if someone had dripped hot water on her. It trickled first to her shoulders, then down her back and at last down between her toes inside the boots Nenet had gifted her.

Her fingers fumbled with the laces, working to free her toes. They needed air, they needed a return to the life of freedom they knew in the Pyramid.

"What yeh doing?" Atsu's voice held a hint of amusement, but a lighter one than usual.

She didn't answer. The laces on the boots undone, she kicked them off. The gravel nestled close around her feet, colder than she expected, but it felt good. She wiggled her toes again. Free. *Grounded*.

The rock she was supposed to Manipulate lay a foot away, motionless. Feel, don't think. Don't think, feel.

A wave crashed into the base of the rock ledge they stood on, water spraying a good ten feet into the air. She could feel that. The pinpricks of ice dotting her exposed cheeks and hands. The breeze lifting the loose strands of her hair and tossing them about her face. The gravel beneath her toes, wet now from the wave. *Water, air, earth.*

The rock shifted half an inch.

The scraping of Atsu's blade against his nail paused. He did not look up.

"More."

It had to move more. Come on. Miki dug her gaze into it, willing it forward. A grunt built in her throat with the pressure of her desire. It hit the air, blunt, annoyed. The rock didn't move any further.

"Too much thinking." Atsu sheathed his blade and picked up the rock. "A Third should only be breathing and be makin' this move." He turned the rock in his palm, squinting as if trying to figure out what was wrong with it. Or her.

"And if I can't?" Gravel shifted under her bare toes and she leaned forward, snatching the rock out of his hands.

"Yeh can."

"But how do you know—"

"Yeh Manipulated the air to Manipulate yerself," he whispered, staring at the ground as if afraid it would hear his words. "I never be meetin' someone who can do tha' successfully." His eyes flitted to hers. "No' even the Third Eshaq had me drown."

"What?" Miki's blood chilled, turning to sludge in her veins. That couldn't be true. Surely he could do it. "Of course you can do it. Just try."

Atsu eyed her, dreadlocks shifting in the wind. He sighed and stepped back. His clear blue eyes darkened to the signature deep blue of Manipulation. The wind picked up with a colder note than it had before. Heat blossomed in Miki's gut, responding to his power. The heat surged, shooting out of her and into the air, drawing the world closer to her, drawing him closer.

Another gust of wind and Atsu frowned. His dreadlocks rose in response. A bead of sweat glistened above his left eye, followed by several more. Closing his eyes, a low moan escaped between his lips. A plea. A cry for it to work.

Miki stepped back. She shouldn't have asked him to do it. The moan sounded again, deeper, more raw. She cleared her throat. This was too personal.

"Atsu, it's okay. I believe you."

His eyes reopened, still the deep blue. He raised one arm, fingers trembling, and muttered words too low to catch. The shaking in his arm passed to his shoulders. Then his whole torso shuddered.

"Atsu—stop." She stepped forward, a hand outstretched as if she might pull him back to reality. But why did she care? This was the man who beat her. But he had also saved her. Fire. Screams. A rush of cool air. Miki blinked the memory of the day before away. "Atsu, it's okay, you don't have to prove it."

"Proving it be all there is," he gasped as he doubled over, body spasming with the effort to Manipulate.

The air resonated with the heat of his power, bringing a sweet stinging sensation to Miki's mouth. Surely she hadn't Manipulated more than this. Surely this was the height of anyone's power. She shuddered, trying to pull away from the power pulsing out of him, but it redoubled, drawing her back in.

"Atsu—"

The heat fell from the air, returning it to the chill of a seaside breeze. Atsu's tan fingers spread over his knees as he remained bent over, but no longer shaking. A prickle crept over Miki's scalp as the wind moved over her. A slip of warmth swirled around her, no stronger than the faint heat of a far-off candle. The wind focused on her, twisting her hair, and settling it back onto her shoulder.

Her fingers traced the lines of her hair before she could stop them. A braid. He had braided her hair. She started, raising her eyes to Atsu's.

He stood erect, a thin smile playing on his lips as if laughing at his own joke. Clear blue eyes again. Light and deep at the same time. Unending pools of mystery.

"I be tellin' ye I canna do it," he said, voice just audible over the wind and crashing waves.

"You could have hurt yourself." The certainty which so strongly held her gut was fainter now.

Atsu shrugged. "I be tryin' it before when I was a boy. Thought I could make myself fly off this island."

The image of a boy Moises's age floating through the sky, waving back to Nenet, stirred something in her chest, an emotion Miki never imagined she would pin on Atsu. Pity.

"I be trying again when the Third came here. I thought he could Manipulate himself out of the drowning hole. He couldna. I be thinkin' I was better," he said, in a tone so low it almost vanished under the roar of the water.

Her hand went back to the braid, fingering over the delicate twists of hair.

"But you can Manipulate air around others?"

He nodded once, eyes flashing.

"I canna do that though. Or the whole camp be knowin' what I am." No fear, just a statement of fact. "Ata be growin' tired o' it." A chuckle this time.

His bright blues stared at her, desperate for her to understand. There wasn't madness behind those eyes. Just an open honesty.

Miki blinked, a wave of lightheadedness sweeping across her, but she couldn't bring herself to tear her gaze from those eyes. How had she not noticed how exceptional they were before?

Atsu looked at the ground, cutting the connection. Miki staggered back two steps, clutching at her chest as the moment ended. Catching her breath, she massaged the feeling away with the heel of her palm. Nothing had changed about him. This was just Atsu, the mad dog of Eshaq.

The air stiffened, warm with Atsu's power. It rolled over Miki as his eyes went deep blue once more.

"Be tryin' again." His voice remained calm, with no hint that he felt anything like she had.

Try again. So simple. She forced back a wry chuckle, but it caught in her throat, refusing to either be swallowed down or coughed out. Stuck, choking her.

Atsu moved forward, the thin lines of his body tightening beneath the leather. Muscle all over.

"Maybe the rock be the wrong thing. Be trying with the air since yeh've done it before."

Air, heavy with the scent of salt and moisture. Her fingers tingled at her side, slick with sea spray. Air. Move the air. She closed her eyes only to reopen them. There was no shift within her, no warmth of power like she felt when Atsu Manipulated. Nothing. Grunting, she threw her hands in the air and spun to face him.

"This isn't going to work! Every time I try, there is nothing there. I don't even know what I am supposed to be reaching for."

She expected Atsu to insult her for failing, but his eyes sparkled, and he leaned closer. "Yer eyes, Miki."

"What about them?"

"Purple," he breathed, awe hinging in his voice.

"What?" She inhaled sharply.

"Ye be Manipulating something, or they wouldna have changed." He stepped closer, eyes intent on her face. His hand hovered in the air between them, fingers searching. Warmth settled in her palm. His hand on hers.

Touching her.

She ripped her hand back and tripped, rear end thudding into the gravel. The world snapped into focus.

"I'm sorry, Miki the Third," Atsu murmured. "I be thinkin'—" He cut off, blinking.

"You thought what?" Though the words came from her lips, they seemed miles away.

He did not expound on his words but massaged his neck with a weatherbeaten hand. Turning away, he retrieved the rock again and threw it into the churning sea. The water accepted it without notice, another wave crashing against the wall of the island.

"Atsu?"

"Again." His voice scratched, and he swallowed with a flinch.

"I can't do it." The confession tore through her, bringing waves of fatigue. She was not as powerful as he, no matter what he insisted. How long had they been at this? At least four hours, surely. The sun burned overhead. The early morning session was long over.

"Do it." He moved back to her, offering a hand up.

She accepted without thinking. Warmth flowed from his palm into hers. Comforting, inviting. Her heart leapt to her throat and she jumped up, ripping her hand away.

"I can't do it," she muttered.

"Air. Go."

The command shivered along her spine. Maybe he was mad after all. Miki planted her feet shoulder width apart. *Feel, not think.* She could do it, prove it to him. The air stilled. The sun slipped behind a looming shelf of clouds, the lack of warmth an abrupt discomfort. She shivered. The air was chilly.

Sweat pricked her brow at her concentration, but the air itself did not change. The water raged below, and the gravel remained at her feet. All was how it had been. No difference.

"I can't do this!" She turned, gravel grating under her bare heel and cutting into her foot. "This is a waste of time." The path back to the camp opened behind Atsu and she made for it.

He raised a hand to his throat as she stalked past.

"Yeh be right. Ye should be better for a Third."

Third. There it was. The ridiculous thing he kept insisting she was and insisting that it made a difference. Heat flared through her gut, bringing with it thing buried for far too long. She spun back to him, hands shaking.

"I am not a Third!"

Atsu's eyes narrowed, no longer as breathtaking as they had been minutes ago.

"Yeh be a liar."

"I'm a Fifth!" The words so long hidden deep within her, behind the wall of Tiye, boiled to the surface. The air shrieked between her and Atsu, expanding as it grew louder. Pressure against her chest, restricting her breath.

The shriek popped.

Gravel, sand, rocks, bits of island brush shot into the air in every direction. The explosion rocked her feet and Miki flung her hands up over her head to block the shrapnel. Dust drifting through the air, the sound of the explosion echoing around the tip of the island, the air thickening, quieting. The waves grew distant, miles away.

The heavy clouds drew closer, the sun entirely gone. Her palms shook with the release of the nineteen-year-old secret and the inability to take it back.

The wind returned, blowing the dust away in one gust. A crater sat between her and Atsu, five feet wide and equally deep.

Atsu stood on the other side, eyes burning over a crooked half smile.

CHAPTER 29

I'm a Fifth!

The words she had unintentionally admitted had haunted Miki as she hiked back to the camp. Even when the dots of fires rose in front of her and the chattering of Thoth's inhabitants replaced the cool calm of the vacant island, she couldn't stop going over the words. The pinging vibrations of her proclamation still resounded through her vacant mind, searching for a place to land. She ducked around the fruit stand outside the cooking tent and slipped into a canvas-lined path. The wind rustled through the path, the only sound in the evening.

A nervous chuckle lodged in her throat. Had she really blown a crater into the island? The dust of her action still clung to her furs and crusted over her still bare toes. The night chill threatened to make her put the boots back on, but if she did, a small bit of who she was in El-Pelusium, the daughter her father loved, would be lost again.

Miki turned toward Nenet's tent. She hadn't been back there since Eshaq took her yesterday. The path twisted past more tents, their wide canvas walls giving shelter against the blustering evening wind.

One more turn and Miki stumbled back as Dalilah stepped into the path, eyes red rimmed. She choked something down from a leather flask, then let it the flask tumble into the rocky path.

"You killed him."

Miki's remaining good hand balled so tight her fingers burned. "What?"

"Lukmon. You—" Dalilah craned her neck to glance up the trail and lowered her voice. "You *Manipulated* and killed him."

Blood pounded in Miki's ears. What Dalilah claimed was only half true, but her cheeks warmed.

"And if it wasn't you that finished him," Dalilah hissed, as if guessing Miki's thought, "it was that mad friend of yours." She stepped in so close, a defect in the white of her teeth shone dully in the firelight that glowed behind them.

"Atsu didn't do it." The defense came before thinking. Miki blinked the image of Lukmon's lifeless face from her eyes.

"He did. You know I can't tell Eshaq, but I can still hurt you. Two men are dead at your hands. Two of *my* men." The words were more of a snarl this time. "You are becoming as mad as the dog." She spit on the ground between them, saliva spraying Miki's bare toes, warm and cool at the same time.

She stepped forward, matching the other woman's action.

"He's not—" she paused, unsure of her next words, "—he is not a mad dog." She drew her arms over her chest to cover the waver in her voice.

Dalilah's eyes narrowed.

"Why do you defend him? He beat you. Several times. Why don't you add him to the list of men you've killed?"

"I haven't killed anyone." Miki tried to shove past, her shoulder thudding into Dalilah's.

The woman's nails dug into Miki's wrist as she pulled her back around.

"Tell me why you are defending him. What did he do to you?" Her eyes widened this time, betraying her desperation.

"Nothing." She hesitated. "Not recently, anyway."

"Then what has he got on you? Why do you care enough to defend him?"

I'm a Fifth! The words echoed again as if she had just yelled them. With a jerk, Miki yanked herself out of Dalilah's grasp, breath thin. If she created a crater where the woman stood—

No. She couldn't. "I don't even know how," she muttered.

"What?" Dalilah made to grab her again, but Miki dodged around her and up the path. The cool earth seeped between her bare toes and she sighed with relief. No footsteps followed, and she turned a corner, putting a large but lopsided tent between her and Dalilah.

A hunched shape filled the path.

"Aye, perfect. I be needin' to speak wi' ye." Eshaq's voice boomed down the still alley, far clearer than his usual gruff, slurred tones. His unkempt hair hung into his face like normal, but his eyes were clear grey beneath. No hint of sour liquor stung the air.

Sucking in a breath, Miki stepped into the deeper shadow of a nearby tent.

Two shapes joined Eshaq, sliding in from behind tents on both sides of the path in perfect unison. His mad twins. Atsu's eyes did not find Miki, but Ata's burned full force. Her brother would have no reason to hide the truth of Miki the Third from her.

Eshaq leaned toward his accomplices, lank hair hanging straight before his face, pale moonlight shooting through the strands. "Lukmon be dead," he intoned.

The twins remained silent figures in the dark.

Eshaq bristled, correcting most of the remaining hunch in his back as he leaned into them. "Did ye hear what I be sayin'? Lukmon, one o' my trusted men, be dead."

"We heard," Ata said dryly.

Atsu ran a hand across his throat.

"Then be tellin' me ye two know somethin' 'bout this? That ye know how it happened?" An edge of worry entered Eshaq's voice, something absent before at any meeting Miki had overheard.

"Drunk," Atsu croaked as if his throat were on fire.

"So the woman who found him be sayin'. Ha," Eshaq chuckled mirthlessly. "He was one fer the liquor, but Lukmon wasna a fool. He wouldna be trippin' blindly into a fire and die," Eshaq mused.

"Even the most un-foolish can have a foolish moment," Ata offered.

"That be it?" Eshaq thumped a hand on each twin's shoulder and leaned in closer, his voice dropping. "Where be yer usual insights? Come on, this isna like ye."

"We aren't perfect." Ata folded her arms across her chest. Atsu shifted from one foot to the other.

"But surely one of ye be seein' something," Eshaq begged.

Atsu shook his head.

"Bah!" Eshaq pulled back, throwing his arms in the air. "I just willna be believin' this!"

The twins stepped closer together but did not exchange any words. Atsu only stared at the blade in his belt as his thumb played along the edge. Eshaq glanced up as if catching movement behind Miki. Her muscles stiffened, taut within her frame. A small ball of heat blossomed in her gut, waiting, wanting to be used.

No! She couldn't Manipulate. Not now.

The heat grew, threatening to burst from her chest. Closing her eyes to the heat, Miki bit into her lip.

Atsu shifted ten feet away, Ata's hand clenched on his shoulder. They could feel it. One slip, one sigh at the wrong moment, and Miki would let it go. Like the crater. Like Lukmon.

No, no, no! She had to think. Thinking overrode the feeling. Feel and Manipulate, think and shut off the power. The blood from her lip pooled in her mouth, thickened, threatened to gag her. A moan, half agony, half ecstasy, slipped through Miki's lips. They vibrated with the sound, a song of longing and denial. The heat wouldn't be silenced much longer. Their plan was ruined. Eshaq would kill her and then Atsu. Her gut flipped. No, Atsu couldn't die. Not until he got off Thoth.

Eshaq was whispering to the twins again. The throbbing in Miki's ears made it impossible to tell what. Ata shot a glance to Atsu but spared no words. Miki opened her mouth to call out to him, only to snap it shut again. With a fragile step, she backed up. Two more soundless steps. A lopsided tent cut the meeting from sight. A stream of campfire smoke wafted in front of it, lazy, unconcerned.

Exhaling with a shiver, Miki turned and sprinted off into the tents. Eshaq hadn't seen her. More importantly, he had not felt her. Silence settled around her as she slowed to a jog and made for the coast. There didn't seem anywhere else to go, to be alone from the threats of Eshaq's camp. The heat dissipated with nothing to show what she had almost done. One moment longer and her uncontrollable power could have swallowed every one of them.

Miki stopped where the scrubby undergrowth met sand and shrank to the ground, legs too weak from the adrenaline pulsing through them. The coastline lay ahead, black land meeting black sea and black sky, only broken by the silver of fog glowing beneath a far-off moon barely shedding any light.

A hand pressed into her shoulder, firm.

"That was close, Miki Not a Third," said a female voice.

So her escape had not been so clean after all. Of course Ata's brother would have told her about the Fifth. Miki pressed her palms into the moist earth and shoved herself upright. A half-delirious laugh slipped out.

"You are right. I am not a Third."

Ata's voice rang out in the dark, hard and without pity. "You came very close to doing something terrible."

Miki flinched, pulling her mangled hand closer to her chest. Words lodged in her throat, choking her.

"You have to be careful. My brother is teaching you too fast." Ata turned and a frown split her face. "I told you to stay away from him."

"I—"

The other held up a slender hand. "I told you to stay away from him before I knew what you are." She stepped closer, eyes narrowing, taking Miki in. "I can hardly handle the one sibling. How did you do it with four?"

Miki held her tongue. The question wasn't meant to be answered, she knew it. Besides, she had no answer to give. Half of those siblings she never really knew. Hemeda was a poor excuse for a sister. If she had been like Ata, always on the lookout for her brother ... life would have been different.

"Look, I'm taking back what I said. If you can control this power and help us, then do it. If not, well ..." Ata's gaze dropped to Miki's half hand.

The scarred skin prickled. Miki cleared her throat.

"We are going to get off this island."

"I am." Ata nodded. "Atsu is. We will see what you can do. You almost got us all killed back there."

"I know." The desperation and helplessness swirling through her gut with the earlier heat she'd felt resurfaced. "I'm trying."

"Well, try harder. Eshaq will figure out what you can do before too long at the rate you keep exposing yourself. If he does, you will never leave. Just like—" she cut off, face darkening. Whatever she might have said vanished inside her tight eyes.

"I don't understand why you two don't just defeat Eshaq. You could take him, beat him. Tie him up or kill him. Atsu alone could do it with his power." The words tumbled out in Miki's desperation to keep Ata talking instead of not thinking about using her knife on the rest of Miki's hand.

Ata inhaled, eyes flashing.

"Oh, aye, he could do it," she snorted. "It wouldn't take more than a minute."

"Then why doesn't he?"

"Because," Ata's voice lowered, "nothing is worth breaking Atsu, and that would cleave him in two." The intensity of her words dug into Miki's chest and she stepped back, not prepared for it.

"Break him?"

Ata matched her step, coming even closer than she had been before, small nose a breath from Miki's.

"Eshaq saved us, raised us. He is our father, whether or not we prefer it. Tell me, Miki the Fifth, could you kill your father?" Her eyes glowed a strange teal and with a lick of the faintest breeze, a rock rose from between their feet, coming to spin slowly in front of Miki's face. It pressed against her cheek, cold pressure. With a jerk, she stepped back.

"Atsu couldn't either," Ata finished in a whisper. "He is more fragile than he appears. Nothing is worth breaking him." The rock settled back into the sand and her eyes faded to their usual blue. "But you have to learn to make this work, or you will die here like Ren." She gazed at the dark sea.

Miki shifted on her feet. This was too personal. Ren must be the Third. She had never heard his name before. But Ata's gaze swiveled back to her, burning.

"I can't control my power," Miki said. Anything to take that look away.

"Yeh be a liar, Miki." Atsu's voice, a cool breeze to Ata's fire, drifted from up the beach.

The skin on the back of Miki's neck tickled under his gaze. She turned to face Atsu. Hard lines under far-off eyes. Blood speckled his leather jerkin. What had happened in the fifteen minutes since she saw him with Eshaq? He shifted in the sand, muscles pulling against the leather leggings, as he reached up to tie his dreadlocks into a bun.

"You'll fix this mess, then?" Without explaining her question, Ata left the beach in two long strides and slipped into the dark.

Atsu turned to Miki.

"Yeh be a liar, Miki. Yeh be sayin' yeh didna control your power."

"I almost drew in power from a fire. It would have exploded out of me. How am I a liar?" She stepped up to him, hair snapping into her face.

The fog cut between them, bringing an eerie glow to Atsu's face as the moonlight reflected off the silver hovering around his cheeks.

"Yeh be stopping all o' that from happening. Yeh be controlling it." He exhaled, eyes alight with excitement. "Maybe this be really workin'." His face lightened with a new emotion, a strange contrast to the musing curiosity it usually held. Hope.

Atsu's smile widened, catching her own cheeks into mirroring it. Perhaps he really had smiled when she made the crater.

"Do it," he whispered, voice soft with lack of accent.

The heat exploded back into her gut.

"Purple," Atsu breathed, staring into her eyes.

Turning to the ocean, Miki raised her hands, the missing fingers leaving a gaping black hole. There was nothing left but to try. The salt of the water stung the air. Fresh, crisp. Mesmerizing. A wave grew closer, ready to break on the beach. Before it could, it paused. Wavering above the sand. Waiting for her command to fall.

"Tha' be it." Atsu's reassuring tone washed over her as he moved in closer, his musky scent filling the air.

The wave toppled and water cascaded across the beach in an erratic pattern apart from the rest. The heat snuffed out. Nothing hummed in her muscles. The night silenced.

"That isn't good enough!" Throwing her hands over her head, Miki thumped into the sand, the cool grains nestling around her rear end.

"Yeh will get it. It be taking practice. I learned by accident when I was five, but it took me until I was thirteen to have fully mastered it." He folded his legs and sat beside her.

"Oh, great. So, I'll figure it all out in eight years." The sand was hard in her palm as she clutched a handful and flung it into the water. "Ata will be pleased to wait that long to leave."

Atsu's fingers snatched her wrist from the air. Surges of heat hit her skin where the tips of his finger pressed against her skin. She wanted to pull away, refuse the touch, but something stayed her hand. His eyes weren't deep blue. The surges weren't from Manipulating.

From something else. Her stomach somersaulted.

"Yeh be a Fifth, Miki. It won't take yeh eight years," he said, voice soft.

She blinked, trying to refocus on learning to Manipulate, but Atsu was too close. His stunning eyes. His lean lines of muscle. His hand holding her arm. The hand that had once beaten her.

With a jerk and intake of breath, she pulled away, the prickles of contact vanishing. Atsu's face fell, but only slightly. Her gaze dropped to her bare feet nestled in the sand and when she looked back up, Atsu's face held nothing. She'd only imagined he regretted the loss of her touch.

"If Eshaq be making me come for yeh, I must do it." His voice scratched against his throat, raw and pained.

She nodded.

"Whatever yeh do, do no' Manipulate with him near. If he makes me take yeh, or Ata, or anyone else, do no' Manipulate until yeh be at the sea—" He cut off, coughing, a hand rising to massage his throat.

"Why does it hurt so much when you talk?" This wasn't what she wanted to discuss with him. But the odd flipping sensation returned to her belly, and the place where his fingers had held her wrist tingled as if he still did.

Atsu shrugged. "Speaking and I do no' be gettin' along." A raw chuckle accompanied the words. "Ata be better at it."

"I rarely like what she says."

Atsu's chuckle doubled. "Most do no'. Yeh be amusing, Miki."

"I'm not trying to be." Her fingers clenched in her lap.

"It be the best thing—" Atsu began, only to roll his lips together and cut off.

She shifted under his scrutiny, heat flaring in her cheeks.

"What is?"

Atsu pulled his knees up to his chest and scooted closer, back to where he had been when he grabbed her wrist. "Havin' yeh here."

The air snuffed from the night, leaving behind a void of fog and stillness. Miki's breath rattled in her ears. She cleared her throat.

"Because I can Manipulate?"

"No ..." He left the word hanging, the reason unsaid, but no hand went to his throat.

The breath in her ears drowned out the waves. Atsu sat only inches away, his hands pressing into the sand just a breath away from hers. One slight movement, and their hands would touch.

The fog surrounding them thickened, driving away the stars and even the water. There was nothing out in the night apart from her and Atsu. His eyes did not lower from hers. A soft weight on her knee. His fingers, including the mysteriously intact forefinger, spread across it, encompassing it with tingles of warmth.

Miki stiffened, throat constricting so she could not swallow or speak. Her own fingers pulsed with the urge to slap his hand away. But she didn't. Atsu's lips moved as if he might speak, but no words came. Finally, he pulled his hand away, both heat and weight vanishing.

The lightness in her chest remained.

"I—" She gulped for a breath, "Why do you still have your fingers? Everyone else on Thoth does not." The words changed at the last moment.

"That be the great mystery," he whispered. "Ata and I be showin' up in a boat alone. They didna be throwin' us off at the Current. We would be dyin'. So we be comin' in a small boat by ourselves. Probably not even a week old and hands bein' normal." His fingers wiggled in the sand between them. "Eshaq couldna be bringing himself to be completing the deed."

"I see." But she didn't. Why had no one cut the fingers in El-Pel? She cleared the rising lump from her throat and looked away. "I should be getting back to Nenet's."

Atsu raised a hand, reaching for her, for something, but it hovered in the air between them. His eyes glowed even in the fog. His hand fell to the sand with a soft thump and he nodded.

"Aye," he whispered, as if he dared not speak louder. He stood, offering a hand to help her up. His olive skin was luminescent in the faint torch light. Hands worn from years of digging in the sand for treasures. Nails immaculately clean for once.

A smile tugged at Miki's lips and she reached for his hand. Weathered, warm. Sand fell from her clothes in a cascading wave as he pulled her up. She faced him, still gripping his hand. Energy fuzzed between her skin and his. Atsu's cheek twitched, and he blinked. His mouth opened, only to snap shut. His fingers slipped out from hers and he pulled the torch from the sand.

He led the way back to Nenet's in silence, and Miki did not intrude on it. Confusion and conflicting emotions thundered through her mind, drowning out anything but the lean form of Atsu and his shifting dreadlocks.

CHAPTER 30

"Get out of the way, old woman."

"You dare to address me that way, *old man*?" Nenet's voice cut through the darkness. Miki stirred, but the cocoon of warmth did not move.

"This isna yer affair. Step aside." Another woman's voice, vaguely familiar.

A thud, followed by a pained grunt.

"Go get her."

Footsteps neared Miki's warmth. She fought the sleep, but it clung too tightly. The warmth ripped away and a musty scent washed across her. A scent far more familiar than the voices outside. Her eyes blinked open. Atsu stood above her, face blank. No quirky stare or curious frown. Nothing.

Her heart spiked, and she scrambled upward, all sleep falling away. Something was wrong. It didn't matter who was outside. It could only be one person.

"Atsu?" she croaked, throat still clogged with sleep.

His eyes flashed, and he shook his head half an inch. His fingers clamped around her good wrist, dragging her off the bed pallet and into the hazy dawn. The smoke of the night's fires drifted into the fog, mingling to make it thicker. Nenet stood before the remains of her own fire, holding a rag to a cut on her cheek. Her eyes blazed.

The woman who held the Steelman's spear stepped up to Atsu, taking Miki's other arm, not being careful with the scar tissue. The remaining finger and thumb throbbed as the woman pinched her hand.

"Ouch! Hey—" She cut off in a groan.

Atsu's fingers tightened around her wrist, but his eyes would not meet hers.

She couldn't Manipulate. Atsu couldn't help. Eshaq had come for her.

He stepped away from Nenet, a sneer on his face.

"Be thinkin' I would be forgettin' 'bout ye?"

Heat threatened in Miki's gut, but just barely.

"Well, that be one mistake ye willna live to regret." He jerked his head to Ata standing behind him. "Keep close, I do no' want her trying to wiggle her way out o' this. Let's be goin'.."

With a jerk, Atsu and the woman shoved her forward. Miki stumbled to the ground, pulling the woman with her. Atsu's fingers slipped away, leaving only the fiery pain in her mutilated hand. Miki jerked out of the woman's grasp and rolled to the left.

"Stop her! Grab her, Atsu!"

Rocks bit into her skin through the furs and cut along her bare hands. Ash clogged her nostrils. The cooking fire. She shot up. Atsu made for her. No sign of help. But then he had already told her he wouldn't be able to help.

She dodged as he came at her, sprinting behind Nenet's lean-two just as Moises poked his head out. Her foot caught him in the jaw and he fell back inside with a cry. Miki dove headfirst to the ground.

"Ata! Be grabbin' tha' wretch!"

Grass wedging between her fingers, Miki pushed off the ground and spun to the right. Atsu's chest met her, firm and cold. Their eyes locked. Something sparked deep within his but then vanished. His fingers snapped around her wrists, twisting her outward and locking her within his arms.

Ata and the other woman sprinted around the lean-to, knives drawn. Eshaq followed, favoring his left leg as if someone had given it a well-aimed kick.

"Cleopetra, be stayin' wi' Nenet and the boy. They be under arrest until further notice."

The woman hefted her spear in salute and vanished around the lean-to.

"Come on. Let's be finishin' this one. She be making me tired." He sighed and nodded at Ata.

She produced a thin strip of cloth and in one quick movement, secured it around Miki's eyes. Darkness took over, leaving only vague shapes in her vision, and Atsu's heartbeat behind hers, his arms still pressing her against his chest. But then his grip lessened, taking away his heartbeat. Cold hands secured her own behind her back. If only she could speak with Atsu.

Someone shoved her in the back, forcing her to stumble forward.

"Move," Atsu croaked.

The sound brought a ball of heat back to her gut.

No. She couldn't Manipulate. The heat diminished at the thought but remained a slip of power within her, waiting. The hand shoved her again. She tried to suppress the rest of the power, but the final shred stayed put, glowing in the far off reaches of her gut.

Someone gripped her elbow, steering her forward. Wind cut into her cheeks, cold and unforgiving.

"Let's be gettin' this over wi'." Eshaq said from behind.

Any hope of speaking with Atsu slipped away. He was right. He had to do it. She wasn't in control enough yet to Manipulate her way out. And if she tried, he would have to stop her.

The slip of heat doubled at the thought, as if willing her to try.

"No," she mumbled.

The grip on her elbow tightened as they continued marching. Rocks caught under her feet, but the hands on her elbows held her upright for the most part. Miki jerked her arm as the pressure doubled to the painful point, but she held back any protest. The twins' breaths rattled in her ears. On the left, the breath was steady and warm as it wafted across her cheek. The right came steady at first but five or ten minutes into the journey several short-clipped breaths intermingled with the rest. A low cough in the back of a throat.

Atsu.

Was he trying to see a way—Miki cut the thought off. The heat in her chest flickered, threatening to grow larger, to force her to Manipulate.

"No," she muttered.

Atsu's fingers gave a squeeze.

A smile might have crept to her face if not for the circumstances. The fire smoldered back down.

The vague outline of the landscape remained unchanged through the blindfold. Eshaq's crooked form strode before her, never slowing. Twice he increased the pace until they were near jogging. They marched for at least two hours. The air was thick with moisture. Fog and sea. They were close.

The heat of the power in her gut remained kindled. Atsu's warning rang clear as if he'd spoken it again, instead of pinching her arm and escorting her to her punishment. *Do not Manipulate if anyone comes to get you. No matter what.*

A hand shoved into her back, thrusting all air from her lungs. She stumbled forward, feet tangling blindly beneath her. Hands out, rough rock scraped her bare skin. No sand shifted as she struggled to right herself, no shrubs crunched. Where were they?

"Be gettin' the chains." Eshaq's voice broke over the relentless pounding of the waves.

"Here?" Ata's voice was subdued, as close to worried as Miki had ever heard it. Footfalls past her head accompanied the words. "You don't want us to take her to the Hanging Rock?"

"No. It be too far today. I canna spare ye to be gone another seven hours and I be needin' to see this done with my own eyes. I be wantin' to watch Lukmon's killer drown."

Drown. The word washed over Miki like water on the verge of freezing. Cold to the point of painful. But beneath the ice, the heat in her gut burned.

A hand gripped her shoulder, fingers digging beneath her collar bone.

"Up," Atsu croaked.

Her knees obliged even as her fingers burst into a spasm of tingles. The power was breaking free. It wouldn't be much longer.

"We haven't—" Ata cut off, clearing her throat in uncertainty. When she tried again, her voice was still quiet, but stronger. "We haven't used this rock for years. Are you sure the chains are still here?" The power threatening to surge through Miki could be distorting things, but did Ata sound hopeful?

"Ye mean we havena used it since tha' filthy Third be tryin' to take my power?" Eshaq's heavy footfalls thudded closer. "This be fitting, do no' ye think? That we be drownin' this Third where the other died?"

The cloth flew off Miki's eyes, the hazy fog blindingly bright. She blinked it back, but Eshaq leaned in, his nose within inches of hers. Sweat stood along his brow from the hike and a drop slid off the end of his bulbous nose.

"Didna be thinkin' I knew, did ye? Didna be thinkin' I could feel yer feeble attempts to Manipulate?" His cracked lips peeled apart to reveal browned teeth.

The fire in her gut sputtered out. That question, more than the concern for herself, brought words to her throat.

"I'm not a Third."

"Perhaps no'. But ye be havin' the attitude o' one. We're goin' to wash tha' out o' ye." He stepped back, only open air and ocean behind him. The massive boulder, or the island itself, jutted out over the churning water. Shrub-covered ground lay at least a hundred yards behind. Too far to run.

As if guessing her thought, Ata pulled her up.

"It's too late for that." She wouldn't meet Miki's gaze.

Atsu's head rose from a crevice in the great rock, something clinking beneath him. Chains, as thick as his arms. With one heave, the chains crashed to the boulder top and Atsu jumped up behind them. His lips moved soundlessly as he worked to untangle the chains.

"Be gettin' her over there. I want this done wi'." Eshaq marched to Atsu and reached for the closest chain. He frowned. "Did we ever cut tha' bastard down?"

Atsu's hands stilled. He glanced at his sister, whose face had gone grey. The veins of her neck throbbed beneath the skin. Atsu looked back to his still hands and shook his head.

"Huh. I be thinkin' there would still be a part o' him still hanging from these." Eshaq shrugged and dropped the chain back to the rock.

"The fish," Atsu croaked as he handed Eshaq the rest of the chains, but he avoided the other's eyes.

"Guess they will be havin' less of a meal wi' this one than they did with him. Ata, be gettin' her over here."

If Eshaq knew of her power, then perhaps he was hiding the extent of his. Any hope of Manipulating before the chains hit her wrists fled. Atsu was too focused on the chains. Her chains. Her death.

"Please, don't do this." The whisper came before she could stop it.

"Sorry, gonna be doin' it." Eshaq held the chain up as Ata shoved her forward.

"No, no, stop! Atsu!"

He stiffened at the call, the chains settling onto the boulder. A muscle throbbed from his temple all the way to his exposed left hand. For a moment, the breath hinged in Miki's throat. He would do it, Manipulate and save her.

Eshaq's rumble of laughter broke the moment.

"Ha! He willna be helpin' ye, wretch!"

Ata shoved Miki's wrists out and Eshaq clamped the open ends of the chain around them. They clanged into place, cold iron on her skin driving a shiver of fear down her back. It couldn't end this way. Never getting back to El-Pelusium, never finding her father. Never seeing the Seconds left free to live unbanished or the babies left to be born.

"No!" She yanked away, but the chains came with her. The weight pulled them down and she slumped at Eshaq's feet. His stench pressed down around her as he reached down for the end of the chain.

A wave roared in the crevice Atsu had climbed up, spraying the top of the rock. Miki struggled backward, every tendon pulling away from Eshaq and the sea, but her bare toes found only wet, slick rock. Her feet slipped out. Stone cracked under her back. White hot pain flared along her spine, filling her vision with speckles of light.

Then someone was dragging her. Air whooshed past her ears and she was weightless. A snap, followed by more searing pain, and the chains bit into her wrists as her feet dangled free beneath her.

The speckles of light cleared in time for a wave to rise and smash into her face. The chain held her in place, but the water shuttered up her nose and throat. Sputtering, she kicked, trying to find solid rock to pull up on to.

The wave receded back into the cove where she hung. Sharp and unforgiving rock rose six feet on each side. The jutting rock where the chain hung stuck out a good four feet. The rock wall was too far to reach.

"Be tellin' the other Third hello," Eshaq chuckled darkly from above.

She craned her neck against the pain shooting down from her wrists. Two faces stood out against the sky. Eshaq's, split by a grin. Ata's, somber and still. With one last chuckle, Eshaq turned away. Ata stared for another minute. Her lips parted as if to say something or apologize, but then her head disappeared as well. There was no sign of Atsu.

Then there was nothing but the pain and the thundering of the water two feet below.

CHAPTER 31

The halls were colder, their deep moisture sinking into Ptolema's skin as it never had before. She tugged the over-toga closer about her shoulders, the fine golden fringes slipping through her fingers like the softest coconut cream. If there was ever a moment to wear the extravagant throw, it was now. The Council must see her as the High One, not just a twenty-two-year-old with only three months of experience. Radames needed to see that as well. He had been helpful, but his time was past.

The doors to the Council Hall brimmed with Council members in their finest. So they knew this was momentous also? Good. All the easier if they could accept the change she was bringing. A man in a purple embroidered toga moved away from the crowd, headdress swaying as he dipped her a bow. Montu spared her no extra deference, and a small smile played on his lips.

"High One."

"Councilman Montu, is everyone here?"

"Yes, apart from Radames."

Ptolema stopped and beckoned him closer, away from listening ears. Montu's eyebrows rose in inquiry, and he stepped so close the smell of lavender rolled off him in waves.

"Radames was not invited to this Council meeting. We will not wait for him."

Montu's left eyelid twitched. Twice. The smile returned to his face.

"Why would we not want the High Advisor to be present?" The smile grew too knowing. "This meeting has been the topic of the Pyramid for the past three days."

"But it is no longer time for advice. A decision has been made." The silk of the throw smoothed flat in her palm.

Montu dipped another false bow.

"Of course. Although—" he glanced into the crowded room behind him and pursed his lips before turning back, "I hear Edrice refused an offer to distract Radames from showing up."

Top teeth ground into bottom but Ptolema said only, "How peculiar."

"Indeed. I don't see why anyone would want to bribe the High Advisor to be absent. If a decision has been made, then it will really be quite the boring affair, wouldn't you say?" A glint in his eye betrayed his underlying meaning.

"I am not sure boring is the right word. Please call the other Council members to order. I shall—" A draft of cold air swept up her toga, prickling her legs with goosebumps. No door stood open, and even if it did, it was a balmy evening. Not a lick of wind or weather colder than midsummer should have been present.

"High One?" Montu's voice broke through the wind.

"Did you feel that?"

"What?"

"It was so cold—" With a prickle of skin, the air slipped around her ankles again. "There! Feel it?"

"High One, are you sure you want to do this meeting now? You do not seem to be yourself." Montu's concern, although mostly feigned, brought a new twitch to his eyelid.

"No, we do it now. Call the Council members." She stepped away without another word to end the conversation, leaving the Councilman with his jaw cocked open. A vague scent of rust stung her nostrils. The door to the side room of the Council Hall stood ajar just an inch. It creaked on its hinges as it swayed in a draft. Heart thudding in her ears, she stepped toward it, knuckles scraping across the polished wood.

The door opened to an empty room. Weeks ago, Miki of Bast stood where the stones were now bare, declaring she was innocent. Bile rose in Ptolema's throat. She would fix it, no matter what needed to be done.

"I'm so sorry, Tiye." Her words echoed against the stone, mocking her. Was she sorry enough to bring her back?

She glanced to the door leading into the Council Hall and inhaled. The air hit her lungs like daggers of ice. She staggered backward, a hand to her chest. The rust scent doubled, working against her lungs.

Spinning, she took the room in again. Brown stone on more brown stone. Nothing else out of the ordinary. She gasped for another breath of the icy air, only to choke on it.

The door to the hall creaked open behind her. She turned, and the headdress slipped in her haste. It landed on the flag stones with a soft *whoosh* and rolled to the door. Open, but empty.

She stepped forward to retrieve the headdress, its feathers already dusted with dirt. She would have to brush it off. There was no time to return to her chambers.

Something flashed at the edge of her vision. Black against brown.

Crack.

Pain flared in her head. She spun at her assailant, but the world faded away, the stones rushing up to meet her.

Crackling filled her ears. Snapping, popping, followed by a burst. Blood pounded through the sounds, her head throbbing with pain. Her face warmed. Someone was watching. Ptolema's skin tickled under their gaze, but the thudding pain in her head prevented her eyes from opening. Something cool and hard registered against her back. She shifted her hips away from it, lessening the dull pain.

Voices rose in the haze of the agony in her head.

"—I am glad. I will give you a house in the Higher Pyramid. Bast's. He won't be needing it. I'm told there is a fine sky-wall."

"Thank you. You are too gracious." The second voice paused, then cut back in, lower. "What do I tell anyone wanting to look in on her?"

"She is too ill for visitors. Give her time. She may be up to making appearances on her own, once she understands."

"You are so certain she will?"

Ptolema raised a hand, the arm so heavy it was like pulling up through a vat of quicksand.

"It is the better option—" The voice cut off with a hiss of breath. "She is stirring. Go."

Feet brushed over stone and water splashed close by. She pulled her other hand up, a low groan escaping.

"Ptolema?"

That voice, why did she know it?

"Ptolema, are you all right?"

Firelight flickered against the walls of her chamber when her eyes opened. Stone was beneath her. The stone benches by her meeting fire. She sat up. Nausea rolled in her belly at the movement, and the pain in her head doubled.

"I am sorry things came to this." Radames moved away from the door, wiping wet hands on his deep blue robe.

Black on brown. The room by the Council Hall.

"You attacked me." The words scratched against her dry throat.

"As I said, I am sorry." He slid onto the bench opposite her.

"I'll have you arrested and hung for your treachery." She stood, only for her shaking legs to give way. With a plop, she landed back on the bench.

A sad smile split Radames's face.

"Should I make you some tea? It will help with the pain."

"You attacked me," she repeated, the words not connecting. "You, my High Advisor."

"The Council was concerned when you did not show up on time for the meeting, so Montu accepted the task of speaking in your place."

"What?" Her temples pulsed under her fingers as she tried to massage the pain away. "He doesn't have that authority."

"I gave it to him."

"You what—?" The words stuck in her throat.

His eyes ...

Green, so dark and deep they were jewel-toned, emeralds set in the copper of his skin. An unnatural glow suffused them, light and dark at the same time. Not human, not his usual plain green eyes. He blinked, the odd eyes only darkening further. The same chill in the air in the room by the Council Hall filled Ptolema's chambers, spiking her lungs with cold.

"I'll have you hung," she whispered.

"I'm afraid my alternative plan for the Seconds was met with such rousing applause that you will find it exceedingly hard to persuade someone to hang me."

"Alternative plan?" A gnawing suspicion replaced the nausea in her belly. "What did you have Montu announce?"

Radames picked a bowl of nuts off the bench with a scrape of wood on stone. Without offering one to her, he popped a handful into his mouth.

"Radames, tell me what Montu announced." Her voice shook.

He swallowed and set the bowl down.

"All known Seconds will be executed on sight. Anyone found to have been harboring one will be arrested. All prisoners on the island known as Thoth are to be summarily executed." His eyes glinted deep and green. A coal in the fire popped, landing on the intricate stones beyond the fire ring.

"How dare you," she breathed. "You know what I wanted."

"And I, along with a great many other people, disagreed."

"I am the High One!" She rose, legs shaking, and not just with weakness.

Radames set the bowl down.

"Are you saying you will not stand with Montu's decree?"

"Montu cannot decree anything. He is just a Councilman." Her headdress sat on the desk, speckled with dirt. She made to step toward it, but a gust of air blowing against the light breeze from the sky-wall pushed back. She staggered at the abrupt strength of it and sat down on the bench. Hard.

Another gust, and the headdress toppled from the desk, rolling toward her, toward the fire. The flames seemed to lick further out than they should have, pulling the expensive feathers and beading closer. She leaned to snatch it out of harm's way. Fire scalded her fingertips. With a cry, she jumped back. The headdress went up in a puff of acrid smoke.

"You will find the Pyramid believes you are sick, taken upon by some mysterious illness, probably brought here by a Second." Radames's eyes glowed a deeper green.

Tingles edged down Ptolema's back. There was something about those eyes ...

"What are you doing?" An answer gnawed in the back of her mind, but such a thing was impossible. He had said he couldn't.

A slow smile tugged at Radames's face.

"I think you know."

"You can Manipulate," she whispered.

Radames blinked and a slip of rope lying beside the bowl of nuts rose into the air. Ptolema bit her tongue. She would not fall prey to fear. But her fingers vibrated against her legs, pressing through the silk.

"Yes, High One, I can Manipulate."

"You lied."

"Yes." With no physical involvement from him, the strip of rope soared over the fire and slipped around her wrists.

Ptolema jumped up, but the rope was too quick. It cinched tight.

"Radames, stop this!" She tried to tug her wrists apart, but the rope only tightened.

"You are sick, Ptolema. No one will call on you, and you will not be expected at the Council Hall. I do not want to kill you, so please make this easier." Radames blinked and his eyes settled back to their ordinary green. "I really am sorry," he added, more subdued.

Ptolema hacked. Spit. The wad of saliva fell short, vanishing among the flames with a sizzle.

Radames stared at her.

"You could have helped me save this great city. You could have been the hero. I didn't want to be. I just wanted to stop the Manipulators."

"You are a Manipulator," she growled, struggling against the unnatural rope.

"The men in my village made me one." His voice lowered and something flickered in his eye. "I didn't want this curse." He closed his eyes with a sigh. "I am doing this to stop the rest of them. To stop the evil they bring. If you can understand that, I can let you free."

"Let me go. I am the High One."

He stood from the bench, sandals smacking stone.

"I still need your signature on the official decree for the Pyramid since, as you say, you are still High One." With a ruffle of paper, he pulled a document out of his robe. "All one hundred Council members signed it, including Edrice." Her name hit the air, heavy and meaningful.

He knew Ptolema had tried to use Edrice against him. He knew everything. He had taken everything. She forced herself to stand.

"I won't sign it."

"Don't make this difficult, Ptolema. I am trying to save your city."

"How dare—"

His free hand cut through the air, smacking into her cheek.

Fire erupted behind her eyes and Ptolema tripped backward. Radames caught her, the hard muscles of his arm pressing into her back.

His hot breath washed over her face. "The Council will understand you are too sick to sign. They will accept my signature as Acting High One."

She twisted in his grip, but his hands only tightened around her. In one quick movement, he stepped toward the sky-wall, depositing her on the moist stones. "I'll be back in the morning. Enjoy the view." He turned away, robes swirling.

"No! Radames, you can't do this!"

But the door snapped shut behind him as if he had not heard. Ptolema scratched against the stone of the sky-wall railing as she pulled herself back up, toga heavy with waterfall spray. She tipped toward the door and flung herself at it. The wood echoed but didn't budge.

"Radames!"

He was going to kill them all. The Seconds. Everyone on Thoth. He was going to kill Miki, if she was still alive.

CHAPTER 32

The wave crashed into Miki full force, spraying up her nostrils, into her mouth, over her head. Salt clogged her throat, her eyes. Air wouldn't come. Choking, she inhaled anyway. More water, ice cold. Then air ... fresh, sweet. Life-bringing. The wave receded, only to return within seconds.

Sputtering, Miki twisted again, flailing her legs out for a place to land among the wall of rock. Her feet found nothing. Again. The pain in her wrists dulled as the blood flowed away, leaving her arms to go numb. Pinpricks of failing nerves ran up them, like a swarm of biting flies.

The wave grew beneath her, preparing to slam into her again. There was no sign of Atsu, a rescue, or a way out. She braced for the wave, fingers clenching around the chain.

It hit her with twice as much strength as the previous waves. There was no time to close her mouth. The water shot up her nose. Searing pain exploded into her lungs. She twisted away from the wave, but it was too late. Gasping for air, she spit out the salt and blood from where her teeth had found her tongue.

She had to get free before another wave came and slammed her head into the stone. Her toes dangled into the cold water now. The tide was rising.

She hadn't felt the ball of heat in her gut since Eshaq snapped the chains on her wrists. But he and Atsu were gone. There was no other option. The water raged beneath her, threatening to come again. Closing out the thin sunlight and fog, the white foam around her toes, and the tingles in her arms, she searched for the power. Felt for it.

She couldn't die. There was too much to lose. Nenet and Moises, Ata and Atsu in their boat fleeing Thoth, her father a beggar until someone beat him to death.

Water slammed into her, as strong as a wall of rock. Even in the pain, she *felt* it. Ice cold tearing at her skin. Salt filling her nostrils. Tingles shooting up her arms, and then a flicker of heat in her gut.

The wave lessened and pulled away.

"I'm not going to die here," she muttered, lips swollen from the salt and pain. She wouldn't die like the Third, and Pilis, and those who came before them.

Water swelled beneath her.

"*I will not die here!*" The heat tripled, oozing between every bit of her intestines, shooting up to her rib cage.

Water. She pushed the field of heat at the ocean, willing it to still. The wave swirling around her toes hesitated, and she was unsure if it would comply. But then the wave didn't matter. The chain was a death sentence alone.

Air.

It blew cool and warm at the same time against the skin of her raw wrists. The air was free, as she needed to be.

The wave surged, ignoring her suggestion for it to pull away. She shut it from her sight as her fingers clenched around the cold chain, the curve of metal too large to fit securely in one palm.

Buzzing filled her ears, too intense to be just from nerves. The wave washed over her. It didn't slam, it didn't roar. It splashed, as if laying itself over her like a blanket. Her eyes flicked open.

The water at her feet still churned madly.

Exaltation, a feeling long forgotten, surged up through her ribs and into her chest. Heat rolled off her, steaming the cove with a sudden humidity. Warm air. Icy water at her toes. The prickles of moisture in the air.

She felt it all. Felt everything.

It all snapped into sharp focus. The beady green moss on the side of the rock. A water spider sprinting his way up a crack to escape the next wave. A mound of seaweed trapped in the far corner of the cove, brown and green strands clinging to the rock. The sun far above, veiled by a layer of mist. The rays of its light joined with the glow of power in her chest, doubling it.

"I feel it," she murmured. The words cut through the churning of the water and the stillness of the rock. In the time she drew air into her lungs, everything was calm.

She exhaled, forcing the air at her wrists to strangle the chain. It creaked, breaking the silence. Pressing harder, the chain groaned under the pressure of the air, and snapped.

She plunged into the water. Shards of ice stabbed at her head. Pain, cold. Things to feel, things to fight back with. Salt hit her tongue, sharp, astringent. She could do this.

Fresh air and the thin sunlight hit her cheeks, forcing her eyes open as she came back up, sputtering. The chains clanked against each other five feet above, the links which had held her hands missing. Cut off with air.

The jubilant cry died halfway out of her mouth. A wave battered into her. Hard stone met her back, pain snapping up her spine. A crack echoed under the water, a muted *thump*. She inhaled on instinct and water rushed in, filling her lungs with fire.

Air was above her. Groping at the rock, her fingers slipped into a crack and she pulled up even as her body convulsed against the pain in her lungs and the salt in her throat.

Air above, water beneath. Earth around.

"Fire within," she gasped, pulling up on another rock ledge. Her maimed hand slipped against the slime covered stone.

Air above, water beneath. Earth around and fire within.

Heat exploded at her fingertips. Sparks shot against the rock she barely held onto. The rock rippled and shook, groaning under the power. An echoing moan filled the cove, breaking free from deep within the rock itself.

Ringing filled Miki's ears, and she shook her head to clear it. It magnified ten times. The rock at her fingertips glowed red, hotter than lava. It moved, groaning louder. With a rush of air and increase of heat, the rock popped. Exploded.

She fell back into the water in a shower of earth and stone. This time it pushed back. The foam of the wave settled around her rear end, lifting her higher, back to the hole she had made in the rock wall.

In one burst of energy, the wave dumped her into the hole, her head narrowly missing the jutting broken bits of rock surrounding the entrance. The water receded, resuming its beating against the stone below.

Her breath echoed in the small makeshift cave. Her heat was gone but she had used it! A giggle of relief echoed against the cool rock. Her fingers steamed as she scrambled backward just in time for another wave to fill the entrance of the hole. There was only time to suck in half a breath of air before it vanished. The water rushed at her. Limbs flailing in the darkness. Her elbow cracked against stone.

Darkness and water rushed past, shoving her further into the rock, further into the ground. The entrance blinked out, the water plunging her into black. Panic rose in her chest where the heat once was, threatening to loosen the little breath she had left.

With one last shove, the water deposited her in an open chamber. Knees cracking against stone, Miki hit the ground and rolled. Stone bit her with the force of a battering ram. Breath gone from her lungs, she splayed flat on the cool ground, gasping.

The sound of it echoed back to her. More cave, more rock walls. Tunnels spread out from the one the water had pushed her through. Was all of Thoth like this? Did Eshaq know? What seemed more likely was that Atsu and Ata knew.

Atsu. Miki sat, clutching at her burning chest. The burning morphed into an ache.

Shoving it off, she half stood, crouching so as to not bash her head into the stone ceiling. Light filtered into the tunnel from the right side. Perhaps that would be her way out. She moved forward, careful not to straighten up. Cold stone met her fingers as she ran them along the wall. She turned right, toward the light. Her foot caught on something in the path. Muttering a curse, she dropped to the floor.

Whatever she had tripped on clattered as her weight shifted against it. Loose rock, probably. The faint light spread across the ground as Miki scooted to the side, revealing a golden brown wooden box.

Not something which should have been in a tunnel on Thoth.

She slid the lid off with ease. Two rectangle slabs of stone sat inside. Tablets. Ancient ones, judging by the odd writing. No language she knew. The box was large enough for a third tablet.

Too bizarre. Just like what she had just done.

Hand shaking, she traced the lines of writing on the tablets, only to pause. Carved across the top of the first one was a language she knew. The words of El-Pelusium.

Royalty Begets Truth.

What truth? The High One was the royalty. But why were only those letters readable? Why would the author bother to carve the rest of the letters in a foreign language when he clearly knew the Pyramid's tongue?

She pulled her hand away, the questions too much, only to choke on her next inhale.

There *were* tablets meant for the High One's eyes that had gone missing three hundred years ago. But why would the lost Tablets of History be in a tunnel on Thoth?

"Oh," she breathed, extending a hand back to the tablets.

Someone who didn't want the royalty knowing the history. Someone who wanted Seconds persecuted. The revelation rang unspoken around her, the air of the tunnel vibrating with it. The fingers of her good hand traced the words she knew again. Deep, but weathered by time. Chips out of the stone decorated the edges. They were older than she and maybe even older than any living person.

"Ptolema has to see these," Miki muttered. No matter how they'd ended up here, Ptolema was the one person who needed them most.

The lid clunked back into place beneath her fingers. The box was heavy, but still manageable. She shrugged off the soaked fur coat and nestled the box into the sopping fibers, then tied the sleeves tight across the bundle. Slipping her arm through the knot, she swung the makeshift bag up onto her back. The tablets didn't clank together. Safe.

Eshaq hadn't killed her. She now knew the extent of her power. She knew how to control it. Eshaq had to be stopped. The persecution had to be stopped. Maybe getting the tablets to Ptolema was a long shot, but she could figure that out later.

The tablets settled heavily to her right side, and she crouched forward toward the light. Perhaps whoever hid the tablets came through this way, as they couldn't have come through the way she had.

The tunnel widened, giving off speckled light. The earth sloped upward and her fingers dug into the soft dirt to pull her up as the stone receded. A breeze hit her cheeks, cool and fresh. The light shifted, leafy shadows splaying across the tunnel. She brushed the tangled vine aside and stepped into the pale late afternoon sunlight. A beach stretched before her, the smoothest, lightest sand on all of Thoth.

The lost Tablets of History, if indeed these were what they were, pulled her forward. Atsu had promised her a boat, and it was time to hold him to his word.

CHAPTER 33

She found him less than an hour later, sitting on the beach, staring out into the waves as if it was just another day, another girl drowned.

The box with the tablets thudded to the sand.

He hadn't been able to help her because Eshaq was there. Or that was what he claimed. Heat flared into her gut, the wind warming in an instant.

Atsu's back went rigid.

She made her move before he could. A rock the size of the tablets at her feet jumped into the air, something she wouldn't have been able to Manipulate even a day ago. It soared toward his head.

Atsu sprung to his feet. He spun in time to dodge the rock, but only just. With a hiss, a hand flew to his cheek. When he pulled it back … red, and the sheen of moisture.

Tears?

Miki's anger faltered.

Atsu's eyes met hers and his jaw hinged open in disbelief. Sand sprayed as he darted toward her. He stopped a foot away, eyes gleaming.

"Yeh be alive," he choked.

"Yes." The earlier urge to be furious at him, to want to crush a rock into his skull still surged through her, but something else intertwined with it, staying the rocks in the sand beside them. She fought it back, struggling to maintain hold on the anger.

"You—" She stepped closer, the sand pressing beneath her bare toes. "—you left me to die."

Atsu shuddered at the last word. The sun beat off a slip of fog for once, its light glinting off the tear lines on his cheek.

"No, I be coming to get yeh."

"When?" she challenged.

"I couldna be going' right away. I be waitin' for Eshaq to get far enough away. By the time I circled back around, yeh were gone. I be thinkin' a wave ripped yeh out o' the chains." A hand to his throat, he massaged it, swallowing as if he'd rather never speak such long sentences again.

"You circled back?" The question brought something apart from anger to life, flaring among the ashes of her ire. Miki clenched her fingers to hold it at bay. Even so, her breath quickened.

Atsu stepped closer, his breath mingling with hers in the seaside air. She glared at him.

"You could have shown up sooner—"

"I be glad yeh be no' dead, Miki."

The rest of her intended rebuke faltered in her mouth.

Miki. Her true name. No false title. She swallowed, the act almost impossible with the lump clogging her throat.

"You've never called me that."

He squinted against the setting sun at her back and his left hand raised as if to touch her cheek, but drew back at the last moment.

"It be a—" he cut off and blinked, "name." It was clear in the twitching of his eyelid that wasn't what he meant to say. His eyes flashed to deep blue, and the air shivered as his power flooded out of him.

The heat still burned in Miki's chest and gut. What did she need it for? To hurt him for almost killing her? A laugh caught in the back of her throat. She couldn't do that. Not now, maybe never. Besides, she would never find the boat without him.

A sharp shock flared at the fingertips of her good hand. Atsu's hovered less than an inch away. His power licked at hers, the air static with the effect of it. Of both of theirs. He didn't stop staring, his hands inches away.

"Were you crying over me, Atsu of Thoth?" The power at her fingertips flickered, but didn't go out.

"Thoth lost a light," he mumbled, accent lessening under the influence of his power.

"What?"

"If yeh were dead, Thoth lost a ..." The words failed him and his hand twitched beside hers, no doubt wanting to massage his throat. He held it at bay, his neck tendons popping beneath the skin.

"Are you all right?"

Thin but warm arms pulled her close. Atsu buried his face in her neck, despite the few inches of height difference. Warmth radiated off him in waves. Miki stiffened, stomach flipping, limbs tingling.

Atsu's fingers pressed against her back as his lips hovered by her ear.

"Miki."

There was only warmth, the beating of his heart through his leather jerkin, and the beating of hers answering back.

And the power pulsing through the air around them.

She pulled away even as her fingers clenched, wanting to hold on to him just a bit longer. "Atsu—"

"I be sorry," he muttered hurriedly, face tinged with pink. The mad dog of Eshaq was blushing.

"No, it's all right." She almost reached for him again, but his next question stopped her.

"How did yeh escape?" He stepped back, as if suddenly aware of the proximity. "Oh." His eyes widened. "Oh, Miki, yeh be Manipulatin'!"

"Yes."

He grabbed her shoulders but didn't pull her back into the embrace.

"The Third couldna be doin' it."

"I'm not a Third. But anyway, Eshaq knows about me now."

Atsu shook his head. "He only be thinkin' he does, and he be thinkin' yeh are dead."

"Will that be enough?"

He nodded, pulling his hands away from her shoulders, taking the energy and warmth with them. Her hands flew up to catch them back before she could stop them, and Atsu started as they made contact.

"I've—" No. The adrenaline of the past few hours was clogging her mind. This wasn't about electric energy and the mismatched pattering of her heart. She cleared her throat.

"I've got something you should see." She crouched down beside the makeshift bag with the Tablets and pulled the box out. "I found this in a tunnel where the waves pushed me."

Atsu's silence settled over her. Stiff muscles under stiff leather.

"Atsu?"

"What be in the box?" he croaked.

She shifted the lid, revealing the gray edges of the tablets. *Royalty Begets Truth* stood out on the topmost one.

"Tablets. I think they may have been hidden here to hide the truth. Atsu, I think they are the lost Tablets of History! I think someone put them there to hide the truth."

He coughed, muscles tightening further.

"No one be hiding them there to hide the truth."

"What? How do you know?"

"Because Ata and I be puttin' them there."

"What?" She stood, sand cascading off her pants. "*You* stole the Tablets of History?"

A quiet chuckle built in the back of Atsu's throat.

"No." The chuckle grew into a round of laughter. He titled his head back and laughed to the sky.

"Atsu? What in the name of all things good and right is going on?" She shoved his shoulder with her fist, the energy snapping from him to her.

The blue in his eyes deepened further, and the box rose into the air beside them. The topmost tablet floated out and Atsu studied it, the smile still on his face.

"Curious."

"What is?" Miki held the annoyance out of her voice.

"Curious that yeh should find these now, when I just aided in trying to kill yeh," he flinched at the admittance. "Fifteen years after I forgot where I be putting them."

"Forgot where you put them?" Maybe he was mad after all.

Atsu nodded, and the tablet settled back into the box.

"When Ata and I be children, around the time we discovered Manipulation, we be determined to be the greatest scavengers of all time." He spoke without hesitation, without gripping his throat. "One day we be digging on the Western coast, Manipulating bits of sand to see how far we could get, thinkin' maybe there would be buried treasure."

Her puzzlement must have shown because Atsu chuckled and shook his head.

"Kids be kids. Anyway, I ended up Manipulating this box out o' the ground." He let the box fall back into the sand. "There be two weird stone things inside. At the time we didn't know what tablets be. There werena any on Thoth. We didna touch them in case they be cursed."

He shook his head with a renewed laugh. "We couldna read them anyway. At tha' age we couldna be readin' any language."

Miki pulled a tablet out and held it up to him.

"It's not a language I know, either."

He squinted and shrugged, only to pause mid-shrug, eyes widening.

"There's another one, Miki the Fifth."

The use of the title and her new name brought a shiver to her spine. It never had when he'd used it before. "What?"

"We be finding it in the Loot Tent. It looks like these. It could be another—" he cut off, doubling up in a coughing fit, the mass of words finally catching up to him.

The tablets clanked against one another and the lid of the box settled back into place. Miki retied the fur and slung it over her shoulder.

"Take me to it, then take me to your boat. We've got to get these back to Ptolema—back to the High One."

Atsu found his breath and straightened.

"Yeh mean, be goin' to El-Pel?" His eyes were no longer the deep blue of manipulation, but clear and narrowed in something almost recognizable as fear.

But Atsu feared nothing.

"Well, you could stay, but I have to go." The words left a hollow pit in her stomach.

His eyes stayed narrowed as if considering the same question.

"Ata be needin' to know." He turned and moved up the beach without another look to the box of tablets or Miki.

At the edge of camp, Atsu slowed, the farthest reaches of smoke swirling about his head. The earthy scent of roasted meat and boiled vegetables mingled with it, tightening Miki's stomach. She hadn't eaten for almost twenty-four hours, but there wasn't time. Eshaq would feel her presence.

"He be knowin' sooner this time, now tha' yeh be findin' yer power," Atsu said without turning back to her. His dreadlocks swayed as he surveyed the camp, no doubt looking for Eshaq.

"Where is the boat?"

"Hidden."

"Where?" She caught up to him, adjusting the tablets on her shoulder. Her muscles ached from the solid weight of them.

Atsu veered to the right of the camp, passing around the back sides of tents.

"Where did you get the boat?"

"Built it," he said, breathless.

"Will it float?"

He gave a sharp nod and picked his pace up again.

A tent flashed between the others, an array of colorful dyed animal skins leaning against another. Nenet. Feet tangling under her, Miki jolted to a halt.

"What about Eshaq?"

Atsu did not respond, but stopped to face her.

"Our deal was I help you get off the island, you bring me along. But I don't want to leave Nenet and Moises to suffer under Eshaq." According to Ata, fighting Eshaq was not an option for Atsu. But to free Nenet and Moises ...

Atsu's face twitched. "It be better if he doesna know what we be up to."

"What are we up to?"

"Getting yeh on tha' boat." He turned away and jumped into a jog.

"What about you, Atsu? What about Eshaq?"

He didn't answer, only heading toward the northeastern edge of the camp.

"Atsu!"

He slowed, turned around and jogged back. He extended a hand.

"Be coming, Miki the Fifth."

"I'm not leaving Nenet and Moises."

"There be—" he turned away, rubbing his head. "We be needin' to tell Ata about the tablets and be gettin' the other one."

"I'm not leaving Nenet and Moises to suffer under Eshaq." Shrubs cracked underfoot as Miki turned on her heel, a broken stick jamming into her exposed arch. With a wince, she walked toward the camp.

"Where yeh be going?"

"To get them!" She spun back to face him, heat rising to her cheeks.

Atsu shifted from one foot to the other and glanced at the colorful lean-to among the tents.

"Yeh should be bringin' them. The boy shouldna grow up here. No one should, Eshaq or no'. I'll be gettin' Ata. Meet us at the North Eastern Rocks. The boat be in a cove under them."

She turned back to the camp, only to have his voice, low and gravelly, pull her back.

"Be careful, Miki." His eyes glinted with something, but she couldn't put a name to it.

She nodded and ducked behind a tent, cutting Atsu from her sight. The electric energy between them fizzled away, but remained glowing in a ball in the back of her mind.

"Stay safe," she murmured, not even knowing what he needed to be safe from, just knowing if he wasn't safe at all costs, something would snap within her. Something she wouldn't be able to control.

"Miki?"

She started, whirling to face Nenet. The woman stood with her usual assortment of shawls draped over her shoulders and a spoon in her hand.

"What are ye doing here? Where did Eshaq take ye?"

"Where's Moises?" Miki grabbed Nenet's free hand.

"I should think playing wi' the other children down a' the beach." She quirked an eyebrow. "Why?"

"We have to get him." With a jerk, she pulled Nenet away from the lean-to. "We're leaving Thoth."

"Leaving?" Nenet pulled Miki to a stop, wrenching her hand free.

"There's a boat. We've got to go. Eshaq tried to drown me. Once he finds me here, it's over. I could kill him—" The thought tingled along her spine, bringing shivers.

Nenet took advantage of her silence.

"If Eshaq wanted ye to drown, I am glad ye did not. But this is my home, Moises's too. He has known nothing else."

"But Eshaq is a monster. You can't stay here with him."

"Ye're right. Someone has to be 'ere to stand between him and everyone else." She smiled knowingly. "I've been fine, lass, and will continue to be." Her hand shot up from her skirts, pulling Miki close. Her voice dropped to a barely audible whisper. "Promise me ye will send someone back if ye change their minds in El-Pel. This place could be different." Her fingers pinched tight.

"I promise."

"Eshaq's here," Nenet breathed.

Craning her neck to the side, Miki caught a shadow passing around a tent several lines ahead. Eshaq stepped from the other side, watery eyes taking in the camp. Searching for something, or someone. Miki's arms tingled still, hours after she escaped the drowning. She sucked in a breath, hoping to pull the power back in, to contain it, turn it off, but it remained the same. The fine dark hairs on her arms stood on end with it, waiting for it to be used.

"I knew ye could do it," Nenet whispered, drawing Miki's attention back to her.

"Do what?" The words hung in the air between them. Noses inches apart.

The skin around Nenet's eyes crinkled as she smiled. "Ye will have to come back and teach Moises. Ye were right about him, and that's how I knew about ye."

"But I—"

"Go," the older woman hissed, wrenching her hand away.

"Nenet!" Eshaq's voice boomed over the silent camp.

Miki dropped into the grass, the pointed ends jabbing into her face. The rich smell of fragrant earth and moist dirt enveloped her, piercing through the thickness in her lungs. If he found her, the power would rip out of her. Explode him, burn him. No matter what happened, he would be dead and with Nenet so near, she might be as well. That couldn't happen. Breath rising to her ears, Miki pressed closer into the grasses, praying they hid her movement as she scooted backward, hands pressing into the moist earth.

"What is it, Eshaq? I am busy making stew if ye didn't notice—"

"Quiet woman, ye be knowin' what it be as well as I. Where is she?"

"Who?"

A smack followed by a grunt.

"Do no' ye dare play me, Nenet. There be only one reason my hairs be standin' on end and my bed leg be twitchin'. Where be the girl?"

"I have a grandson, not granddaughter. Perhaps ye'll remember next time ye decide to come accost me."

A clatter of stones echoed behind Miki's feet as she shifted further back. Breath hovering in the back of her throat, her fingers froze, half into the dirt, ready to push up and run.

There were two sharp intakes of breath above her. The grass chilled her hands, fresh with an evening dew from the fog, but she couldn't wipe them on her shirt. She couldn't do anything.

"If tha' be her, and I expect it is, ye'll be payin' the price. Or tha' grandson of yers." The air stiffened with the presence of another power, the faint heat of it running along Miki's arms.

"Don't ye dare—" A pop of air cut Nenet off.

The tingle in Miki's arms shifted into a barrage of electricity. She shifted, pushing her head above the grass. Eshaq stood ten feet away, hand outstretched above Nenet, who lay on the ground, a hand to her head.

"Do no' be makin' me do tha' again, Nenet. Ye know I be respectin' ye." He stepped closer, the air still thick with his Manipulation. "Where be the girl?"

"I wouldn't tell ye even if I knew." She struggled back to her feet, shawl disheveled across her back.

The heat radiating from Eshaq flickered hotter.

"Do no' be lyin' to me. I be puttin' up with ye fer long enough." He raised both hands to the sky, his fingers channeling air that was almost visible in the lines of sweat streaming down his arms, staining his sleeves a dark grey.

Much more effort than it should have been, but still enough to harm Nenet. Miki rolled her fingers into her palms, the missing ones aching in a phantom pain. When the last nail pressed into her skin, a shock erupted. A wall of air slammed forward, knocking Eshaq to the ground beside Nenet.

Miki sprinted forward, the force of the power vibrating within her enough to propel her almost past him. Eshaq's eyes widened as she leaned over him, hands shaking in an effort to not wrap around his sweaty neck.

"I be knowin' it," he rasped. "I be knowin' ye didn't die."

"No thanks to you." The air thickened again, willing her to crush him.

"I'll make ye wish ye had, girl." His eyes glowed a dull orange, as dull as the power flickering out of him. A rock shifted by his head. One command and it would crush his skull. Eshaq's eyes narrowed as if guessing her thoughts.

"Ye canna kill me. Who will be watchin' out fer Thoth?"

"Is that what you call what you are doing?"

"Aye—" furs and leather flapping, he rolled to his feet. The rock flew for his head, but too late.

A rush of air hit Miki, but not enough to make her move. She flicked her wrist to the side, the campfire beside Nenet roaring four feet high. Eshaq started, wasting a precious second to glance behind him. She lunged. Wood cracked against the base of her skull. Pain, white hot, flared along her spine and up into her head. She hit the ground. Grass and rocks bit into her exposed skin as she rolled. The woman who often accompanied Eshaq stood above her, outlined in the fiery red of the sunset. Her spear flashed, a blur of gray and brown.

"Get her! Get the wretch!"

Miki rolled again, the spear brushing past her face to sink inches deep in the soil she had just vacated. With a grunt of frustration, the woman yanked the spear back out and tried again. Miki braced her knees against the moist earth and shot upward.

Feel, don't think.

Teeth sinking into her lip, the sharp sting of pain took away the frantic thoughts, replacing them with a rush of pain. Of fear. The heat boiled up again. A flame shot out from the fire, wrapping itself around the woman's leg. She fell to the ground, screaming a curse.

Clammy fingers slipped around Miki's throat, pinching tight.

"Ye'll be dyin' under my hand, ye wretch." Eshaq spat.

A cooking pot clanged against his head, the sound so close to Miki she staggered forward, ears ringing.

"Go, Miki!" Nenet shoved her toward the beach, toward wherever Atsu had gone.

Movement in her peripheral vision. Miki shifted in time to avoid Eshaq's guardwoman's spear again. She dropped to the ground, rolling to the left. A pair of ash-stained legs flashed by. The fire had died too soon.

Nenet's grunt of warning came too late. A fist-sized stone cracked against Miki's back, flattening her further into the grass.

"No one goes,'" Eshaq growled, the stench of him rushing over her with the tingle of his Manipulation. "Do tha' again, Nenet, and I'll be killin' yer grandson. Then I'll be hangin' ye in the sea." Weight pressed against Miki's back, firm. "I'll no' be riskin' the sea again wi' ye."

The box with the tablets dug into her side, her arm pressed fiercely against it. Where was Atsu? He couldn't leave without her power, just as he hadn't for the past two decades.

The foot pressed harder, squashing the breath from her lungs.

"Thought ye could Manipulate better than I?"

"I don't think so. I know I can. You do too." She spoke into the grass, every word an effort against the weight on her back. Her power certainly was greater, but without being able to come on command, it was almost as useless as his.

Nenet grunted above her. With a hiss, Eshaq drew away. Skin slapped skin. Nenet, if she had been slapped, said nothing. Miki stiffened in the grass, muscles poised. Her father's face hung somewhere in the void where the heat of her power boiled. With one steadying breath, she forced it out.

Air, hotter than the fire beside her, exploded upward. Eshaq's scream was proof enough. Miki shot upright as the woman with the spear stumbled in front of her, face covered in a mass of blisters. Her eyes went dark at Miki's movement and she lunged, spear tip grazing the edge of Miki's shoulder.

Ignoring the pain, Miki whirled around. Someone screamed behind her. Her feet tangling beneath her, almost threatening to trip her, she sprinted ahead, dodging between tents.

CHAPTER 34

"She be findin' them, Ata."

"I told you. I *told* you not to save her." Ata raised a finger of warning, her face tightening with the movement. She stepped away from their pile of loot, the torch in her other hand spreading a myriad of shadows across it. "You've started a full-out war now against Eshaq. I know you aren't prepared for that." Something flickered deep in her eyes, sorrow and annoyance intermingling.

"I didna. She be savin' herself. Manipulated."

"What?" The torch lowered half an inch. The stern cheek bones slackened. "What do you mean?"

"I be meanin' Manipulated. Blasted rock and chain."

"But he couldn't do it. Ren couldn't do it," she muttered, breathless.

"Aye, but Miki be a Fifth. She be crawlin' to safety and be findin' the tablets we hid as children."

Ata glanced over her shoulder to where the other tablet sat nestled at the bottom of the pile.

"She couldn't have. We forgot where we put them."

"She did. I be seein' them. They be the same."

A slight slip of wind brought a creak to the small cavern, and the boat pulled against its binding. Ata set the torch into a holder on the stern. She stooped, pulled a bundle of clothing off the deck, and turned back to her brother.

"It's all here. Two togas and belts. I even found sandals last week and managed to bring a shine into them. The ones for you might be too big, but I figure it's better than nothing."

Atsu squinted at her. She looked fine in the boiled leather, why would she spoil it by wearing the silly toga?

Her brow furrowed as she guessed his thought. "They don't wear leather in El-Pel. We have to fit in."

"Ata—" words clogged his throat. So much to make her see, but no way to say it.

She set the togas back in the boat.

"I got one for Miki as well, just in case. Does she know where we are?"

Glad for the change of topic, Atsu shook his head.

Ata cursed under her breath.

"And you just left her up there—no, it's too late," she whispered.

Tingles shot up his arms.

Someone was Manipulating, and judging by the twin pulses of heat, it wasn't just one person. Eshaq and Miki. Atsu turned and ran through the thin tunnel back to the exit. Feet thudded behind him. His fingers scraped the rocks as he climbed up the hole, ignoring the specks of blood left by his careless climb. The low sun sitting on the horizon flared into his eyes as he pulled up out of the cave.

Ata surfaced right behind him, but he didn't wait. Boots slapping rock, he sprinted down the stony coast, waves crashing to the left and grasses waving to the right. The enormous rock face hiding the camp ended abruptly, layers of tents unfolding across the plain.

"There!" Ata pulled up beside him. Movement among a scattered outcropping of tents. The heat was almost visible, thin red lines swirling through the air as if they wished to create a beacon to their Manipulations.

A body forcibly shot through the tents closest to them, tripping over its own feet and careening into the ground. The filth-encrusted shawl shifted, and Miki raised her head. Deep purple eyes sparked, relief flooding her features. Atsu stepped forward, covering the ground between them in fifty long strides, pulse hammering through his ears.

"Where's the boat?" Miki staggered to her feet. Warm skin brushed his as her fingers clamped around his arm for support.

He pulled her the rest of the way up and jerked his head back over his shoulder. "It be there. Yeh be all right?"

Her arm stayed under his fingers and her eyes met his, purple fading back to brown.

"Yes."

"Come on you two, we've got to go!" Ata moved for Miki. "Where are the Tablets?"

"I've got them—"

"Atsu! Ata! Kill her!" Eshaq's heaving bulk stood twenty feet behind Miki, just past the last tent. His face twisted into a mass of anger, the faint heat of Manipulation streaming off him like a good sweat.

Ata hissed in a breath behind Atsu.

"If we run, we will be gone before he can see we went into the cave," she muttered.

Atsu tightened his grip on Miki's arm. He couldn't let go. Not when they were so close.

"There be no time to run," he heard himself saying but he couldn't be saying it. Those words implied something far worse than running.

"Atsu! Kill her!" Eshaq stepped a foot closer as Miki pulled up to Atsu.

"We have to fight him. I'm not leaving everyone here to suffer under him." Her words were hard, determined.

Atsu's fingers slipped down her arm, settling over the mangled stump of a hand his sister had given her. Miki shuddered at the touch but said nothing. Atsu faced Eshaq. The man's eyes widened slowly, as if seeing him for the first time. His gaze settled on Atsu and Miki's locked hands and then back to the determination on their faces.

"Atsu ... what?" was all he managed.

"We be leaving."

"*We*?" Eshaq's faint strips of hair stood off his head as a rush of wind swept past them. "Atsu, that no' be funny. Ata, talk some sense into the lad!"

Ata shifted at Atsu's side, the arm brushing his tense and stiff. She said nothing.

"Kiddos, I raised ye." The words floundered in the air. Lost, confused.

"Aye," Atsu croaked, refusing to pull his hand from Miki's to massage his throat. "And now yeh'll no' stop us from goin'."

Eshaq's face tightened, the disbelief morphing into something worse. "I be yer father. Ye shallna leave!"

Atsu inhaled, the air coursing through his body like the courage he needed.

"We have to do this," Ata whispered, tensing further.

He nodded once. It was too late to pretend otherwise. Too late to hold on to a shred of fantasy that Eshaq was their father, or anything close. So why did something in his chest hurt as if he *was* betraying his father? A sidelong glance to Ata proved she felt the same. She grimaced, neck muscles so tight they could snap.

"Atsu, be killin' this wretch. She be playing with yer mind. Slit her throat and come over here." Eshaq pulled himself up as if the action might assert authority over Atsu.

A clammy finger and thumb wrapped firmer around his. Atsu cleared his throat and gave the fingers a small squeeze in response. Miki's grip relaxed. He found Eshaq's eyes, red, wide, and angry.

"I be sorry." The words just rose above the wind and the distant waves.

Eshaq's eyes widened further.

A roaring pulse of heat swept from his body as he opened himself to Manipulation. Miki's grip on his hand slackened, and she stepped away, mouth formed into a small O of surprise.

Ata fell back as well, not bothering to bring her limited power into it. Judging by the rapidly whitening face of Eshaq, Atsu's power was enough.

"Ye?" the man gasped.

"Me," Atsu whispered. Whatever heat the other man might be feeling, it was cool relief to Atsu. A lifetime of secrets released. The faint taste of mint tickled his tongue. Yes, earth would do. His eyes flicked shut. He didn't want to see. He didn't need to.

Miki inhaled sharply behind him. Ata said nothing. She had seen the like before. Eshaq grunted, cursing the grasses rising at his feet, slithering around his legs, fighting to constrain him.

Atsu's eyes opened despite his effort to keep them shut as a strangled cry left Eshaq. He lay on the ground, wrapped in a tight cocoon of grass, twenty times longer than they should have been, driven out of the ground by Atsu's Manipulation. Only his foster father's eyes showed through the rings of grass, with the end of his red splotchy nose poking through.

"He will get out of that. You've got to do more," Miki urged.

Ata didn't nod in agreement or curse in disagreement.

Cleopetra, spear held aloft, stepped around the tent. Her jaw tightened, jutting through her yellowish skin. She moved, but a slew of pebbles bombarded her before she finished the step. Hands over her head in useless protection, she dropped to the ground, screaming.

With Atsu's attention on Cleopetra and off the tangle of grasses, Eshaq shook himself free and bounded to his feet.

"I be guttin' ye for this, Atsu!"

"Atsu, stop playing around. We need to go!" Steel glinted as Ata drew her knife.

His fingertips tingling, Atsu let loose another spray of rocks, this time including ones larger than Eshaq's head. The man threw his arm up, a stone half the size flying to protect him. It cracked against the others, breaking apart and thudding to the ground. Eshaq grunted as the rocks struck him in the abdomen.

Cleopetra jumped up and fire took her in the face, her screams dying before they began.

"I be sorry," Atsu muttered, looking away.

Gripping Miki's hand again, he turned away. What he had done needed to be enough. Ata shoved past him, the knife in her fist.

"Ata—"

"He did this to us. He made us mad. He killed Ren—" The rest of her words were lost as she flew at Eshaq, ramming one foot into his chest.

"Ata, I be beggin' ye—" But Atsu couldn't finish. His nails bit into Miki's palm.

"Ata, daughter, please," Eshaq wheezed.

"I am *not* your daughter." The knife sank into Eshaq's chest. He grunted, eyes wide, bright crimson spurting onto the grass beneath him.

Atsu flinched as the knife withdrew, but he could not take his eyes off Eshaq. Another father gone to join the one who'd abandoned him years ago.

"Come on." Miki tugged him away, a gentle but persistent urging.

Ata stepped away from the corpse as a shout rose among the tents, echoed by others.

Thoth was theirs.

Turning on his heel as Ata caught up with him, Atsu sprinted back to the cave entrance, Miki in tow. The shouts followed them but didn't grow any closer. Atsu's breath rattled in his ears.

Eshaq was dead.

Ata had killed him, after he had spent years begging her not to. But Eshaq had tried to kill Miki and made Atsu help. And Ata ... the Third had been her Miki. He couldn't fault her fury.

The sharp scent of sea spray tore through the evening. The rocks rose beneath him. Everything was happening too fast, but there was nothing for it. He slid through the cave opening and thudded to the stone beneath. Ata and Miki followed. Miki said nothing of the cave, only following him to the loot pile and the boat. She inhaled at the gleaming pile and made for the tablet without hesitation.

"Everything we need is on the boat. We have to leave the loot here." Ata turned away from the twenty-some years' worth of scavenging. Two decades of finding the best and hoarding it for a day they would need it, even if needing it meant they left it. She swung up into the boat and moved to unwind the tie.

Miki tucked the tablet into the box, where it fit snugly as if it had always belonged there. She glanced at Atsu, a thin smile playing on her face.

"Ready?"

No. Not at all.

His fingers bit into the solid wood of the boat anyway, a splinter catching under his nail. Choking back a hiss of pain, Atsu flung himself over the side. A thud answered beside him. Miki exchanged a glance with Ata, possibly the friendliest they ever shared, if untrusting frowns were friendly.

Ata let the rope tie off fall to the bottom of the boat.

"Are you sure you two have enough power to move us past the Back Current?"

He wasn't sure of anything, except leaving Thoth was not a good idea. Atsu moved to the front of the boat, waving Miki to follow. The boat jerked under his feet as a slip of wind caught the sail and pulled them several feet out into the cove. Rough wood scraped across his knuckles as he lunged for the side to steady himself against the unfamiliar sensation.

A hand rested against his back, a ball of warmth to the cascading chills down his spine.

"Are you okay?" Miki asked.

A grunt was all he managed in answer. The wind doubled, ripping past his face cold and fierce. They would need their powers soon. He pulled up on the salvaged sandalwood railing and faced the looming entrance of the cove where open ocean foamed beyond.

"The Back Current will meet us in fifty yards," Ata explained before he could. "Miki, can you Manipulate through it?"

She shifted behind Atsu, boat floorboards creaking. "Yes."

Atsu straightened, raising his arm to point to the waiting sea.

"Yeh focus on the water above. I'll be takin' beneath." Fire racked his throat, and he swallowed, but the movement only brought more pain.

"Above?" Miki raised her own hands.

A rush of power filled Atsu, the pain in his throat vanishing. With an exhale, he raised his other hand.

"Aye. Be tellin' it to part." The words came easier than any all day, despite what they meant.

Miki nodded, black hair flipping about her face in the increasing wind as they sailed within a foot of the opening to the sea.

"On my count," Ata began. "Five, four, three—" The boat jolted backward ten feet as a wall of wave foam slammed into them.

"That's it," she shouted, as she struggled to catch the flying rudder steer.

"Now, Miki!" Atsu gripped the edge of the boat with one hand to save himself from flying overboard and raised the other hand higher. Cold sea spray danced along his face and arms. They were on the sea. They were fighting the Back Current. His power threatened to flicker away, but he focused on the feel of it, of the heat in his gut and the rush in his head.

The water at the bow of the boat jerked unnaturally, the foam on the tip of the latest wave swirling against the rest of the churning water as if trying to flee the opposite direction.

"Yes! Keep going!" Ata's voice rose from behind.

Miki grunted in concentration. Another peak of foam followed the first. She was doing it. Atsu closed his eyes, envisioning himself ten feet down, swimming amidst the Back Current as he had as a foolish child.

The boat jerked unceremoniously forward.

"Ha!" Ata whooped, only to be cut off as they skipped backward again, the sail tossing about madly above them.

"I can't hold this for long, Atsu! You've got to hurry!" Miki was pale, purple eyes shining against waxy skin. She shot him a strained smile. Darkness shut her out as he returned to the water, to the mammoth force of the Back Current. Wood shuddered under his feet. Wind shifted around him, tugging his dreadlocks in every direction. Tugging, biting, pulling.

A burst of heat radiated from beside him, from Miki. Ata screamed. Maybe he did as well, the sound echoing against his abused windpipes. Another savage yank from the Back Current. An answering gust from Miki, or from him. It was hard to distinguish anymore. Someone else screamed. A woman maybe, but the tone didn't match his sister or Miki. Still, it was vaguely familiar.

Kind blue eyes sparkled over a wide smile, the mouth so like Ata's. Atsu tried to pry his eyes open again, to see if she was really there, but he couldn't. The motion of the water pulled him back into his Manipulations, back into the drum of water on the wooden hull.

The woman ... why did he know her?

"Atsu! One last push!"

The early evening sky glinted overhead, only the rising moon watching their endeavor. Miki leaned against the side, teeth digging into her lip as she concentrated. Her eyes flicked to him, then back to the water.

The water.

Raising both arms above his head, Atsu screamed. Heat rippled out of him, rending the cold air. Water shifted. The boat lurched. Ata cried out, accompanied by the thunk of limbs hitting the wooden deck. Miki dropped from the side, head cracking against the boat.

Everything stilled. The water lapped happily at the base of the boat. The sail tugged in the wind. They moved forward, the Back Current behind them, trapping everyone else on Thoth as it had for the past three hundred years.

But not them. They were free.

Or doomed.

CHAPTER 35

Miles of open ocean, the grey-blue waves lapping on all sides, giving no hint to where land might be. Occasional birds dove for the water, coming back up with a fish trapped in talons or beak. If there were birds, there had to be land somewhere. A sailor in the cloth shop once said if he ever got lost, he always followed the birds. Ata agreed and had used them as guides.

But Miki's fingernails still bit into the wood railing of the boat as she pushed down the fear that they would float on, lost forever.

"This is the right way." Ata's insistence in the matter hadn't lessened in what must have been at least the last twenty hours they had been on open water. The rope of the sail creaked as she gave it a firm yank, letting loose more canvas.

"Where did you learn to sail?" Miki pulled away from the edge, rump thunking against the wooden bottom of the boat. The second trip on water did not prove to have cured the nausea swirling in her gut at the constant motion.

"Books. Scavenged one from Eshaq's pile when I was seven and found one myself on a dead man on the beach last year. Same way I learned to build this." She ran a hand over the rough olive wood, a rare smile creeping up.

"Impressive—" Hand flying to her mouth, Miki shot upward and retched over the side of the boat.

A hand pressed against the nape of her neck, cool but shaking.

"Ye be all right?" They were the first words Atsu had spoken since they'd broken through the Back Current yesterday evening, and he still managed only a little more than a whisper.

Miki closed her eyes to the water sloshing against the edge of the boat, and the nausea lessened. With a sigh, she turned around and sank to the bottom again. Atsu sat beside her, hand twitching in his lap as if he would reach out and stroke the loose strands of hair sticking to the sweat of her cheeks.

"I also read a book of stars. That one I didn't have to steal. A present on my thirteenth birthday from—" Ata stopped, knuckles white against the rope.

Atsu sat beside Miki, his knee brushing against hers.

"Ye sure yer all right?"

"I will be when we get off this cursed boat," she muttered.

"It won't be long now," Ata said. "I charted the stars last night and there is no doubt we were heading North East when the sun rose. I haven't changed my course since. These birds prove land is close. Maybe in an hour we will see it." Ata squinted into the late afternoon sun, hand over her eyes. Silence hovered for several minutes. She remained gazing into the horizon. "Do you think they are still alive?"

Atsu's hands balled into fists in his lap, and he stared at them without answering.

"Who?" The moment the word was out, Miki sucked in a breath. There was only one thing Ata could have meant.

"I'd like to think they are," Ata murmured. "They roam the Pyramid, thinking of the children they lost, wishing to have us back."

"Or they be dead." Atsu stood without warning and moved the few steps it took to get to the back of the small vessel.

"Atsu, we aren't on Thoth anymore. You don't need to be so negative." But a shadow of doubt passed over his sister's face.

Miki forced her wobbly legs out from under her and stood. The boat rocked with each step, but she made it to Atsu's side without toppling over. Breath lingering in the back of her throat, she reached for his hand. His fingers were stiff, clammy, and she yanked hers back. She could have mistaken everything between them.

The hair on the back of her neck prickled, and she turned to meet Ata's level gaze. Intense, but not threatening. She raised one warning eyebrow. *Don't hurt him, he's fragile enough,* it seemed to say. Miki pulled the left corner of her mouth up in response and stepped away. This wasn't the moment.

"He could have come with us. If things had gone differently, if we had hidden him in our cave and Eshaq hadn't come for him, he might have been on this boat with us today." Ata's voice rose just above the lapping of the waves on the hull of the boat as she leaned next to Miki at the edge. "We could have used his power to sail away then, but we weren't ready to leave."

Ata stared across the waves.

"Ren should have been able to free himself like you did, Miki. He was powerful enough. He had learned to Manipulate years before coming to Thoth as an outcast sneaking around the streets of El-Pelusium."

Atsu shifted beside Miki, wary eyes taking his sister in. "Yeh no be speakin' so much o' him since—"

"Since he died," Ata finished, reserved.

"You mean the Third?" Miki's good fingers brushed her wrist where the chains had held her in that terrible cove. The skin prickled, as if feeling the cold iron again.

"Yes. He didn't deserve to die like that." Ata's hands balled at her side. "He was a ray of light on an island full of darkness."

Thoth would be losin' a light. Atsu's words from the beach when he discovered Miki lived. A light. The Third was Ata's light. Her blue eyes were far away, full of a sadness that she couldn't wave away. Had she loved this stranger who could Manipulate as well as her brother?

"His name was Ren?"

Ata glanced up, the sorrow lifting for a moment. "That's what I called him. His full name was Beren."

Miki's heart stopped. The wind, though warmer than it had been, sliced through her shirt. The cloth snapped with a vehemence, but she stood her ground, unable to think past the name Ata had just spoken.

"Miki, what be the matter?" Atsu croaked from the side, no longer leaning over the rail.

Ata's eyes widened with realization.

"Did you know him in El-Pelusium?"

Numb fingers fumbled with her sleeves. Miki pressed her thumb to the soft flesh of her inner elbow. "Did he have a birthmark here? A chestnut shape?"

The color left Ata's face, but she nodded. "Yes, he did."

Miki's sleeve fell back into place as her hip thumped against the railing of the boat.

"Beren was my brother. Third born of Bast."

Ata took a step back, staring at Miki as if for the first time.

"He mentioned his family once," Ata said. "He said he ran away as a child because he couldn't stand hiding any longer. He never meant to leave for good, but he got lost. By the time he remembered how to get home, he didn't want to. He found a way to have a life in the shadows. He never told me his family name, and I never thought to ask. No one has family names on Thoth."

Miki rested her head against the railing. The sky above was blue with layers of white cloud. Beren had stared at this same sky on his way to Thoth.

"We waited years for him to return, but he never did. The last time I saw him, I was seven. My mother died hoping he'd made it across the sea, or at least out of the city. But I always saw the truth in my father's eyes. He thought Beren was dead." Beren had been alive the whole time. Alive, somehow learning to Manipulate, he had been banished and then murdered. The skin on Miki's wrist prickled again. He had died a terrible death, one she had almost shared in.

"Beren, I'm so sorry," she whispered.

"I loved him." Ata mumbled more to herself than anyone else. She raised her head and set a hand on Miki's shoulder, firm and warm. "I suppose that might make us sisters."

It might. Miki tried to smile back, her muscles pulling against the lead in her heart. Beren had lived. Her father needed to know. Hemeda needed to know, even if she wouldn't care.

A small wave rocked the boat.

Ata squeezed Miki's shoulder. "He was happy, you know, on Thoth. He often spoke of his time in the Pyramid before. It was a lonely place for him. Thoth was a relief ... until it wasn't anymore." A shadow of pain flickered across her face. "He said when a merchant caught him stealing and accused him of being a Second, he pled guilty on the spot. Let them cut his fingers that same moment and never even had a trial. I suppose your father would not have heard of him at all."

High One Khentimentiu must not have wanted people to panic.

"We never knew." If they had, would things have been different? More painful, but not better. She said nothing else, just stared out over the same water her brother had drowned in.

"Be that the place, Miki from El-Pelusium?" Atsu whispered. A shaking finger pointed at the horizon.

A lump rose in her throat. Where the unending water met the line of sky, there now stood another thin line in the middle with a jutting tip hovering above it.

Land, and the Pyramid. Her neck ached as she nodded.

Ata inhaled behind them. "We did it."

But there was still so much more to do. Sneaking in without being noticed. Even with the togas, the twins did not look like citizens of the Pyramid. Atsu with his dreadlocks and Ata's harsh, sun-weathered face. The wind that had warmed the farther they got from Thoth tickled Miki's mangled hand. That alone would be cause for suspicion on her part if no one recognized her. *If*. Then, if they weren't apprehended, there was still the journey to the Higher Pyramid and getting to Ptolema. Making her understand Seconds deserved life. Showing her the Tablets.

Atsu moved away from the end of the boat, head lowered to avoid any sight of the Pyramid as it grew larger on the horizon. He stooped to collect the box with the Tablets as if reading her mind.

"Yer Ptolema be knowing what to do wi' these?"

"I hope so. She is royalty."

He nodded and pulled the togas out of their bag to stuff the box in. Ata moved away from the bow of the boat and peeled her leather jerkin off. Beneath she was thin and pale, a startling contrast to the sun-tanned skin of her face. A strip of cotton secured her chest, and she left it in place as she wrapped the toga on. She grabbed one corner and slung it over her shoulder. It fell off, taking the rest of the fabric with it.

"Here." Miki gripped the toga, the silk sliding through her fingers as easily as any of the most expensive cloth at Jabarre's shop. "Wrap it all the way around your waist and then bring the two ends up one shoulder. It ties like this." Her hands fell to the task as if it had only been yesterday and not a month ago that she had tied a toga on herself.

The fabric flowed across Ata's body, accentuating the curves she hid so well under the leather. She glared down at herself but raised a finger to stroke the silk.

"Is it all this soft? I imagine it makes it hard to fight and too easy to sleep."

"Few people fight in El-Pelusium, but I suppose they do sleep more than on Thoth." Grabbing the other togas, Miki turned to Atsu. He shied away from the white fabric. "You have to wear it. It's the only way we can get into the Higher Pyramid. That is where Ptolema will be." Miki moved closer.

"This is what we've wanted for a long time, Atsu. It's okay." Ata gripped his shoulder.

"It be what yeh wanted," he muttered. "I no want it, sister." He glanced up, eyes wide. He flinched as her fingers pinched harder.

"What would you prefer? To go back to Thoth and rule in Eshaq's place? To deal with his men who are probably dumb enough to still be loyal or wish the throne for themselves? Do you want to live like a barbarian, no better than who Eshaq taught you to be?" Her eyes blazed. This was it, her goal within arm's reach.

"Yeh know tha' isna what I be wantin'!" He jerked away from her grip. "Four years we be buildin' this boat! Four years of me sayin' nothin'! But I no be wantin' this, Ata!"

She stepped back as if he had punched her, paling as much as her sun weathered skin would allow.

"But why?"

"It does no' matter, does it? Yer mind be made." Grabbing the toga, he flung it out of the boat where it ballooned with air and settled against the calm water. There was no point in telling him the cloth was worth more than the boat.

"You could have told me this years ago. This isn't my fault, Atsu." Ata came nose to nose with him, one twin staring the other down.

"Aye, I should have. I'll be helpin' right this city, but tha' be all. I willna be stayin' here." He folded his arms over his chest, leather squeaking on leather.

"But you look a fool. They will know there is something up—"

"He's a traveling shepherd. We—" no, not *we*, Miki thought, "—they see them occasionally. No one will think to be suspicious." If a man like Radames, the gnat who corrupted Ptolema's mind, was accepted so easily, why not a shy man like Atsu? Miki nodded to him encouragingly. "We can do this. It's all right."

His shoulders relaxed. "If yeh be sayin' so, I be believin' yeh."

The shape of the Pyramid jutted into the sky behind him. Hundreds of feet of city, people, and lies.

"Ata, steer us away from the main dock. We need to hide the boat somewhere to the side of the river mouth." Miki shrugged off her dirty furs and leather, leaving only the thin cotton shirt and leather pants Nenet had provided her with. Draping the toga about herself, it felt almost constricting.

Tiye. The name blinked through her mind. *You are Tiye.*

"No," she whispered.

"Miki?" Atsu's hand gripped her elbow.

"It's nothing." She cinched the toga ends tight across her left shoulder, maimed hand smarting at the effort.

Tiye—no, she was not Tiye. Putting the toga on one more time wouldn't change that. But with the Pyramid rising to her left and the faint drum of the waterfall, her heart pattered with the threat of her old anxiety attack.

The boat lurched forward, settling into the soft clay of the land.

"Is this good?" Not waiting for an answer, Ata hopped over the edge and secured the rope to a gnarled tree.

Miki nodded, but words wouldn't come past the lump of anxiety.

"You'll be okay, Miki," Atsu's words tickled her ear. "I'll no be letting them harm yeh." His hand brushed her arm, a current cutting through the fear building in her mind.

"I won't let them hurt you either," she answered.

He gazed down at her, blue eyes tight as his hand dropped to her good one. He coaxed his fingers between hers.

"This be all right?" His words barely made it over the distant roar of the falls.

"Yes," she breathed.

His fingers squeezed. "Thank yeh, Miki. For everything."

"We can do this," she murmured.

"Aye. Yeh said so already." But he didn't move away.

"Come on!" Ata's voice punctured the moment, accompanied by the crackling of brambles.

Miki jerked her eyes from Atsu. White flickered between scrubby, twisted, trees. Ata was already leaving. She couldn't get too far. She didn't know where to go.

Fingers wrapped around Miki's chin, pulling her back to face Atsu.

"This be how they be doin' it 'ere?" He leaned down, breath hot against her cheeks.

"I wouldn't know," she breathed, any anxiety evaporating into the thin pounding in her ears.

"Good." Atsu leaned the rest of the way, lips planting on hers. Warm, moist, eager.

Miki stiffened, unsure of the odd sensation of a man's lips against hers. But this wasn't just a man. This was Atsu. She leaned into him, taking the kiss in full, breathing him into her. All the air left her lungs, but it didn't matter.

There was only him on her and her on him. The fingers fell from her chin only to press against the small of her back. Then Atsu stepped back, face tinged red.

"I—" But her words wouldn't come.

A small smile pulled at Atsu's lips and he turned. He jumped off the boat. Miki stood still for a moment longer, torn between falling onto her bottom or following him.

"Come on, Miki the Fifth." The smile widened.

She pulled the bag with the tablets over her shoulder. Accepting Atsu's hand, warm in the best way, she jumped into the sand.

CHAPTER 36

Ata was waiting for them on the other side of the small thicket of trees. Her gaze shot to Atsu, then back to Miki. Was jealousy hiding in those blues? Was she thinking she should have had this same moment with Beren? She deserved it as much as they. Beren did too. But it would never happen.

The moment passed and Ata waved them over.

"Let's go."

There was no path to the city from where they stowed the boat. Miki led them through low-lying brambles that fought them every step of the way for ten minutes before they came to the outer wall. A gate sat a hundred yards farther down it. An animal gate, most likely. Grass lay trampled in all directions, the farmers having no choice but to push the animals through the thick grass to the gate. The horizon glowed the light lilac of dusk behind Miki as she slipped against the cool stones of the city.

She pressed her hands to the cold iron bars.

"It's not locked yet. We need to hurry. They could lock it at any moment."

Ata slipped up to the gate and wrenched it open with a squeal of poorly oiled hinges, but she didn't step through. "I didn't expect it to be so large," she said offhandedly.

There wasn't time to ogle. Miki pushed past, her fingers wrapped firm around Atsu's. He followed, but his hand was colder than the waters of Thoth.

"If you stick to the side roads, it doesn't seem so big."

"How could men have built this?" The gate clinked shut as Ata entered the short tunnel.

"It took many years and many deaths"—Atsu's hand shook within hers—"but it is just stone." Miki slowed as the tunnel ended, the smooth stone giving way to the Lower Pyramid and its markets.

The twins froze. Two straight backs, breaths rattling in echo of each other. Miki squeezed Atsu's hand, but he did not respond, his eyes only for the lines of people moving across the road ahead. There were dozens, so many Miki's breath clipped short. Had there always been so many people in the Pyramid? Surely it had grown since she left, or the loneliness of Thoth had made her forget.

"How do they do it?" Ata cringed.

"Do what?"

"Not kill each other?" Her knuckles curled against the stone wall at her right.

The rough laugh slipped out before Miki could stop it.

"Life here is much different. There is no need for killing."

"Unless yeh be a Second," Atsu cut in, voice thick with hidden emotion.

"Is the city safe?" Ata did not leave the shelter of the wall, her eyes tight and lines around her mouth rigid.

"Safe enough, unless they discover who we are. People here do not know what a Second really is, or what someone from Thoth may look like. Even if we are found out, they won't just kill us in the street. There are rules. Trials—" Miki cut off as a flash of teal across the street caught her eye. She moved out into the street, tugging both Atsu and Ata along with her. A toga- clad woman cursed as they cut off her path. Miki shot her a half smile of apology, but the woman was already continuing her way up the street.

Miki stopped before a merchant's stall two feet past the tunnel exit. The stall was dark, whoever owned it gone for the day. A teal feather signaling a royal decree draped from the exterior wall where a small shelf jutted from the side. A stone tablet, the words carved with little care, sat alone in the middle.

"By decree of the High One, Ptolema of Khentimentiu, all Seconds will be executed immediately. Anyone found consorting with them shall be put to death. Anyone suspected of being a Second will be put to death. All citizens are encouraged to aid in this search for Seconds. All inhabitants of the island known as Thoth are to be executed ..."

Miki stopped reading, head light. Ptolema couldn't. This wasn't the kind girl seeking truth she'd met just two months ago.

"We've got to find Ptolema. Maybe they haven't sent the executioners to Thoth yet." The desperate hopefulness of the words was almost laughable.

Neither twin laughed. Atsu ground his teeth with an audible grating before speaking.

"There be no trained Manipulators left there. They be helpless." He pulled his hand from Miki's, the clammy warmth evaporating.

The street's traffic had not slowed, but perhaps that provided more cover for them. A group of cloaked travelers hurried past the merchant stall, muttering amongst themselves.

"Because we are here, stopping it. Come on!" Miki stepped after the group, straightening her shoulders as she had when she lived in the Lower Pyramid, sending the message that she did not want to be addressed.

The twins fell in step with her, Ata beside and Atsu behind. She longed to reach for him again, but it was not the time. There was too much to do. The group they followed made an abrupt left turn, heading toward the finer markets. Her feet almost followed on instinct.

"Which way?" Ata's words overrode her thoughts.

"Straight. Follow this road until it comes to a large gate in the wall. We will go through the Inner Pyramid. Fewer people to see us in there."

"How many blasted parts are there to this city?" But Ata charged ahead, stepping around a group of giggling teenagers. They shuffled back in surprise, one glancing up as Atsu stalked past. Her eyes widened and with a thin intake of breath, she dug her bare arm into a friend's ribs. The other girl yelped and turned to curse but stopped dead at the sight of Atsu. If it wasn't the leather, then it was the dreadlocks. They swung heavily with each step, almost a physical representation of his power.

Miki glared at the girls. They turned away, giggling. Atsu had not noticed the moment, and that was probably for the best.

"There!" Miki stopped before a door three times the size of any other in the Pyramid. It still stood ajar as it was not yet dark.

"Stick to the main road inside and we will come out near the Higher Pyramid. From there getting to the top will not be difficult as long as there are no Steelmen in the way."

"What if we run into these men of steel?" Ata's muscles tightened to the breaking point.

"Some of them know me—" Miki cut off with a hiss, good hand shielding her face as she turned away.

Bare feet slapped stone. Hinges squealed. The door to the Inner Pyramid thudded closed with enough force to rattle the jars in the shop behind them.

"Go back. Each part of the Pyramid is sealed off tonight. You must remain where you are." The foremost Steelman in a group of half a dozen stepped forward, his voice cutting out into the street of curious onlookers.

A woman stepped up beside Miki, a basket clutched on her head. "I live in there. Am I not allowed to go home?"

"No. A search is being conducted for Seconds. The door will reopen in the morning."

Miki stepped back, face hidden still behind her hand. Atsu moved with her.

"What do we do now?" Ata whispered under her breath.

The crowd that had gathered for the announcement thinned away, only the woman with the basket looking up hopelessly at the massive door.

"There is another way. If we go back and turn into that tunnel," she jerked her head toward the way to Jabarre's, "there is a small door to the Inner Pyramid. Once inside, there is a trap door that will bring us to a house at the base of the Higher Pyramid."

"Won't they have that other door blocked?"

Miki nodded but pulled them closer, lowering her voice. "Yes, but not as well and you should have no trouble taking out one Steelman. It's a door for commoners and servants. No one of respect would go through without risking their reputation."

A smile flickered on Ata's face, then vanished almost as quickly.

"You are not coming?"

"I'd risk exposing us if I do. People might recognize me—"

"Be climbin' the waterfall," Atsu whispered.

"What?"

"Yeh can be doin' it. It be water, like the Back Current. Yeh can Manipulate it. Climb it and be meetin' us at the top. Didna yeh say it be startin' at the High One's room?"

"Yes, but that's hundreds of feet up."

"Atsu, that would be suicide. I thought you liked the girl."

Atsu ignored his sister. "Yeh must be choosin' now. There be no time."

The waterfall thundered overhead, only a slip of it visible from their position in the city. Miki craned her neck, taking in the powerful rush of water before it vanished behind a hundred houses and shops. Could it be climbed? A shiver wracked her body.

"This is madness. How will we know which trap door to take once we are inside the Inner Pyramid?"

"Three lefts, follow the long main road for ten minutes. Turn right. It sits at the back of a dusty alley. There are three sets of initials carved into the base of the door." Miki closed her eyes, seeing the childish markings as if she and her siblings had carved them only the day before, not more than a decade ago. "KB, BB, MB."

Her eyes opened to Atsu and Ata exchanging a look. "Whose house is it?" Ata scowled, unconvinced.

"My father's."

Ata started but Atsu turned intense deep blue eyes on Miki.

"Three lefts, be followin' the long main road, turn right until we be comin' to a dusty alley. Door be at the back."

"Yes." The warm sensation of his Manipulation power shimmered up Miki's arms, a soothing embrace. If Ata was not there, if six Steelmen did not stand twenty feet away—the kiss from the boat glowed in her mind, her breath quickening.

Atsu must have felt the same, for his eyes lowered.

"What did you Manipulate?" Ata glanced over her shoulder to the half-toga-dressed men gripping spears in their fists.

"Nothing. I be ready."

Miki drew in a deep breath of the warm, humid air, so foreign to her lungs after the time on Thoth.

"We've got to go. Miki, find a better covering for your face—"

"I'm climbing the waterfall." The words stabbed the air, hard, determined.

Ata turned toward her, eyes wide. "But you can't possibly make it!"

"I will. I have to." Miki's eyes met Atsu's.

A small smile tugged at his lips and he nodded.

"Yeh can do it."

"I know." She pointed back toward the other tunnel. "The smaller doorway is just through there. Hurry, before they decide to send more Steelmen to guard it."

Ata pressed her hand to her waist where a bulge in the toga gave away her knife. Stiff-faced, she stepped into the street. It had cleared after the news of the shutdown, leaving the way to the other market area clear. She waved for Atsu to follow before jogging to the tunnel and slipping inside.

Fingers fizzing with the power of Manipulation brushed Miki's cheek.

"Yeh be careful." Atsu stared into her eyes, as he had before the kiss, but he didn't lean toward her, didn't pull her in. "I'll be seein' yeh at the top."

She nodded again, concentrating on the sparks at his fingertips and not the waterfall roaring above them.

"Thank you."

Atsu's gaze flickered, and a smile pulled at his face again.

"No, thank yeh." He squeezed her shoulder, the heat radiating from him doubling at the impact. The blue of his eyes deepened.

"Be careful Manipulating."

"No one here be knowin' how, do they?"

"Not unless there are Seconds hiding somewhere."

"Then I be fine." His hand withdrew and his Adam's apple bobbed as he swallowed something down. He turned away, following his sister across the street and into the tunnel. The absence of his heat hit Miki like a bucket of ice water thrown from two stories up.

CHAPTER 37

Miki shivered, pulling the loose ends of the toga closer. The waterfall raged, the rhythmic pounding drawing her gaze upward. It was just like the waves in the cove where Eshaq had left her to die. White-topped walls of power, slamming into her, leaving her without breath.

Killing Beren.

Shuddering, she tore her gaze from the waterfall. There was no help stewing over it. Where was the best place to begin the climb? The waterfall vanished behind a building whose roof jutted into the evening sky. Perhaps that would aid her. She moved for it before she could change her mind. The stones were still warm beneath her bare toes. She should have told Ata only a few people wore sandals.

The Steelmen guarding the large entrance to the Inner Pyramid turned as she crossed the street, but no one called out a warning. Even in the dimming light, the newly lit torches cast an array of odd-angled shadows, aiding to hide her face. She reached the building she sought. The windows were dark. Another empty shop. Testing the strength of the sack containing the box of tablets, she smiled grimly. It would hold.

The window of the shop remained open. Someone's forgetfulness was her ally tonight. Hand against the window frame, she pulled herself inside. Rows of linen, as fine as the ones in Jabarre's shop. She leaped to the floor with only the sound of skin scraping stone.

"If you think you can steal my goods, you had better be prepared to lose a hand." A raspy voice spoke from the darkened corner. A familiar voice, even after two months. Miki jerked upright, hand flying to the bag in protection.

Jabarre stood with arms crossed over his chest, a thin sliver of gleaming metal hanging idly in one hand. He stooped and pulled a clay jar from the bench along the wall behind him and with a flick of his free wrist, lit it. The flickering lamp cast shadows as far as Miki, the faint heat of it reminding what the light exposed. She jerked her head away, but too late.

Jabarre gasped. "You—" He stepped forward, knife held aloft, the wry smile gone from his face. "Tiye?"

Clenching her teeth, Miki turned back to face him. Better to not let him know how nervous she was.

"What are you doing in this shop?"

He sucked in a breath again and stepped closer. "So it is you." His eyes widened, then narrowed. "Aren't you supposed to be on Thoth?"

"Supposed to isn't the same as being there." The heavy cloth of the bag rolled between her hands as she clenched it. There wasn't time for this.

"You escaped? How?" His gaze shifted to the window and the Steelmen beyond. He swallowed, eyes narrowing as he clearly weighed his options. The knife faltered in his grasp. He turned back to her, a congenial smile on his thin lips.

"I'll admit I was sorry when I heard what happened and even sorrier when I heard you were to be executed. But none of it makes up for the fact I had to move my shop. When word spread that a Second had been in my employ ... it nearly ruined me, Tiye." As if it was all her fault and there was nothing more at stake than his business. "Your lies cost me dearly and—" He stared. "My word! What in the name of Kemet happened to your hand?"

She jerked the mangled hand behind her back on instinct. He was stalling, he had to be. Even speaking with her meant death for him if he didn't turn her in.

"Get out of here, Jabarre. This doesn't concern you."

His eyes glowed darkly in the lamp's light.

"I'm afraid you made it my concern when you jumped through my window." Light reflected against the blade of the knife as he raised it. "There are Steelmen right outside. Come quietly and I won't use this."

"They will kill me."

The knife wavered. "For that, I am sorry. Even with your unforgivable lie, you were a wonderful worker." His eyes scanned her, from feet to eyes, slowing at her chest. He clicked his tongue and shrugged the moment off. "But you are not worth my life."

He couldn't ruin this, not when Ata and Atsu were depending on her. When all Seconds and everyone on Thoth was depending on her, even if they didn't know it. The surrounding walls held nothing with which to defend herself. The anxiety she had fought her entire life surfaced in the shaking of her hands and shallow breaths in her lungs. A ball of heat, the familiar warmth and accompanying power she was growing to love, exploded into life in her gut.

Manipulation was the only way out of this. The fire pushed harder inside of her, begging to be used. The air burned with it, the air smelling sharply of sulphur. Jabarre didn't move, didn't react. He had no clue of the power swirling within her, desperate to escape. There was no one to feel it, no one to care. So different from Thoth. No wonder the ancient High Ones feared Manipulation. They had every right to do so. Miki chuckled, only catching it at the last moment.

Jabarre scowled. "Am I to assume you won't come quietly?"

"No, not quietly," she whispered. The heat erupted out of her, catching the lamp in Jabarre's hand. Flames shot to the ceiling.

With a shriek, he dropped it. Fire erupted higher, blocking him from sight and filling the windows. The Steelmen could see the windows. Cursing herself, Miki tried to rein the power back in, to call the heat to herself. A flash of cool air cut through the flames, dimming them down.

She dropped from sight below the window. The flames grew dimmer still, revealing Jabarre's stricken face as he sat huddled against the wall, hands over his head.

Her fingernails needled into her palm as she clenched her hand. Air slammed into Jabarre, blasting him against the wall with enough force to shake the building. The remains of Miki's fire extinguished, plunging the shop into the hazy gray of late evening. Jabarre did not try to regain his footing, eyes closed and body still.

Miki's breath rattled in her chest, the only sound in the shop. No noises from outside. The scent of smoke hung in the air. She craned her neck to the window, even though her body screamed, demanding she run, abandon the mission. The Steelmen lounged against the gate, their backs to her, table standing between them. The breath loosened in her chest. They had not seen after all.

She moved for the shelves. The silk tore easily enough. She bound Jabarre's hands behind his back. For good measure and four years' worth of poor behavior, she tied a strip around his mouth. Maybe it would prevent him from calling out the moment he woke. By then she would be at the top of the waterfall.

Maybe.

A set of stairs sat at the back of the shop. If they went to the roof, her job was that much easier. The stone steps accepted her footfalls without so much as a whisper. With a shove, she pushed the door open. Warm wind brushed past her face, blowing the loose strands of hair out of her eyes.

Water rushed along the end of the building, flying from far above and disappearing into a blackened canal just past the roofline which led it outside of the city. Lights glimmered far above, dotting the line of structures along the top of the Pyramid. Ptolema's apartments. Only a few hundred feet up.

Miki's stomach dropped. How well would Manipulating work on a force like the waterfall? It had flowed for centuries, unfettered by any power, especially by a novice in Manipulation. A lump rose in her throat and she choked it back down. Somewhere beneath the tangle of houses and lines of shops, Atsu and Ata ran in the dark of the Inner Pyramid.

Forcing back a shivering breath, Miki stepped up to the water. A wall of cooler air swirled around it, both intoxicating and terrifying. She raised a hand as she had seen Atsu do on many occasions. Mist caressed her fingers. Soft, welcoming. Water spray dotted her toes, refreshing. Stones glimmered beneath the surface of the rushing water, slick with green algae. They would be slippery.

Feel. Don't think. Her other hand met the water mist, and she wiggled her fingers through it.

The mist jumped back, ready for her. The water at her toes gurgled out in concentric circles as her foot lowered onto the outermost rock. The slime shifted beneath her but did not send her flying down the waterfall. Another step proved as successful. The water shifted, making a small path for her even as the water roared above her knees on all sides. The waterfall cascaded toward her, crashing wave after crashing wave ripping down the aqueduct ancient engineers had constructed long ago.

She hesitated a moment too long. A rogue blast of water slammed into her. Miki jerked backward. Water roared around her ears and flooded her eyes. Forced its way down her throat. A rock scraped her back, pain flaring along her spine.

Another blast of water and she lost her place, falling another ten feet down. The faint sunset winked from sight as the canal began. She couldn't get trapped below the city. She had to get up!

With a rush of heat and air, the water flew away from her. The pocket of safety expanded, doubling in size to the one she had created before. Algae oozed between her fingers as she pulled herself upright, limbs shaking with the effort. The toga hung heavy, only working to trip her up. The darkness fell away behind her and Miki struggled to the top of the flat rock she had slipped off beside Jabarre's shop. She shrugged the sopping toga off. It squelched to the rock and disappeared into the rushing water. The leather from Thoth was heavy as well, but she couldn't climb naked.

Bare toes gripped the next rock, digging through the inch of slime to hold her steady. The water, so unlike Thoth, merely cooled her skin instead of freezing it. Exhilaration rippled through Miki, the fine hairs on her arms standing on end.

She was going to do this.

She had the power to do this.

Raising her arms out to both sides, she took another step. The water pushed out further from her with the movement, creating a wall reaching to her head in a circle around her. Could the inhabitants of the Pyramid see it? A laugh rolled through her belly. She didn't care. Let them see, let them marvel.

She was Manipulating the Waterfall of El-Pelusium.

She stepped forward, the water-free space moving with her. Fingers dug into the cracks between stones. She pulled, good hand over maimed hand, ignoring the treacherous algae and the water hovering just inches away. Twenty feet up. Then thirty. Pain flared through the stump end of her left hand as her remaining finger and thumb worked to compensate for the missing fingers. Muck clogged her nails as she dug them deeper into the algae, gritting her teeth against the agony. One more pull and she would be up to a large flat rock.

Seven fingers weren't nearly as good as ten, but she flung her legs out to the side. Cold stone cracked against her knees. Biting back a cry, Miki pulled up onto the ledge. She stood on shaking legs in the middle of what should have been one of the largest collision points for the waterfall. It rose directly above her, raining down on the bubble of air encapsulating her. There was nothing above her but a hundred and fifty feet of free falling water on its way down from Ptolema's apartments.

The rest of the journey should be easier. Slime covered the rock behind the waterfall as well but it was blessedly free of the forceful waves. Miki stepped out of the water, ears ringing with its force. It crashed back into place in the absence of her air bubble. The heat in her gut lightened, as if relieved it didn't have to keep the waterfall at bay any longer. Droplets misted the back of her neck as she tucked her soaked hair into a topknot. The restraint was odd after the weeks of letting it fly free.

Eyelids closed, Miki exhaled, the heat and mingling cool air of the mist surging around her.

Good. Whole.

Two arms straight up. The air pocket expanded, sending a good bit of the cascading water shooting out of the way. She couldn't be too careful. A stray bit of water could ruin the climb. The brown, shining rock shone with flecks of green and black, its own rainbow of living fungi and algae waiting to make her bad hand slip.

But what if she didn't have to climb?

"Yeh be Manipulatin' air to be Manipulatin' yerself ..."

Atsu's voice, from weeks ago, floated on the roaring water. The algae was cool at her raw fingertips, the brief climb she had already done having left its mark.

A shiver worked its way up her arms, hot and urgent. With a hiss, her arm dropped from the rock. Someone was Manipulating. The time to contemplate was over.

Stepping back, she curled her arms around her body, closing out the thunder of the falls. Closing out everything. It was time to fly.

CHAPTER 38

The pen slipped from Radames's grasp, leaving a long black smear across a list of suspected Seconds. He cursed, reaching for a rag sitting on the far end of his desk. He had imagined it, of course. The faint tingle in his arms, the heat glowing in his belly. Decades had passed since he felt them, but it still wasn't long enough to forget. He shrugged the feeling away.

He blotted the edge of the rag against the line of ink, only smearing the names further and leaving the paper smudged black.

"Curse it all," he muttered, and flung the rag to the side. A new list would have to be drawn up, and quickly. The Council expected results after his rash actions of the past week. Montu had made that much plain while they shared a toast to the solution of the Ptolema problem.

The paper crunched as he crumpled it.

"Acting High One Radames." A Steelman garbed in the vivid teal headdress normally assigned to Ptolema's personal guards stuck his thin head into the room. "Councilman Montu is here to see you."

The crumpled paper soared through the air to the fire with a flick of Radames's wrist.

"Send him in." The annoyance stayed out of his tone, thankfully. What did the bothersome man want now of all times?

Before the Steelman had finished stepping out of the room, Councilman Montu shoved past, purple striped toga swirling about him.

"The list. Do you have it?"

"Almost, my dear man." Radames relaxed into the chair, folding his hands in his lap. "Were you not pleased to wait in the Hall for me to bring it to you?"

Montu flushed about the ears but dismissed the comment with a wave of his hand.

"I figured I might expedite the process. Also, I have good news."

Radames leaned his neck to one side, gratified with a small pop. "And what is that?"

"After the last near escape—" Montu swallowed and forced a smile, although the memory of the High One shrieking obscenities against both him and Radames through the Higher Pyramid corridors could be anything but amusing, "—we now have her sufficiently secured. The only way for her to leave those rooms is if she follows her mother off the balcony into the waterfall."

"You are sure?" Radames cracked his knuckles this time. He was sure, even if Montu couldn't know about the wall of air shutting Ptolema off from the world. He should have left it up to begin with, but then he had never expected the girl would overcome the Steelman and make a run for it.

"Positive. The Steelman barred the outer door with a chain thicker than my arm and called in a second guard to back him up."

"And the chain does not look suspicious?"

Montu shook his head, eyes glinting with the genius of his plan. "No, they draped a decorative silk over it, a sign of the High One's illness. A warning to all who may want to enter. The walls are too thick for anyone to hear her cries." A shadow crossed his face for half a second.

"Something the matter with this wonderful plan?"

"Eventually we will have to say she is healed. She can't continue to be sick for months on end. Weeks are perhaps acceptable, but longer than that and something will have to be done."

"Are you suggesting we get rid of her?"

Montu came close to blushing again. "This would not be the first time someone poisoned a High One for the good of El-Pelusium."

"I am sure." Radames stood, the chair scratching across the stone floor. "Thank you for the update." There it was again, there was no mistaking it. The prickling heat bumping the flesh of his arms. Radames sucked in his next words to Montu with a sharp hiss.

Someone was Manipulating in the Pyramid.

"When will the letter be—"

"Out. Get out!" Radames stepped around the desk and slapped Montu. "Do not leave the Council Hall until I come for you, understood?" The words vibrated along his nerves, anxiety and excitement mingling together.

A red hand-shaped splotch stood out on the white of Montu's cheek as he blinked, wide eyed, uncomprehending. But of course he couldn't comprehend. He couldn't feel it. He hadn't been subjected to years of torture to make him feel it. Radames strode for the door, dark blue robe snapping at his ankles.

"Do I need to repeat myself?"

Montu choked back a few unrecognizable words. He dropped a small bow, and he fled the room. In the ensuing silence, Radames closed his eyes, the world dulling apart from the tingles in his skin. The evening had deepened, and it was too late for the Pyramid to be bustling anymore. The Steelmen had orders to round up the four names he had already sent out. Was it one of them?

The excitement overrode the anxiety. It was here, the end of his search. There were Manipulators who needed wiping out. Squeezing his eyes shut further so dots of light spotted the black behind his eyelids, he raised his nose as if to sniff them out.

The tingles surged into a current of energy, bringing a ball of heat to his belly again. He took a step back, hand pressing against the warm stone of the doorway. The Manipulator was strong. Too strong. His eyes snapped open. It wasn't possible. An untrained fool couldn't be so strong.

The scar tissue in his leg throbbed, as if he was back in Iztklarigkitsch when the wound first happened. Radames's breath thinned with his nerves. Where were they? He stepped into the deserted hall, the Manipulator's energy calling to him.

"I never imagined this, Atsu, even if we had a thousand years on Thoth to dream it up." Ata stepped out the door of Miki's house, the hinges squealing as she shut it.

Atsu did not respond to her latest statement of disbelief. He hadn't imagined it either, nor had he imagined anything like Miki's cellar. To spend her life in such a dark hole, waiting for someone to recognize her as a person when she could have been free, Manipulating on Thoth as he had. He avoided the closing door. He couldn't see the place again, couldn't picture the unique tortures of her life. Ata had remained silent as well as they passed through, her thoughts no doubt turning to Miki's brother. She had fingered the 'BB' engraved in the door and whispered, "I'm sorry."

But now Ata was back to her assertive self.

"Which way now? She never said." Ata stepped into the covered street. To the left, the tunnel wound up. To the right, it ended in an open expanse of road.

Atsu jerked his head to the left before fingering his throat, raw and pained as it had never been. Ata eyed him, but he held a hand up.

She snatched it out of the air.

"This better not be the death of you, brother, not after all we have gone through together."

He blinked wordlessly.

Ata sighed, and she and Atsu turned up the torch-lit tunnel. The walls seemed to move with each step Atsu took, threatening to strangle him if he went much farther. The stones were dark, a blood-tinged red almost. He tore his gaze away, but the cobbled street was the same.

"Ata," he croaked, any more words rendered impossible by the stinging in his throat.

"What is it?" Her arms wrapped around him, pulling him to her as they had when they were children. The scent of juniper and sweat clung to her.

He grunted, a half guttural moan. His feet tangled under him as the walls loomed closer.

"Atsu, listen to me. We are so close. We have to finish this!" Her fingers dug into his armpits, hefting him upward.

"Is he all right?" A man's voice cut through the thudding of blood in Atsu's brain. He jerked upright, knife slicing free of his belt in one swift movement even as his throat burned worse.

Ata remained cool, not drawing her own knife. A man sat against the wall. A patch of red skin stood against the copper of his bald forehead, twisted into a circle with a line cut through it. A swath of wrinkles covered his face that at once made him appear both ancient and ageless. He wore a dirty toga and no shoes. His gaze shifted to the knife in Atsu's hand and his eyes, pale brown, lit in surprise. A vaguely familiar brown.

"Do you wish to live, old man?" Ata stepped closer, features taut, back rigid.

"Yes, I do." The man raised a hand to cover a cough following the words. His eyes met Atsu's over the marked hand and a smile played on his lips.

Atsu looked to the ground, driving back the familiarity. It was just an old beggar man. Even Eshaq did not mark his beggars. The air was humid with the mist of the nearby waterfall. It tickled Atsu's nose, begging to be used. Without thinking about it, he Manipulated the mist into the beggar's bowl, filling it with water.

The man stared levelly at the bowl, then looked up to Atsu, head cocked in interest. But no surprise shown in those wrinkles. No alarm or fear.

"Atsu, no." Ata pulled on his sleeve.

But the old man was on his feet now, moving toward them without a limp or any sign of age. He brought the bowl to his lips as he stopped three feet away.

"Come on." Ata yanked his arm this time.

Atsu turned to follow, but the man spoke.

"You seem familiar to me."

Ata pulled harder. The beggar made no other move to follow, only standing in the middle of the road, sipping his Manipulated water.

"The next time you feel the urge to show kindness, wait until we aren't on a mission." Ata tugged him up the tunnel, leaving the stranger behind.

They emerged out of the tunnel. A gust of warm air washed over Atsu. The sun no longer shone, but torches still lined the open road. The pain in his throat subsided for a moment as he sucked in the air, just to be sure. Rich, soft, and warm. Disgusting.

"We're almost there. Just hold yourself together for another minute, okay? There's the waterfall again. She must be getting close."

She was right. Miki was depending on them. He stepped after his sister, only to stumble to a halt a foot away.

"What is that?" Ata slowed, eyes darting to his. She felt it too.

The skin of his arms tickled with a fury so great, it could be a swarm of island bees peeling his skin off. Atsu stiffened. That wasn't all. He spoke through cracked lips.

"Someone here be Manip—"

A door cracked against the stone as a man stepped into the street just inside the next tunnel. Tall, with dark robes. A stark contrast to the rest of the togas in the Pyramid. But beyond that, a red ring of hazy light hung about him. Manipulation. Powerful Manipulation to be so visible.

Atsu raised his arms just as the man spun to face him.

"Atsu—no!"

A boom of stones crashing to the road drowned out Ata's warning. The man darted left, a barrage of steaming air shooting toward Atsu. He dropped and rolled with the man's movement, jumping up on one knee. A stone from the wall he had collapsed shot into the air. The man diverted it with a jet of water from the waterfall without so much as a flick of his wrist.

He was good.

Atsu grunted and threw himself to the side again, shoulder crunching into the hard ground. Flames roared past his face with the acrid scent of burning hair.

Someone moved close by. Pressure against his arm, accompanied by urgent tugging. A voice drifted past, but with no intelligible words. He rolled away, pressed his palms flat against the stone and pushed upright.

The man stood ten feet away, eyes glowing a green so dark they were almost black. He cocked his head.

The pile of rubble jumped into the air. Atsu met them with a wall of flames from the torches. A curse rose above the crackling fire, but the stones didn't stop at the wall of flames. They plunged through, a fist sized rock taking Atsu in the gut. A cry rose behind him, but he couldn't turn to see. The air squeezing into him from all sides made it impossible. He jerked his elbows out, but the air only pressed in harder, threatening to steal even the air from his lungs. They constricted, coming closer to giving in. He pulled against the unnatural air, gasping for a breath, but it wouldn't come.

One finger tugged free of the constricting air. The wall of fire slammed into his opponent. The stranglehold of air vanished as the man stumbled backward, throwing a water stream from the waterfall at the flames. He collapsed to the ground, a sopping, smoking mass.

Atsu turned, only to choke out a strangled cry. Ata lay in a heap of limbs, a bloody rock next to her head. A trickle of blood ran from a blue-black bruise covering her cheek.

"Ata!"

The tingles flared back into life along his arms. Spinning, he blocked a wave of fire with a funnel of air.

The man stood five feet away, frowning, eyes shining jewel-tone green.

"Who are you?"

The tornado of air swirled at him, guided by the panic cresting in Atsu's chest. Ata couldn't be hurt. She couldn't.

The man dodged to the left, whipping his arms up into the air to summon more fire. More water. Pushing Atsu back, away from the Higher Pyramid. Away from Miki.

Something caught under Atsu's heel and he tripped to the ground. Ata's arm. She didn't groan at the impact. Atsu rolled over her prone form and jumped back up to face the stranger. The man's attack hesitated as he drew in a breath of air.

Atsu struck. Flinging his arms out, two strips of air worked like ropes, flicked around the man's ankles. Atsu jerked. The man toppled to the ground. Ten feet and Atsu would be inside the next tunnel. That much closer to Miki and finishing this. He sprinted left, even as his heart groaned for him to stay near Ata. She would want him to go on, no matter her condition.

The pungent scent of burning fibers engulfed Atsu and a ball of air struck his back. He gasped, dropped, and rolled forward. The air didn't stop. Scalding hot, blistering his skin wherever it was exposed beyond the leather, it picked him up, slowly raising him off the ground. His feet dangled an inch above the paving stones, but a jerk to kick his legs and break the Manipulation did nothing.

The black-robed man, thin face alight with the exhilaration of the fight, stepped up to him. His breath came in short, clipped bursts, but with a wave of his hand the pressure around Atsu doubled. It held him firmer, crushing his appendages against his body.

"I am quite sure you weren't on my list," the man mused, breathless. "I'd have known if there was a beast such as you."

Atsu blinked. Ata remained motionless behind his captor. Please, she had to be all right. Please.

The man's eyes narrowed. Water plunked off his arms to the ruined streets.

"The men who tortured me would have loved to get their hands on you. Where did you learn to Manipulate? Why are you so strong?" The air pinched tighter. "Answer me!"

"Here be my answer."

The air popped.

Ears ringing, Atsu forced the man's power away from him and fell to the pavement with a crack of elbow on stone. Pain flared along his bones, straight to his head, but he jumped up and sprinted down the corridor, toward the door at the end.

A rush of power licked at his heels.

CHAPTER 39

The air around Miki trembled, ruining her carefully kept balance. She jolted downward, losing twenty-five feet of altitude. Screaming, she reached out to the air again. It grabbed her with a jerk, her shoulder smacking into the rock face at her side. Fire gripped the right half of her torso, but she gritted her teeth and focused on Manipulating.

The last rays of sun vanished, leaving the waterfall awash in pale gray. Countless torches and fires twinkled far below her. Light rimmed Ptolema's balcony a hundred feet above her.

The power vibrating through the air was too much to be just Atsu. Was he fighting someone? Sweat beading her forehead, she pushed upward with her hands as if swimming, pushing through the air and returning to the point from which she fell. The base of the waterfall lay more than a hundred feet below her dangling toes, with nothing between them. She wouldn't look down. Her head swam. She was doing something Atsu claimed was impossible. Even her own brother, a Third, could not do it.

But she was a Fifth.

She gulped for air. Her limbs trembled, but she couldn't spare a moment to halt, nor was there anywhere to rest. There was only wet rock and open air. Rest meant death.

Another tremble shook the air. Urgency spurred her on. She kicked upward again, curling her arms around her torso as she had at the beginning. For some reason, the curled-arms position made it easier to Manipulate the air around herself.

The ledge jutted sharply out only twenty feet ahead. Miki gave one final push. She shot upward.

Vibrations wracked her body. The air shifted. Another vibration broke her concentration, and she fell.

Hands flailing. Gut churning. Her good hand smacked stone and wedged into a crevice in the rock surface. She crunched into the wet stone and her mangled hand grasped desperately for something to hold, scraping across algae and mud. A lump on the rock surface caught under her two remaining fingers and she clenched around it.

She was alive for the moment, dangling one hundred fifty feet above death. Fingers burning, she swung her feet to the side and dug her bare toes into a crack five feet below the balcony, craning her body as far as she could manage. She grabbed another rock and pulled up. Muscles aching in protest, she forced her limbs into action one more time. She sprawled across the rock like a spider, her breath trapped between her mouth and the cool rock. A drop of water slipped down the green-black moss and trickled into her mouth.

Air. She needed air again. Her fingers dug into the rock.

Earth. Real and solid.

"I feel it," she gasped. She didn't need air.

A crack shook the stone wall as a rock dislodged itself. It pressed against her rear end, pushing up. It was enough. With a grunt, Miki launched toward the balcony railing. Her seven fingers dug into the stone, pain flaring along the tips.

Legs swung. A rush of warmth. Her knees cracked into the balcony floor, body trembling with adrenaline and strain.

Fabric rustled across the room, followed by a jolt of movement. Ptolema sat upright on the benches by the fire, paler than Miki remembered. The scar above her left eye was an angry red, and the bones of her face were more defined as if she had not eaten in a good many days. Her brown eyes, normally so bright with life, were dull.

Miki forced her weakened legs to hold her again, gritting her teeth against the pain in her side and the fire in her maimed hand.

"Ptolema—"

The High One started to her feet, ash-smudged robes wadded around her, with none of her finery in sight.

"How did you get in here? Who are you? One of Radames's assassins sent to get rid of me?" Her voice cracked at the accusation and she tipped forward as if drunk.

Miki reached her in five strides. The woman's hand was stiff beneath hers as she gripped it.

"Ptolema, you have to make all this stop."

Ptolema wrenched her hand away, a snarl in the back of her throat.

"Get out."

"You have to end the decree against the Seconds. Stop the executioners from reaching Thoth. Why did you agree to it?"

The dull eyes widened, disbelieving. Ptolema blinked twice. She took a step back, taking Miki in again. The breeze stabbed at her damp hair, no longer constrained by the top knot. The dirty shirt was heavy against her chest and the leather chilled her legs. Of course Ptolema hadn't recognized her.

"Tiye—" Ptolema stopped and swallowed hard. "M-Miki." Her eyes met Miki's with a flicker of fear.

The heat of Manipulation still burned in Miki's belly. With a jolt, she blew it out. It acquiesced without a struggle. Ptolema's face relaxed, but only just.

"Your eyes are like his," she whispered.

"Ptolema, you have to make an announcement."

"Would you control me as he does? Do your eyes change colors because you are like him? Evil?" The woman's face snapped up, lines around her mouth tight.

"No, Ptolema. I just climbed a waterfall to help save this city. I don't want to control you."

Ptolema's already pale skin changed to ashen. "You climbed the Waterfall?"

"Well, the Manipulation helped, but—"

"Manipulation?" Her mouth screwed into a sneer and she stepped back. "So you *are* like him. He was right."

This wasn't the headstrong High One who had ruled El-Pelusium when Miki left. She stepped up to Ptolema again, grabbing her wrists. The High One struggled backward, but Miki yanked her closer.

"I am not evil. I risked death, several times, to come save this city. The people on Thoth are just like you. Most of them can't even Manipulate. I only learned so I could leave and convince you to change your mind. I can't believe this was your idea." Miki released Ptolema and sank to the floor, her legs finally giving out.

Ptolema rubbed her left wrist and her eyes caught Miki's missing fingers. She jerked them behind her back, but Ptolema didn't ask about them. Instead, she sank beside Miki, dirty toga splaying out around her like the feathers of a dead dove.

"I don't want to kill them," she whispered.

"Then send out an edict and a rider to stop the executioners. Look—" Miki swung the bag off her shoulder, its weight vanishing as it thudded to the floor. "The lost Tablets of History. I found them on Thoth. The answer is in here."

Ptolema's mouth hinged open as she stared at the box's corner peeping out of the bag. "You found them?"

"Yes. You must read them. You must tell the truth to the Pyramid."

Ptolema's hand quivered as she reached toward the box. With a scrape of wood on wood, she slid the lid off. Miki lifted the topmost tablet. She ran a finger along the only words she recognized.

"Royalty begets Truth?" Ptolema scooted closer. "What does that mean?"

Miki held it out to her. "You are royalty. Read it and see."

Ptolema accepted the tablet, thin fingers wrapping around the edge of the stone. "What does—"

A low groan shook the stones beneath Miki, and the tingles in her arms redoubled.

"You have to hurry."

Ptolema stared at the tablet, upper lip pinned between her teeth. She reached for the other tablets. Miki slipped them into her hand, breath hovering in the back of her throat. Ptolema squinted. She glanced at each tablet in turn.

"I can't read it. And this one—" she pointed to Atsu's tablet, "is just a story." Leaning closer, she studied the tablet one more time.

"Just a story? But Atsu said it went with this one."

"Well maybe it does, as I don't understand a word of what either say." The tablet fell from her fingers with and hit the floor with a thud.

"Try again! You have to be able to read it!"

"I can't." A wry laugh caught in Ptolema's throat. "It's all too late." Anger burned in the brown flames of her eyes.

"No, it's not. The people of Thoth are still alive. There's still time."

"You don't understand. I'm not doing this." Ptolema drew in a shaking breath. "It's him. He is doing everything." She glanced back up, eyes bloodshot. "He can Manipulate. He was lying the whole time."

The tingles of Atsu's Manipulation and the other odd sensation redoubled in Miki's gut and arms. Someone else could Manipulate. The saliva in her mouth turned to ash.

"Who—"

A screaming crunch of metal tore through the air. Half of a wooden door trailing chains shot through into the room and crashed against the balcony wall. A body flew through behind it, dreadlocks twirling in the air. Atsu collapsed into a heap of limbs beside the desk, crimson splattered across his face.

"No!" Miki jumped up.

The remains of the door cracked out of its frame, the room shuddering with the force of it. The heat in her gut flared, pulling her back around. Without needing to be asked, the fire from the grate streamed to her fingertips, ready for use.

A man stood in the doorway, dark blue robes hanging in strips around his knees. A beak-like nose under gleaming deep green eyes. The eyes of a Manipulator.

Radames.

His chest heaved with the effort of his fight with Atsu but there was no victorious gleam on his face. His gaze met Miki's and understanding filled his face. "So, it's you, not him."

There was no other warning. The fire betrayed Miki, turning back onto her.

The heat licked at her fingernails, eyebrows, and scalp. She pushed back with air, but he was strong. The heat was insanely intense. A scream ripped through the chamber, then died just as quickly. Miki tried to push past the flames, but she felt them everywhere, a cocoon of his power attempting to devour her.

She could *feel* it. A mad laugh gurgled up inside her chest even as the fiery pain bit into her hands. It didn't stop, and she didn't try to make it. Instead, she opened herself to the pain, to the power.

A startled grunt rose beyond the roar of the flames in her ears. The muscles of her forearms went taut and she jerked her arms upward. The flames tore away from her body. Away from Radames's control. The laugh filled her chest again as she channeled the flames toward him.

His eyes widened. He threw himself to the side and collided with the shattered door just as the flames seared past. Then he was up on his feet again, air pressing around Miki before he was even straight. Miki balled her good fist and flung her power at a tree growing beyond the next room in Ptolema's gardens. She knew the one she wanted. Tall, laden with plums. It crashed through the doorway, spilling its precious contents across the room. The roots, showering dirt to the floor, spun to catch Radames in the face.

The stones vibrated, cool and humming against his side. Atsu shifted, agony shooting up his torso. Yells, crashes and the surging of heat that only came from Manipulation hung around him. Miki was there. She was shouting, grunting. Cursing someone. Atsu pushed upward. His arms threatened to give way, but he held steady. He had to help Miki.

A tree blocked most of his view of the pair of fighters. Black hair and black robes flashed between the branches. Fire erupted, devouring half of the tree in one breath, as the black-haired man raised both arms. Atsu dodged the next jet of fire, only to have a rock slam into his side.

Pain flared hotter than the blaze before him, but he didn't stop to groan. The man had Miki. Her arms were pinned to her side. The man's green eyes shivered, alive with his power.

Miki groaned.

Atsu lunged at him, all power forgotten. His hands wrapped around the stranger's throat and the stranger spun, eyes wide. Nails bit into Atsu's skin, but he did not release until a gust from Miki threw the Manipulator to the floor. She advanced, hand out to press him down with air.

The man struggled through it anyway, gasping out words.

"You are in over your head. You can't understand three hundred years of evil." The heat of the man's Manipulations pulsed under the air holding him down. There wasn't much time.

"No one can understand the evil," he whispered, eyes wide and black hair hanging lank around his face. The air holding him snapped. Miki shot across the room, back striking the broken fragments of the door. Atsu moved for her, but she shifted and pulled herself up, grimacing. The Manipulator stood on the other side of the room, heaving with the effort of his power. His arms raised again.

Atsu matched his movement. He could kill him. End it all.

"It be over—"

A splintered limb of the tree rose faster than was conceivable, even for Manipulation. The chaos in the room melted away. Someone was screaming.

Atsu tried to block the spinning limb with air, but the attack was too fast. Too sudden. Pain, white hot and surprising more than agonizing, blossomed in his chest. The end of the limb jutted out of him.

"Miki—" The words became impossible as his breath was clipped short. His legs crumpled, the stone floor rushing to meet him.

"No!" The fire at Miki's fingertips died as the scream tore from her throat. She tilted forward toward where Atsu lay in a pool of his own blood, body heaving. Something caught her in the chest before she could reach him.

Radames stood two feet away, triumph on his face because he had taken Atsu down. Triumph because he thought he could defeat her as well. Triumph because he thought the Pyramid was his.

But it wasn't.

Behind Radames, the waterfall raged. Thousands of pounds of pressure and water roaring over the lip of the roof. *Thousands of pounds of power.* Miki reached for it even as the air sent by Radames pressed against her lungs. In one long stream, the water of the falls diverted, redirected to her chosen course.

To Radames.

It flowed over him, cutting off the air pressing in her chest. Gulping in a liberating breath, Miki pulled more water. It bubbled around Radames, sealing him in a floating tomb made of her power. His eyes shone through the ripples, wide and glowing.

Water surged at Miki's feet, quickly rising to her knees. No sign of Atsu in the foamy water, only a stain of red in the swirling blue.

No!

Miki jerked her arms down. The water sucked away, back to its original course. Radames dropped like a stone, head cracking against the edge of the desk. His body jerked, then lay still. The deep green in his eyes winked out.

"Atsu!" Miki slipped over the blood and water-slicked stones. Her knees cracked into the edge of one of the tablets, pushed next to Atsu by the raging water. Pain shot through her kneecaps, but it didn't matter. So much blood pooled around him. His skin was waxy pale and his eyes bulged. A hand to his cheek—too cold. A sound, strangled and full of pain, scratched in his throat. His hand hung limply in the air, searching for something. She grasped it, fingers intertwining with his. A shudder passed through him and his eyes closed.

"Atsu!" Her fingers pinched around his. "Atsu, don't—" Her words failed.

His eyes flickered back open, and he exhaled with a gasp. The tree limb moved with his chest, more blood gurgling out. Her maimed hand rested against his shoulder and a smile spread over his lips at the touch even as his skin grew more ashen. His fingers clenched around hers, knuckles white.

"I—" He gulped for a breath, the branch in his chest slipping deeper. He coughed, blood trickling down his chin.

"I be free ..."

The words ended as his chest stopped shuddering for another breath. He stilled. The fingers around hers relaxed and slipped away.

"No! No, no, *no!* Atsu!" He couldn't be—the words refused to surface. He just couldn't.

His limp fingers dropped lower, landing on the Tablet. Miki leaned over him, hot tears spilling across her cheeks.

"This can't be it. He can't be gone." Her maimed hand came down on his chest, beating him, willing him to stand back up. "Get up," she muttered, then louder, into a shout as she pounded on him. "Get up, Atsu. *Get up!*"

Get up, to berate her for Manipulating poorly. To kiss her. But he never would again.

Atsu's body was drenched like everything else, but it didn't matter. Miki pulled him closer and sank her forehead against his.

"Miki?" Ptolema's voice punctured the steady dripping of water. "Who was he?"

"He didn't even want to come," she mumbled. He'd wanted to live freely, Manipulating how he pleased.

"Was he from Thoth?"

Miki nodded. He *was* Thoth. Fire and ice. Atsu had been wrong. She, Miki, wasn't a light on Thoth. He was. Or had been. Bright crimson polluted his wet leather, its fingers of red reaching out from the wound in his chest.

Atsu was dead.

"Miki?" Her father's voice rang in the distance.

"Councilman Bast!" Footsteps slapped the wet stone again.

"I'm sorry, I'm so sorry," Miki sobbed.

"Miki?" her father said again.

Miki pulled Atsu's hand into her lap and squeezed it.

"I'm so sorry, Atsu," she whispered. Neck smarting, she turned. Her father stood in the doorway. Dirt dusted his head and smeared his cheeks. A symbol screamed angrily from his forehead, all too recently branded.

Miki groaned and leaned over Atsu. Too much pain for one day.

"We're all right, Miki," her father said.

She looked back to see if he was lying. A weary smile lit his face. Ata clung to him, blood on the side of her head and face far paler than it should have been. Her eyes were closed as if blocking out pain, but then they flickered open to find her brother on the ground in a pool of blood and water.

"Atsu!" She pulled away from Miki's father, legs shaking beneath her. She thudded to the ground but pulled herself forward until her hand squelched in the pool of her brother's blood.

"Atsu," she breathed, paling further. "Is he ...?"

The nod pulled against every muscle in her neck and Miki looked away, unable to see her own pain mirrored in Ata's face.

"No, no, no," Ata stuttered. "No. He can't be. Atsu, talk to me. Atsu!" She cupped his face, stroked his cheek. He didn't respond. A groan built in her throat, growing to an aching cry.

Miki glanced away. This was Ata's brother. The only person she'd had on Thoth for twenty-two years. This was Atsu.

A few moments later, Miki's father spoke.

"Ptolema, Miki, there's something you need to know." He came further into the room. "What are your friends' names?"

"He didn't even want to be here," Ata muttered between sobs. "I should have listened to him, because now he's dead!" She wrenched one of the Tablets of History off the floor near her foot and threw it across the room with a scream. It struck the benches by the fire and cracked in two.

Clammy fingers clenched around Miki's hand holding Atsu's. Ata yanked her closer and embraced her, weeping in great racking gulps. Miki's own tears couldn't hide any longer. She held the woman who had loved her brother, and whose brother she had loved, and together they cried.

CHAPTER 40

Ptolema's face burned. Her fingers trembled at her side, wanting to touch the charred skin on her head, but she kept them still. She bit her lower lip to draw her attention away from the pain.

Miki seemed to be in far worse pain. Who were these mysterious people? They had to be from Thoth. The man could Manipulate but had died trying to stop Radames. And Miki ... she could Manipulate.

The strange woman's sobs ripped through the room again, sending shivers down Ptolema's spine. This moment wasn't for her. She turned away. The Tablet the woman had broken scraped on wet stone as Ptolema's foot knocked it. She froze.

The room snapped into a sharper focus. A small noise echoed in the back of her throat.

The words of the tablet, once so foreign, had changed. No longer obscure symbols, but plain, readable text. Ptolema retrieved the Tablet fragments with shaking fingers.

"See the other one," Bast said beside her. He pointed to the Tablet of History resting under Atsu's hand.

"Impossible!" Ptolema gasped. Another readable tablet. And where was the third one?

Bast held it. The tablet was still covered in the strange runes. He looked down at it and muttered, "It has to be."

"Councilman Bast?" Ptolema winced as she took a step, the motion sending ripples of pain through her burned face.

Bast crossed to the two grieving women and held the tablet out to the stranger.

"Take it, please."

She stared at him with red-rimmed eyes for a second before glancing to Miki, questioning.

"He's my father—and Beren's," Miki said, as if that explained something.

The woman's eyes widened, and she looked back at Bast. She hesitated a moment longer but then accepted the tablet with blood-stained fingers, streaking the artifact with red. She gasped and almost dropped it.

Ptolema rushed to her side, no longer caring about the fire screaming through her head. The letters on the Tablet had changed from obscurity to readable text, as if a breath of magic blew across them.

"She's not Royal," Ptolema whispered, horrified. But the letters didn't morph back to unintelligible scribbles.

Miki leaned over the dead man. "Ata ..."

"We never touched them as children," the woman whispered. "We always Manipulated them. It was fun. I—I don't think I've ever touched them."

Ptolema slid the stone out of the woman's fingers. It was strangely warm beneath her fingertips. Across the top the words *Royalty Begets Truth* still shone.

"You have to be Royal," she muttered. But that was impossible.

"She is. You—" Councilman Bast said gently to Ptolema, "—are not."

"What is going on, Bast?" The words took all her strength. She grabbed her head, only to pull her hand away with a hiss.

Bast sighed. He guided Ptolema to the stone bench. He glanced at Miki and frowned down at her missing fingers.

"I should have told you this sooner, but didn't want to endanger you with the knowledge. Either of you." He squeezed Ptolema's hand.

Miki clenched her hand tighter around the dead man's. The man whose other hand had changed one of the Tablets of History.

"Would you like to call for someone to care for the body, Miki?" Bast said gently.

"No. He should have heard this. He should have known what he did with the tablet."

Did Miki love this Manipulator from Thoth? The revelation brought a knot to Ptolema's gut, but Bast was speaking again.

"I alone was privy to a detail so awful, so scandalous, it was never uttered past the walls of that bedchamber." Bast pointed to the doorway to the left. "Khepri, wife of the High One—"

"My mother," Ptolema emphasized.

Miki's father only smiled, a light of sadness filling his gaunt face.

"Khepri was heavily pregnant. One day I was summoned to her chamber. Khentimentiu and I were good friends, and he needed someone to confide in. Something was wrong with his wife's pregnancy. I didn't understand what it was until I was inside this very room. She was carrying twins."

Ptolema couldn't hold back the gasp. *Twins.* She had heard of it happening, but it was rare. The last mention of twins had been over ten years ago. A woman sold her twin babies to a caravan across the sea. She was arrested later, of course.

"This led to a terrible dilemma," Bast said. "If they nullified both, they could never again produce an heir. If they allowed both to live, they would break the most sacred law." He sank down beside Ptolema. "Khentimentiu decided the best course of action was to nullify one child and leave one inside his wife."

"But how could they know which was the First and which was Second?" Ptolema twisted a length of toga in her grip.

"They couldn't know. It was a blind guess. The best they were hoping for was to kill the Second and save the First. It was never to be mentioned that the child had a twin, and even if it was a Second, no one would know. Not even they would know.

"Khentimentiu brought me in at his wife's request. She knew I wasn't a hardline nullifier. But it was too late. The physician's forceps already had one baby by the leg. The moment I walked in—" he glanced over his shoulder to the bedroom doorway, and a shadow crossed behind his eyes, "—I demanded they stop. I'm surprised they didn't figure out how many children I had hiding back home right then, but they didn't. I had enough sense to plead the logic of their mistake. They could kill the First. It was too risky to let a Second become heir to the throne, even if no one knew.

"The physician was able to stop the procedure and allow the pregnancy to continue as before, though Khepri only had a few weeks left. I knew that once they broke her water to begin the nullification, they would have had to deliver the babies soon. No one knew what damage had already been done, but we all hoped for the best. Khentimentiu didn't mention any of this. He just thanked me and sent me from the room. I never heard the incident spoken of again. I didn't even know what they did after that."

"But how do you know I am not royal?" Ptolema twisted the knotted toga further.

Bast sighed.

"As with all pregnancies, Khepri's proper time finally came. The babies might have been born early due to the attempted nullification—no one really knew, because they didn't announce the birth for three weeks. When they did, the small girl child they presented to the Council had a shock of copper hair and fair skin. So different from the dark-toned High One and his wife." His eyes flicked to the woman bending over the dead Manipulator, face in her hands, not even listening. "A rumor circulating through a small circle said that the child was not theirs. I could only guess what they had done about the twins. Either they nullified both and found a replacement, or they had sent one away and kept this one—though it seemed too pale to be theirs."

Ptolema's hair stuck to her blood-glazed cheek, tickling her nose. She pulled the strand off with a wince. Copper. Lighter than her father's by three shades.

"But my final guess, that they had sent both babies to Thoth, or somewhere else, was proven correct twenty minutes ago when these two passed me in the street." He inclined his head toward the silent man on the floor, and his voice dropped.

"Thank you. You were a good man."

Miki stifled another sob. "Atsu wouldn't like this."

Ptolema's breath hitched in her chest. Those two savages from Thoth, and not she, were heirs to El-Pelusium, the chief city of Kemet? Not her, the one raised by Khentimentiu. Trained since she was four to be High One. Ptolema dropped her head into her hands, only to pull up sharply as her hand touched the charred skin on her scalp.

"Everything I know is a lie." The words were small, inadequate. But the truth of them threatened to strangle the breath from her lungs.

The dead man ... The same long face as the man Ptolema had called Father. The woman had the same sharp facial lines and high cheekbones that Ptolema had hidden from when she knew she had done wrong. Even her coloring, tanned with jet black hair, was the same. This woman was a descendant of High One Khentimentiu and Khepri, his wife, if Ptolema was remembering her correctly from the few short years she had known her.

A shadow crossed Bast's face.

"Khepri must not have adjusted as her husband hoped." He glanced to the sky-wall. "I think she found the only way she could out of her guilt. Her suicide only strengthened my resolve of what happened, but I was not able to stop it."

Ptolema traced the line of the scar above her left eye.

"My mother said I tripped when I was learning to walk, but there is something I see sometimes in my dreams ..." A cry of frustration. A crack of pain splitting her vision ...

"She didn't want me. I—I think she deliberately dropped me." The mother she hadn't known, who wasn't even her mother. "She wanted her own children back, not me." Ptolema ended in a whisper.

"Our parents are dead?" The woman clenched a white hand around her brother's shoulder.

Bast nodded.

"Yes. Ata, is it?"

The woman blinked before looking back at her brother. Miki grabbed her wrist. "Atsu deserved to know."

Ata swallowed. "He's better off not knowing."

Bast retrieved the Tablets from the floor. He inhaled, eyes closed, breathing in the ancient letters.

"Ah," he said as he exhaled. "There it is. Truth." He held the Tablet out to Ata. "As descendant of the High One who wrote this, it is up to you to divulge that Truth to us."

Ata shifted on the floor.

"I can't. Not now," she whispered.

Bast nodded and set them beside him on the bench.

"We will all have to face this soon."

"Atsu is dead," Ata mumbled into her arms. "Nothing else matters."

This Atsu was dead, not knowing he was heir to the Pyramid, the same Pyramid to which Ptolema no longer held any claim. Had her real parents died of some sickness and the High Ones swept in to claim her? Was she even from the Pyramid? Kemet? Too many questions. Perhaps Bast knew. Ptolema pulled her arms to her chest. Her whole life was a lie.

Miki stood. "Let's take him out of here, Sister."

Ata glanced up from her crossed arms. Tears ruined her face. "Sister," she agreed in a whisper, and slowly stood, pain etched across her face.

Ptolema's heart ached. These two had something she never would.

With little more than a sigh, Miki raised Atsu's body from the floor. Ptolema stifled a squeak. Manipulation. And Miki did it without shame and as much ease as breathing. Even Bast straightened as if startled by the sight, but he said nothing.

Atsu's dreadlocks swung beneath him as he hovered three feet from the floor, straight as a plank.

"He didn't want to live here anyway," Ata mused, voice thick with emotion.

Miki stepped across the chamber, Atsu floating before her.

"But what happens now?" Ptolema stood from the bench. "If I'm not royalty, I have no right to be here."

Miki's father tugged her closer, an arm around her shoulder. "We will figure it out."

But there was one thing they needed to do. Ptolema stared at the sopping dark mass that was Radames's body, crumpled against her desk. Lifeless.

"I want him gone."

Five Steelmen pushed their way through the ruins of the door. Five pairs of eyes swiveled to Atsu's floating body. The closest Steelman was the only one to react. His spear rose.

The spear jerked from his grasp just as Miki slashed her arm through the air.

"They are not to be harmed," Ptolema commanded, though her voice still shook.

She cleared her throat and crossed to the remains of the tree beside Radames's body where her secondary teal headdress floated in a pool of water. She'd worn the secondary ever since Radames had burned her other one. She shook it out, water cascading across his distorted face. She didn't look at those dead eyes, but turned and put the headdress on. Water trickled coolly down her back and over the burns on her face, a sweet relief. She was still High One, even if the Steelmen didn't know she had no right to be.

"Take The High Advisor's body away and dispose of it. He tried to kill me. These Seconds saved me." She didn't move, willing them to challenge her.

The man who had thrown his spear gaped.

"Seconds? Shouldn't we arrest them?"

Three hundred years reversed in one evening. Dangerous territory, but it hardly seemed to matter anymore.

Ptolema held herself straight. "No. We won't be arresting any Seconds, effective immediately. Now go."

Miki's father inhaled sharply. The Steelmen glanced at each other. A minute stretched into two, but then one moved for Radames's body. The others followed. Miki and Ata stepped out the door, Atsu's body floating in front of them.

CHAPTER 41

Atsu would never know he'd been heir to the Pyramid he despised. Would never know what his final act of touching a tablet had meant. His subjects had been told of High One Khentimentiu's lie and the events in the Palace, but they would never truly understand who Atsu was.

Two weeks since his death, and life in the Pyramid continued. It wasn't entirely normal, but what else could be expected? The Tablets of History had been made public after three hundred years. People would need time to get used to all of it.

But Miki would not hang around to see what that looked like.

The doors of the Council Hall creaked inward just as her fingertips brushed the rough wood. Councilman Montu met her. All color vanished from his face.

Well, not everyone would get over their fear of Seconds, or Fifths, as easily as Ptolema had.

"Ah, M-Miki," he stuttered. "Good to see you."

She brushed past him. He jumped back as her hand touched his, and he fled the room. If wounding his pride was the closest she could get to repaying the beating he had ordered on her father, she would see it done.

A group stood huddled in the center of the room, deep in conversation. Ptolema, in embroidered gold and purple but with no headdress. Edrice, frowning as if being berated for something. And Miki's father. A weight lessened in her stomach at the sight of him. He hadn't had time to regain the weight he'd lost, but there was a clear light in his eyes.

The brand would never leave his forehead, but he didn't seem to notice.

Ptolema looked up as Miki's sandaled feet swept the stones.

"Ah, Miki! Just who we were talking about." She pulled away from the Council members. The scent of rosehips and vetiver crushed Miki as Ptolema yanked her into a hug. "Things really are going to be okay," she said into her hair.

"So the Council agreed?" Miki gave Ptolema a gentle push back.

"They had little say in the matter, but it helped that Edrice was one of the first to take my side once she saw the evidence. Montu threw quite a fit, but I reminded him we could dispose of him if he didn't agree. He will go along with it, though I won't be surprised if we need to accept applications for his replacement before the month is out." Ptolema giggled and turned back to wave Edrice over.

"Have you met Miki? I mean, other than the last time she was in this Hall?" A shadow washed over her face. "Oh Miki, I'm sorry, I didn't mean to bring that up."

"It's fine." Though the thought had surfaced before Miki had resolved to come. On the other hand, if they hadn't banished her, she would never have met Atsu or found the Tablets.

"Miki, it's an honor." Edrice dipped a bow. Though the woman had always seemed more genuine than Montu, she still gave off an aura that added to the gurgling in Miki's gut.

But she wouldn't need to worry about that again. Miki peered around the room, but there was no one else there.

"Where is Ata? Wasn't this whole thing about her, anyway?"

"She left as soon as the meeting was over. Scooted past all the Council members on her way out the door. They toppled over to get out of her way. Seems they are a bit afraid of their new High One." Bast set a hand on Miki's shoulder and chuckled. "I suggested she tone down the dark stares and snide remarks."

"She's working on it. There wasn't much reason to be diplomatic on Thoth." Miki hadn't been surprised by her father's suggestion that Ata and Ptolema rule together. They really were the two halves of a whole. Both were fierce, determined. But where Ptolema was finely educated, Ata understood the real grit of life the royal-raised never would.

Was Ata truly satisfied with this new life? She had accepted the proposal so quickly and eagerly. A way to move past Atsu's death, perhaps, and to honor Beren's. Ata and Miki had broken the news about him to Bast a week ago. They weren't even finished with the story when he pulled Ata into an embrace and called her daughter. Perhaps that had helped Ata accept her new role as well.

Miki frowned at her father's brand. Would the redness and anger of it never fade?

"It's all right, Miki. A reminder of the family I lost. And regained." He touched the ruined skin with a small smile that quickly faltered. "I may not have your brothers or other sisters, but Hemeda will come around eventually to the new way of things."

"I'm not so sure," Miki mumbled. Her sister still refused to see her.

Her father shrugged. "She will. Thank you again for the news of Beren. I'd be lying if I didn't admit the guilt over his choice to run away has been eating at me for the last twelve years. At least we know he found a life of his own. And love, if only briefly."

Miki smiled. Such like her father to find the positive in anything. But then the smile slipped away at the weight of the bag digging into her shoulder.

Her father gestured at the bag.

"I see you made your decision."

"You're really going to do it? Leave us?" Ptolema grabbed Miki's good hand. "Ata will want to say goodbye."

"I'll see if I can find her on my way. But I need to go. They have him ready for me." Would Atsu look any different, once embalmed? Those gleaming dark blue eyes ... whatever he looked like, those eyes would always be his.

Her father's arms enveloped her in a cloud of warmth and citrus. She melted into the embrace long enough to choke back a sob before pulling away.

"If you ever need us, we will be here," he said.

Ptolema squeezed her hand. "Thanks, Miki, for everything."

Miki couldn't stop a small smile, even with the events of the past days. How would things have been different if Khentimentiu hadn't chosen this woman to replace his children? If they hadn't been blessed with a High One who longed for truth? She squeezed Ptolema's hand back. "Thank *you*, Ptolema."

Ptolema smiled.

"Please promise me you will visit."

Bast shifted beside Ptolema, a frown flickering across his face. Miki grabbed his elbow. Thinner than it should have been. But that would change now.

"I will visit, though I can't guarantee it will be soon." If luck favored her, it wouldn't be. "Goodbye, Father. Ptolema." She dipped an abbreviated bow.

Edrice said nothing. It was better that she did not.

Miki turned away, hitching the bag higher on her shoulder with trembling hands. An almost giddy sense of euphoria swept through her as she hurried from the Hall. None of this would ever be her problem again.

"Have you heard the truth of the Seconds' Rebellion?" a woman gushed to a friend as Miki passed through the market.

"Who hasn't? It's all anyone has been talking about the past two weeks," a two-chinned merchant answered.

The deeper voice of a Steelman joined the two women.

"The Seconds' Rebellion was a farce. The High One's second son decided he wanted to rule when the time came for his sister to inherit the High One status."

"Because his sister was corrupt, taking the people's profits for herself!" The first woman joined back in, voice ringing with the surety of her knowledge. "The sister refused to give up her seat and tried to kill her brother. Their father, the High One, died instead—"

The Steelman cut back in. "So the sister blamed it on the brother. He was a Manipulator."

"No!" The second woman gasped. "So he was evil?"

"Not necessarily. That's what the tablets claim. Manipulation wasn't the evil, it was the corrupt sister."

"Yes, before the rebellion, Manipulation was widespread and even considered a point of cultural pride. Pride. Can you believe that! We were known for miles around for it!"

"Yes, with schools to teach all those who could learn."

"Well, I would never send my child to one of those. There are probably," the woman's voice dropped, "*Seconds* at those places."

"But that's what we are saying! High One Ata, the woman from across the sea, has struck down the law against Seconds!"

"No!" The woman gasped.

"Yes, and High One Ptolema says she agrees! I just don't see how the pair of them plan to get along—" The conversation faded away as Miki stepped around the final corner of sandstone wall that encompassed the Lower Pyramid, the wide gate displaying open pasture and beyond, the sea.

The sea.

Freedom from the gossips. It was a miracle their wagging tongues spoke something so remarkably close to the truth. Miki had not thought gossips knew how to tell the truth. But with news so alarming, it was far more exciting than any story they could dream up.

The wind shifted, blowing a faint breeze carrying the light scent of sea spray. The grasses shifted on either side of the road leading out of El-Pelusium, as if beckoning her forward. The Steelmen guarding the gate did nothing as she approached. No spear lowered, threatening to arrest her. No man shouted for her true name. Nothing at all. They simply looked on, bored as they would be on any other day.

With a sigh of years' worth of regrets left behind, Miki stepped through the gate.

"Miki! Wait!"

At that, the guards stiffened. Another rumor the gossips got mostly right, with one glaring error. The closest Steelman's face said he'd heard those rumors. His eyes went wide, his lips parting in surprise. He was looking at Miki The Manipulator. The woman who had flown across the sea to free the Seconds and restore the rightful heirs to the throne.

Except she hadn't known what she was doing.

A woman stepped through the gate behind her, short hair fluttering free in the breeze. Without the traditional headdress, Ata was almost unrecognizable. She still wore her sandals from Thoth, something a proper High One would never stoop so low to wear. The toga clung tight, complete with the toga leggings so many outgoing women wore. Another thing a High One would never do.

But this was Ata, daughter of Thoth.

A smile split her face, but it slid off as her eyes found the cart and its precious bundle, pulled by the donkey Miki had picked up at the bottom of the Higher Pyramid.

"So it's true then. You are taking him back?"

"Where else do you think he would want to be?"

Ata shrugged.

"You're right. He would hate to be buried in those Tombs of the Kings Ptolema keeps going on about. Can you imagine it? Atsu locked deep in the earth underneath this city?" A sad smile pulled on her lips.

No, Miki could not imagine him there at all. Atsu deserved more. He deserved open air and sea spray. He deserved to be alive, but life was one thing he would never have again.

Ata crossed her arms over her chest, an eyebrow rising to her hairline.

"I promised Ptolema I would at least ask you to return when you are done."

"High One!" A merchant with a cart stopped short in the gate behind him, his eyes widening far enough to pop as they found Ata. The cart handle fell from his grasp, pears and figs scattering over the roadway, as he prostrated himself on the dirt road before her.

Ata blushed. She would have to learn not to do that.

"Get up, go on your way."

"But you have no headdress! They must punish me—"

"That rule has been struck down. Go." Her voice hinged on annoyance.

The man muttered something unintelligible but scrambled back to his feet. His cart dislodged pebbles in the road with a crunch as he hurried away, only throwing back two or three glances before he vanished down the road.

Miki turned to Ata, the only true sibling she knew.

"You already know my answer."

"I do," Ata nodded, "but Ptolema is so cursedly persistent." The frown playing on her lips hid the hint of a smile beneath. Whatever she might say, the two women were getting along like old friends.

The donkey shifted in impatience beside Miki, his rear end nudging her arm. He was right, it was time to go. The road down to the docks lay before her, travelers milling up and down, but the lesser known path to the left called out to her. Absently, she gave the donkey's reins a tug and stepped off the road. The animal gate they had entered through lay just a hundred yards back along the wall, and their boat should be where they left it two weeks ago.

"Good bye, Miki the Fifth. I'll look out—" Ata's words disappeared under the rising wind.

The grasses parted easily before the donkey cart. At the edge of the brambles cutting off the land from the water, Miki ran her hand over the coarse hair of the beast as she untied him from the harness.

"Go on, go home."

Heat flared into her gut. The power had been waiting, anticipating her return to Manipulation for the past two weeks. The act might finally be legal, but the thought of Manipulating in the Pyramid—where Atsu died, left a sour taste in the back of her throat.

His body lifted from the cart, free and peaceful. The donkey started, as if aware of the unnatural power being exercised.

Except it was more natural than anything.

The animal leapt into a trot, disappearing back through the grasses. The wrapped form of Atsu's body floated over the brambles ahead of her. Crunching filled her ears and the next moment her feet sank into sand. The boat stood as they had left it, as it had been when they shared their first and only kiss.

Her lips tingled as if tasting him again, and her eyes threatened to close—to release the tears she had long held back.

Instead, rough wood met her fingers as she jumped over the edge of the boat. Her feet thunked against the bottom. The leather pants a merchant had volunteered to give to Miki The Manipulator fit almost as good as the ones from Nenet. The leather was soft beneath her palms as she wiped the sweat off. The time had finally come.

With a whoosh of air, the boat slid off the bank. The water lapped hungrily at the sides, pulling it further out as the heat in her gut expanded. Manipulation was so natural now she hardly had to think. Atsu would have been proud. His body rested at the base of the boat, linens covering him entirely.

With a lurch, the boat hit the open sea. The wind caressed her cheek as it had done so many times on Thoth. The island lay out there, just a day away, less if she Manipulated the whole way. She would Manipulate the boat through the Back Current herself. If she could Manipulate the whole waterfall, one Current couldn't stand against her.

A day, and she would be back. Nenet would stand on the beach as Moises, the little Manipulator, ran down the beach to greet her. All Eshaq's men would be sent off the island if they didn't comply with the new peace and the new society Miki would establish, if Nenet hadn't already done so.

Thoth. The one place she had wanted to leave for weeks, and now the only place she could imagine being.

Maybe at night she would roam the eastern rocks as Atsu used to. Maybe his cave could become her home. Maybe she would be the new mad dog of Thoth.

A laugh vibrated along her lips, the first real joy swelling in her since the kiss. The sky's reflection glistened in the endless expanse of water, the usual blues interspersed with streaks of midday yellows. The sun itself was a shifting sphere against the motion of the waves. The water beat against the hull of the boat, a dull, rhythmic *thunk thunk,* but her breath hitched in the back of her throat.

There was a voice in that rhythmic beating, words meant only for her from a halting and familiar tongue.

Yeh be all right, Miki the Fifth.

ABOUT THE AUTHOR

Abigail L. Wilkes finds life in Truth-filled stories and sees every wonderful story in the world pointing to Jesus, her Savior. She studied creative writing in Iowa but now lives in the mountains of Colorado with her husband and two kids. She promises one day she will write a book for each of them.

That you will know the Truth,
and the Truth will set you free.
—John 8:32

Made in the USA
Columbia, SC
21 July 2021